"Who are you? And what the devil do you think you're doing?" Maggie snapped.

The stranger rifling through her father's desk looked up. His rugged face remained impassive, but those silver-gray eyes pinned her.

Immediately visions of murder and mayhem flashed through her head, and fear slithered down her spine. For an instant she considered running, but it was too late. He would catch her before she made it out the front door.

Left with no choice, she lifted her chin and stood her ground.

The man was big and tough-looking—at least six-four. The rolled-up sleeves of his shirt revealed muscular forearms dusted with dark hair, wide wrists and powerful hands. He had the kind of broad-shouldered, impressive build that didn't come from working out in a yuppie gym three times a week.

She braced herself, but instead of rushing her, he straightened, crossed his arms over his chest and looked her up and down. "Well, well. If it isn't the prodigal daughter come home at last."

GINNA GRAY

THE
PRODIGAL
Daughter

ISBN 1-55166-603-0

THE PRODIGAL DAUGHTER

Copyright © 2000 by Ginna Gray.

All rights reserved. Except for use in any review, the reproduction or utilization of this work in whole or in part in any form by any electronic, mechanical or other means, now known or hereafter invented, including xerography, photocopying and recording, or in any information storage or retrieval system, is forbidden without the written permission of the publisher, MIRA Books, 225 Duncan Mill Road, Don Mills, Ontario, Canada M3B 3K9.

All characters in this book have no existence outside the imagination of the author and have no relation whatsoever to anyone bearing the same name or names. They are not even distantly inspired by any individual known or unknown to the author, and all incidents are pure invention.

MIRA and the Star Colophon are trademarks used under license and registered in Australia, New Zealand, Philippines, United States Patent and Trademark Office and in other countries.

Visit us at www.mirabooks.com

Printed in U.S.A.

To Brad.
My husband, my love, my best friend.

One

In Ruby Falls, Texas, population 3,418, the sleek Viper convertible stood out like a tuxedo at a barn dance.

Heads turned and jaws dropped when the stunning redhead roared into town behind the wheel of the hot car, the top down, her long hair streaming behind her like a fiery banner, The Best of Kenny Rogers blaring from the speakers.

The car's cream leather seats and green exterior were the perfect foil for her ivory skin and vibrant hair. The emerald color was only a shade darker than her eyes, a fact that escaped few of the gawkers who followed her progress through town.

Though her eyes were currently hidden behind a pair of Christian Dior sunglasses, there was scarcely a person in the country, or even the world who didn't know their exact color. Periodically over the past seven years, Maggie Malone's face, usually wearing a sexy smile while those fabulous eyes danced with wicked amusement, had graced the cover of every major magazine in the U.S. and Europe.

Noticing the stunned faces out of the corner of her eye, Maggie experienced a rush of satisfaction.

The reactions were exactly what she'd hoped for when she'd made arrangements to have the Viper delivered to the Dallas-Fort Worth airport in time for her arrival.

Seven years ago, she'd left Ruby Falls in disgrace, but by heaven, she was returning a success. And nothing drove that point home better than a classy fireball of a car.

Reaching the center of town and a bit of traffic, Maggie downshifted, and the Viper responded with a throaty rumble as she slowed behind Miss Agnes Purvey's 1964 Chevy II, which, Maggie noticed, still looked as though it had just rolled off the assembly line.

The traffic light up ahead at the north end of the town square had been green for several minutes. If she hadn't been stuck behind Miss Agnes and a U.P.S. truck she would have punched the accelerator and made the first turn around the square with seconds to spare before the light changed.

"Ah, jeezlouise, Miss Agnes! Move your skinny little butt, will you?"

Even as Maggie muttered the words she knew she was wasting her breath. Occasionally Miss Agnes cranked her speed up to a hair-raising thirty on the highway, but she never drove over twenty in town, and then only when someone was impertinent enough to honk or tailgate, as Maggie was doing.

That was why Miss Agnes never put more than five gallons of gas at a time in the Chevy. The prim little spinster swore that a full tank made the car go too fast.

The U.P.S. truck swung a right and started the

counterclockwise circuit around the square. Miss Agnes, her permed silver hair a halo of tight curls around her head, clutched the steering wheel with both hands and chugged along behind him. The U.P.S. truck hung a left onto the second side of the square before the old lady completed the first turn, leaving Maggie facing a red signal light.

She braked with a little squeal of tires and a huff of exasperation. After only a few seconds, though, she shook her head, a hint of a smile on her lips.

In all honesty, Maggie didn't really mind Miss Agnes's pokiness. During the past seven years she'd dreamed often of returning home someday, and in her mind's eye she'd always pictured things in Ruby Falls exactly as they'd been the night she'd left. It was comforting to know that at least some things hadn't changed.

Drumming long, cinnamon-colored fingernails against the padded leather steering wheel, Maggie glanced around while she waited. Obviously, she needn't have worried. From the look of it, not much of anything had changed in Ruby Falls.

On the way into town she had noticed a new Safeway grocery out on the Dallas highway next to Rowdy's Bar and Grill, and where the old abandoned gas station had been at Mimosa and Main a Jiffy Lube had sprung up, but other than that everything was wonderfully familiar.

The same white-trimmed, redbrick shops lined the square. Still anchoring the four corners were the First National Bank, Purdue's Pharmacy, Handyman Hardware and the Elks Lodge. Two blocks off Main to the east, the white spire of the Calvary Baptist

Church still rose above the oak, sweet gum and pecan trees.

For almost one hundred and thirty years, the sandstone courthouse had sat smack in the middle of the square. The ancient oaks dotting the surrounding grounds had reached their full growth long before Maggie was born. On this fine September afternoon, as they had every warm day since anyone could remember, old men played dominoes in the shade beneath the gnarled branches. Over the years the faces had changed as old-timers passed on and others took their place, but the cutthroat games continued, regular as the seasons.

Maggie recognized several of the silver-haired men—Ned Paxton, Oliver Jessup, the Toliver twins, Roy and Ray. Jeezlouise, there was even old Moses Beasley. The old coot had to be pushing a hundred. The World War I veteran had been a fixture in the square all of Maggie's life.

A group of women poured out of the Elks Lodge onto the sidewalk just a few feet away from the car, chattering among themselves.

Ah, yes, another thing that remained constant, Maggie thought. Come hell or high water, the first and third Thursday afternoons of every month the ladies' auxiliary met at the lodge. Apparently, the meeting had just ended.

Leading the pack was Edna Mae Taylor, Dorothy Purdue and Pauline Babcock, the three biggest gossips in town.

The instant the women spotted her they came up short, gaping.

Immediately the others plowed into them from behind.

"What in the world? Goodness gracious, Dorothy, why'd you stop like th...? Oh, my stars! Isn't
that...?"

"Yes," Pauline snapped.

"That's her, all right."

"What's she doing here? She hasn't been back
even once since she lit out of here seven years ago."

"I expect she's come to see her daddy. You
know, what with him being so ill an' all."

"And about time, I say."

"Humph. I can't imagine that seeing the likes of
her will be good for him." Pauline sniffed. "I heard
tell he disowned her years ago."

"Oh, surely not. Lily would never let Jacob do
that. She loves that girl somethin' fierce, you
know."

"Well, all I know is Lily goes to New York to
see her two or three times a year. Alone," Edna Mae
added with a knowing look. "And Lucille was told
by Inez, who got it on good authority, that Jacob
hasn't so much as spoken to the girl on the telephone since she left."

"And who can blame him? She was a wild one.
Used to drive poor Jacob crazy with her shenani-
gans. And after what she tried to do...well..."

"True. That was shameful. Still, blood is blood,
and in times of crisis, a man wants his family gathered around him."

"Yes, well, you'd think, under the circumstances,
she'd at least have the decency to arrive quietly. But
oh, no. Not Maggie," Pauline huffed. "She has to

make a spectacle of herself. Why, just look at that car. And listen to that loud music. You mark my word—''

The traffic light turned green. Flashing the women a grin, Maggie reached over and cranked up the volume on the stereo. She squealed a right, "Love, or Something Like It" blaring from the speakers in Kenny's whiskey voice, the heavy throb of the base reverberating in the air like a giant heartbeat.

Nothing much distracted the domino players from their games, but the rumble of the Viper and the honky-tonk music grabbed their attention. Heads came up and swiveled in unison, following the sleek machine as it growled its way around three sides of the square.

Maggie waggled her fingers in a flirtatious wave, then winked, puckered her luscious red lips and blew them all a kiss.

At their slack-jawed astonishment, she laughed and hung a right, speed-shifted into second and peeled rubber down Main on the south side of the square.

No, nothing had changed in Ruby Falls.

Before she'd gone a block her laughter faded and she made a wry face at her own behavior. Lord, how easy it was to fall back into old patterns. Back in town five minutes, and already she'd deliberately baited the gossips. She hadn't resorted to that sort of thumb-your-nose-in-their-faces defense since she'd left here.

But then again, there had been no need.

Those few minutes in the square had distracted Maggie, but now, drawing close to home, the nervousness was back and growing worse with every rhythmic thump-thump of the tires on the paving.

Ever since that awful telephone call four days ago she'd been wound as tight as an eight-day clock.

The call had come in the middle of the night while she had been on a photo shoot on an island off the coast of Greece. At her mother's first words she had bolted upright in the bed, her heart pounding.

"Maggie, you have to come home."

"Momma? Is that you?" All she'd heard was a sob, and she'd gripped the receiver tighter. "Calm down, and tell me what's wrong."

"Please, Maggie, you have to come home. I'm begging you."

"Oh, Momma, you know I'd like nothing better. But I can't. Nothing has changed."

"Yes, it has," her mother had cried tearfully. "Your daddy is dying! Oh, God, Maggie, my Jacob is dying."

The words had hit her like a fist to the stomach. Remembering the shock and pain of that moment, Maggie gripped the steering wheel tight and bit her lower lip.

"Wh-what?" she had replied weakly, sinking back against the pillows. "But...but you told me just a few days ago that he was holding his own. That the tumor in his lung was shrinking. If I had known he was so ill I wouldn't have flown halfway around the world."

"I know, I know," Lily said in a chagrined voice. "But I knew you had this important job, and I didn't want to worry you. And for a while the treatment did seem to be working,'' she added quickly before Maggie could take her to task. "Then his condition worsened."

"Oh, Momma, why didn't you tell me?"

"I should have, I know. But at the time Dr. Lockhart seemed so positive that another round of chemotherapy would halt the cancer, so I didn't see any point in alarming you needlessly. But it didn't work, Maggie,'' Lily said, her voice quavering. "That horrible, insidious disease is winning. It's going to take my Jacob from me."

Lily barely choked out the last, and Maggie fought back tears of her own as she listened to her mother's pitiful sobs. It was several seconds before the wrenching sounds turned to sniffs and Lily regained enough control to speak again.

"The doctors sent him home. There's nothing more they can do for him at the hospital other than make him as comfortable as possible. They give him three or four months. Five at best."

"Oh, Momma,'' Maggie murmured in a stricken voice, closing her eyes. She felt as though the ground had just dropped out from under her. Her father? Dying? No. No, it couldn't be. It was too soon. She needed more time!

"So you see, you have to come home."

"But…Daddy doesn't want me there."

"No! No, you're wrong! Believe me, when a man knows he hasn't much time left he sees things differently. Trust me, dear, your father wants you to come home."

"Did he…did Daddy actually say he wanted to see me?" She tightened her grip on the receiver, doing her best to clamp down on the hope swelling inside her.

"Well...maybe not in so many words—"

"Oh, Momma—"

"But he hinted at it," Lily insisted.

"Momma, please—"

"Maggie, I've been married to your daddy for almost twenty-nine years. I can read him like a book. He wants to ask, but you know his stiff-necked pride. He took a stance and now he thinks he can't back down. But he needs to do this, sweetheart."

She waited a beat, then added, "So do you."

No fair, Maggie thought, tipping her head back to stare at the ceiling in an agony of doubt. No fair.

Lily's voice lowered, quavered with urgency. "This is the end of the line, Maggie. Your last chance to make peace with your father. If you don't, you'll always regret it."

Sighing, Maggie closed her eyes and massaged her forehead with the fingertips of her free hand. "You make it tough to say no."

"Then don't. Come home, Maggie. I'm begging you. Please, *please* come home. Before it's too late."

The pathetic little catch in her mother's voice had been her undoing. That, and her own helpless yearning.

She had been only one of five top models on the shoot. The photographer, Jean Paul Delon, was notoriously temperamental but a brilliant artist who ran his shoots like a fascist dictator. Luckily, he was also a softy when it came to family. With the complete agreement of the other models, who were all sympathetic and supportive, Jean Paul worked only Maggie the next day to complete her part in the shoot.

After the grueling dawn-till-dusk stint in front of the cameras, she had caught the red-eye for the first leg of her journey. It had taken her the better part of three days just to get home.

In flight, Maggie had contacted her agency and explained her situation and given instructions to clear her schedule for the next four months—or at least, whittle it down drastically.

It had not been easy. The job had required all the diplomatic skills of Val Brownley, the owner of the Valentina Modeling Agency, to handle the disgruntled clients.

Those photo shoots, TV appearances and promotions that could be delayed without causing a major crisis or a lawsuit were rescheduled, and other models were assigned to those accounts that would accept a substitute.

Unavoidably there were some commitments Maggie would have to honor. Her exclusive contract with Eve Cosmetics, for one. The Stephano Perfume shoot for another. Plus a few other contractually binding deals.

Which would mean flying back and forth every few weeks, but compared to her normal frenetic schedule, that would be a piece of cake.

Val was not happy. She had thrown a fit and tried every argument and threat she could dream up to change Maggie's mind. In the end Maggie had informed her that if the agency didn't reduce her workload for the next few months, she would be forced to quit.

What choice did she have? Her father was dying, and he wanted to see her.

On the south side of town the houses were older, bigger, farther apart, more elegant—Victorian-colonial- and mission-style homes with wide porches flanked by massive azalea bushes, set far back off the street among enormous shade trees. This was where the old guard had always lived— the founding families who owned the businesses, ran the town and were what passed for society in Ruby Falls.

Maggie passed the impressive white colonial where her sister Laurel lived with her husband and father-in-law, but she clenched her jaw and drove on without so much as a glance at the place. The mere thought of her sweet sister married to Martin Howe made her physically ill.

A mile past the city limits sign Maggie turned off the highway onto the black-topped farm road, and the knot of tension in her stomach tightened. Her breathing became shallow and her palms began to sweat. No longer in the mood for music, she snapped off the CD player. Now the only sounds were the wind, the throaty purr of the engine and the hum of the tires.

A mile down the blacktop road, Maggie turned right onto a narrow lane. The Viper growled as she reduced speed. Gravel popped beneath the tires and bounced off the undercarriage, but her heart was knocking so hard and fast all she heard was its pulsing beat drumming in her ears.

Bordering the lane on the left, the Malone home orchard flashed by, five hundred acres of mature peach, plum and pear trees marching in precise rows as far as the eye could see. Absently, Maggie noticed that the seven-hundred-acre tract of virgin forest still bordered the lane on the opposite side, and an amused smile tugged at her mouth.

That land had been in the Toliver family for more than a hundred years. For at least the last fifty her grandfather, then her father, had tried to buy the property so they could increase the size of the home orchard, but the Tolivers wouldn't even discuss the matter.

More than eighty years ago her great-grandmother and namesake, Katherine Margaret Malone, had refused Wendell Toliver's marriage proposal. The Toliver family was still miffed over the supposed insult. People around these parts didn't let go of a grudge easily.

The thought had barely run through her mind when she rounded a curve and her family home came into view. Maggie stared, equal parts joy and nervous anticipation flooding her.

The large house sat far back from the lane on a two-acre patch of land dotted with towering oaks and pines and surrounded on three sides by the fruit orchard.

Heart pounding, Maggie turned into the drive and moments later brought the Viper to a halt in the circular section in front of the house.

For several minutes she sat motionless, still gripping the steering wheel, staring at the two-story, red-brick house. Her nerves hummed like a plucked guitar string. Tingles raced over her skin, making the fine hairs on her arms stand on end.

She was swamped with so many different emotions that she could barely breathe—grief and joy, regret and anticipation, sorrow and excitement, all tangled together.

The shutters and wood trim were still a crisp white. So were the swings and rocking chairs scattered along the porch. The azalea and camellia bushes bordering the wide veranda were perhaps a bit larger, the crepe myrtles at the corners taller, but other than that the house looked exactly the same.

Which didn't surprise her. Since her great-grandmother had built the house in 1927, what remodeling that had been done had been minor. The sunporch across the back of the house had been enlarged and made into a family room, the kitchen and bathrooms had been updated twice and central air-conditioning had been added.

Today, however, all the doors and windows stood open to take advantage of the unusually pleasant fall weather. Maggie eyed the screen door, expecting someone—either her mother or Ida Lou Nettles, their housekeeper—to appear at any moment, but no one came, nor were there any sounds from within.

Then Maggie remembered that Thursdays and Sundays were Ida Lou's days off, which meant she wouldn't be home until around ten. Every Thursday for as far back as Maggie could remember, Ida Lou ran her personal errands in the morning, joined her cronies for an afternoon of bridge, then had dinner at the City Café with her best friend, Clara Edwards, and the two of them capped the day off either with a movie or an evening of bingo over at the Grange Hall.

A sweet scent hung in the air. Maggie inhaled it deep into her lungs and smiled. Ah, peaches.

Automatically her gaze darted beyond the house in the direction of the cannery on the opposite side of the property, though it wasn't visible through the trees. These days, the Malone Cannery offered a full line of canned fruits and vegetables, but it was the smell of peaches stewing that she would always associate with home.

Home. Fixing her gaze on the house again, she drew a deep breath and reached for the door handle.

After shaking the travel wrinkles out of her blue-and-burnt-orange broomstick skirt, Maggie started up the short walkway and climbed the steps.

No one watching would ever imagine the turmoil going on inside her. She walked with her head high, her shoulders back, her hips swaying with sassy confidence. Maggie'd had years of experience at hiding her feelings. And one thing she'd learned since leaving home was how to project an image.

At the door she paused, not sure whether to ring the bell or just walk right in.

Cupping her hands on either side of her eyes, she peered in through the screen down the long central hallway. There wasn't a soul in sight.

She hesitated, reluctant to call out or knock, in case her father was resting.

Oh, what the hell? This was her home, wasn't it? she thought, and opened the screen door and stepped inside.

She had barely taken a step when she heard a faint

sound coming from her father's study, to the right of the front door.

One of Maggie's eyebrows rose. Apparently he wasn't as sick as her mother had led her to believe if he felt well enough to work.

Her nerves began to jump. She had been longing for, praying for this meeting for seven years. Now that it was finally about to happen she was almost sick with nerves.

Pressing her fist against her fluttering stomach, she drew a deep breath and stepped to the open doorway...and froze.

"Who are you? And what the devil do you think you're doing?" she snapped.

The stranger rifling through her father's desk looked up. His rugged face remained impassive, but those silver-gray eyes pinned her.

Belatedly, Maggie recalled the numerous reports she'd heard on the evening news in New York about people who'd had the misfortune to stumble across a burglar. Immediately visions of murder and mayhem flashed through her head, and fear slithered done her spine.

For an instant she considered running, but it was too late. He would catch her before she made it out the front door. Besides, her knees were trembling so much she wasn't sure her legs would support her.

Left with no choice, she lifted her chin and stood her ground.

The man was big and tough-looking—at least six four. The rolled-up sleeves of his chambray work shirt revealed muscular forearms dusted with dark hair, wide wrists and powerful hands. He had the kind of broad-shouldered impressive build that didn't come from working out in a yuppie gym three times a week.

Clearly, she was no match for him.

But dammit, she was no wimp, either. Barefoot, she stood six feet tall and was in excellent physical condition. Maggie narrowed her eyes. *I may not win, but lay a hand on me, buster, and you'll damn well know you've been in a fight.*

She braced herself, but instead of rushing her, he straightened, crossed his arms over his chest and looked her up and down. "Well, well. If it isn't the prodigal daughter come home at last."

The drawled statement—snide though it was—reassured her as nothing else could have.

The awful fear and tension left her in a *whoosh*, like air rushing out of a balloon. A burglar might have recognized her, but he wouldn't have had any knowledge of her personal life.

"Ah, so you're a local, are you?" While that discovery allayed her fear of being attacked, it produced a different kind of uneasiness. His only knowledge of her had to have come from others, and she could just imagine the kind of stories he'd heard.

As a teenager Maggie had learned to hide her insecurities and pain behind saucy humor and flippancy. During the past seven years she'd acquired self-esteem and poise, but she'd found that the strategy still worked when dealing with men, particularly with a bit of audacious flirting thrown in. The harmless ones either dissolved into stammering wrecks or ran for the hills, and the macho types never seemed to know quite how to handle a confident woman who possessed sass and style. Either way, it gave her an edge.

Turning on a sultry smile, Maggie cocked one hip, planted her hand on it and gave him a slow once-over. "Do I know you, handsome?"

"I doubt it." Instead of the reaction she expected, he turned the slow perusal back on her.

His pale eyes skimmed her dispassionately, examining her famous face feature by feature, her bright, wind-tousled hair. When he was done his gaze slid downward over the burnt-orange knit top that clung to her curves, then down farther to her ankle-length skirt. His attention lingered there before continuing down to the cinnamon-colored toenails peeking out of her sandals, only to return seconds later to linger again in the region of her thighs.

Maggie realized that, backlit as she undoubtedly was by the light streaming in through the front door, he could see through her gauzy skirt, but she didn't move. Let him look at her legs. It would take more than this brawny workman to fluster her. Besides, she had fantastic legs, and she'd shown them—and a whole lot more—in dozens of swimsuit layouts.

When he was done his gaze met hers again. The disdain in his eyes and the slight twist of his chiseled mouth was not the reaction she was accustomed to receiving, and it gave her a jolt.

"But I know you," he said finally in a flat voice.

Anger curled in Maggie's stomach but she controlled it and feigned amusement. "I doubt it," she mimicked. "You can't believe what you read in the gossip columns, you know. Or what you think you see in the photographs of me."

"I wouldn't know about that. I don't read gossip columns or look at many magazines. But you can't grow up in Ruby Falls without knowing about the Malones. And you have to admit, as a teenager, you made your mark around here."

"Ah, I see. My misspent youth has come back to haunt me," she drawled, strolling into the room. She hitched one hip onto the corner of her father's desk. "You still haven't told me who you are or why you were going through my father's papers."

"I was looking for an account file that Jacob was reviewing last night. And the name is Garrett. Dan Garrett. I'm general manager of the cannery and orchards."

"Oh, I don't think so, sugar. Harry Putnam has been the general manager for over twenty years."

"Harry retired two years ago."

"Oh, right. I guess I forgot." Forgot, hell. This was the first she'd heard of it. When it came to business matters, her mother might as well be on another planet.

"So Daddy made you the new general manager, huh? Odd, I would've thought he'd give the job to an older hand. How long have you worked for Malone Enterprises?"

"Twenty years."

"*What!* That's impossible. I've only been gone seven, and I don't remember seeing you around here at all."

He shot her a steady look, then bent and went back to searching the desk drawers. "Hardly surprising. I was seven or eight years ahead of you in school. I started working on the picking crew part-time on weekends and after school when I was fourteen. When I graduated I was hired on full-time as a crew boss. By the time you took off I'd worked my way up to foreman in the cannery.

"But as I recall, in those days you didn't spend much time hanging around the orchard workers or on the cannery floor. And our families sure as hell didn't move in the same social circles."

Maggie frowned. The implied accusation of snobbery didn't set well. Growing up, she'd spent most of her free time at the cannery, but mostly in the office trying to learn the business. Her father would have skinned her alive if she'd gone down onto the cannery floor or into the orchards during harvest time.

Tipping her head to one side, she studied him curiously. "You don't like me very much, do you?"

"No," he replied without the slightest hesitation, startling a laugh out of her. He didn't bother to look up.

"Oh, gee, don't hold back. Spit it all out, why don't you? What's the matter, sugar? Don't you like redheads? Or is it just me?" When he didn't bother to answer, she went on. "Surely you don't hold my teenage rebellion against me. I was a little wild, I know, but I was just a kid, for heaven's sake."

"From what I hear, nothing has changed. But that's not it. I don't give a rat's ass about your teenage pranks or what kind of dissolute life-style you're into now." He straightened with a file folder in his hand and pinned her again with those cold eyes. Absently, he raked back a lock of dark hair that had fallen across his forehead. "I happen to think you're a spoiled, self-centered brat who doesn't care about anyone but herself.''

Maggie's jaw dropped. Before she could find her tongue he went on.

''Your father was diagnosed with cancer over two years ago. Two *years!* He's been through ten kinds of hell since then—chemotherapy, radiation treatment, a barrage of tests—and he's grown weaker by the day. And not once in all that time have you come home or even bothered to call him.''

Maggie stiffened. ''I talk to Momma about him every day.'' The flirtatious, honeyed tones disappeared as anger sharpened her voice.

''It's not the same. He needs to talk to you, to see you.''

Maggie shot off the desk and drew herself up to her full six-foot height. ''You know nothing about me or my feelings for my father. Or what my father wants and needs. Furthermore it's none of your business.''

''Your feelings?'' Dan snorted. ''What feelings? Since you walked in you haven't even asked where he is.''

Maggie blinked, thrown off guard. Uneasiness trickled down her spine. ''I assumed he and my mother were napping.''

''Jacob is in the hospital in Tyler. At two this morning Lily and I had to rush him to the ER.''

Two

"The *hospital!* For God's sake! Why didn't you tell me right away? Which hospital?"

"Mercy."

Maggie spun around and tore out of the office and out the front door. She cleared the steps in one leap and almost made it to her car before the screen door banged shut behind her.

In only seconds she'd slid behind the wheel and the Viper roared to life. "Oh, God. Oh, God. Please don't let me be too late. Please. Oh, please, God, please."

From the corner of her eye Maggie saw Dan Garrett standing on the other side of the screen door, watching her, but she had more important things on her mind. Tires squealing, she spun out of the circular loop in front of the house and smoked down the long drive toward the road.

The forty-two-mile drive from Ruby Falls to the Tyler city limits normally took forty-five to fifty minutes, and then another fifteen to negotiate the city traffic to the hospital. Maggie made it in thirty-five.

The first person she saw when she rushed off the

elevator onto the second floor of Mercy Hospital was her mother.

Lily Malone stood beside a nurses' station, talking to the women behind the counter.

"Momma!"

Lily looked around, her face lighting. "Maggie!" She hurried forward with her arms outstretched. "Maggie! Oh, Maggie, love, I'm so glad you're here."

Eight inches taller than Lily, Maggie had to stoop to return her mother's hug. Fear had her heart knocking against her ribs, her nerves screaming, so for an instant she allowed herself the comfort of her mother's embrace. Clasping her close, she squeezed her eyes shut and breathed in the familiar scent of violets that always seemed to cling to Lily's skin, and absorbed the unconditional love that flowed from her.

"How is he?" Grasping her mother's shoulders, Maggie eased her back and searched her face.

At fifty-two, Lily was still a beautiful woman, Maggie thought, as she did every time she saw her. With her fair coloring and small build she had a delicate look that made everyone want to protect her, her husband most of all.

Jacob Malone adored his wife and treated her as though she were a fragile angel. Seeing the fear and strain in Lily's face, Maggie knew that he was probably more worried about what his illness was doing to his wife than what it was doing to him.

Fatigue smudged dark circles beneath Lily's blue eyes and deepened the lines that ran from each side of her nose to the corners of her mouth. Her blond hair had a few more streaks of silver than when she'd visited New York six months ago, Maggie noticed. However, it was the worry in her mother's eyes that concerned her most.

"He's all right, dear," Lily assured her firstborn gently. "He's weak, but he's resting comfortably now. Thank God."

"What happened? When we talked yesterday you said he was resting comfortably at home."

"He was. Then last night he began to have difficulty breathing. His lungs were filling with fluid, so we brought him here. They drained it off, and he's doing better now."

"By 'we' I take it you mean you and that Dan Garrett person I met at the house."

"Oh, you met Dan. Good, good. He's a wonderful young man, and he's been such a help to your daddy. And to me, too."

"Mmm," Maggie hummed noncommittally. She fully intended to question her mother about Mr. Garrett, particularly about how he came to hold such a responsible position in the family business, but that could wait until later. "What caused the fluid to build up, and what's the doctor doing about it?"

Pretending not to notice the agog stares of the nurses behind the station, Maggie slipped her arm through her mother's and nudged her down the hall toward her father's room before one of the women could work up the nerve to ask for her autograph.

Though she didn't understand what the fascination was, normally Maggie went out of her way to be cordial to fans. At the moment, however, she simply wasn't up to dealing with their adulation. Later,

when things were more settled, she'd make a point
to stop by the station for a chat.

"It's just part of the disease," Lily explained,
oblivious to the stir her daughter's arrival had created. "The tumor prevents his lungs from functioning as they should, and the fluid builds up gradually.
This is the second time they've had to be drained.
The doctors have adjusted his medication and want
to watch him for a few hours, but barring compli-
cations, we can take him home tomorrow."

"Is it all right if I go in and see him?"

"Of course it's all right. He's allowed visitors.
Your sisters are with him right now."

"Oh, wonderful. I can't wait to see Laurel and Jo
Beth."

"Well, come along, then. Jacob was sleeping
when I left to get some coffee, but he should wake
up soon."

Maggie eagerly walked with her mother down the
hall. She had missed her sisters terribly these past
seven years. Her mother visited her regularly, but
never Laurel or Jo Beth. Whenever she talked to
them on the telephone their conversations never
lasted long, and they always had an excuse why they
couldn't accompany Lily to New York. Maggie had
never pressed her mother for an answer, but she suspected that her father had forbidden them to have
any contact with her.

Lily opened the door a crack and peeked into Jacob's room. "He's still sleeping," she whispered to
Maggie over her shoulder. "We'll have to be
quiet."

She stuck her head inside the room and said

softly, "Look who's here, everyone." Pushing the door open all the way, she dragged Maggie into the room with her.

"Maggie!" A look of blinding joy flashed across Laurel's face. She took an eager step forward, but her husband's barked warning halted her in her tracks.

"Laurel!"

Laurel's gaze darted to Martin, and instantly her expression sobered and the light went out of her eyes. Visibly reining in her emotions, she clasped her hands together. "Hello, Maggie," she said in a flat voice.

Maggie had no intention of settling for such a cool greeting. Surging forward, she threw her arms around her sister. In return she received a lukewarm hug, but she pretended not to notice.

"Oh, it's so good to see you," she declared, squeezing her much-shorter sister in a bear hug. "I've missed you so much." Holding Laurel by her shoulders, she eased back with a warm smile. "How are you, sis?"

"I'm fine. Just fine."

She didn't look fine. She looked pale and listless, and there were dark circles under her eyes. Laurel had always been a delicate beauty, but now she wasn't just slender, she was almost skeletal, her arms and legs bony and her classic facial features pared down to sharpness. Her natural blond hair, which had always been her sweet sister's one vanity, was clipped at her nape and hung lank and limp down her back like an old rag.

Jeezlouise, Maggie thought. Laurel was only

twenty-six, a year younger than she was, but all her sparkle was gone. She looked used up and drab, and so skinny a good wind would blow her away.

Was she anorexic? Or had worry over their father's condition done this to her?

Most worrisome of all, Laurel wouldn't quite meet Maggie's eyes.

"What's *she* doing here?" Martin demanded.

Maggie stiffened. Up until that moment she had studiously avoided looking at her brother-in-law. Now the outrage in his voice fired her temper. Before she could turn and deliver a cutting retort her mother stepped in.

"Maggie is here because her father is gravely ill. And because I asked her to come. She's our daughter, too, Martin. She has as much right to be here as her sisters."

"I don't agree at all."

"That may be, but it isn't your decision to make, is it?" Lily smiled slightly to take the sting out of the words, but her voice was velvet-covered steel.

The exchange flabbergasted Maggie. She knew her mother wasn't fond of Martin, but, good, genteel southern lady that she was, she always treated him cordially, for Laurel's sake and because of Jacob's determined support of the man. Her mild-mannered mother usually went along with whatever her husband wanted, leaving the decision-making to him. That she had taken a stand against Martin, especially in that emphatic tone, was amazing.

Maggie noticed that she wasn't the only one surprised by Lily's uncharacteristic firmness.

Martin was so taken aback he was speechless for

a full five seconds. Then he clenched his jaw and stalked to the window, presenting his rigid back to the room as he stared out.

Laurel's face turned even paler than before, something Maggie hadn't thought possible. Her sister darted a worried look at Martin, then she turned away and needlessly fiddled with the items on the nightstand beside Jacob's bed.

To break the tension, Maggie turned to the teenager sprawled in the room's only chair with her legs draped over one of the arms. Small, dark-haired and pixie cute, in looks, her seventeen-year-old baby sister favored their father as much as Laurel favored Lily.

"Don't tell me this is little Jo Beth? I can't believe it."

The girl rolled her eyes and made a disgusted face.

"For heaven sake's, child, stop that slouching and come here and say hello to your sister," Lily ordered.

"I can do that from here. See." She barely spared Maggie a sidelong glance. "Hi."

"Jo Beth." The warning in their mother's voice was unmistakable, and instantly the teenager's attitude turned from surly to belligerent.

"What? You want me to turn cartwheels for her? Why should I? She hasn't bothered to visit us in seven years. Miss Big Shot Supermodel thinks she's too good for her family and Ruby Falls."

Martin turned from the window with a smirk on his face.

Laurel gasped. "That's a terrible thing to say!"

"Jo Beth!" their mother snapped.

"What? It's the truth!"

"Really, child," Lily scolded, wringing her hands. "You should be ashamed of yourself, speaking to your sister that way. Now, be nice and apologize."

"When pigs fly!" The girl shot out of the chair, glaring at Lily. She clenched her fists at her sides and her face screwed up in over-the-top teenage outrage.

"Jo Beth! How dare—"

Maggie touched Lily's arm. "No, Momma, please. It's all right. She's entitled to her opinion."

"I don't need you to defend me," the girl snapped.

"Good, because I'm not. Just your right to speak your mind. Look, if you want, we'll have this out later. You can take your best shot." Maggie glanced at their father and tipped her head in his direction. "But now isn't the time for this kind of discussion."

The girl looked as though she was about to argue, but after a few seconds she flounced back to the chair, plopped herself down and sulked.

Unable to avoid it any longer, Maggie looked directly at her brother-in-law for the first time. "Hello, Martin."

His mouth tightened, but he gave a curt nod. "Maggie."

The terse reply made no attempt at civility, and that suited Maggie just fine. The less he said to her the better. She'd be happy if he never spoke to her at all.

"Has he wakened since I left?" Lily asked in a whisper, moving to stand beside her husband's bed.

Laurel shook her head. "No. He's really sleeping soundly. He hasn't even stirred."

Maggie joined her sister on the opposite side of the bed from Lily. Laying one forearm along the side rail, she reached out and smoothed her father's hair away from his forehead.

He, too, was thinner. And older, she thought with a pang.

Deep lines scored his forehead and bracketed his mouth, and his once-dark hair was now salt-and-pepper. Maggie had always thought of her father as strong and invincible, and it came as a shock to realize that he wasn't.

In the faded blue-and-white-striped hospital gown he looked old and sick and vulnerable. His eyes seemed to have sunk into his head and the exposed skin on his neck and arms appeared soft and crepey. Even the hair on his chest, visible through the V-neck gown, had turned white.

Tears threatened, but Maggie blinked them back. Time and illness had taken their toll, certainly, but Jacob Malone was still a big man. So what if his shoulders were a bit bony and his chest not quite as broad or as firm as it had once been? Both were still wide enough to nearly span the narrow bed, weren't they?

A terrible longing twisted inside her as she gazed at those shoulders, and a sad smile quivered around her mouth. How many times had she longed to be held in her father's strong arms? To put her head down on those broad shoulders and be cuddled? To hear him say "I love you, Maggie girl"?

She battled back the wave of grief and pain and clenched her jaw.

He couldn't die, dammit. The doctors had to be wrong. Fifty-eight wasn't old. He could still fight this.

Oh, God, Daddy, please don't die.

"Laurel, it's time to go," Martin announced. "I have to get back to the cannery. Jacob is depending on me to look after the business now. I can be more help to him there than standing around here."

"You go on, Martin. I can take Laurel home when visiting hours are over."

"No, thanks, Lily. She has things to do, as well. C'mon, Laurel, let's go."

"I'll go with you, too," Jo Beth announced, bounding up out of the chair. "You can drop me off on your way."

"Call me tonight when you get home, will you, Momma, and let me know how Daddy's doing?" Laurel asked, casting one last worried glance at their father.

"Of course I will, honey."

"Laurel, I haven't got all day."

"Coming." Snatching up her purse, she kissed Lily's cheek and scurried out the door her husband held open without so much as a "goodbye" for Maggie.

"Does he always treat her like that?" Maggie asked when the door swung shut behind them.

"Hmm. Most of the time he's a bit more subtle about it, but, yes, Martin tends to be bossy. I'm afraid I haven't set a very good example, always deferring to your father, but I do so because I love and respect your father. Jacob has never demanded blind obedience the way Martin does.''

Lily shook her head. ''I've tried to talk to her. I've told her she shouldn't let him dominate her the way he does, but she just laughs and brushes my concerns aside. She claims she's perfectly happy and says I'm worrying over nothing. Jacob's no better. He says that Martin simply believes that a man should wear the pants in a family.''

''Huh. If it were me I'd strangle him with them. How does she stand it?''

''She loves him, I suppose.''

''Daddy loves you but he's never treated you that way.''

On the contrary, Jacob adored her mother, and even after almost twenty-nine years of marriage he still treated her as though she was the most precious thing on earth. Maggie was quite certain her parents could count the few serious arguments they'd had on the fingers of one hand. Neither she nor her sisters had ever heard a cross word pass between them.

Lily sighed. ''I know. But everyone is different, Maggie. And as much as Martin's attitude concerns me, a marriage is between the two people involved. It's not our place to interfere.''

''I'll never understand what she sees in him,'' Maggie said, giving a little shudder of distaste.

''Now, Maggie—''

Jacob made a small sound and shifted, and both women forgot all about Martin Howe as they leaned anxiously over the railings on either side of the bed.

"Well, now, did you finally decide to wake up?" Lily teased, and slipped her hand into her husband's.

Jacob blinked twice, then focused on his wife's face. His eyes warmed with so much love that Maggie felt her throat close up. His mouth twitched in an attempt at a smile. "Hi, love."

"Hi, yourself." Lily squeezed his hand. "Look who's come to see you, dearest." She glanced across the bed at Maggie, and he slowly turned his head.

Shock raced across Jacob's face.

Maggie's stomach took a fluttery jump, but she managed a smile. "Hello, Daddy."

"You." His face hardened and his eyes turned to ice. "What the hell are *you* doing here?"

Three

Maggie's gaze flashed to her mother.

It was all a lie, her eyes silently accused. He didn't want to see me. He doesn't want me here at all. You *lied* to me!

Lily at least had the grace to look guilty, but that was small consolation to Maggie.

Hurt and disillusion sat on her heart like wet cement. There were only two people in the world whom she felt she could trust without question—her mother and Aunt Nan. Now her mother had lied to her. Tricked her.

Oh, God. What a fool she'd been. She should never have come. And to think, she'd been so elated that her father had finally wanted to see her. Fool! Fool! Fool! When will you ever learn?

"I asked you a question. What are you doing here?"

Ruthlessly tamping down her hurt and disappointment, Maggie flashed her father a cheeky smile and drawled, "Well now, Daddy, you know what they say about a bad penny. It just keeps turning up."

Jacob's mouth tightened. "I might have expected a flippant remark from you. You haven't changed a bit, have you. You're still the same disrespectful smart mouth you always were."

She shrugged and flashed another smile. "Works for me."

Inside, she was shattered and fighting to hold herself together. The only way she could do that was to act blasé.

The instinctive response bothered her, though not for the same reason it annoyed her father.

Why did it matter so? Why did she *let* it matter?

Dammit! She was a grown woman. A competent, intelligent, successful woman, a woman with the poise and confidence to hold her own in any society. She had rubbed elbows with all manner of celebrities, from movie stars to politicians to the power brokers of the world. She was a celebrity in her own right, for Christ's sake!

Yet, one harsh word from her father and she reverted to the hurt child she had once been.

And like that hurt child, her instinctive defense against his dislike and the pain it brought was the same one she had employed as a teenager—irreverent humor and in-your-face provocation.

It was childish and nonconstructive, but it was either that or cry. Damned if she would let him see how much she longed for his approval.

Jacob's mouth tightened. Even as weak and sick as he was, his animosity was so strong it was palpable. It radiated from him like hundreds of tiny poison darts stinging her skin, making her stomach cramp. Shredding her heart.

"I made it clear when you left that you were no longer welcome here, Katherine."

"Jacob!"

He ignored his wife's shocked exclamation. Maggie barely heard it herself. Her focus was centered on her father. "Oh, yes. You certainly did that."

Trust him to call her Katherine, she thought. At her mother's insistence, as firstborn, she had been named after the family matriarch, his grandmother, Katherine Margaret Malone, who had also gone by the name Maggie, but from the time she was born Jacob had stubbornly insisted on calling her Katherine. He had never actually said so, but Maggie suspected that Jacob hated the idea of her carrying his beloved grandmother's name.

Catching her lower lip between her teeth, Lily wrung her hands and shifted from one foot to the other. Her worried gaze darted back and forth between Jacob and Maggie.

"Knowing that, you have a lot of gall showing up here. Did you think I'd be too sick to toss you out again?"

"Jacob, please." Lily's face was white with distress. "If you're going to be angry with anyone it should be me. I asked Maggie to come. I told her you wanted to see her."

"What! Dammit, Lily, you shouldn't have done that! You know—"

The door swung open, and a young man in his mid-thirties strode into the room. "Afternoon, Mr. Malone. How're you feeling today? Better, I hope."

Even had he not been wearing a long white medical coat with a stethoscope stuffed into one pocket, Maggie would have known he was a doctor. He had that scrubbed, antiseptic look.

He stopped in his tracks and gaped when he spotted Maggie. Accustomed to the poleaxed reaction, especially from men, she pretended not to notice and even managed to force a smile.

To his credit, he recovered his composure quickly and stepped forward, extending his hand. "Hello, there. I'm Dr. Neil Sanderson. Dr. Lockhart's new partner. Say, aren't you...?"

"This is our daughter Maggie," Lily supplied in a quick, nervous voice, anxious to dispel the angry tension in the room. "Maggie is a model, Neil. You've probably seen her picture somewhere."

"Yes. Of course. I should have realized. Your face is on the cover of over half the magazines in the waiting rooms." Dr. Sanderson's blue eyes glowed as he flashed her an eager smile. "It's a pleasure, Miss Malone."

Maggie shook his hand and murmured something in return. What, she couldn't have said. It took all her concentration to maintain her nonchalant expression.

"Maggie has just arrived. She flew in all the way from Greece."

"I see. Well, I wouldn't want to interrupt your visit. Why don't I come back later?"

"You're not interrupting." Jacob's gaze pinned Maggie. "She was just leaving."

Maggie forced a chuckle and sent the young doctor a twinkling look. "Not very subtle, is he? That's Daddy's way of telling me to get out while you examine him." She winked and whispered behind her hand, loud enough for everyone to hear, "I think he's afraid your delightful hospital gown might be too revealing for my delicate sensibilities.''

Dr. Sanderson looked appalled. ''Oh, no, please. Don't go on my account. I can just as easily stop by at the end of my rounds.''

Maggie laughed again and gave his arm a pat. ''I'm kidding, Doc. Daddy's just being thoughtful. The only sleep I've had in four days has been cat-naps on airplanes. Jet lag is catching up with me. If I don't find a bed soon I'm going to drop in my tracks. I just stopped by on my way home to let my folks know I had arrived.''

''Oh. I see. Well, in that case, it was a pleasure meeting you. Perhaps I'll see you again before you leave.''

''Perhaps,'' she replied with a flirtatious smile, and had the pleasure of seeing color rise in his neck.

For the first time in her life, Maggie was furious with her mother, but for Dr. Sanderson's benefit she gave her a quick hug. ''I'll see you at home later.''

Leaning down, she kissed her father's forehead, ignoring the way he stiffened at her touch. She winked at him and drawled, ''Now, Daddy, don't you go chasing any pretty nurses, you hear?''

Pretending she didn't see Jacob's mouth tighten, Maggie sauntered out the door with her head high, as though she hadn't a care in the world.

The nonchalant pose vanished the instant the door swung shut behind her. She slumped against the wall next to her father's room and clamped her hand over her mouth. Oh, God. Oh, God. Oh, God.

The pressure in her chest was unbearable. A sob forced its way up past the knot in her throat, and though she struggled to hold them back, tears filled her eyes, blurring the long hallway.

Maggie's face contorted. Her shoulders hunched forward and began to shake. She fought for control, but she was no match for the unspeakable sorrow. With a great, gasping sob the last of her composure crumbled, and she turned her face to the vinyl-covered wall and gave in to the flood of tears.

That was how Dan Garrett found her when he arrived a few minutes later.

He spotted her the instant he stepped off the elevator and came to an abrupt halt, stunned. The last thing he expected was to find Jacob's audacious, self-assured daughter huddled in a ball of misery.

Dan darted a quick look around. The three nurses behind the station were busy and hadn't yet noticed her. The youngest one looked up and smiled as he strode past, but he merely nodded and kept going.

As Dan walked he positioned himself to shield Maggie from the nurses' view. Not for her sake. He didn't particularly like the woman. But she was Jacob's daughter, and any gossip about her would probably upset him.

There was no one in the world Dan respected or admired as much as Jacob Malone. He owed the older man a lot. Others had dismissed him as no-account trash from the wrong side of town, but not Jacob. He had given him a chance when no one else would. Dan would do whatever it took to protect him.

Maggie was so distraught she didn't hear him approach. Her sobs were barely audible, but the effort at silence was costing her. The awful, muffled sounds threatened to choke her, and the force of them shook her whole body. They sent a chill down Dan's spine. What the hell had happened?

He hesitated, then touched her shoulder. "Are you all right?"

Maggie jumped like a scalded cat. She bolted away from the wall, straightened her spine and stood tall. Lifting her chin, she squared her shoulders and busied herself with fluffing her hair and brushing imaginary lint off her knit top. "Of course I'm all right."

"Then why are you crying?"

"I'm *not* crying," she denied vehemently, even as she swiped at her wet cheeks with her fingers.

"Yeah, right." He had a sister. He'd seen the signs enough to know a weepy female when he saw one.

Maggie sniffed and shot him a killer look out of the corner of her eye, but before she could voice a comeback he stared at the door to her father's room and frowned. "Ah, hell, is it Jacob? Is he worse?"

"Oh, my father is in fine form, I assure you."

"Then why are you upset?"

"I am *not* upset. I told you I wasn't crying. Not that it's any of your business."

"Then why're your eyes red and your eyelashes spiked with tears?"

"If you must know, I had something in my eye. I was trying to get it out."

"Uh-huh." He stared at her, making no attempt to hide his skepticism. Something in her eye, be damned. He'd seen plenty of tears, some out of anger, some out of frustration or hurt feelings or deep sorrow, but in his experience, women didn't cry like that over something trivial. Or over a cinder in the eye.

Maggie bore his scrutiny in silence for as long as she could. Then she lifted her chin at a haughty angle. "If you'll excuse me, I was just leaving."

He had her hemmed in, but she shoved him aside with surprising strength, brushed past and headed toward the elevator with that leggy model stride, her hips swaying enticingly.

Dan stood with his feet braced wide, thumbs hooked in the back pockets of his jeans, watching her. "Damned screwy woman," he muttered under his breath. First she's bursting with confidence and sass, then she's bawling like a lost child. Then she has the nerve to get pissed off when he tries to help.

He watched her until the elevator doors closed, then he shot a hard look at the door. If Jacob was doing okay, what the hell had brought on that bawling jag?

The instant Dr. Sanderson left the room, Lily turned sad eyes on her husband. "Oh, Jacob, how *could* you? Maggie came all this way, hoping to heal the breach between you two. How could you treat her like that?"

"Lily, we've been over this before. Let it go."

"No. I can't." Her soft voice quavered, but she forced herself to go on. "I've let it go too many times in the past. And that makes me partly to blame."

"The blame is Katherine's, not yours or mine."

"Does it really matter? Oh, Jacob, you must make

peace with her while you still can. Surely you know that. For your own sake, and for Maggie's.''

He closed his eyes and gave a weary sigh. "Lily, please. I'm just not up to this right now.''

Instantly terrified, she grabbed his hand. "What is it? Are you in pain? Are you having trouble breathing?'' She laid the back of her free hand against his forehead.

"I'm just tired,'' he said weakly. "So very tired. Seeing Katherine was a shock.''

Lily studied her husband's face. Was he faking fatigue to bring an end to the discussion? He often used diversionary tactics with her to avoid unpleasantness. Not that he shied from confrontation normally. Though it was almost never directed at her, Jacob had a formidable temper. He could bellow and rage with the best of them. However, he headed off any arguments between the two of them for her sake, knowing how much disharmony upset her.

And, God help her, she had always taken the coward's way out and let him.

He did look pale and exhausted. But then, lately he always looked that way. Lily gnawed at her lower lip. They really needed to talk.

She shifted uneasily, torn between letting him rest and doing what she knew was right. What she should have done long ago.

The matter was taken out of her hands when the door opened and Dan walked in.

Maggie was so upset and angry she had no trouble staying awake on the drive back to Ruby Falls. She even shaved another two minutes off the trip.

Approaching the house, she was relieved to see that no vehicle was parked in the long driveway. All she needed was to run into Martin again. She'd just about used up her supply of civility those few minutes in her father's hospital room.

She parked her spiffy little car in the circle before the front entrance.

Bone-weary and emotionally drained, she wanted only to escape to her old room, curl up in bed and pull the covers over her head, but after turning off the engine she didn't move. She simply sat there, gripping the steering wheel, her gaze fixed on her childhood home. Remembering.

Her hands tightened around the steering wheel. No. Don't go down that road, Maggie told herself. It doesn't matter anymore. Remember? You've made a new life for yourself, a good life that's given you success and fame and wealth beyond anything you ever imagined. Poking at the past will only bring more pain.

It was too late. The meeting with her father had reopened all the old wounds, and memories began to surface, fresh and painful as ever.

Why? Maggie's throat tightened, her heart squeezed. Why couldn't her father love her? What was it about her that was so terrible? So repulsive? So unlovable?

As far back as her memory went, she had known, or at least sensed, that Jacob merely tolerated her. It was nothing overt or dramatic. He had never been mean or abusive or even too strict. Just…distant.

He had provided her with a good home, an education and all the material things she'd needed, the same as he had Laurel and Jo Beth.

But those things had been given to her sisters with love and warmth. Jacob doted on his two younger daughters, showering them with love and attention, but all of Maggie's life he had been remote and stern with her.

And she didn't know why. She never had.

As a little girl she'd thought Jacob ignored her because she didn't have Laurel's delicate beauty or Jo Beth's pixie cuteness.

The irony of that tugged Maggie's mouth into a crooked smile.

Today she might be one of the top five models in the world, but during those years, whenever she'd looked into a mirror all she'd seen was a too-tall, skinny girl with freckles, horrid red hair and a mouth that was much to full for her thin face.

Just when she'd become absolutely convinced that she couldn't be any more unappealing, she'd grown to be six feet tall and so damned gangly she'd been all arms and legs and knees and elbows.

Remembering those days and the lengths to which she'd gone trying to compensate for her shortcomings brought a painful heaviness to Maggie's heart.

She had gotten it into her head that maybe, if she were really, *really* good, Jacob would be proud of her, and then he would love her.

It had been a child's foolish quest from the start. Looking back, Maggie doubted that Jacob had even noticed.

By the time she reached her teens she finally accepted that it wasn't going to happen and said ''to hell with it.'' After that, she'd set about breaking every rule she could think of, thumbing her nose at not only her father, but all the small-minded busybodies in Ruby Falls, as well.

She hadn't done herself any favors, of course, but after years of battened-down emotions, Lord, it had felt good to cut loose at last and kick up her heels.

Still, despite getting into one scrape after another during her early teens, she'd loved school too much to neglect her studies. By age sixteen she'd managed to graduate from Ruby Falls High School with a perfect four-point average.

The achievement hadn't impressed her father, but it had gotten her accepted at Harvard. Her first semester there, distance and maturity had ended her rebel phase. Thank God.

She'd worked her tail off in college, and in just under four years, at not quite twenty, she'd graduated with top honors and returned home with both her bachelor's and master's degrees in business, flush with success and full of dreams.

Remembering, Maggie snorted. Fat lot of good it had done her.

Her achievements didn't mean zip to her father— not then and not now.

After that delightful reunion at the hospital, it was obvious that no matter what she did or how successful she became, his heart would always be closed to her.

"Face it, Maggie. To him, and probably most of the people in Ruby Falls, you'll always be that wild, teenage hell-raiser, Jacob and Lily Malone's no-account oldest daughter."

She pushed the button that raised the car's roof. When it had settled into place she unfolded her long length from the car, snatched up her leather tote and headed up the walk. There was no sense bothering to unload the rest. Tomorrow morning, as soon as she hashed things out with her mother, she was outta there.

Now that Maggie was on her feet, fatigue hit her like a semi going ninety. She was so exhausted her legs wobbled.

She'd hoped to have a talk with her mother tonight, but there was no chance of that. Lily would stay by Jacob's side until the nurses ran her out, and the way she drove it would take her an hour to get home. Even if Maggie could somehow manage to stay awake that long she would be too wooden-headed to think, much less engage in a head-on confrontation.

It was barely twilight, but all she wanted to do was fall into the nearest bed and sleep the clock around. She wasn't even sure she had the strength to undress and get into her nightgown.

The windows and doors of her parents' home were all still open, the front screen door unhooked. Anyone could walk in. To Maggie's knowledge, the locks on the doors had never been used. She doubted that anyone in her family even knew where to find the keys. Growing up in Ruby Falls, where almost no one locked their doors, she'd never thought anything about it, but seven years in New York had imbued her with a healthy sense of caution.

Maggie shook her head and stepped inside. Her friends back east would have a fit if she told them.

New Yorkers tended to barricade themselves in their homes behind steel doors with multiple locks, bolts and chains.

Light and television sounds spilled into the long central hallway from the family room at the back of the house.

Jo Beth.

Maggie grimaced. She probably ought to go say something to her little sister, but she was angry and sick at heart and too punch drunk to go even a few rounds of verbal sparring with a seventeen-year-old with attitude.

Hefting the tote bag's strap a little higher on her shoulder, she trudged across the entry hall and started up the stairs.

"Oh, it's you. I was hoping it was Ida Lou, coming home from bingo."

Maggie stopped with her foot on the fourth step. She looked down at Jo Beth and did her best to smile.

"Nope. Just me." She glanced up toward the second floor. "Is my old room still available? If Momma's using it for something else these days, I can take one of the guest rooms."

"It's just the same. Like some kinda freakin' shrine." The teenager crossed her arms over her chest and gave Maggie a sullen look. "Don't tell me you're actually going to stay here with us peons?"

"This is my home. Of course I'm staying here." For tonight, anyway. Even if she had the energy to drive back to Dallas, she doubted there were any flights available until tomorrow.

"Well aren't we the lucky ones. The princess is going to honor us with her presence," Jo Beth jeered in a singsong voice. "I'm all aflutter."

Maggie sighed and started trudging up the stairs again. "Not now, baby sister. I've hardly slept in four days. I'm not in any shape to take you on just yet."

"Are you sure the accommodations are up to your standards? We don't have any silk sheets, you know," Jo Beth called after her.

Maggie kept going.

"And I'm *not* a baby!"

Four

Maggie slept for thirteen hours. She awoke a little after eight, rested and ravenous, but still sick at heart.

After showering, she applied a minimum of makeup, dressed in jeans and a short-sleeved T-shirt and denim-and-leather vest and went downstairs in search of coffee, food and her mother, preferably in that order.

Following her nose, she poked her head into the kitchen and sniffed appreciatively.

"Mmm, something smells heavenly in here."

The woman at the stove spun around, her stern face lighting up. "Maggie!" She bustled across the kitchen with her arms outstretched.

"Oh, Maggie, child, it's so good to see you."

Ida Lou Nettles had worked for the Malones ever since her husband died more than twenty years ago. She and Barney had been childless, and she treated Maggie and her sisters as though they were her own.

A tall, rawboned country woman, Ida Lou stood barely an inch shorter than Maggie. She had gray-streaked, mouse-brown hair, which she wore scraped back in a bun, broad shoulders and even broader hips, and she was strong as an ox. She snatched

Maggie into a bear hug, nearly knocking the breath right out of her.

"No one told me you were coming home. I just found out from Miss Lily this morning that you were here. Why, if I'd known, I would've stayed home yesterday and cooked a feast to celebrate."

She backed up a step, holding Maggie by her shoulders, and gave her a critical once-over. "Lord knows, you could use fattening up. Lord'a' mercy, child, you're skinny as a stick. Don't those folks up in Yankee land eat decent food?"

Maggie grinned. "Not the kind you cook." She sniffed. "Is that biscuits I smell?"

"And what else would I cook your first morning home, I'd like to know? Soon as I heard you were back I whipped up a double batch. I haven't forgotten how you used to put away my biscuits. Gonna whip up some eggs and sausage and hash browns and sausage gravy to go with 'em. I was just waiting for you to wake up to start 'em cooking."

"And your boysenberries and honey? And fresh-churned butter?" Maggie asked hopefully, practically salivating.

"Of course. Now, go on out to the terrace while I finish up. The table's all set for breakfast and there's juice and coffee on the cart. Your momma and Jo Beth have already eaten. Miss Lily's in the study right now, talking to the folks at the hospital. I expect she'll join you for coffee when she's done. Here, you can take a biscuit to tide you over," she said, lifting the cover on the bread warmer.

"Why don't I take two?"

Ida Lou chuckled. "Lord'a' mercy, I never saw

the like. Always did eat like a lumberjack. By rights, child, you oughta weigh three hundred pounds. Instead you're so skinny you look like a good puff of wind would blow you away.''

Maggie didn't argue the point, but she knew she wasn't that thin—especially not by model standards. She ran three or four times a week and was slender and well-toned, but she wasn't emaciated like many models were. But Ida Lou had her own ideas on what constituted beauty. ''Men like a woman with a little meat on her bones,'' she was fond of saying.

''I know, I know. I just can't seem to gain weight, no matter how much I eat.''

Maggie took her biscuits and went out to the terrace. The glass-topped table and serving cart sat in the shade of the wide pergola alcove. Morning glory vines twined around the posts and draped the lattice roof with swags of green leaves and blue trumpet flowers, still glistening with morning dew.

She poured herself a cup of coffee, took a sip and closed her eyes. Heaven.

Breaking open a steaming biscuit, she added a generous dollop of butter and heaped on the satiny lavender puree of boysenberries and honey. With the first bite she gave a sigh of ecstasy and closed her eyes again as melted butter dribbled down her chin.

Nobody made biscuits like Ida Lou.

She had barely finished the snack when the housekeeper bustled out with a plate piled high with steaming eggs, sausages, gravy and potatoes and a basket of warm biscuits.

''Now, see that you eat every bite,'' the older

woman said, plunking down the plate in front of Maggie.

"Yes, ma'am." Grinning, she picked up a fork and dug in. As always, Ida Lou had given her enough for two men, but after days of nothing but airline food, Maggie was ravenous, and she polished off the gargantuan meal without the least effort.

When finished, she took her cup of coffee and strolled over to the edge of the terrace. Her gaze softened as she drank in the familiar scene with longing and sadness. How she wished she could stay forever.

The tall pines and ancient oak and pecan trees dotting the grounds had stood sentinel for hundreds of years, long before the present house was built. The backyard, surrounded by a waist-high white picket fence, flowed down a gentle slope. The orchard butted right up to the fence all around, the smaller peach trees marching away over the rolling land in precise rows.

The sun had not yet cleared the tops of the tall trees, and the grass still glistened wetly. One set of big footprints tracked across the dew-drenched lawn, leading from the back gate up to the terrace, then back out again, disappearing through the gate and into the orchard.

Dan Garrett? Had he already paid her mother a visit? Maggie wondered.

Birdsong trilled from one of the oaks, and Maggie smiled, the sweet ache in her heart expanding. Lord, how she loved it here. How she missed her home, she thought bittersweetly.

Then her gaze lit on the gazebo to the right of the

terrace, and she clenched her jaw. Bitterness nearly overwhelmed her.

While she was growing up, the gazebo had been her special place. With its white latticework railings and gingerbread trim, the sweet smell of honeysuckle drifting from the vines that twined around the posts, the rhythmic squeak of the old fan hanging from the cone-shaped ceiling, the small bower had seemed like a magical place to her.

As children, she and her sisters had played with dolls and had tea parties there. In her teens it had become her special place, the spot where she could be alone, where she went to think or simply to daydream, or sort through whatever was troubling her.

Then the events of that fateful evening seven years ago had forever stripped her favorite spot of its magic and tranquillity, and changed her life forever.

A terrible fight with Laurel had driven her to seek the sanctuary of the gazebo on that balmy June night so long ago. Maggie closed her eyes, remembering the frustration and despair and utter helplessness that had caused her to pace the octagonal wooden floor.

She had returned home from Harvard just a week earlier, so happy and proud, full of plans to join her father in the family business. Jacob had resisted the idea at first, but she had expected that and had been prepared to convince him otherwise.

What she hadn't expected—or been prepared to accept—was to find her sister engaged to marry Martin Howe in a ceremony that was to take place the following Saturday.

To her further horror, Laurel had expected Maggie to be her maid of honor. The dress had already been made and was hanging in her closet. At Laurel's request, no one had contacted Maggie at college to inform her of the engagement. Her sister had wanted it to be a surprise.

It had been that, all right.

Maggie could not believe it. Throughout their school years Martin had been a bully and a sneak, and both she and Laurel had despised him. What had happened while she'd been away to change her sister's opinion?

Maggie had tried every argument, every bit of logic, every cajoling plea she could think of to get Laurel to reconsider, but that only resulted in them getting into a terrible shouting match.

It had ended when Maggie stormed out of the house. She'd raced across the back lawn, straight to the gazebo, where she'd paced and railed and shaken her fists at the heavens. She couldn't abide the thought of her sweet sister married to that asshole, Martin. She *couldn't!*

Ten minutes later, she was still cursing and pacing the gazebo when Martin stomped inside looking like a volcano about to erupt.

"There you are! I thought I'd find you here."

Maggie shot him a blistering look. The sight of him made her sick to her stomach. She wanted to run at him, claws bared, and scratch and kick and pummel.

"Get out of here, Martin," she snarled. "I've got nothing to say to you."

"That's too damned bad, bitch, 'cause I've got

plenty to say to you. You've got a hell of a lot of nerve bad-mouthing me to Laurel.''

She jutted her chin. ''You bet I do. Where my sister's happiness is concerned I'll dare anything. I know you, Martin Howe. You're narcissistic to the bone. You're incapable of loving anyone but yourself. Why don't you just admit it? The only reason you want to marry Laurel is to get your hands on Malone Enterprises!''

''So? It's none of your business, so just butt out. Anyway, I'm doing her a favor. There are plenty of women who would like to be Mrs. Martin Howe, you know.''

''*You're* doing *her* a favor? Why, you conceited pig,'' Maggie spat. ''You're not worthy to kiss my sister's feet!''

''You're just jealous because I didn't pick you.'' His disparaging gaze traveled over her, and his mouth curled into a sneer. ''As if I'd ever choose a homely, redheaded scarecrow like you to be my wife.''

''You'd never get the chance. If you were the last man on earth I wouldn't let you touch me. You disgust me,'' she jeered, each word dripping with loathing and revulsion.

Martin's arrogant smirk dissolved. His nostrils flared and his face tightened and flushed a mottled red. The gazebo was lit by only a single carriage lamp, but even in the dim glow Maggie could see the rage in his eyes, and for the first time since he'd stormed into her sanctuary she experienced a prickle of fear.

''We'll just see about that,'' he ground out.

Maggie's heart gave a quick bump, but she set her jaw and moved to step around him. "I have nothing more to say to you. I'm going inside."

"You're not going anywhere, bitch." He side-stepped in front of her, and before she realized his intent he grabbed a handful of her blouse. A ripping sound and the rapid-fire click-click-click-click of buttons hitting the wooden floor followed.

Maggie let out a yelp. Her eyes widened with stunned disbelief and horror, and for the space of three heartbeats she stared down at her ruined blouse and exposed breasts, barely covered by her lacy bra. Then delayed reaction set in and she moaned and tried to cover herself, but Martin grabbed her wrists and twisted her arms behind her back.

"Stop it! *Stop* it! Get your hands off me!" Maggie shouted, twisting and straining against his hold. Martin was a couple of inches shorter than her, but he was stocky and muscular, and she was no match for his strength. "Let go of me!"

"Oh, no. Not yet. No one messes with me and gets away with it. I'm going to teach you a lesson you'll never forget, bitch," he snarled through clenched teeth.

"Dammit, Martin, I said let go!"

She punctuated the order with a sharp kick to his shin. Giving a grunt of pain, he released her so quickly that Maggie staggered backward into the railing. Martin spat out a vicious curse and grabbed his leg, hopping in place.

Heart pounding, Maggie eyed him cautiously and tried to sidle around him, but she'd barely taken a step when his feral gaze stabbed into her like a knife.

"Why you...!" With a roar of fury, he straightened and backhanded her across the face.

Pain exploded in Maggie's jaw, then more bursts erupted in her hip and shoulder when she hit the floor. Her cry of agony turned into a scream as Martin came down on top of her, but he quickly clamped his hand over her mouth, cutting off the sound in midshriek.

Over the top of his hand, Maggie's eyes widened with real terror when she read his intent in his eyes.

In a frenzy of panic, she bucked and kicked and squirmed, but she couldn't dislodge him. She tried to bite his palm, but his grip tightened so painfully she thought her jaws would surely snap.

She fought with all her might and even managed to pull his hair and get in a few good blows, but all that she succeeded in doing was to fuel his rage. Despite her struggles, Martin managed to ruck her full skirt up around her hips, and with one rough jerk he ripped away her bikini panties.

Icy horror suffused Maggie when he worked his hands between their bodies and unzipped his trousers.

"Now, bitch, you're going to find out what it's like to have a real man between your legs!" he growled.

No! This couldn't be happening! Oh, God, no!

In despair, she squeezed her eyes shut and silently cried, Help me! Someone please help me!

"What the *hell* is going on here!"

Jacob's irate roar whipped through the gazebo with tornado-wind force.

The effect on Martin was instantaneous. He shot to his feet as if he'd been jabbed with a cattle prod. Whimpering with relief, Maggie shoved her skirt down, curled on her side in a fetal position and began to weep softly.

Sweating and pale, Martin fumbled to fasten his pants and met Jacob's glare with a phony look of contrition and gratitude.

"Jacob. Thank God you came when you did. I know this looks bad, but it wasn't my fault. This was all *her* doing."

"Wh-what?" Blinking back tears, Maggie sat up and stared at him with disbelief. Martin had more gall than anyone she knew, but this was too much, even for him. "How can you *say* that?"

He ignored her and focused on Jacob. "Maggie has been coming on to me ever since she got home. I've told her over and over that I wasn't interested, that I love Laurel, but she just wouldn't take no for an answer."

"That's a lie!" Maggie cried, but Jacob shot her a quelling glare.

"Be quiet, Katherine. You'll get your chance to talk after I've heard Martin. And for heaven's sake, cover yourself!"

Mortified, she glanced down at her ruined blouse and snatched the gaping edges together, her face flaming.

"The closer the wedding came, the bolder Maggie became," Martin continued. "Tonight I was out here enjoying a quiet moment alone, waiting for Laurel, when she threw herself at me.''

"No, Daddy, that's not what hap—''

"I said quiet!''

Martin shot her a quick, taunting look while Jacob wasn't looking. When he turned back, Martin assumed a desperate expression and raked a hand through his hair. "Maggie is jealous of Laurel and she was determined to take me away from her. She's been relentless in her attempts at seduction. Tonight...well, I...I guess she caught me in a weak moment.''

His gaze fixed on Jacob. His pathetic expression reeked remorse and pleading. "I know it was wrong of me to respond, and I can't tell you how sorry I am. I wouldn't hurt Laurel for anything. But hell, Jacob, I'm only a man. There's just so much temptation a red-blooded male can endure before he cracks. I'm just grateful you came along before I made the worst mistake of my life. Thank you.'' He closed his eyes and hung his head. "Thank you so much.''

Slowly, Jacob turned to Maggie, and her heart sank at the look in his eyes. "Well, Katherine?''

"He's lying! *He* attacked *me!*'' She scrambled to her feet, clutching the edges of her torn blouse together. "I love Laurel. I would never do anything to hurt her. I certainly would never try to take Martin from her. I loathe and despise him.''

"She's the one who's lying,'' Martin insisted. "She's so jealous she'll do anything to break us up. Not twenty minutes ago she tried to get Laurel to call off the wedding. If you don't believe me, just ask her.''

"Is this true, Katherine?"

"Well...yes. But it wasn't like he said. I was just—''

"Quiet!" Jacob roared, and Maggie flinched as though he'd struck her. The fury and disgust in his eyes when he looked at her sent a frisson of dread down her spine. "You haven't changed at all, have you, Katherine? Not one bit."

"No, Daddy, that's not tr—''

"I said be *quiet!* I'm finished listening to your lies.'' He paced away a few steps, then swung back. "Dammit, I should have known you'd cause trouble somehow. I just never imagined you would stoop so low you'd try to harm your sister.''

"I would never—''

This time Jacob silenced her with a glare so fierce that Maggie shrank back.

"For days now, ever since you returned from college, you've been telling me that you've changed and matured and put all that foolishness behind you, but you haven't. You're the same reckless hell-raiser you were when you left here four years ago.''

"No, that's not true. Daddy, please. If you'll just listen to—''

"I will deal with you later,'' her father snapped, cutting her off. "Your sister and Martin are getting married in a few days, and I don't want anything to upset her or mar her big day. So you are not to say anything to anyone about what took place here tonight. Not one word. Do I make myself clear?''

Maggie nodded, too numb to speak.

"Good. Because I'm warning you, if you do or say anything to ruin Laurel's wedding, you will answer to me. Remember that. Now, get out of my sight."

Maggie fled the gazebo in utter despair and defeat. She went straight to her room and threw herself facedown on her bed and cried into her pillow.

After a night of weeping, she awoke the next morning with a pounding head, puffy eyelids and gritty eyes, convinced that things could not be worse, but she hadn't counted on Martin.

He, of course, had gone straight to Laurel and told her his version of the incident. Hurt and angry, Laurel refused to talk to Maggie at all. Whenever she entered a room where Laurel was, her sister either wouldn't look at her or else got up and left.

Martin, however, hadn't counted on Laurel's tender heart. He had succeeded in driving a wedge between them, but her sister refused to give in to his demand that she order Maggie to drop out of the wedding.

Maggie would have preferred it if she had. The next two days were miserable. Not only was her father furious and disgusted with her, and her relationship with Laurel strained, in her heart she knew that her beloved sister was making a terrible mistake. And there was nothing she could do to stop her. Not one thing.

The day of the wedding Maggie walked down the aisle ahead of Laurel with a heavy heart and an awful sense of foreboding.

Somehow she got through the ceremony and the reception in the garden with what she hoped was a semblance of a smile on her face. However, she wasn't surprised when, barely moments after the newlyweds left on their honeymoon, her father summoned her to his study.

Aware that he was still angry with her, she entered the room on shaking legs, her stomach tied in a knot.

Jacob stood with his back to the door, turning the combination lock on the wall safe. She wasn't sure he'd heard her enter until he spoke.

"Don't bother to sit, Katherine. This won't take long," he said without looking around.

Maggie had expected anger, and had braced herself for a blistering tongue-lashing. His flat, unemotional tone sent a chill slithering down her spine.

She shifted from one foot to the other, her nerves winding tighter with every passing minute. Finally Jacob closed the safe, replaced the picture that covered it and turned with a fat envelope in his hand. Only then did he look at her, and what she saw in his eyes did nothing to ease her anxiety.

"Ever since you turned thirteen you've been a disruptive force in this house. Up until now I've tried to be tolerant, but you have pushed me too far this time, Katherine. I cannot forgive what you tried to do to your sister."

"I didn't try to do anything to Laurel. Martin's the one who lied. Not me. I swear it, Daddy."

"I'm afraid your reputation doesn't inspire trust, Katherine. I see no reason why I should believe you."

"But I'm telling the truth! I tried to talk Laurel out of marrying Martin, yes. But because I think he's despicable, not because I want him. You have to believe me!''

''No, Katherine, I don't have to do any such thing. The fact is, I don't trust you. And the matter is not open for discussion. I've made my decision.'' He gave her a long, steady look. ''I want you out of this house. Tonight. There's a Dallas-bound bus leaving the Greyhound station at midnight. You're going to be on it.''

His words struck Maggie like a knife to her heart. She sucked in a sharp breath and stumbled back a step. ''You're...you're throwing me *out?*''

It was her worst nightmare come true: total rejection by her father.

''Here, take this.'' He shoved the envelope into her hand. She stared down at it, too numb and shocked to think.

''What...what is this?''

''Five thousand dollars. It should be enough to tide you over until you get established somewhere else.''

Maggie was shaken to her core. The world she knew had suddenly tilted on its axis, and she had fallen off into space. Her heart began to pound and panic clawed at her throat.

The iciness in the pit of her stomach spread outward, suffusing her entire body, setting off a violent trembling deep inside her. Tears filled her eyes and streamed down her face, and her chin quivered pathetically.

Pride vanished. So did dignity and self-possession. All that was left was fear—cold, stark fear. She gazed beseechingly at her father through her tears. "Please, Daddy. Oh, please, don't send me away. I'll do anything you say. I promise. Anything."

Jacob stared at her, unmoved. "It's over, Katherine. As of tonight, you are no longer a part of this family and no longer welcome in this house. When you leave here, don't come back."

The words were blunt and brutal. Reeling, she stared at him. He wasn't merely tossing her out on her ear. He was disowning her.

A low, keening wail tore from Maggie's throat. She bent forward, as though she'd been punched in the stomach, and braced herself with her palms flat on his desk, her head hanging between her stiff arms. Tears splashed on the mahogany surface and her shoulders shook with each choking sob. "I...I don't want to l-leave, or...or get a jo...job somewhere el...else," she gasped. "A-all I've ever wa...wanted was to wor-work in the fa...fa...family business."

"You should have thought of that before you tried to seduce your sister's fiancé."

"I di...didn't. I didn't." She shook her head mournfully, her voice quivering with hopelessness. "I didn't."

Her father turned away and stared out the front window. "If you're trying to make me change my mind by crying, it won't work."

On some remote level, Maggie was as surprised and appalled by her reaction as her father. A quick wit and impudent tongue were her weapons of defense. She never cried. *Never.*

But she was beyond stopping. The anguished sobs

came from some place deep in her soul, awful animal sounds of raw pain that tore from her. They were harsh and raspy, and they hurt her throat and shook her entire body.

"Come, come, Katherine," Jacob ordered in an impatient tone. "Control yourself. It's not as though you're going to be destitute and live on the streets. You have a good education. With your scholastic record, you should be able to find a decent job. Thousands of new college graduates leave home and strike out on their own every year."

But they weren't being tossed out of their family. The thought brought a fresh rush of panic and pain that threatened to take her to her knees and made her tears flow faster.

They hadn't the least effect on her father.

"These histrionics are not going to gain you anything. Dry your eyes, Katherine. The bus will be leaving in a little over an hour. I suggest you use that time to pack a few things. When you get settled, you can let Ida Lou know where to send the rest."

Maggie fought for control. It was painful and required a tremendous effort, but somehow she choked back the sobs until they gradually reduced to harsh, hitching sounds, then silent spasms that shook her body and rippled her throat.

Slowly, like an old, old woman, she straightened. Taking several tissues from the box on the desk, she dabbed at her eyes and runny nose.

It was over. Finished, she thought, and despair and hopelessness settled over her like a lead cape.

She looked into her father's unyielding gaze, trembling inside, a freshet of hot tears rushing to her eyes. "Goodbye, Daddy. I..." Her voice quavered and cracked, and she knew if she didn't go now she would break down again.

She turned to leave, but stopped when she noticed that she still held the envelope of money in her hand. Numb to everything but the excruciating hollow ache in her chest, she stared at the bundle for an interminable time. Finally, gathering her tattered dignity, she placed the envelope on the desk.

"Don't be a fool, Katherine. Take the money. You'll need it."

She looked at her father then and shook her head. "No. I don't want your money." All she wanted— all she'd ever wanted—was his love, and she knew now that he would never give her that.

Holding on to her fragile emotions by sheer will, Maggie headed for the door on legs that seemed to have turned to wooden posts. Her steps were jerky and stiff, but she walked out of the room with her head held high.

Five

Maggie swallowed hard, her gaze still blindly fixed on the gazebo. Even after all this time, she remembered every detail of that awful night, every nuance and inflection in her father's voice, every word they had exchanged, every lash of pain each one had inflicted.

As a rule, she tried never to think about that parting scene. It hurt too much. But she supposed that, returning here for the first time since that night, it had been inevitable.

She would think of it as a catharsis, she told herself. Something she'd had to face. Now that she had, she could move on.

Dragging her gaze away from the gazebo, Maggie realized she had been so lost in the memory that she had forgotten to drink her coffee. She'd forgotten she was even holding the cup and saucer.

With a rueful shake of her head, she slung the cold brew out into the grass beyond the terrace and turned back to the table. She refilled the cup, then sat down again, this time with her back squarely toward the gazebo.

She had just taken the first sip when her mother

stepped through the French doors from the family room.

"Ah, there you are, dear." Lily hurried across the terrace. "I just talked to the head nurse on your daddy's floor. He's doing well enough that he's nagging to come home. She expects Dr. Lockhart will release him this morning, so I'll be leaving to go get him in an hour or so."

As always, Lily looked immaculate, makeup perfect and understated, her hair a shiny cap of blond curls that enhanced the delicate beauty of her face. This morning she wore a casual but elegant deep rose pantsuit with a single strand of pearls.

As a plain young child, and later a gawky, unattractive teenager, Maggie had often wondered how someone like Lily could have produced a daughter like her. Next to her mother and sisters, she had felt like a lumbering giraffe.

All of her life, Maggie had thought her mother looked like a fairy princess, with her misty beauty and dainty build. There was something fragile about Lily, an ethereal quality that made everyone she met want to shelter her from life. Maggie had been no exception.

This morning, however, she wasn't feeling in the least protective. She had not forgotten her mother's deception.

Lily's smile faded when she saw her expression. By the time she slipped into the chair next to Maggie's and reached for her hand, her blue eyes were moist and contrite. "I know, I know. Oh, my dear, I'm so sorry."

"Why? Why did you do it, Momma? I trusted you, and you lied to me. How could you do that?"

"I *had* to. You wouldn't have come home otherwise. And I was desperate."

"But what was the point? You must have known how he would react. Especially springing me on him like that."

"No. No, I thought that knowing he was going to…" Her chin quivered, and she stopped to look skyward and blink back tears. "Knowing that his time was short would make him do some soul-searching and realize that the most important thing was family. I was so certain that when he saw you he'd regret all the lost years and be happy to have you back home where you belong."

"Oh, Momma, you are such a Pollyanna. When have you ever known Daddy to relent once his mind was set?"

Maggie knew it was futile to point out that the chasm between her and her father went deeper than just what had happened seven years ago. Lily either couldn't or wouldn't accept that Jacob didn't love his oldest child. That he never had.

Such a thing was unthinkable to her. She steadfastly refused to even consider the possibility.

In the past, whenever Maggie had broached the matter, her mother had always rushed to assure her that she was wrong.

"Don't be silly, sweetheart. Your father loves you very much. Truly, he does. He's just not a demonstrative man, that's all," she had insisted.

Jacob had been demonstrative enough with Lily, and with Laurel and Jo Beth, Maggie had noticed.

However, pointing that out had merely brought more denials and platitudes and caused her mother unnecessary distress. After a while she had stopped asking and kept her hurt to herself.

"You're right," Lily said in a dispirited voice. "I suppose I do insist on seeing the bright side, even when there isn't one." Sighing, she slumped back in her chair and ran a shaking hand over her eyes. "This is all my fault. I shouldn't have tricked either of you. I should have had it out with Jacob years ago and put an end to this stupid estrangement."

"Why didn't you?"

A part of Maggie felt heartless even posing the question, especially seeing the stricken look on her mother's face, but she was still raw and hurting from the scene with her father yesterday so she ignored the twinge of guilt. It was something she'd wondered about for years, and time was running out. She wanted some answers. She needed them.

"Because I'm a coward," Lily whispered, surprising her. "When I found out that Jacob had thrown you out, we had a terrible fight."

"You? You had a fight with Daddy?"

Maggie made no effort to hide her skepticism. Her mother was sweet-tempered and biddable by nature and had always been perfectly happy to acquiesce to her husband's wishes. In addition, anger and harsh words unnerved her. Lily went out of her way to avoid strife of any kind. It was difficult, if not downright impossible, to imagine her having the grit to take a stand against Jacob.

"I know you think of me as a meek little mouse,

but mothers of every species, even the most docile ones, will fight for their young, you know.''

"Sorry. I was just surprised, that's all. Go on.''

"Jacob laid down the law and said that neither I nor the girls could ever see you or speak to you again. When I refused he was nearly as shocked as I was.

"I made it clear, though, that while I would not overrule him where Laurel and Jo Beth were concerned, there was no power on earth that could make me abandon you." Her chin came up at a defiant angle. "I told him that I would leave him before I would give up one of my children.''

Maggie stared, stunned and touched at the same time. Lily had threatened to *leave* her father? Never in a million years would she have thought her mother capable of such a thing.

She had never discussed with her mother what had taken place in the gazebo that night, probably because the habit of protecting Lily from unpleasantness had by then become so ingrained she kept quiet without thinking. The closest they'd come to talking about it had been the first time her mother had visited her in New York.

She had asked, point-blank, if Maggie had tried to seduce Martin away from Laurel, as he claimed, and when Maggie had said no Lily had accepted her word without question, and that had been the end of the matter.

A wave of tenderness washed through Maggie. For her timid mother to take that stance against the man she loved had been an act of courage and love that touched her to her soul.

But then, she had never had any doubts about her mother's love for her.

"Jacob didn't like it," Lily continued. "Things between us were strained for a time after that, but for once I refused to back down, and he finally accepted my terms. He had no choice.

"Since then we've rarely discussed you. Whenever I announce that I'm going to New York to see you, an uneasy silence hums between us for days, both before I leave and after I return. Whenever I try to tell Jacob about your life or how you're doing, or even mention your name, he gets quiet and remote or changes the subject. I've learned not to talk about you to him."

Lily's mouth wobbled pathetically and her eyes filled. "I shouldn't have let this go on so long, but I've always been afraid to force the issue, for fear of starting another frightful argument. Even now, knowing I'm going to lose him soon, I still can't do it."

Her mouth twisted. "I tell myself that he's so ill I can't bear to upset him, and that I don't want to spend what little time we have left together arguing. But the real reason I don't push him to work things out with you is...I just can't handle that kind of angry confrontation. It's selfish and cowardly of me, I know, but...I just can't."

Dropping her face into her hands, Lily began to weep softly. "I'm sorry. I'm so sorry. I know I've failed you. You must hate me."

"Oh, Momma, of course I don't hate you," Maggie said wearily, but Lily's sobs did not lessen.

Torn between resentment and pity, Maggie studied her mother's downbent head and shaking shoulders, and after a moment she sighed. Oh, what the hell. Trying to stay angry with Lily made her feel like she was abusing a defenseless kitten. Anyway, her mother couldn't help it. She was simply one of the world's noncombatants.

Maggie patted her arm. "C'mon, Momma, don't cry. You're not to blame. You can't help it if you're sensitive. Anyway, I'm a big girl now. I can fight my own battles."

Lily sniffed a few times, wiped her eyes on a napkin from the table and struggled to compose herself. "I know, but—"

Jo Beth burst out of the French doors onto the terrace, her face alight with excitement. "Whose car is that out front?"

"Jo Beth, if you don't hurry you're going to be late for school," their mother admonished gently, but the girl ignored her.

"If you're talking about the Viper, that's mine," Maggie said.

"Yours? Yeah, right. Tell me another one. Like the car rental places offer brand-new Vipers."

"Oh, I imagine there are some that do, but that car isn't a rental. I bought it in Dallas yesterday. I called the dealer before I left New York, and he was nice enough to meet me at the airport with the papers and the car."

Instantly the excitement in Jo Beth's face vanished and her mouth tightened. "Huh. I guess because you're a famous model people fall all over themselves to do stuff like that for you."

Maggie shrugged. "There are times when celebrity does have its advantages."

"Yeah, I'll bet."

Ignoring the sarcasm, Maggie lifted one eyebrow. "So…do you like the car?"

"What's not to like? It's bitchin'."

"Jo Beth!"

The teenager groaned and rolled her eyes at her mother. Maggie took a sip of coffee, hiding her smile behind the cup.

"What's the big deal? It's just an expression," Jo Beth said.

"Well, it's not the kind of language I want a daughter of mine using."

"Do you have a driver's license?"

The question earned Maggie a narrow-eyed look. "I'm not a baby. I'll be eighteen soon. Of course I have a license. Why?"

"I just thought if you did, maybe you'd like to take the car for a spin sometime."

Excitement lit Jo Beth's eyes, but she quickly tamped down her delight and assumed a sullen expression. "No, thanks. I'm not impressed with your expensive car and your glamorous image. So don't think you can come waltzing back after all these years and wheedle your way back into this family with bribes."

"Jo Beth!"

The teenager sent Lily an eye-rolling look of disgust. "You just don't get it, do you, Momma. She only bought the car to show off what a big deal she is."

"That's not true," Maggie said calmly. At least,

impressing her former friends and neighbors hadn't been her sole reason. "I've always wanted a sports car, but they aren't practical in New York. Here, with so much wide-open space, it's different. And since I was planning to fly out on assignment every few weeks, and I could hardly expect Momma or you or Laurel to chauffeur me back and forth to the Dallas airport, I figured I'd better have my own transportation.

"At the time it all made perfect sense. Of course, that was when I thought I'd be staying for a while."

Lily shot her a look. "You're not leaving?"

"Oh, get real. You didn't really think Miss La-di-da Supermodel would hang around here, did you? The only reason she came at all was because it would've looked bad if she hadn't."

Before Lily could answer, the girl whirled around and stomped back to the house. "Well, go on back to New York. See if we care. Nobody wants you around here, anyway!" she yelled over her shoulder, and slammed into the house.

"Pay no attention to her." Lily leaned forward and grasped Maggie's hand. "Please, Maggie, you can't leave."

"What did you expect, Momma? That I'd stay where I'm not wanted? That I'd stick around for more scenes like that one at the hospital yesterday?"

"*I* want you to stay. Please, Maggie, I *need* you here."

Pulling her hands free, Maggie pushed back her chair and stood up. "You don't need me. You have Laurel and Jo Beth, and they're sure as hell all

Daddy needs. Besides, if I stayed I'd just be a thorn in his side and make his last days miserable.''

"Maggie, no—''

"I'm sorry, Momma. Now, if you'll excuse me, I'm going to get my things and say goodbye to Ida Lou.''

She turned and headed for the house.

"No, please, you have to stay. I need your help, Maggie. The business is in trouble. If we don't turn things around soon, Malone Cannery will have to close its doors.''

Maggie jerked to a halt and whirled around. *"What?* That can't be!''

Particularly since she personally had funneled a huge amount of money into the company through her aunt Nan just over a year ago.

"Malone Enterprises has been successful for over eighty years. What happened?''

"I don't know.'' Lily wrung her hands. "Jacob explained it to me, but you know I have no head for business. All I know is the company is in financial trouble, and for months now Martin has been badgering your daddy to sell the business to Bountiful Foods.''

"Sell? Martin knows that's impossible. Daddy's grandmother set up Malone Enterprises as a closed corporation so that it would always remain in the family. The charter and articles of incorporation forbid the sale of shares to anyone who isn't a direct descendant of hers. Not even spouses are allowed to own shares.''

"Martin wants Jacob to call an emergency meeting of the shareholders and vote to change the articles and the charter so that everything can be sold.''

That earned Lily a sharp look. "Everything? You mean the orchards, too?''

Lily nodded.

Maggie ground her teeth and began to pace. Some of that land had been in her family even longer than the cannery. Bountiful Foods was a huge company that had bought up small canneries all over the country. Now they wanted to gobble up Malone Enterprises, as well?

Not if she could help it.

Maggie reached the far side of the terrace and swung around. "I might have known that Martin was behind this somehow. That self-serving, arrogant maggot.''

"Now, now, dear, I don't care for Martin any more than you do, but I don't think you should let your feelings blind you. I didn't say that he was to blame for the company losing money. I really don't see how he could be. Jacob has never given him any real power. He's a vice president, yes, but only because he's married to Laurel.''

"That's not a good enough reason to make someone a VP. What was Daddy thinking? Martin is, always has been and always will be a lazy, incompetent screwup who is so spoiled and egotistical he thinks he's entitled to whatever he wants. By making him a vice president Daddy merely affirmed Martin's inflated opinion of himself.''

"He did it for Laurel's sake. But at least the title carries absolutely no authority. Martin is in charge of customer relations. He calls on clients and prospective clients, wines and dines them and keeps everybody happy.''

Maggie snorted. "That ought to be right up his alley, since it doesn't involve any real work." She slanted her mother a look. "So, what's being done to turn things around?"

"Lately, since Jacob has been so ill, nothing. When things first began looking bleak he was still well enough to work. At that time he got a loan from Nan to bail the company out of debt."

"Oh? And did the infusion of capital put us back in the black?"

Maggie asked the question innocently, but she couldn't quite meet her mother's eyes. She knew all about the transaction. More even than her father did.

"For a while it looked as though it had. But lately, the situation is worse than ever. And we still haven't paid back the loan from Nan."

"I wouldn't worry about repaying Aunt Nan right away. Uncle Edward left her comfortable financially, so she isn't hurting for the money. Besides, the family business means as much to her as it does to the rest of us."

"Yes, but the worse things get, the more Jacob worries, and the more Martin pressures him to sell out. I've asked Martin over and over to stop, but he just pats me on the shoulder and smiles in that condescending way of his. He says I don't understand how dire the situation is—and maybe he's right—but I do know that his constant badgering can't be good for Jacob."

Lily sighed. "I'd like to think that Martin is just trying to help us avert financial disaster. I truly would. But in my heart I know it's more likely that he's simply panicked that we'll go broke and he'll go down with us.''

"You're probably right. He won't find another cushy position like the one he has. I'm sure his father would give him a job at the bank, but I doubt it would be as a vice president. Rupert has other shareholders to answer to.''

Maggie paced the width of the terrace twice more, then stopped beside the table. "At the hospital, Martin said he was in charge of the business now. Is that true?''

"Jacob hasn't authorized him to take over, if that's what you mean. Martin has just taken it upon himself to step in. But I have to say, your father knows and he hasn't objected. And to be fair, until you came home, who else was there?''

Maggie made a face. With her brother-in-law at the helm, they'd be lucky if the business survived another six months.

"What about this Dan Garrett person? You made him general manager, so you must have a lot of faith in him.''

"Oh, we do. Dan's a fine man.''

A fond look came over Lily's face. "You probably don't remember, but in his youth, Dan was a bit of a hell-raiser. Mind you, even so, he's always been a hard worker. He started working here part-time after school as a teenager, picking fruit during harvest season. I understand that in his senior year in school he earned a college scholarship, but he had to give it up when his father died and go to work full-time to help support his family. Such a pity.

"Early on, Jacob sensed there was something special about Dan. He might have been a rowdy kid from the wrong side of town, but he had drive and ambition and a keen intelligence. And he's proved himself to be absolutely trustworthy.

"Over the years, Jacob has steadily promoted him to positions of greater and greater responsibility." Lily shot Maggie an amused look. "Two years ago, over Martin's strenuous objections, he made Dan general manager. It proved to be one of the best decisions Jacob ever made.

"Dan knows Malone Enterprises top to bottom. He can repair every piece of machinery in the cannery, and he knows exactly what each individual tree in every orchard needs in order to stay healthy. He can judge to the day when the time is perfect for picking. He also has a knack for overseeing the workers and coordinating the harvest and canning and shipping. Frankly, I don't know what we'd do without him. When it comes to the actual day-to-day operations, Dan is Jacob's right-hand man."

"Hmm. He sounds almost too good to be true," Maggie drawled. Her two meetings with Dan Garrett had not endeared the man to her, but she was reserving judgment. The very fact that her brother-in-law disapproved of him was a point in his favor.

"Your daddy relies on him heavily, particularly these days. Jacob has never said so, but I think, in many ways, Dan is the son he never had." A wistful look flickered over Lily's face. "I've always regretted that I couldn't give your daddy a son, but after Jo Beth was born the doctors said another child wasn't advisable."

Lily blinked and squared her shoulders, visibly shaking off the old sadness. "Oh, well, we have to live with what we can't change. Anyway, much as Jacob trusts and relies on Dan, the financial end of the business is just not his area of expertise."

"I'd hardly call it Martin's, either."

"True, but Martin is family, whether we like it or not."

Maggie made a face. She didn't like it. She hated to even think about it. "What has Martin told you about the current situation?"

"Martin? Absolutely nothing. Now, with Dan it's a different story. At least once a day he comes by to keep Jacob and me current on the schedule and whatever problems have arisen. It seems that we've had a lot of costly breakdowns of the automated equipment and shipments have gone astray, and a number of other setbacks that have had an adverse effect on our profits.

"Dan usually drops by for coffee before going to the cannery. He had breakfast with Jo Beth and me earlier this morning, as a matter of fact."

Maggie's gaze flickered to the footprints in the dewy grass. The sun had just cleared the tall trees in the backyard, and the moisture was quickly evaporating, but the prints were still faintly visible.

"But Martin wouldn't dream of consulting with me," Lily continued. "He's just like his father. He and Rupert think that women should be confined to the kitchen and the bedroom, and be a pretty ornament on a man's arm, and they assume all other men feel the same."

"You could demand that he keep you informed."

"To what end? Even if I understood the problems, I wouldn't have the foggiest idea how to fix things."

Lily caught Maggie's hand in both of hers. "That's why you have to stay. I need you, Maggie. The whole family needs you. And not just us. Think of all the people in Ruby Falls who work in the cannery and orchards who stand to lose their jobs. Bountiful Foods is notorious for conducting wholesale layoffs and bringing in cheap labor when they take over a cannery.

"You're smart as a whip and you have a master's degree in business, Maggie. You're our only hope of surviving this."

The desperation in her mother's eyes pulled at Maggie. Still she hesitated. "Momma…first of all, it's been seven years since I earned my degree, and I've never put my training to use. And second, even if I could pinpoint the problem or problems, there's no guarantee that I could turn things around. Provided, of course, that Daddy would even let me get near the office."

"I'll talk to your father. I promise."

Maggie gave her a skeptical look. Her mother said that now, but she knew that one harsh word from her father and Lily would fold. If Jacob needed convincing, she'd have to do it.

"But what about what's best for him? You know my being here will upset him. I don't want to make his last days miserable."

Nor was she anxious to subject herself to more of Jacob's animosity and coldness. She had put all that behind her years ago. Or tried to.

"He'll be a darn sight more miserable if we lose the business. He's worried sick about what will become of us when he's gone. It's preying on his mind, I can tell you. That can't be good for a man in his condition."

Us, meaning her mother and sisters, Maggie thought. She was quite certain that Jacob didn't trouble himself over her future.

"Please, dear," Lily pleaded when she continued to hesitate. "Please. All I'm asking is that you try."

Maggie looked into her mother's frantic eyes. She was acutely aware that except for Ida Lou, Lily was the only one who wanted her there.

Her father certainly didn't, nor did Laurel or Jo Beth. Nor that macho hunk of a general manager. Unlike most men she encountered, Dan Garrett wasn't in the least impressed with her looks or her fame.

If she stayed she would be letting herself in for all manner of grief from all directions.

But what choice did she have?

Maggie exhaled a long sigh. "All right, Momma. I'll stay and do what I can. Just don't expect miracles. Okay?"

Beaming, Lily surged up out of her chair and threw her arms around her daughter. "Oh, thank you, sweetheart. Thank you, thank you, thank you."

Maggie returned the hug, rocking her mother's slight body as she made a wry face over the top of her head.

"Am I interrupting something, ladies?"

Tensing, she turned her head and saw Dan Garrett emerge from the orchard and amble up the slope of the backyard. For a big man he moved with surprising grace, his stride long and loose. Everything about him—from his big, fit body, pale eyes and rugged face—radiated quiet strength and intensity.

Maggie's skin prickled. The man was too self-assured...too rawly masculine for her taste. Still, there was something about him...

Lily pulled out of Maggie's arms and turned to Dan with a welcoming smile. "No, of course not. I was just thanking Maggie for agreeing to stay awhile with us."

One dark eyebrow cocked and his eyes turned cold as they switched to Maggie. "Oh? I didn't realize there was ever a question of her *not* staying."

Maggie's hackles rose. Lily seemed oblivious to the censure in his voice, but she heard it, loud and clear. She wanted to tell him that either way it was none of his business what she did, but she smothered the urge. Instead, as always when she felt under attack, she instinctively turned on the flirtatious charm.

"Oh, there wasn't one doubt, sugar," she purred, giving him a sultry smile. "I came prepared to stay for as long as I'm needed. I ran into a little glitch yesterday, and that upset Momma, but that's all straightened out now. So you better get used to having me around, handsome."

Lily looked confused by Maggie's familiar manner, but she recovered quickly. "Oh, that's right. Maggie told me yesterday that she'd met you."

"Yes, we met," Dan said with insulting indifference.

He turned his full attention on Lily, leaving Maggie with the feeling that she'd just been dismissed, which, she was certain, was what he intended. "I took care of what I needed to at the cannery. I'm ready to go when you are, Lily."

"Just let me get my purse." She smiled at Maggie. "Dan is going to the hospital with me to bring Jacob home."

Maggie experienced an instant stab of jealousy that her mother had asked Dan to help with a family matter instead of her. "There's no need for Mr. Garrett to take time away from work, Momma. I can help you fetch Daddy home."

"Thank you, dear, but it will be better if Dan goes with me. He's stronger than you and can help lift Jacob into the car. Dr. Lockhart has arranged for a live-in male nurse. He'll stay with us until—"

Lily pressed her lips together, her eyes suddenly stricken. She fought for composure and won, but when she continued her voice sounded hollow and strained. "He'll stay with us for the next few months, but he won't be here until Monday."

Looking a bit uneasy, Lily lowered her voice to a murmur. "Plus, I think it would be best if I...you know...prepared Jacob for the changes he's going to find around here."

In other words, her mother wanted to warn him that she would be staying, Maggie realized with a pang.

"Why don't you spend the morning getting settled in? Dan and I will be back with your daddy before you know it."

"I'll go get your car and bring it around front."

Without so much as a glance toward Maggie, Dan headed for the garage.

Five minutes later, from the window of her bedroom, Maggie watched Dan drive Lily's Cadillac into the circular drive and come to a halt in front of her Viper. Her mother hurried down the front walk and climbed into the passenger seat. A vague sense of resentment and envy squeezed Maggie's chest as her gaze followed the deep burgundy car around the circle and down the long drive toward the road.

Dan Garrett had the trust and admiration of both her parents and had firmly established a place for himself in the family business and in their lives. That was more than she'd ever managed—at least, with her father.

Dammit, it wasn't fair.

The instant the thought whispered through Maggie's mind she felt guilty and childish. It wasn't Dan Garrett's fault that her father didn't love her. She was just directing her anger at him because he was handy.

Making a disgusted sound, she rolled her eyes. "Knock it off, Maggie. Nobody said life was fair," she grumbled. "And the only thing feeling sorry for yourself will get you is a bad case of the 'poor me's.'"

The Cadillac disappeared around the curve in the road, and Maggie let the lace curtain drop back into place.

Turning away from the window, she wandered over to the four-poster bed and trailed her fingertips along the ruffled edge of the bedspread. Her mouth quirked. Jo Beth was right about one thing—her room was exactly the same.

The ruffled white-and-green bedspread and the mountain of frilly pillows piled against the cherry headboard, the soft-green wallpaper sprigged with tiny white flowers, the white lace curtains, the delicate Queen Anne furniture and Dresden figurines and vases had all been part of her mother's tireless efforts to make her feel feminine and dainty. Instead, they had emphasized her gangly height and awkwardness.

Not that she hadn't loved it. It was a truly beautiful room, one to delight the heart of any young girl. It just hadn't suited her.

But Momma had meant well, Maggie thought, giving the delicate bentwood rocker a poke with her forefinger to set it in motion.

With a brisk step, Maggie went downstairs and out to her car. In only a few minutes she'd hauled the rest of her luggage out of the cramped rear of the Viper and carried it upstairs.

She hadn't brought much with her, only the essentials. Aunt Nan, bless her, was shipping the bulk of her fall wardrobe, and Maggie would fly in and out of New York often enough to pick up whatever else she needed.

In no time at all she was unpacked.

Thinking about her aunt had reminded Maggie that she had promised to call and report on her father's condition and how their reunion had gone.

Sitting down on the edge of her bed, she picked up the telephone on the bedside table and dialed her aunt in New York.

Nan answered on the second ring.

"Hi," Maggie said softly, smiling with affection.

Seven years ago, she had instinctively headed for New York and the only person other than her mother from whom she knew she would receive solace and help.

Aunt Nan had not failed her. One look at Maggie's shattered expression and she had folded her in a loving embrace and taken her in. While Maggie had licked her wounds her aunt had showered her with the love and attention she had so desperately needed.

"Maggie, darling. I was hoping it was you calling." Nan paused, and her voice grew husky with concern. "How is Jacob?"

"He's doing okay now. He had a setback and was in the hospital when I arrived. They had to drain his lungs. But he's being released today. Momma has gone to get him now."

"Well, I suppose we can expect those kind of things with this ghastly illness." She waited a beat, then inquired, "How did it go between you and Jacob?"

Blinking furiously, Maggie looked up at the ceiling and pressed her lips together. "Awful. Momma made up the whole thing to get me to come home."

"Oh, Maggie," her aunt murmured with such heartfelt sympathy that the lump in Maggie's throat threatened to choke her. "Sweetheart, I'm so sorry."

"I know. I should have known better than to believe that he really wanted to see me, just because he's dy—"

Maggie's throat seized up on her, making speech impossible for a moment. She squeezed her eyes shut and pressed her balled fist hard against her breastbone, trying to ease the hideous pain. "Just because he…hasn't much time left."

Like Lily, she could not even think about her father's impending death without grief nearly overwhelming her. No matter what he did or didn't feel for her, he was still her father. In every other way he was a good and decent man, and she loved him with all her heart.

"Oh! I'm furious with that blind, hardheaded, stiff-necked brother of mine!" Nan fumed. "And with Lily, too. How could she lie to you like that and let you walk in there and get blindsided, thinking he was going to welcome you the way he should have all along? How could she *do* that to her own daughter? I thought better of her. I really did."

"To be fair, she was desperate. Momma's terrified that Daddy and I won't resolve our differences before it's too late."

"Humph. And whose fault is that, I'd like to know. Bringing the two of you together through deceit was a stupid way to promote a reconciliation. What she needs to do is what she should have done seven years ago, and that's pound some sense into Jacob's granite head."

"I know, but you know Momma. Confrontation just isn't an option for her."

Nan made a disgusted sound and murmured something uncomplimentary under her breath about fragile females.

Maggie didn't take offense. She knew that Nan

loved her mother. She was so sweet-natured and gentle it was impossible not to, and when Nan was around Lily she cosseted her as much as everyone else did.

However, being a strong, confident woman, Nan had never understood and had little patience for Lily's pathological fear of conflict.

"So, when are you leaving?" Nan asked.

"I'm not. I'm staying to the end, like I planned."

"What? Maggie, child, that's crazy. You tried. That's all anyone can expect. Why subject yourself to abuse for months?"

"Because Momma needs me," she replied quietly.

"Oh, for Pete's sake. For once in her sheltered life Lily will just have to pull her socks up and handle a difficult situation on her own. I won't stand by while you—"

"Aunt Nan, it's not just Daddy. The company is in deep trouble again."

Shocked silence hummed through the line.

"But that's impossible!" Nan finally said in an incredulous voice. "I loaned Jacob more than enough money to shore up the financial problems."

"I know, but apparently something has gone terribly wrong." Maggie quickly related all that her mother had told her. "So I'm going to stick around and see what I can find out, and hopefully take steps to get the company back into the black."

"Hmm. That might not be easy. Jacob won't appreciate you poking around in Malone Enterprises business. Neither will that slug, Martin."

"I know. I'm going to be as discreet as possible,

but whether Daddy or Martin like it or not, I *am* going to get to the bottom of this."

There was a long silence, then Nan said quietly, "You do realize that if you meet too much opposition and Jacob bows his neck you're not going to have a choice. You'll have to tell him."

Maggie rubbed the pounding in her temple with her fingertips. "I know, I know. But I'd rather not do that until I absolutely have to. I'm just not ready to face that hurdle yet."

"Well, prepare yourself, sweetheart, because the time is coming when you won't have a choice. And trust me, it isn't going to be pleasant. Jacob is going to be livid when he finds out that you now own forty-seven percent of the stock in Malone Enterprises."

Maggie grimaced and rubbed her temple harder. "I know, I know."

It had all seemed so simple when she'd purchased her aunt's stock in Malone Enterprises.

"Maybe you ought to go ahead and tell Jacob and get it over with," Nan suggested. "You know, catch him off guard. Come in with guns blazing."

"I don't think so." Maggie barely suppressed a shudder when she imagined forcing a showdown with her father.

A wry smile tugged at Maggie's mouth. Maybe there was more of her mother in her than she'd thought.

"Well, if you're determined to do this, I'm flying down there to help you deal with Jacob. As long as he thinks I still own forty-one percent of the stock, he'll have to listen to me. Short of calling a share-holders' meeting and starting a war within the family, he can't do anything about it if I insist on putting you in charge. He and I hold equal shares of stock. Or at least, he thinks we still do.''

"Aunt Nan, that's sweet of you, but you don't have to do that. I don't want to cause a rift between you and Daddy.''

"Nonsense. You're like a daughter to me, child. Besides, when it hits the fan down there—which, sooner or later, it will—I intend to be there to take my share of the heat. It's only right, since we cooked up this scheme together. You wouldn't have those shares if I hadn't sold them to you.''

"I know, but—"

"I'm flying down there, and that's that. You're going to need someone in your corner, and we both know you can't depend on Lily. Besides, I want to spend what time is left with that fool brother of mine. He may have a blind spot when it comes to you, but I love him all the same.''

When their conversation ended and Maggie hung up the telephone she wandered aimlessly around the room for a few minutes, then sank down into the fragile bentwood rocker in the bay window alcove. Leaning her head against the high back, she began to rock. Her eyelids lowered partway until the room became a surreal blur through the heavy fringe of her lashes. She sighed.

Nothing was working out as she'd planned. A year and a half ago when the family business had

run into trouble and her father had appealed to Nan
for a loan, the solution had seemed an easy one.

Her father had already poured all he could of his
own money into the company, and his appeal to Nan
had been a reasonable request. She had been the
only other major shareholder and Edward Endicott,
her late husband, had left her financially well off.
But what her father hadn't realized was, all of Nan's
inheritance was tied up in the complicated trust that
provided her income. The only asset she'd had that
could be liquidated was her Malone Enterprises
stock, and that could only be sold to a direct descendant of the first Katherine Margaret Malone.

When her aunt had explained the problem, Maggie had immediately offered to purchase enough of
her stock to provide the money her father needed. It
had not been necessary for Nan to sell all of her
Malone Enterprises stock, but she had insisted that
she wanted Maggie to have it.

"I was going to leave all my shares to you, anyway, just in case that brother of mine had cut you
out of his will. I'm not about to stand by and let
him rob you of your rightful inheritance.

"Anyway, it's only right that you have the lion's
share. You're the only one of Jacob's children who
is qualified to run the business or has an interest in
doing so," Nan had insisted.

Nan's shares, added to the six percent that grandfather Michael had left each of his granddaughters,
gave Maggie forty-seven percent of the family business.

At the time, Jacob had recently been diagnosed

with cancer and Maggie had not wanted to upset him more. If he found out that not only had she been the one to come to his rescue, but that she now owned the largest single chunk of the business, he would have been livid. To hide the transaction, she had set up a blind trust of her own—the Malone-Endicott Trust—of which she was the sole owner and beneficiary. Nan, however, was the trustee of record.

On paper the shares had been sold to the trust. When Jacob had questioned the change in ownership, Nan had simply told him that it had been done for "estate planning purposes." Since all the stock reports continued to go to Nan, so far he had not questioned the matter further.

As she rocked, Maggie rolled her head against the chair back and gave a wry chuckle. "Eighteen months ago it had all seemed so simple, so foolproof," she murmured to herself. She'd play the white knight and save the company, and her father would never know.

Of course, at the time she hadn't counted on ever returning home, at least not while Jacob was still alive. And she certainly hadn't expected to actually get involved in Malone Enterprises in any hands-on way.

What strange twists and turns life took, she mused. All of her life there had been only two things that she'd ever really wanted—her father's love and a chance to work in the family business. After the scene with her father the day before she no longer harbored any hope of gaining the first. Now, how-

ever, it appeared she was about to attain her second
goal by default.

Maggie's mouth quirked again, this time her smile
more sad than wry. How ironic, after all that had
happened, that she was the one being asked to save
the company.

Six

"Pull around to the back. I've been cooped up in that damned hospital for two days. I want to sit outside for a while."

Dan met his boss's gaze in the rearview mirror as he turned the Cadillac into the driveway. "Whatever you say."

It was the first complete sentence Jacob had uttered since they'd driven away from Mercy Hospital. He had been cheerful and anxious to get home when he and Lily had first arrived, but something had occurred between the two of them while Dan had gone to bring the car around.

When he returned Jacob was stone-faced and Lily was upset, and it was obvious that she'd been crying. The tension between the couple was thick enough to cut with a knife.

All the way home Lily had seemed anxious and overeager to please, but Jacob had ignored her nervous chatter for the most part, staring out the side window in silence. When he bothered to respond at all it was with grunts or sharp, one-word replies that cut Lily off and brought a sheen of moisture to her eyes.

It was aberrant behavior for Jacob, and that puzzled Dan. More than any man he'd ever known, Jacob adored his wife and cosseted her as though she were made of spun glass. What the hell had passed between these two during those few minutes while he'd been gone? Whatever it was, Jacob was furious.

Dan drove past the circular section of drive in front of the house and around to the side. He parked by the brick walkway that led from the drive to the terrace, then hopped out and retrieved the wheelchair from the trunk.

Though weak, Jacob waved him away when he attempted to lift him from the car, struggling out and into the wheelchair on his own. By the time he was settled his face was white with the effort.

"It's good to be home again," Jacob said with a sigh. He sagged with weariness as Dan pushed the chair up the walk. Lily scurried along beside them, fussing with the blanket that covered her husband's legs, smoothing his hair.

When they rounded the massive crepe myrtle bush at the back corner of the house, Jacob stiffened. His oldest daughter sat in a lounge chair on the terrace.

Jacob's bony hands gripped the arms of the wheelchair until his knuckles whitened. Even from behind, Dan knew he'd clenched his jaw.

Maggie rose with languid grace and sent Jacob a tentative smile. "Welcome home, Daddy. How're you feeling?"

Jacob's hard stare pinned her. Dan began to think he wasn't going to answer when suddenly he snapped, "I'm not ready to die just yet, if that's what you're asking."

"Jacob!"

"Even if I were to, you wouldn't benefit," he added, ignoring his wife. "You may as well know, my shares of Malone Enterprises will be divided between your sisters. So if you're hanging around hoping to collect an inheritance, you're out of luck, Katherine."

"Jacob! How *could* you?" Lily shot a pleading look at her daughter. "Pay no attention to him, dear. He didn't mean it. Truly. He's just out of sorts. He always gets this way when he has to stay in the hospital."

If Dan hadn't been watching Maggie he might have missed her flinch and the flash of hurt in her magnificent green eyes.

She recovered quickly, though, he'd give her that. In a blink the wounded look was replaced by a saucy sparkle. Paying no more attention to her mother's dithering than her father had, she heaved a theatrical sigh. "Ah, well, you win some, you lose some. I guess I'll just have to muddle along on my own salary."

Dan almost smiled. He wondered if Jacob knew that his daughter's annual income ran well into eight figures. From his expression, he suspected the older man hadn't a clue what a top model earned.

Not surprising. The idea of anyone being paid millions simply to pose for pictures or strut down runways would be incomprehensible to a salt-of-the-earth type like Jacob.

"Your mother tells me she's asked you to stay, Katherine. And that you've agreed."

"Yes, I'm staying. For Momma's sake." The

amused smile remained in place, but she raised her chin a notch, those emerald eyes daring him to object.

Dan's gaze sharpened and swung back and forth between father and daughter. What the hell kind of reunion was this? These two were circling each other like a pair of wary dogs. And what was this ''Katherine'' business?

''I'm sure you're aware of my feelings on the matter. However, I do realize that the next few months are going to be difficult for your mother, and apparently it's important to her to have you here,'' he said in the stiffest voice Dan had ever heard him use. ''I love Lily too much to deny her that comfort, but I'm warning you, girl, you cause any trouble— any at all—and you will leave this house. Is that clear?''

''As a bell. Daddy, I'm twenty-seven, not sixteen. Believe it or not, I haven't painted a racy limerick on a water tower or attended an all-night beer bust with my school pals in over eleven years.''

''There are ways to cause trouble other than juvenile pranks, Katherine. Some quite serious. And as I recall, you were quite adept at discovering them.''

Confusion, then dawning comprehension flickered over Maggie's face. Both gave way to a devilish twinkle and a husky laugh.

To Dan's surprise, the throaty sound sent a shaft of pure lust coursing through him.

''Ah, I get it. I hate to disappoint you, Daddy, but I haven't seduced a man in...oh...at least a week.

But if it'll make you feel better, I promise to control myself."

Lily winced and fluttered her hands.

"You make a joke of everything, don't you, Katherine?"

"I try," she replied, grinning.

The glib comeback infuriated Jacob, but whatever retort he'd been about to make died on his tongue with the appearance of the housekeeper.

"There you are." Ida Lou bustled across the terrace carrying a tray loaded with a pitcher of iced tea and plates piled high with chicken salad and fruit. "I thought I heard your car drive up. Lunch is ready. Y'all sit yourselves down while I go fetch the rest."

"None for me, thanks," Maggie said.

"What nonsense is this? How'm I ever gonna fatten you up if you don't eat, child?"

"Sorry, Ida Lou, but I'm still stuffed from breakfast. In fact, I think I'll take a little walk through the orchard to work it off."

"If you don't mind, I'll go with you. I need to get back to the cannery." Because he was watching for it, Dan saw the flicker of annoyance in Maggie's eyes, but it was quickly subdued.

She hitched her shoulder. "It's a free country, sugar." Without waiting for him, she headed for the terrace steps.

"I swear, I don't know what's wrong with you young people today," Ida Lou groused. "You're gonna dry up and blow away, that's what."

Since he was over six four and two hundred and twenty pounds, that didn't seem likely to Dan, but he merely winked at the elderly woman. "Now, Ida

Lou, you know I'm crazy about your cooking, but I really need to get back to work. That is, unless you need me for something, Jacob? If you need help getting into the house I'll stay.''

"Just go on with you. I'm a healthy, able-bodied woman, aren't I? If Mr. Jacob needs help, I'll see to it just fine. Truth is, I don't know why we have to have no male nurse, anyways. Just plain foolishness, if you ask me. Some stranger underfoot all the time. Always gettin' in the way,'' the housekeeper muttered, stomping back to the house.

Lily rolled her eyes. Even Jacob looked amused.

"I'm sorry about that, Dan. Ida Lou's had her nose out of joint ever since I told her we were getting a nurse to help out,'' Lily explained.

Maggie made no effort to slow down and let him catch up, though Dan was certain that she knew he was coming up behind her. Perverse woman. She flirted outrageously, then turned a cold shoulder when male company was offered.

Those long legs of hers covered a lot of ground, but Dan's covered more, and he steadily closed the gap between them. He could have let her outdistance him, but he was curious about this oldest Malone daughter.

Lily and Ida Lou obviously adored Maggie, and they were two fine women whose opinions he respected. However, most of what Dan had heard about her wasn't good. His own dim recollection of Maggie was of a wild, in-your-face, sassy teenager. From what he'd seen so far, the woman wasn't much improved.

Still, he had to admit, she was a treat for the eyes.

A man would have to be dead, blind or a eunuch not to appreciate that easy, hip-swiveling walk of hers.

He caught up with her at the back gate, in time to reach around and hold it open for her.

After an initial start, Maggie gave him a sultry smile and purred, "Mmm, a gentleman. Good manners are *so-o-o* sexy in a man."

Dan made no comment. He hadn't figured out yet whether flirting was merely an automatic reflex for Maggie or a shield she hid behind. Either way, it meant nothing and he wasn't fool enough to snap at the bait. Or even interested.

For several seconds they walked along in silence. The narrow dirt lane they followed through the dappled shade between the trees was an extension of the Malones' driveway and led to the old cottage in the middle of the orchard.

The sun was starting its long, slow slide toward the western horizon. The air was redolent with the sweet scent of ripening peaches and sun-warmed earth. A light wind played through the branches, and the leaves ruffled with a papery whisper. Out of habit, Dan scanned the bobbing fruit for ripeness and any sign of infestation or blight.

This section would be ready for the pickers by the middle of the following week, he decided. Scowling at the green shoots poking up through the rich red dirt, he made a mental note to start a crew weeding in this section at first light Monday morning.

Maggie gave a husky chuckle and waved away a persistent butterfly fluttering around her bright hair. The sound drew Dan's attention. He studied her out of the corner of his eye, and irritation rippled over his skin like prickly rash.

Jesus, the woman was absurdly beautiful.

In all the glossy magazine pictures he'd seen of Maggie over the years, she'd looked so stunning it took your breath away, nothing at all like the scrawny, funny-looking kid he and everyone else in Rudy Falls remembered.

He'd chalked up her impact to the artistry of makeup and photography, and perhaps a weird affinity for the camera lens, and dismissed her. He'd always figured that if he ever saw her again in the flesh she wouldn't look so hot. At the very least, he'd be able to spot some flaws.

Damned if there were any that he could see.

She wore a minimum of makeup, yet her skin was porcelain-smooth and the color of cream. Not a freckle in sight. Unusual for a redhead.

Her features were perfection, or as close as humans were likely to come, he thought sourly—high cheekbones, delicate nose, firm jawline, luscious lips and big green eyes that sparkled like emeralds. The last were framed by winged auburn brows and lashes so long and thick he would have sworn they were fake if he hadn't been close enough to see otherwise.

And that hair. That alone was enough to drive a man over the edge. He didn't even like the woman, but still his fingers itched to dive into that sexy mane, feel it slide across his skin.

Jesus! Get a grip, Garrett, he silently berated himself. This is Maggie Malone, the town hell-raiser, you're drooling over.

Still, no matter how hard he tried he couldn't seem to tear away his gaze from that glorious hair.

It was the color of flame, shiny as satin, and so thick and curly it seemed to have a life of its own. Yesterday, it had been wind-tossed and loose. Today, pulled up in a banana clip, it cascaded down her back in a riot of curls, only slightly more tame. When struck by the sunlight coming through the trees it caught fire.

Very few true redheads ever made it big in modeling, he'd noticed. But then few had Maggie's vibrance.

It was more than just her coloring, spectacular as that was. There was that self-assured walk, the proud tilt of her head. She almost crackled with a feisty "look out world, here I come" kind of sass.

It showed in the laughter that so often danced in her eyes and tugged at the corners of those full lips. As if she had a secret that no one else knew.

That touch of mystery was intriguing as hell, and almost impossible to resist, beckoning to a man, daring him to try to discover what lay behind that devilish twinkle.

Small wonder she had rocketed to the top of the modeling world only a few short months after landing in New York. In a field dominated by cool, sophisticated blondes and sultry brunettes, Maggie Malone stood out like a bright butterfly in a flock of moths.

And apparently, she was just as elusive and aloof as that pretty creature.

Strolling along with her fingertips stuck in the back pockets of her jeans, her gaze drifting around the orchard, Maggie had tuned him out as though he weren't there.

"Looks like I was wrong about Jacob wanting to see you."

She jumped at the sound of his voice, then slanted him a droll look out of the corner of her eye.

"Gee, ya think?"

"It was a natural assumption. Most fathers and daughters would be happy to see each other after so long apart."

"I'm sure that's true," she concurred agreeably. Her mouth twitched. "But then, Daddy and I have never been like 'most fathers and daughters'."

Dan waited for her to elaborate, but she focused her gaze straight ahead and resumed her silent stroll.

"Judging from that exchange between you two back there, I gather it's safe to assume that old story about you is true?"

She chuckled, but it was a bitter sound that had little to do with mirth. "And which story would that be, sugar? Don't forget, I was the gossips' favorite target for years. For all I know, I may still be. There are more rumors about me flying around this town than there are peaches on a tree."

"The one about Jacob throwing you out because you tried to seduce your sister's fiancé."

"Oh. That one."

The change in her demeanor was subtle but unmistakable. All trace of amusement vanished from her eyes. She withdrew her hands from her back pockets, folded her arms across her midriff and seemed to draw into herself.

"So, did you do it or not?"

Maggie gave a startled laugh. "You sure are plainspoken, aren't you. I've known you less than twenty-four hours, and twice already you've been painfully direct. No shilly-shallying around for you, just go straight for the heart of the matter."

Dan shrugged. "It's honest and leaves little room for misunderstanding."

"True, but I wouldn't try for the diplomatic corps if I were you."

Maggie fell silent again, and Dan realized that the little jibe at his manner had merely been an attempt to sidetrack him.

"Aren't you even going to bother to deny the story?" he prodded after a moment. "Most women would if they knew a rumor like that was circulating about them."

She shot him another one of those looks, and for a moment he thought she wasn't going to answer. Then she shrugged. "Why should I bother? My father thinks I'm guilty. Therefore, so does everyone else in town."

"Is that a yes or a no?"

"It's whatever you want it to be, sugar. I stopped defending myself to the people of this town years ago."

Interesting. It wasn't exactly a denial, but it wasn't a confession, either.

"Are you saying you don't care what people think of you?"

"I'm saying that people are going to believe what they want to believe, and there isn't a blessed thing I can do about it. And you can bet your boots that everyone around here wants to believe I'm guilty.

I've got about as much chance of convincing them otherwise as I do of jumping over the moon. So why should I tie myself up in knots trying?''

''Maybe. But some would say that a person who is wrongly accused would at least deny it.''

Maggie stopped and turned to face him, forcing him to come to a halt, as well. ''What is this about? Why do you care whether I'm guilty or innocent, anyway?''

''I don't. My only concern is what effect your being here will have on Jacob. He's sick and weak, and he has a lot of business worries to contend with. He doesn't need any more on his plate right now. So if you came back here with any idea of coming between Laurel and her husband, or stirring up any kind of trouble that might upset your father, it would be best if you just turn around and head back to New York right now.''

Maggie managed a smile, but it was strained and it didn't reach those snapping green eyes. ''Oh, really? You know, sugar, I hate to tell you this, but my relationship with my father is none of your business.''

''Too bad. I'm making it my business. Jacob Malone is a fine, decent man. In my book, they don't come any better. He's honest and absolutely fair with everyone. I figure, if he's got a problem with you, he's got good cause.

''Jacob took a chance on me when no one else would. I owe him a lot. I'll be damned if I'll stand idly by and let you or anyone else put any additional burden on him in his final days.

''Cause him any grief, Red, and you'll answer to me. And I warn you, I'll do whatever I have to do to protect him.''

Seven

Maggie was still simmering when she reached the cannery.

"Come between Laurel and Martin, indeed," she muttered to herself as she stalked toward the main building. "I'd like to come between them, all right, but not in the way Dan Garrett seems to think."

Did he honestly believe she'd been pining away for that creep all these years? That was about the most insulting thing anyone had ever said to her. Maggie shuddered and made a face. "Yuck."

She didn't know why she had allowed Dan's comments to get under her skin. Or why she had this dull ache in her chest or this stupid urge to cry. It wasn't as though she hadn't dealt with that kind of unfair criticism before. In the past, she'd let it roll off her like water off a duck's back.

The problem was, during the past seven years she'd grown accustomed to being treated with respect and admiration. She'd almost forgotten what it was like to have to defend herself at every turn.

"You're out of practice, Mag," she muttered. "You're going to have to toughen up again. And fast."

What had she expected, anyway? Dan Garrett was

her father's general manager, after all. The man knew where his loyalties lay.

Besides, she couldn't fault his reasoning, since she agreed with him. Her father *was* a decent and honorable man, a scrupulously honest and fair man...with everyone but her.

At least she'd managed to hide her upset with a flippant remark. "Don't worry, sugar, home-wrecking isn't on my agenda this trip. Maybe next time," she'd drawled with a taunting twitch of her lips, though she hadn't felt in the least like smiling.

To her relief, only moments later they had parted company when Dan stopped by his place to change into his work clothes.

Until then, Maggie hadn't realized that Dan lived in the old manager's quarters. The Victorian cottage had been her great-grandmother's home when she'd started the family business, and it had previously occupied the site on which their present home sat.

In 1927, when the big house had been built, the cottage had been moved to the clearing in the center of the orchard, a small patch of ground too alkaline to grow healthy fruit trees, halfway between the original site and the cannery. Ever since, the three-bedroom cottage had been home to the cannery manager and his family.

Over the years the old place had been renovated and kept in top condition. Still, Maggie was surprised that Dan had opted to live there, charming as it was. She would have thought a good-looking bachelor would have wanted the privacy of an apartment in town.

But then again, what did she know? Maybe Dan

Garrett was one of those men who conducted his love life someplace other than his home.

Maggie entered the minuscule lobby of the main cannery building and started up the stairs to the second-floor offices. Stepping into the reception room at the top of the stairs, she paused to look around and experienced a sharp tug of nostalgia.

The computer that hummed on the corner of the desk was new and so was the carpet, but everything else was just as it had always been—the same sturdy mahogany furniture, the same paintings on the walls, the same seven-foot-tall bamboo plant in the corner.

An ever-changing geometric shape careered silently around the computer screen, but there was no one manning the receptionist's desk.

The hallway on the right led to various offices and the marketing and accounting departments. Faint sounds of voices and activity came from that direction, but Maggie turned left toward her father's office.

Taking a hard look at the books was going to be a top priority, but she wasn't ready yet to begin any serious digging. Today she would just lay a bit of groundwork—reintroduce herself to the staff and meet any new people, let them get used to seeing her in the office again, maybe get the lay of the land and pick up some useful tidbits of information. And the best place to start was with her father's secretary.

Anna Talmadge had worked for Malone Enterprises for twenty-two years, the last thirteen as Jacob's secretary. Not only did she know the company inside out, she knew all the office gossip, as well—

all the rivalries, the petty jealousies and office politics.

Anna was staunchly loyal to her boss and guarded him and his business dealings with the fierceness of a junkyard dog. However, the starchy old woman had always had a soft spot for the Malone girls. Maggie figured if she handled things right, Anna could be a fountain of information.

Without a doubt, she would be of immeasurable help to Maggie on a purely practical level in the coming weeks.

Besides, Maggie knew the pecking order. Dan Garrett might be her father's right-hand man on the production end and Martin probably thought of himself as second in command, but it was Anna who ran the office.

Her father's secretary wasn't at her post in the outer office when Maggie poked her head inside. If she hadn't known the woman to be a "neat freak," she would have thought she wasn't there. There wasn't so much as a piece of paper or a pencil on her desk, not even a paper clip, just a rigidly aligned blotter and desk calendar. Even her computer was covered.

Maggie crossed the room and entered her father's office, but Anna wasn't in there, either. "Maybe she's taking a late lunch," she murmured to herself, checking her wristwatch. If so, she would be back soon.

Deciding to wait, Maggie wandered aimlessly around the room.

No modern office furnishings or wall-to-wall carpet in here. This office retained the look of old-world elegance that Katherine Margaret had given it over seventy years ago—walnut wainscoting topped by embossed ivory wall covering, dark oak floors polished to a satiny sheen, and an enormous wine, blue and ivory Oriental rug anchoring the antique furnishings.

Smiling, Maggie trailed her fingertips along the edge of the massive walnut desk and her father's big chair. She closed her eyes and breathed in the scents that she had always associated with this office— lemon oil, leather and fine cigars. The latter came from the humidor her father still kept on his desk, even though he'd given up smoking years ago.

A distant rumble drew her attention, and Maggie walked over to the floor-to-ceiling glass wall behind her father's desk that overlooked the cannery floor. Heavy draperies could be drawn over the wall to block out the faint sounds, but her father, like his father and grandmother before him, liked to feel connected to the actual work being done in the vast cannery.

The prep rooms, where machines did the work of washing, peeling, scraping, slicing and chopping, and the "kitchens" where the fruits and vegetable were cooked in enormous vats could not be seen from this vantage point. Jacob's office overlooked the part of the operation where the foods were put into cans or bottles, then sealed, labeled and crated for shipment.

Maggie's gaze drifted over the workers and machinery, all of which seemed to be in perpetual motion. Hundreds of times she had stood in this very spot, but she never tired of watching the process.

Her eyes scanned the lines of empty cans and bottles jiggling along on miles of ball-bearing tracks at
various levels. She watched the precision machinery
fill one container after another, seal them and send
them on their way to the next machine, which, in a
blink, wrapped and glued a label around each one
and shot them out to be trundled away on wide conveyor belts, to be neatly slotted into packing cases.

Her gaze followed the cases of canned and bottled
foods as they moved along on conveyors to the loading bay at the back of the building. There they were
stacked on pallets and transferred by forklifts to the
various storage warehouses around the grounds.

As always, the process mesmerized Maggie, but
she was jarred out of her trance when the door to
the general manager's office, on the far side of the
building, opened and Dan strode onto the cannery
floor.

Maggie's entire body tautened and a tingle rippled
over her skin. Annoyed, she gritted her teeth, but
the sensation wouldn't go away.

Dan was dressed as he had been the day before
when she'd first met him, in jeans and a chambray
work shirt. From far away he looked big and utterly
masculine, even a bit dangerous. Maggie thought of
those cool silver eyes that could see right through
you, and shivered.

The instant he stepped onto the floor he was be-
sieged from three sides by workers wanting to have
a word with him.

Maggie watched him converse with the three men
and two women on the fly. All of them practically
had to trot to keep up with him as he strode through

the maze of machinery and people on the floor. Every once in a while he stopped to say something to one of the workers, or gesture, or inspect a piece of machinery, but he wasted no time.

Even viewed from above at this great distance, Dan Garrett stood out from the rest of the workers. There was just something about him, an innate air of confidence and authority that marked him as the man in charge.

Without warning he looked up, straight at her, and Maggie's heart gave a little leap. In a panicked reflex, she took a half step back before she realized what she was doing and halted the retreat. From this distance she couldn't see his expression clearly, but she felt those pale eyes drilling into her. Squelching the urge to escape his penetrating stare, Maggie smiled and waggled her fingers.

For several seconds he didn't react, but finally he nodded, then continued his rounds. When he headed toward the kitchens and disappeared from view, she let out the breath she hadn't realized she had been holding and pressed her hand against her midriff.

What was it about that man that rattled her so? Exasperated with herself, Maggie pushed the question aside and turned back to the room.

All thought of Dan Garrett flew right out of her mind when her gaze fell on the large, ornately framed photograph of her great-grandmother that dominated the wall opposite her father's desk. Maggie strolled over to stand before the picture, her lips curving into a warm smile.

Katherine Margaret Malone, her namesake and idol.

The photo had been taken when her great-grandmother had been in her mid-forties. As a young woman Katherine Margaret had been a beauty, and even in middle age she had been what in those days had been described as a "handsome woman," but it was the fortitude and intelligence and determination in that clear, steady gaze that had always fascinated Maggie.

Growing up she had been awed by the stories about Katherine Margaret, and it had been her fervent hope to be like her great-grandmother and someday follow in her footsteps as head of the company.

Left widowed and penniless, with a small son to raise, she had done what few women of her day would have dared. Young Katherine Margaret had started a small, in-home business and eventually built it into what was today Malone Enterprises.

"We owe it all to you, Great-gran," Maggie murmured. "And I swear to you, I'll do everything I possibly can to see that the business continues to thrive, and that it remains in the family."

"What are you doing in here?"

The querulous question startled Maggie, and she jumped and turned her head sharply. Standing in the open doorway was a small, prim-looking woman of about thirty-five who was glaring at her as though she were a thief whom she'd caught with her hand in the safe.

The woman wore her brown hair in the straight, chin-length bob that was currently popular, but the severe style did nothing for her sharp features. Her thin mouth was pinched into a disapproving line, and she held herself so stiffly she looked like an advertisement for a full-body corset.

"Hi. I didn't hear you come in," Maggie said pleasantly.

The woman didn't bend a fraction. "I'm afraid you'll have to leave."

Maggie laughed. "You must be new here. Trust me, there's no problem. I'm Maggie Malone. This is my daddy's office."

"I know who you are, Miss Malone," she woman said in a haughty voice, and Maggie could have sworn that her upper lip curled ever so slightly. "Although, I must say, we weren't expecting to see you here. Mr. Howe called the hospital this morning, and your father told him you were leaving today."

So, Martin had called to be sure she was going to be given the boot again, had he? Typical. He must have made the call before her mother and Dan arrived at the hospital. He was going to have a conniption when he found out she was staying. And why.

She almost laughed out loud, imagining it.

"Yes, well…my plans have changed," she said.

"So I see. Nevertheless, you still have to leave."

"Excuse me?"

"Mr. Howe is using this office, since he's in charge now. He instructed me to keep everyone out of here whenever he's not around."

"Oh, really?"

We'll just see about that, Maggie thought. No way in hell was she going to stand for Martin commandeering her father's office. Or his company.

"And where is Martin? Perhaps I'd better talk to him."

"Mr. Howe is on his way to the Dallas airport. He's flying to Albuquerque to meet with the buyer for the Thrifty Pantry supermarket chain."

"On Friday afternoon? Isn't that a bit odd? By the time he gets there their offices will be closed."

The woman tilted her chin at an imperious angle. "Business is often conducted in places other than an office, you know. It so happens, Mr. Howe is participating in a charity golf tournament on Sunday that Thrifty Pantries is sponsoring. He committed himself to playing months ago. Of course, had he known you would be here, I'm sure he would have canceled."

Oh, I'm sure he would have, Maggie thought. The last thing Martin wanted was to leave her alone on what he considered his turf.

"Well then, isn't it fortunate that he didn't know? I certainly wouldn't want to interfere with his work schedule." If you could call playing golf work. "So, when do you expect him back, Miss...?"

"Udall. Elaine Udall. Mr. Howe won't be back in the office until next weekend. He's been so busy running the company for Mr. Malone that he's neglected his own work, so he'll be spending all of next week flying around the five-state area, calling on our major customers."

"I see. And just what is it that you do here, Miss Udall?"

"I head the accounting department."

"Really? What happened to Miss Franklin? She's

held that job for years, but I don't believe she's old enough to retire.''

"Yes, well…Miss Franklin really was past it, you know. The woman never made the adjustment from keeping books by hand to doing them on the computer. A year ago your father gave her a very generous early retirement pension. I was promoted to take over her job.''

"I see. Have there been many other changes in office staff since I left?''

"I really wouldn't know. Now, I'm afraid I must insist that you leave.''

Maggie waved her hand in a dismissive gesture. "Oh, don't worry about it. I'm sure Martin won't mind me being here. I'm just waiting for Anna to return from lunch.''

"Anna doesn't work here anymore.''

"*What?* Don't tell me Daddy retired her, too. I don't believe it. He would be lost without her.''

"Actually, uh, Mr. Howe let her go yesterday. He felt that since he will be running the company he should hand-pick his own secretary.''

Maggie's eyes narrowed. "He let her go? You mean he pensioned her off like Miss Franklin?''

"Well…'' Elaine Udall twisted her hands together and did not quite meet Maggie's eyes.

"Wait a minute. Are you saying Martin *fired* Anna? After twenty-two years with the company? Does Daddy know about this? No, of course he doesn't,'' she supplied before the woman could answer. "He would never have approved such a move.''

"As acting president, Mr. Howe has the authority

to make such decisions. And I must say, he was right to get rid of her. The woman took entirely too much upon herself. Why, the way she acted you'd think she was the one running the company.''

Anna probably had been, for the most part, since Jacob's illness began to take its toll, Maggie thought. And no doubt she'd been doing a helluva lot better job of it than Martin even came close to doing on his best day.

Maggie was so furious she was shaking inside. Martin had been running things only a few days, and already he was wreaking havoc. Had he been there she would have marched into his office and throttled him with her bare hands.

She was careful, however, not to let her anger show, since she was certain that Miss Udall would report this meeting to him, verbatim. She wasn't ready to show her hand to Martin just yet.

''Well, since Anna's not coming back, I guess I'll be on my way. First, though, I'll just pop in and say hello to the rest of the staff.''

''Oh, dear. I really don't think that's a good idea,'' Elaine protested, but Maggie had already sailed out the door, her long legs taking her quickly through the outer office and down the short hall. The older woman hurried after her at a trot, catching up in the reception room.

''Miss Malone, I don't think Mr. Howe would approve of you taking up the staff's time during working hours.''

Maggie's patience snapped. It had been her intention to let everyone think that she had no interest in the business, that she'd merely stopped by for a friendly visit, but she'd had more than enough of Elaine Udall.

Coming to an abrupt halt, she whirled on the woman so suddenly that Elaine gasped and almost bumped into her.

"Miss Udall. A word of warning," Maggie said in a voice so silky smooth the other woman's eyes widened. "This is a family-owned company. You would do well to remember that not only am I a member of that family, I'm also a stockholder. Mr. Howe is merely an employee."

"I...he...he's a *vice president!* And your sister's husband," Elaine protested.

"True. But he's not an owner. Which means, if he's not careful, he can get his ass fired. And so can you." Bending slightly from the waist, Maggie jutted her chin at the woman. "Do I make myself clear?"

Maggie spent the rest of the afternoon at the office. She deliberately took her time, dawdling by each desk and stretching out her conversations in order to needle Miss Udall. The woman pretended she was working, but she hovered close by the whole time, looking as if she'd swallowed a lemon.

Maggie could sense that morale in the office was not what it should be, and she wondered how much of the blame for that could be laid at Miss Udall's feet.

In the past Malone's had always been a cheerful, relaxed place to work, but from the nervous glances the people in accounting cast Elaine Udall's way it was clear that the woman ruled with an iron hand.

Even people who did not work in her department seemed leery of her.

That kind of whip-cracking approach to management did not go over well in small towns like Ruby Falls, where everybody knew everybody, and it had never been Malone's policy. Maggie was surprised that her father had allowed the uncomfortable work atmosphere to develop.

At closing time she left the office along with the staff. A storm was brewing toward the south. Lightning forked from the dark thunderheads. With every clap, the rumble of thunder grew louder, and the smell of approaching rain hung in the still air.

Anxious to get home before the storm broke, Maggie hurried through the orchard, mulling over all she had learned on the way. If she and her father had been on better terms she would go to him and discuss the situation, but until she had something concrete to report he was sure to brush aside her concerns.

As she came through the garden gate the first drops of rain began to fall, big drops the size of grapes that pelted her like hail. A crack of thunder almost directly overhead sent Maggie sprinting for the house.

She burst through the kitchen door, out of breath and laughing, her top plastered to her skin. Startled, Ida Lou whirled around.

"Lord'a' mercy, child, you're soaked. Here, dry yourself before you take chill and catch your death of cold," she said, tossing her a towel.

"Thanks." Maggie blotted her arms and face, then rubbed the towel over her hair while she sniffed the air. "Mmm, something sure smells good. And I'm starving."

"It's roast beef, and it's not done yet, so there's no use in hintin' around for a bite. Dinner'll be ready at seven as usual, so just go on with you."

"Not even a little bite? Pretty please," Maggie cajoled, doing her best to look pitiful.

"No. Those who skip meals can just go hungry, I say," she stated with a huff. Then she flapped her apron. "Now, shoo. Get out of my kitchen, you're dripping all over my clean floor."

"I'm going, I'm going." Chuckling, Maggie pushed through the swinging doors.

Her sisters were in the family room with their parents. They didn't notice her when she paused in the doorway, and as she took in the scene Maggie felt the same sense of isolation she'd experienced growing up.

Laurel sat beside their father on the sofa, and Jo Beth was curled up on the floor beside his feet, her head leaning against his knee. Jacob absently stroked his youngest daughter's cap of dark hair, but his gaze was focused on Laurel's face as she pleaded earnestly.

"The doctor I spoke to in Houston is willing to take you into his study. This new medication they're testing may be just the answer for you, Daddy. If you agree, we can take you to Houston first thing Monday morning. They'll put you through a battery of tests and start you on the program. Of course, you'll have to stay in the hospital there, but—"

"I don't think so, baby."

"Daddy, please—"

"No, Laurel. I know you mean well, but you have to accept that it's too late for me. I'm going to spend my last days at home with my loved ones, not in a hospital being prodded and poked and studied like a lab rat."

"But at least this offers some hope, Daddy."

"Oh, sweetheart, we both know the chances of me finding a cure at this late date are zero to none. No, baby," Jacob said softly, patting her hand. "I thank you for caring, but no."

The look of absolute love in his eyes as he gazed into Laurel's anguished face pierced Maggie's heart like a spear. Without making a sound, she turned away and went upstairs to her room.

The storm had leveled off to a steady downpour by the time Maggie came downstairs. When she entered the dining room she was startled to find Dan there with her parents and sisters. After only an initial blink of surprise, she smiled and drawled, "Well, hello there, sugar. I didn't know you were joining us."

"His name is Daniel, Katherine," her father snapped.

"Yes, Daddy, I know. And mine is Maggie," she replied, and slipped into the chair next to her mother's at the opposite end of the table from him. Her father's mouth tightened, but she pretended not to notice.

As usual, Laurel and Jo Beth took the chairs flanking Jacob's at the head of the table. Dan sat down across from Maggie, on her mother's left.

Throughout the meal Maggie remained silent except when someone directed a remark to her. Usually that was Jo Beth, getting in one of her "zingers," followed by Lily doing her fluttery best to play peacemaker and smooth things over. Once or twice Dan made a polite remark or asked a question. Each time Maggie dredged up a glib reply, but otherwise she kept her eyes on her plate and didn't encourage conversation.

Neither her father nor Laurel addressed her.

Several times Maggie glanced up and caught Dan staring at her, but she ignored him and applied herself to the delicious meal.

It wasn't difficult. Ida Lou had outdone herself, and after skipping lunch, Maggie was ravenous. She put away two plates piled high with roast beef and gravy, mashed potatoes, green been amandine and pickled beets, then topped it all off with a piece of lemon meringue pie.

When she'd finished the last bite she looked up and discovered that Dan was watching her with a look of mild amazement.

"I thought models only ate salads."

Maggie chuckled and patted her flat tummy. "Not me. It takes more than rabbit food to satisfy my appetite. Besides, I tend to get crabby when I'm hungry."

"Oh, dear, we wouldn't want that," Jo Beth jibed. "Heaven forbid Miss Glamor Queen is anything but perfect."

"Jo Beth," Lily warned, but her tone had grown weary from repeated reprimands.

Other than to cast the teenager a quizzical glance, Dan went on as though she hadn't spoken.

"Somehow I don't think there's much danger of that happening tonight."

"Daddy, are you all right?"

Laurel's worried tone drew everyone's attention to the head of the table. A painful tangle of emotions knotted inside Maggie. Merely eating a meal had sapped Jacob. He sagged in his chair like an old, old man, his face ashen.

Instantly, Lily was on her feet and hurrying to her husband's side. Maggie and Dan followed right behind her.

"Time to get you to bed, dearest," Lily gently declared. "It's been a big day and you're worn out."

"You'll get no argument from me. Sorry to poop out on you, Dan. Maybe we can go over those reports tomorrow morning at breakfast."

"No problem. There's nothing that can't wait."

"I'll get Ida Lou," Laurel offered, but no sooner had she spoken than the housekeeper appeared in the doorway.

"What's this now? Plumb tuckered out, are you? Well, let's get you upstairs."

"I've got him." Dan scooped Jacob up in his arms as though he weighed no more than a sack of flour and strode out of the room.

Watching, Maggie stared after them, biting her lower lip. "Oh, God, it breaks my heart to see him so sick and weak," she murmured.

"Yeah, right. Like you really care. If you did you would've come home to see him before now."

Maggie exhaled a long sigh. "You know, little sister, I'm getting tired of your constant sniping. Do you honestly think I didn't *want* to come home? That I didn't *long* to see my family? It nearly killed me to stay away. But I had no choice. By now you must know that Daddy threw me out seven years ago and told me never to come back. He's only tolerating my being here now for Momma's sake."

"Yes, and I know why he threw you out," she shouted, jumping to her feet so suddenly her chair tumbled over backward. Shaking with fury, she glared at Maggie, her young face flushed with outrage and hurt and confusion. "Everybody in town knows. It's so humiliating. I don't know how Laurel can stand to be around you. I certainly can't!"

With that parting shot, she whirled and ran from the room, leaving a thick silence behind.

The two sisters stood frozen in place as Jo Beth's footsteps pounded up the stairs, then faded down the upper hall. A few seconds later her bedroom door slammed.

Maggie sighed again and looked at her sister, wincing. "I'm so sorry, sis. I didn't mean for that to happen."

Laurel stood ramrod stiff, staring at the floor, her face stricken. She shook her head. "It doesn't matter."

"I think it does. Otherwise you wouldn't look like you'd just been slapped. Laurel, don't you think it's time we talked this out? We never have, you know."

Laurel's head snapped up. Her wide-eyed expression was one of absolute horror. "No!" She shook her head again, so hard the clip that held her lank hair back went flying. "There's nothing to talk about."

"Nothing to *talk* about? Dammit, Laurel, that night changed my life. It changed all our lives. I'd say we have plenty to talk about. And it's long overdue."

"No. It's over and done with, and I just want to forget it ever happened."

"Laurel—"

"I have to go. Tell Momma good-night for me. And that I'll call her tomorrow." Before Maggie could protest she darted past her and out of the dining room.

"Laurel, wait!"

Laurel pushed open the front screen door on the run, but before it could swing shut all the way Maggie shoved it open again and followed her out onto the veranda. The screen door slammed shut behind her, but the sound was barely audible over the noise of the storm.

Rain poured down in torrents. It danced and splattered against the sidewalk and the railings, creating a fine mist that roiled up under the veranda roof.

At first Maggie didn't see her sister. She halted in the pale rectangle of light slanting through the screen door and looked around. How could she have disappeared so quickly? Then jagged lightning flashed across the night sky, and she saw her fumbling in the darkness for the umbrella she'd left on the porch earlier.

Locating the umbrella, Laurel snatched it up and headed for the steps as thunder cracked and rumbled with a force that vibrated the ground. Maggie sidestepped in front of her, blocking her way.

"Laurel, listen to me. I didn't try to seduce Martin that night. I swear it. Dear God, Laurel, we were so close back then, you and I. How could you believe I would do something like that?''

''Martin said you thought I'd call off the wedding if you could get him to sleep with you. You had just tried to convince me to do just that.''

''Jeezlouise, Laurel, I love you dearly, and there's not much I wouldn't do for you, but I draw the line at sleeping with Martin.'' Even the thought sent a little shudder through her.

''Martin said—''

''Martin lied. For God's sake, he tried to *rape* me! He would have succeeded if Daddy hadn't interrupted. Then the weasel turned it all around and claimed that *I* came on to *him!*''

Laurel's chin came up. ''Daddy believed him.''

''Because Daddy *wanted* to believe him. Daddy has always wanted to believe the worst of me. You know that.''

Laurel's mouth began to quiver, and even in the dim light Maggie could see the sheen of moisture in her eyes. Still she shook her head. ''No. No, he…he wouldn't do that. He wouldn't.''

With jerky movements she raised the umbrella over her head and turned to step out into the rain.

''Dammit, Laurel, listen to me!'' Maggie grabbed her sister's arm to stop her but let go instantly when Laurel cried out.

''What's wrong? Oh, God! Did I hurt you?''

Grimacing, Laurel cradled her arm against her side and shook her head. ''No. No, of course not. I…I just have a little bruise, is all.''

''Let me see.''

"No, really, I'm fine," she began, but before she could stop her, Maggie grabbed her wrist and pushed up the loose bell sleeve of her dress.

She sucked in a hissing breath and stared, appalled, at the livid bruises that discolored her sister's skin from mid-forearm to her shoulder and beyond.

Slowly, she raised her head, and her shocked gaze met Laurel's uncomfortable one. "I wondered why you were wearing long sleeves on such a warm night. Did Martin do this to you?"

"Of course not." Laurel jerked her wrist from Maggie's grasp and quickly pushed down the loose sleeve. "I, uh, I just had a little accident."

"An accident? What kind of accident? And why didn't you tell anyone about it?"

"I fell down the stairs. It's nothing. And I didn't mention it because I didn't want to worry Momma and Daddy. They have enough on their minds already."

"Are you sure? Laurel, you would tell me if—"

"There's nothing to tell. I had an accident, that's all. Now, I really have to go."

She darted down the steps into the rain and hurried to her car. Maggie didn't dare try to stop her, for fear of hurting her again.

Frustration and uneasiness niggled at her. The mist dampened her skin and the air seemed suddenly chilly. Absently, she rubbed her hands up and down her arms, and watched the taillights on her sister's car grow dim though the rain and recede down the drive.

"You're worried, aren't you?"

Maggie's heart leapt right up into her throat. Her

head snapped around toward that deep voice as Dan stepped out of the shadows.

Her heart still clubbed against her ribs, but with an effort, she swallowed down the jolt of fear and cocked an eyebrow.

"Eavesdropping, were you? Why, sugar, you surprise me. I never would've taken you for a snoop."

"It wasn't deliberate."

"No? Then what were you doing skulking around in the shadows."

"I was hardly skulking. I know it embarrasses Jacob for me to see how weak he is. So I carried him upstairs and left him to Lily's care as quickly as I could. When I came downstairs I started to stop by the dining room to say good-night, but when I heard you and Laurel arguing I decided the best thing to do was leave quietly. I was just standing here waiting for the rain to slack up a bit when the two of you stormed out onto the porch."

"You could have let us know you were here."

"True, but I didn't want to embarrass your sister."

Maggie tossed her hair back and gave a mirthless laugh. "But you don't mind embarrassing me, is that it?"

"I doubt that you embarrass easily."

He stepped farther into the light. Those pale eyes zeroed in on her face. "So, do you think Martin is abusing her?"

Sighing, Maggie hugged her arms tighter around her body and for once let her glib facade fall away. She was too tired and too emotionally drained to bother. Her mouth flattened into a grim line. "I wouldn't put it past him. But I can't prove it. It's possible she did fall down the stairs, I suppose.''

Crossing his arms over his chest, Dan tipped his head to one side and studied her serious expression. "Did Martin really try to rape you?" he asked quietly. ''Or was he telling the truth about you trying to come between him and Laurel?''

Maggie slanted him a look. "If you have to ask, there's no point in me answering, is there?'' She looked away again and shrugged one shoulder. ''Believe what you like. It makes no difference to me.''

''Nice try, but it won't work this time. You lied to me, Red.''

''Excuse me?''

Dan edged closer. ''Earlier you led me to believe you didn't care what people think. That's not the impression I got from your conversation with Laurel.''

He was standing so close, Maggie had difficulty concentrating on his words. As though her sensory perception had been heightened by the drama of the storm raging around them, she became acutely aware of several things at once—the heat from Dan's body, his clean, masculine scent, mingled with the smell of laundry soap and woodsy cologne, the dark chest hair peeking out of the V-neck of his sport shirt. He was big and powerful, and utterly male, and something about him pulled at her. It almost felt as though there was a strong magnetic current flowing between them.

Lord, Mag, get a grip. You're tired, and the strain of the last few days is getting to you, she told herself, but it didn't help. Just being this close to him made her skin tingle and started a trembling deep inside her body.

He felt the attraction, as well. She could see the awareness in those silvery eyes, feel it radiating from him, along with a powerful resentment for his own weakness.

He still looked at her with suspicion, but that didn't seem to matter. A part of her—the young girl deep inside starved for love, no doubt, she thought scornfully—longed to lay her head on that broad chest, feel those strong arms enfold her.

Maggie turned her head away sharply, unsettled by the foolish yearning. "I *don't* care what most people think."

For a long time she gazed at the faint spots of glowing red disappearing around the bend in the road. "Only those who matter."

Giving a little huff, she eased away to put some space between them. "Not that it matters or changes anything. Laurel doesn't believe me any more than Daddy does."

Turning, she tilted her chin and looked him square in the eye. "Or you."

Eight

Tuning out his sister's cheerful chatter, Jacob sipped his morning coffee and gazed out across the sloping backyard and surrounding orchard, drinking the familiar beauty of it all deep into his soul.

Lord, how he loved this place, he thought with fierce pride. He'd been born here, lived in this gracious old house all of his life, knew every inch of it—the house, the land, the cannery—like the back of his hand. It was inconceivable that he would leave it soon.

Yet every day the end drew nearer.

The knowledge filled him with sadness and, yes, a touch of fear, but most of all a consuming desire to seize each precious moment left to him. Coming face-to-face with his mortality had given him a new appreciation for the simple things, things he'd taken for granted for so long—the beauty of a sunrise, the smell of honeysuckle, the sparkle of dew on the grass, the sound of a mockingbird at dawn, the touch of a loved one's hand against his skin. Even his coffee tasted better now.

How he wished that he could spend his final days just taking in those simple pleasures, instead of worrying about the business and what was to become of his family if they lost it.

He couldn't let that happen. He had to *do* something.

But what? He'd already tried everything he could think of, short of borrowing from the bank, and he'd be damned if he'd do that. He wouldn't give that prick Rupert a toehold into Malone's, even if the man was his darling Laurel's father-in-law.

Maybe Martin was right. Maybe the offer from Bountiful Foods was the only way to ensure a secure future for Lily and the girls.

The instant the thought slid through Jacob's mind, everything inside him recoiled from it. No. No, dammit, there had to be another way. There *had* to be.

"Are you all right, Jacob?"

The gentle touch of Nan's hand on his forearm brought him back to the present. Only then did he realize that he was gripping his cup so tightly it was rattling against the saucer like a castanet. "Yes, of course. I'm fine." He quickly drank the rest of the coffee and placed the cup and saucer on the table.

"You sure?"

"Yes, I'm sure. Actually, I'm having one of my better days. It seems to go that way. I have days when I feel I'm on a fast downhill slide, then for no apparent reason, I have a good day or two when I don't feel half-bad. There's no explaining it, but I'll take what I can get."

Nan put down the toast she was buttering and touched his arm once again. Her blue eyes, so like his own, swam with painful emotions. "Jacob, I'm so sorry. I'd give anything if I could—"

"I, know, sis." He covered her hand with his free one, giving it a little squeeze. "I know."

Deep affection for his sister filled him. Like all siblings, he and Nan had teased and tormented each other as youngsters and they'd had differences over the years, but they shared a special bond that neither time nor distance could diminish. The raw pain and sorrow in her eyes made him ache for her.

Nan had arrived the evening before. As always, she'd brought a mountain of luggage with her, which had forced Katherine to pick her up at the Dallas airport in Lily's Cadillac instead of that impractical sports car of hers. By the time they returned last night he'd been so tired he'd barely done more than kiss his sister hello before retiring.

As though just thinking about her had somehow conjured her up, the door from the kitchen opened and his oldest daughter stepped out onto the terrace. At once, Jacob's tender smile faded. He tried to remain calm and indifferent, but as he watched her walk toward them the old resentment rushed up inside him like bile rising in his throat, and he clenched his jaw.

Nan withdrew her hand from his and quickly dabbed at her eyes with her napkin before turning to the girl with a welcoming smile.

"Well, good morning, sleepyhead. I was wondering when you'd wake up. Come, join us. As usual, Ida Lou has made twice what Jacob and I can eat. Which ought to be just about enough for you," she added with a teasing twinkle in her eyes that irritated Jacob all the more.

He'd never understand his sister's attachment to

the girl. There was no doubt that she loved Laurel and Jo Beth, but she'd always had a soft spot in her heart for Katherine—or Maggie, as everyone else insisted on calling her. It had been no surprise to him when she had turned to Nan for sympathy seven years ago. Or that his sister had given it.

"Actually, I've been up for hours. I went for a run at dawn, then had a snack with Ida Lou before I showered."

"Mmm, but I'll wager you can still eat some breakfast, right?"

She grinned. "Right."

Changing direction, she went to the food cart and piled a plate high with pancakes and bacon and scrambled eggs. "Where's Momma and Jo Beth?" she asked as she took a seat at the table and poured a cup of coffee from the carafe.

"They've gone to early church service. Something that wouldn't hurt you to do once in a while."

"I'm sure you're right, Daddy," she replied with an impudent grin, and scooped up a bite of pancake dripping with butter and syrup. She chewed thoughtfully, then waggled her fork at him when she'd swallowed the bite. "But you know, I'm not too sure Brother Taylor and his congregation would be pleased to have a sinner like me at their Sunday morning service."

"What nonsense. Shame on you, child, teasing your daddy that way," Nan scolded. "And as for you, Jacob, I don't know why you assume she doesn't go to church. Maggie and I attend services together every Sunday morning when she's in New York."

Jacob knew he should be pleased by the information, probably should offer an apology, but he couldn't bring himself to do so. Instead he felt his frustration rise another notch. Trust Katherine not to do what you expected.

Ignoring him, she glanced at her wristwatch and addressed Nan. "We can make the next service if you'd like."

"I'm a bit jet-lagged this morning, love. You go on without me. I'll just sit here and visit with Jacob."

The kitchen door opened again, and Ida Lou stuck her head out. "Maggie, there's some woman named Val on the telephone for you. You want me to bring the phone out there?"

"That's okay. I'll take it inside." She took two more quick bites of pancakes before dabbing at her mouth. "That's Val Brownley, the head of the modeling agency. She probably wants to twist my arm to take a job."

"A job?" Jacob snorted. "Surely you don't call what you do work? It's an embarrassment, is what it is. Posing for pictures wearing practically nothing.

"Why, the whole town was buzzing about that sports magazine cover a few months ago. There you were, prancing around on the beach in two little scraps of cloth, for all the world to see."

Maggie laughed. "It's called a swimsuit, Daddy. A very expensive one, I might add, by a top designer."

"You wore more than that to go swimming when you were a baby."

"Ah, but I'm not a baby anymore."

"You made that patently obvious to every ogling fool who cared to look. Every place I went in town, there was that magazine with that picture of you on the cover, flaunting yourself like a prostitute. It was embarrassing.

"I didn't send you to Harvard to become an exhibitionist. You have a good brain and a master's degree, but do you use them? No, you'd rather take up a useless, narcissistic career that doesn't require an ounce of intelligence and allows you to make an indecent spectacle of yourself."

As usual, his anger didn't find a target—not with his daughter, at any rate. Nan bristled and muttered, "Jacob, really!" but Maggie merely shrugged and flashed another impudent grin.

"A girl's gotta do what a girl's gotta do." She rose and patted his shoulder as she passed him and murmured, "Look at it this way, Daddy. Every family has to have a black sheep."

She headed for the house with that sassy walk of hers, as though she hadn't a care in the world. Simmering, Jacob watched her go, the old corrosive feelings he'd thought he'd buried years ago churning inside him.

"You're an idiot, Jacob Patrick Malone. A complete dunderhead."

"Don't start, Nan. I don't want to hear it."

"Well, you're going to hear it!" she snapped, jumping to her feet. "For your information, being picked for the cover of *The Sports Gazette* is an honor. Every model dreams of snagging that job.

"And another thing," she went on before he could respond, angrily thumbing her chest. "If you've got a complaint about her career choice, take it up with me. I'm the one responsible for Maggie becoming a model. Believe me, she would never have considered it on her own. In fact, the first time I suggested she give it a try, she was so startled she burst out laughing.''

On a roll now, Nan began to pace beside the table, punctuating her words with sharp hand gestures. ''Growing up in this family with a mother and two sisters who looked like Dresden dolls, the poor girl had always thought of herself as homely and awkward.

''Granted, she did go through an unfortunate stage during her early teens, but what no one, most of all Maggie, seemed to notice was that by eighteen she had blossomed.

''At first, she resisted the idea, but I kept badgering until finally she gave in and went to the Valentina Modeling Agency just to shut me up. She was convinced they'd take one look at her and laugh her out of the office, but to her surprise, they signed her to a contract on the spot. Within a year she became one of the most sought-after models in the world. And with good reason. In case you haven't noticed, Jacob, your oldest daughter is a stunning beauty.''

He opened his mouth to make a pithy comment, but she cut him off.

''Regardless of what you think about the modeling profession, at that time it was the best thing that could have happened to her. When Maggie arrived on my doorstep she was a shattered wreck, thanks to you. Modeling has given her poise and self-confidence and rebuilt her sense of self-worth.''

Nan stopped and regarded him, her accusing expression tinged with sadness and confusion, and when she spoke again her voice was soft, almost pleading. "How could you do that to her, Jacob? How could you throw her out of your life that way? Your own precious child."

Jacob clenched his jaw so hard his teeth hurt. Trust Nan to take him to task. Ever since he was diagnosed with cancer his family and friends had tiptoed around him, treating him with kid gloves, but mollycoddling had never been his sister's style. It was a trait he'd always admired in her. Until now.

Dammit, she didn't understand. No one did.

"Katherine didn't leave me any choice. What she tried to do was unforgivable."

"You mean what Martin claimed she tried to do," Nan shot back. "I'll never understand how you could take that little worm's word over your own daughter's."

Jacob shot his sister a stern look. "Kindly remember that you're talking about the man Laurel loves."

Nan responded with an unladylike raspberry and rolled her eyes. "Oh, that's right. Heaven forbid anyone should fault Laurel for anything, even if it is only her poor taste in men. God alone knows what she ever saw in Martin Howe. Oh, he's a good-looking charmer, I'll grant you that, but underneath he's still the spoiled, overbearing bully he was as a child.

"Frankly, we both know if he wasn't married to Laurel you would have given him the boot years ago. If I were running the company, I'd do it, anyway."

"Now, Nan, you're too hard on the boy. Martin does his job," Jacob protested, but deep down he knew his sister was right. He would never have tolerated such poor performance from any other employee. Much as it galled him to do so, he'd turned a blind eye for Laurel's sake, but the truth was, his son-in-law was a slacker. He had to constantly prod and push the man just to get him to do his job.

"Oh, please, Jacob. The man's a complete screwup and you're a fool for siding with him against your own child."

Jacob stiffened. "Regardless of what you think of Martin, Katherine's reputation didn't exactly inspire trust."

"That may be the excuse you've given yourself to ease your conscience, but we both know that your animosity toward Maggie started long before that night."

"That's absurd."

"You've always doted on Laurel and Jo Beth, but you're distant with Maggie."

"Not this again," he groaned. "Look, Nan, I've told you at least a hundred times over the years, I don't treat Katherine any different than her sisters."

"Horsefeathers. If either of the younger girls was one of the world's top models you'd be busting your buttons, but you rake Maggie over the coals. You can deny it until you're blue in the face, but you know and I know that from the day Maggie was born you've tried to ignore her existence."

"That's ridiculous. She's received exactly the same advantages and privileges as her sisters—a good home, a top-notch education, dance lessons, music lessons, nice clothes, almost everything she ever wanted. Even a car when she was sixteen."

"Things. Those are all *things,* Jacob. Not once did you ever show her the least bit of love or warmth."

Unable to deny the charge, he gritted his teeth and looked away, but Nan was relentless.

"Admit it, Jacob. You know I'm right."

"If I didn't show her as much affection it's because Katherine wasn't an easy child to love," he muttered. "She still isn't."

"What rot. For the first twelve years of her life she practically turned herself wrong side out trying to please you. I'm telling you, it was painful to watch.

"Maggie was born with an exuberant nature, but she clamped down on it and struggled to become the perfect child—quiet, helpful, studious. Obedient and polite to the point of nausea. And she did it all to win your love and approval."

"Well, she certainly made up for lost time when she hit her teens," he snapped. "She should have been valedictorian. She had the highest grades of anyone in her high school class. But because of her abominable behavior her mother and I had to sit there and watch that Janowich boy give the valedictory speech at graduation."

Nan stared at him and shook her head. "You just don't get it, do you. What did you expect? After twelve years she finally figured out that pleasing you was hopeless, so she said 'To hell with it.'

"I think, subconsciously, she decided that if she couldn't get your attention by being good, she'd get it any way she could." She paused a beat to let that soak in, then added, "And it worked, didn't it, Jacob?"

"Oh, she got my attention, all right. It's easy for you to criticize, but that girl has caused her mother and me many a sleepless night and quite a lot of embarrassment and expense. I was constantly being called to the school. And I had to make reparation for those stupid stunts she pulled, you know."

To Jacob's astonishment, a grin twitched Nan's mouth. "Oh, I don't know," she drawled. "Personally, I thought some of them were quite clever. Smuggling that cow onto the second floor of the high school in the middle of the night, for one. I would have loved to've been a fly on the wall when Principal Davies arrived at school the next morning.

"By the way, did they ever find out how she did it?"

"No. But that little prank cost me a bundle. I had to hire a crane and have the animal hoisted out a window. I also had to pay a cleanup crew to scoop up the mess the frightened beast left behind and have the entire second floor repainted and fumigated. Dammit, Nan, stop laughing. It wasn't funny. There was cow dung everywhere."

"Actually, it was hilarious."

She stifled her chuckles and studied her brother's angry profile. "Tell me something. Didn't Maggie always own up to what she'd done? Did she ever once try to deny her guilt, or put the blame on someone else or feign ignorance of a deed?"

"No. I'll give her that," he admitted grudgingly.

"Yet...you chose to believe Martin."

Surprise, then a niggle of guilt rippled through Jacob, but he scowled and ignored both. "They're not the same things at all."

"Hmm. Anyway, my point is, you've wronged that girl, Jacob. And that isn't like you. She's a bright, beautiful, warm person, but you've always been distant with her. Why? How could you treat her that way all these years?"

He looked away toward the orchard, emotions boiling inside him. "I don't want to talk about it."

"Dammit, Jacob, you're dying. For your own sake, as well as hers, you have to make amends while you still have the chance. For pity's sake, she's your daughter!"

Something inside Jacob snapped. He shot his sister a furious glare. "That's just the trouble," he snarled. "I don't think she *is* mine."

The statement had the impact of a bomb going off. Suddenly it felt as though all the oxygen had been sucked right out of the air. Slack-jawed, Nan could only stare at him for several seconds.

"Oh, Jacob. You can't believe that Lily was unfaithful to you."

"Of course not! Don't be ridiculous." His mouth thinned, and he looked away, the muscles in his jaws working. When he looked back at her, fury and reluctance warred inside him. Fury won.

"She was raped," he said in a flat voice. "Exactly eight months and twenty-three days before Maggie was born."

"Dear God, Jacob!" Nan sank down onto the chair beside his as though her legs were suddenly too weak to support her. "I didn't know. All this time, and I had no idea."

"No one knows. At least…no one in this town. Just Lily and me and the Houston police."

"It happened in Houston?"

He nodded, staring into the middle distance, only remotely aware that Nan had taken hold of his hand. "I went there to call on several of our accounts, and Lily went with me to do some shopping. I dropped her off at Neiman Marcus that morning on my way to my first appointment. She returned to the hotel before I did. When she unlocked the door to our room a man pushed her inside."

Shaking his head, Jacob squeezed his eyes shut against the painful rush of memory. Other than the police who investigated, he'd never told the story to anyone before, had tried not to let himself think about what happened, but now that he'd started he couldn't stop.

"She fought him, but she didn't stand a chance. I found her an hour later, beaten unconscious, so bloody and bruised I hardly recognized her. Oh, God," he groaned, cupping his free hand over his eyes. "I blame myself. If I had just come back sooner, instead of having a drink with my last customer, that bastard wouldn't have touched her. Or if I'd taken her with me. I should never have left her alone."

"Jacob, don't! It wasn't your fault. You didn't do anything wrong. The blame lies entirely with that animal who attacked Lily. Not you."

"That's…that's what the police said, but—"

"No buts. They were right. And I'm quite sure

that Lily doesn't blame you.'' Nan massaged his hand and shook her head mournfully. ''Poor Lily. No wonder she's always seemed so fragile. Did the police catch the man who did it?''

He shook his head, and Nan made a disgusted sound.

''Lily and I stayed in Houston until her physical wounds healed. We let everyone, even Dad, think that we were taking a long vacation. Lily couldn't bear for anyone in Ruby Falls to know what had happened to her.

''But it was the emotional damage that animal inflicted on her that worried me most. For months after we returned she was still like a zombie. She was so shattered I was afraid to leave her alone, for fear that she'd take her own life.''

''Then she found out she was pregnant, and she snapped out of the depression instantly. It was like flipping a switch. It never seemed to occur to her that the baby might be her attacker's. I think she blocked the whole thing out of her mind.

''She was so overjoyed, I didn't have the heart to mention it myself. I was afraid of what it would do to her.''

''But you wondered, didn't you, Jacob?''

''I tried not to. Lily was happy. And there was a possibility the child was mine. We'd been trying for several months to have a baby. I told myself that the odds were in my favor.''

Jacob sighed. ''Then she was born, and I was almost certain that she wasn't a Malone.''

''What made you think that?''

''For heaven's sake, Nan, all you have to do is

look at her. She's six feet tall, and Lily and her sisters are petite. She doesn't resemble Lily or me in the least, or anyone else in our family, for that matter. And there's that red hair and green eyes. No one in our family has coloring like that."

"So? That doesn't mean anything. You're six one. Maggie could have gotten her height from you and her looks and coloring from someone far back in our gene pool. Maybe those genes skipped a few generations."

"Maybe," he conceded grudgingly. "But it doesn't seem likely."

"I take it you didn't get the doctor to test for paternity? I know that a blood test wouldn't necessarily have identified you as the father, but it might have told you if you weren't."

"I couldn't do that. Lily didn't want anyone to know, not even the doctor. And she became hysterical if I so much as alluded to the attack. I couldn't upset her with my doubts and risk her slipping back into depression."

"Jacob, she should've had counseling," Nan said gently. "She needed to work through it and put it behind her, not block it out."

"I know, I know, but she resisted the idea so vehemently, and I was afraid to force the issue."

Nan sighed. "That's why she's so fragile, isn't it? Why she avoids conflict and strife at all cost? And why you've always babied and protected her?"

Jacob's shoulders slumped. "Yes." Tears filled his eyes as he met his sister's gaze, but he didn't care. "If you could have seen what that animal did to her, how devastated she was afterward, you would understand.''

''Oh, Jacob, I'm not blaming you—at least, not for that. I'm not sure that wrapping Lily in cotton wool all these years was the best thing for her, but I understand why you did it. What I have a problem with is that for twenty-seven years you've allowed this thing to fester inside you. And Maggie has borne the brunt of it.''

The accusation pricked his conscience and his anger flared. ''Dammit, do you have any idea what it's like to live every day tormented by the possibility that the child who bears your name might have been fathered by the beast who attacked your wife? Well, I'll tell you,'' he ground out. ''It's hell. Pure, unmitigated, living hell. I tried to love her. I swear to God I did. But every time I looked at her, I thought of him.''

''All the more reason to find out for certain. These days DNA testing can provide conclusive proof whether or not Maggie is your child.''

''I told you, I can't do that to Lily.''

''She doesn't have to know. Neither does Maggie. Although, personally, I think the whole thing should be brought out into the open.''

''Absolutely not.''

''Fine, then. I can take a few strands of hair from Maggie's hairbrush and a saliva sample from you and send them to my physician in New York and ask him to have it tested.''

Jacob looked out at the orchard, his chest suddenly tight.

''Time is running out, Jacob. You owe Maggie

this much," she urged quietly. "And you owe it to yourself."

He shook his head. "No. I won't do it. And I want your promise that you won't order the test on your own."

"Jacob—"

"Your promise, Nan. I know you. You always want to step in and put things right, but this isn't your decision to make. So I'll have your promise."

Nan glared at him, fuming. Finally she gave a huff and snapped, "Oh, all right. I promise. But you're a fool, Jacob Malone."

He watched her storm away into the house and winced when she slammed the door behind her. Then he turned his head and stared out at nothing in particular. Ethically, morally, even intellectually, he knew that Nan was right. But emotionally—that was another matter.

The only thing that had allowed him to accept Katherine's presence in his family all these years was the possibility, no matter how slight, that she might be his. How would he bear it if after all this time he discovered, beyond all doubt, that she wasn't?

Or worse...that she was?

Nine

Maggie's head snapped up. What was that?

She looked around her father's office, her heart pounding. Only the green-shaded desk lamp and indirect lighting along three sides of the ceiling lit the room, but it was enough to see that no one was there.

She swiveled her father's big leather chair around and peered through the glass wall at the cannery floor. As always on Sundays, the place was deserted and quiet.

Unlike some canneries that operated around the clock, Maggie's great-grandmother had made the decision years ago that Malone's would work a six-day week. Those employed in the orchards and the office worked the usual forty hours, but cannery workers put in three twelve-hour days per week, allowing them to earn a decent wage and still have plenty of spare time.

"We could make more money operating all the hours that God sends, but the workers pay too high a price for the additional profit. It's just plain unnatural for people to work at night," she had contended. "Besides, folks need time with their families."

Maggie agreed with her great-grandmother's philosophy and was amused that these days many other businesses were adopting the schedule. At that moment, however, the unnatural quiet and emptiness gave her the willies.

Security lights spilled dim pools of illumination throughout the cavernous space, turning the machinery into hulking shapes in the shadows.

Maggie scanned the floor as far as she could see, but nothing moved.

With a self-deprecating chuckle, she turned the chair back around. "You're letting the emptiness spook you, Mag. Remember, this is Ruby Falls, not New York." Scooting the chair closer to the desk, she turned her attention back to the ledgers spread out on the top.

Within seconds she was totally absorbed in scanning the columns of figures. Every now and then she stopped with her index finger on a number while she reached across the desk to flip through another ledger and check the amount against another one.

"What the hell are you doing here?"

Maggie let out a strangled cry and nearly jumped right out of her skin. Her pencil went flying, and in full flight mode, she'd cleared the seat of the leather chair by eight inches before the voice and the face of the man standing in the doorway registered fully.

Pressing her hand against her heart, she collapsed back into the chair and closed her eyes. "Jeezlouise, handsome, you scared the living daylights out of me. Don't sneak up on me like that. You'll give me a heart attack."

"I was driving home and I saw a light up here.

Since Jacob is too sick to work and Martin doesn't put in long hours, I thought I'd better check it out. And you haven't answered my question. What are you doing here at this time of night?''

Just coming home, was he? Maggie cast a surreptitious glance at the clock on the corner of the desk. Almost midnight. Had he been on a date?

She was surprised at how much the idea bothered her. For heaven's sake, you only met the man three days ago.

What did you expect, anyway? He's a healthy, red-blooded male in his prime, and good-looking and single to boot. Of course he has girlfriends. For all you know, he could be hot and heavy into a serious relationship. Maybe even engaged.

He might feel the same tug of attraction that you do, but he doesn't like it one bit. He doesn't like you. So, get a grip, Mag.

Lying didn't come easy to Maggie. In any case, the ledgers spread out over the desk left little doubt as to what she'd been doing. Stalling for time, hoping to sidetrack him, she leaned back in the chair and gave him a sultry smile.

''Is there a problem? I'm a member of the Malone family. Why does everyone act like I have no right to be here?''

He didn't answer right away, merely stood there with his big workingman's hands splayed on his lean hips, those silvery eyes studying her from beneath half-closed eyelids.

''Does Jacob know you're up here snooping around?''

"No. But Momma does. Actually, I'm here at her request."

"Oh? That's funny. I've never known Lily to get involved in the business."

"True. But with Daddy so sick, somebody in the family has to. Since Momma has no experience or training, she asked me to take a look at things."

Tilting her head to one side, Maggie studied him and debated just how much she should reveal. In the end, she went with her instincts. "I don't know if you are aware of it, but our profits have been steadily dropping for months."

Dan leaned a shoulder against the doorjamb, crossed one booted foot over the other and folded his arms over his chest. "Yeah, I know. Jacob told me."

"Did he also tell you that if we don't turn things around soon we're going under?"

"Yeah. Either that or sell out to Bountiful Foods, like Martin wants him to do."

"Not if I can help it."

Cynical amusement flickered in his eyes and twitched his mouth. "So, you're just going to prance in and pull all of Jacob's chestnuts out of the fire, is that it?"

"I don't know about the prancing part. I usually save that for the runway. But I am going to do my best to find the hole in the dike and plug it." She arched an eyebrow at him. "Do you have a problem with that?"

Dan's gaze shifted toward the pile of ledgers. "Do you know what you're doing?"

"Well…it's not my specialty, but I did take a few

accounting courses when I was working toward my master's in business. I think I can muddle through."

He appeared not in the least discomfited by the revelation. On the contrary, he didn't turn a hair but continued to study her in that inscrutable way. Maggie couldn't be certain, but she thought she saw a glint of admiration in those cool eyes.

Of course, with the lighting so low, she could have imagined it.

"Why are you working now? Why not during normal office hours?"

"I thought it best not to upset the normal routine around here. I don't want to panic the employees. And to be honest, Miss Udall seems—how shall I put this? An extremely territorial type? I'd rather not pull rank." Maggie shot him a grimacing smile. "Any more than I already have, that is."

Nor did she want to alert Martin to what she was doing and have him go running to her father. Of course, now that Dan knew, that point might be moot.

This time, though it was no more than a lopsided twitch of his mouth, there was no doubt about Dan's smile. "Locked horns with her already, have you? Careful, Red. The woman's hell on wheels."

"Maybe so. But I think I can take her in a fair fight."

The saucy comment produced another twitching smile. "You're probably right."

Dan straightened away from the doorjamb. "I guess there's no harm in you taking a look at the situation. Things can't get much worse than they are now."

"Yes, well, I've done about all I can for one evening. I've looked at so many figures my eyes are beginning to cross. Time to call it a night."

"I didn't see your car downstairs," Dan said as she rose and came around the desk.

"No, I walked."

"It's late. C'mon, I'll give you a lift back to the house."

Maggie's heart gave a little bump. She was tempted, but common sense told her it would be a foolish move. "That's okay. I don't mind walking back through the orchard in the dark. Really."

Maggie fished a small metal cylinder out of the pocket of her skirt and held it up for him to see. "See, I've got a flashlight."

"That thing won't light up the ground more than a few feet ahead of you. It won't take me but a couple of minutes to drive you home. C'mon," he ordered, taking her elbow and steering her out the door.

Normally, Maggie would have balked at such high-handedness, but the touch of his callused fingers against her skin seemed to have short-circuited her brain.

She was acutely aware of that broad palm and each individual finger, wrapped around her arm just above her elbow. From the point of contact, an electrical current zinged up her arm and spread tingling heat over her neck, back and chest and set her heart to beating absurdly fast.

This close, she could smell his scent, feel the heat from that deliciously fit body, see each individual lash surrounding his silvery eyes and the shadow of beard stubble just beneath the skin along his jaw. Despite the mildness of the night, a shiver rippled through Maggie. Sweet heaven, Dan Garrett was one potent hunk of man.

"This won't be anywhere near as fancy as that sexy little number you drive, but it'll get you home," he said when they stepped outside and he steered her to the only vehicle in the row of parking spaces in front of the building.

"I'm from here, remember? You can't grow up in Ruby Falls without riding in a pickup," she reminded him as she climbed up into the cab of the battered work truck.

"But lately your mode of transportation has been Jaguars and limos. And Vipers."

She could hardly deny that. Before she could come up with a snappy response, he slammed the door, circled around to the driver's side and climbed behind the wheel.

In one easy motion that spoke of long experience, he cranked the engine, slung his right arm onto the back of the bench seat and looked over his shoulder out the back window while he reversed out of the slot. Within seconds they were out of the parking lot and speeding down the gravel road that encircled the Malone orchard, cannery and homesite, heading for the opposite side of the property.

Dan didn't seem inclined to talk, and for one of the few times in her adult life, Maggie couldn't think of a thing to say. She was too acutely aware of that muscled arm stretched out along the back of the seat. Her hair brushed his fingers every time she moved the slightest bit, and she could feel the heat from them on the back of her neck.

The only sounds were the rumble of the engine, the crunch and pop of the gravel beneath the tires and a symphony of rattles the truck made.

He drove the same way he walked and moved, with an effortless, loose-limbed grace. He steered the truck with his left wrist draped over the top of the wheel, his big, lean body slouched against the worn seat.

The interior of the truck, though clean, was as battered as the outside. A bucket of tools sat on the floorboard—hacksaw, pliers, hand drill and several others Maggie didn't recognize. The vinyl seats were cracked and several of the springs had seen better days. Jagged cracks spiderwebbed out from a deep pock in the windshield on the passenger side.

Maggie wondered if many of the women he dated objected to being picked up in the beat-up old truck. Then she glanced at the man behind the wheel and almost laughed at the foolish thought. Not likely.

In the dim light from the dashboard, she studied Dan's strong profile. Her gaze slid down over his rolled-up sleeve to the muscled forearm with its liberal dusting of dark hair and farther still to the broad wrist propped on the top of the steering wheel and to that hand hanging loosely on the other side.

Calluses ridged the broad palm and the pads of the long, blunt fingers, and the skin across the top bore small nicks and scars, but his fingernails were clean and neatly trimmed. Though utterly masculine, there was something so oddly graceful and appealing about that rough hand that just looking at it made Maggie's mouth go dry.

She tore her gaze away when he gave the wheel a counterclockwise twirl and turned into the driveway of her parents' home.

He pulled to a stop in the circular portion of the drive next to the front walk but left the engine running. Turning his head, he gazed at her through the dimness and waited, not saying a word.

Maggie felt that look like a physical touch. Without any contact at all, without so much as moving, he affected her as no man ever had. She felt as though she were melting from the inside. The air in the cab seemed to pulse with awareness.

This is insane, Mag, she told herself. Go. Get out of here, before you do something foolish.

Swallowing hard, she reached for the door handle. "Well, uh, thanks for the ride."

"No problem." Dan removed his arm from the back of the seat and his fingers brushed against the side of her neck. He jerked his hand away as though it had been scalded.

Maggie froze with the door half-open. She shot a startled look over her shoulder and knew by his expression that the touch had been an accident. And that he, too, had felt that stunning zap of electricity...and he wasn't pleased.

She felt as awkward and jittery as a teenager on her first date. And just as tongue-tied. Retreat seemed her only option.

Muttering a quick good-night, she hopped out of the cab, but when she turned to shut the door, a thought occurred to her, and she paused and mustered a coaxing smile.

"Uh...sugar, I would really appreciate it if you wouldn't mention to Daddy what I'm doing. It would only upset him. I'll tell him myself soon, but I'm hoping I'll find some concrete reasons for the losses and take steps to correct the situation before that becomes necessary."

He looked at her across the bench seat, his eyes a pale glitter in his shadowed face. Maggie's heart speeded up and her breathing became shallow. He remained quiet for so long she began to think he wasn't going to answer.

"Tell you what," he said at last. "I won't mention seeing you in the office. But I won't lie to Jacob if he asks. That's the best I can do."

Considering this man's loyalty to her father, it was more than she'd expected, and the relief she felt helped to calm her skittering nerves. "Fair enough," she said with a wink. "Thanks, sugar."

The pickup engine continued to idle after she closed the door and headed up the walkway. Maggie could feel him watching her. Smiling, she put a little extra sway in her saunter.

Charles Minze, the male nurse, arrived the next day, much to Lily's relief and Ida Lou's annoyance. There were some initial skirmishes and vying for territory between the two, but Charley was an affable sort and a born diplomat. By the end of the first day he had won grudging acceptance from the older woman with lavish compliments about her cooking. Before day two was over he had completely won her over by asking her advice on all manner of things, particularly those concerning his patient.

In his late thirties, Charley was a strapping man with bulging muscles and an appetite that outstripped even Maggie's, which went a long way toward softening the housekeeper's resentment. Bald as a cue ball, with fearsome tattoos on each biceps, he looked more like a professional wrestler or a Hell's Angels biker than a nurse, but when dealing with Jacob he was a soft-spoken, gentle giant.

Having Charley's around-the-clock assistance made life easier for everyone, particularly Lily, and before long the household had adapted to his presence. For the most part, Charley stayed in the background, but when needed he always miraculously appeared. After only a few days it was difficult to imagine how they'd ever gotten along without him.

During that first week Maggie developed a routine. She spent the daylight hours visiting with her mother and Nan and Ida Lou, ran errands for them and did her best to stay out of her father's way.

When Jacob retired each evening immediately after dinner, Maggie walked through the orchard to the cannery, staying there until late, poring over the books and scouring the files for answers. She never used her car to drive to the cannery for fear her father would hear and want to know where she was going. Before leaving the office every night she carefully put everything back exactly where she'd found it so as not to arouse Miss Udall's suspicions, as well.

Just before dawn each morning Maggie rose and went for a three-mile run around and through the orchard, returning home in time to shower and change for breakfast with the rest of the family.

Jacob continued to have good days and bad days, but he was always at his strongest and most alert in the mornings, more like his old self. He talked fondly with Lily and Jo Beth and engaged in lively banter with his sister. Dan joined them every morning, for breakfast or coffee afterward, and when the conversation turned to business matters Jacob displayed his usual sharpness.

Listening to the morning discussions, Maggie could almost pretend that her father wasn't sick at all. He spoke to her as little as possible, but there was normalcy in that, as well.

Thursday morning, one week after her return, Jacob and Nan reminisced over breakfast about how, as kids, they used to swim in Catalpa Creek. Listening to their teasing, Maggie contentedly consumed the stack of waffles on her plate and indulged in the pleasant fantasy that her father was the same vigorous man she had always adored.

"I'll never forget the time you tossed that piece of rope into the water and yelled 'snake!'" Nan recalled, giving her brother a playful poke. "Nearly gave me a heart attack."

Jacob chuckled. "Yeah. That's the closest I've ever come to seeing someone walk on water. You were on the bank before the thing sank. And when you saw what it was you chased me all the way home."

While everyone else laughed Jo Beth pushed her chair back and bounded to her feet. "I gotta go."

"Hey, what's the rush, short stuff?" Dan said, coming up the terrace steps. "I just got here."

Lily checked her wristwatch and frowned. "Why are you leaving so early? You have plenty of time. It's over an hour before school starts."

"Drama Club is holding auditions before school for our first play of the year. I don't want to be late."

She started to bolt, but Jacob stopped her.

"Whoa, there. Just a minute. Did you fill out those college applications?"

Jo Beth rolled her eyes. "Not yet," she replied in that put-upon voice only a teenager can achieve.

Maggie stared, her fork suspended halfway to her mouth. Since returning home, she'd come to expect surliness from her sister, but she was stunned to hear Jo Beth address their father in that tone, especially given his condition.

"Young lady, I specifically said I wanted you to mail those applications today. How many times have I told you, in order to get into a good school you have to apply early? As it is, you're running late. You should have taken care of this during the summer."

The teenager's expression turned mulish. "It doesn't matter if I get accepted or not. I'm not going to college. It would be just a big waste of time. As soon as I graduate next spring I'm going to go to New York and become a professional actress."

"Jo Beth!" Lily gasped.

Nan arched an eyebrow and looked with interest from her brother to her youngest niece. Well, well, well. What is this? her expression plainly said.

Dan picked up the coffee carafe from the table and rose from the chair he'd just taken. "I'll go get Ida Lou to refill this," he said, and headed for the house, diplomatically taking himself out of the family argument.

Maggie kept her head down and her eyes on her plate. She drew enough flack from her father on her own. She wasn't about to get embroiled in her sister's battles.

"You'll do no such thing!" Jacob snapped. "That's childish nonsense. You're going to go to college and get a degree in business, then you're going to come back here and learn the cannery business from the ground up so that you can take over someday."

Maggie's head came up. He was going to give Jo Beth the job she'd always dreamed of having? The job she'd worked so hard for all those years? It wasn't fair.

"No! I won't do it! I don't know anything about business. I don't *want* to know anything about business. I don't *care* about the stupid business."

"Jo Beth, you mustn't talk like that. You're upsetting your daddy."

"I'm sorry, Momma. I don't want to upset anyone, most of all you and Daddy, but I won't sacrifice my dream to please you. If you want someone to take over the company, let Maggie do it. She's the brainy one in the family and she loves that stuff. I hate it."

"Jo Beth—"

"No. I don't care what you say, I'm going to be an actress. I'm going to be in plays and maybe even movies. What do I need with a stupid college degree?''

Jacob's fist struck the glass-topped table, rattling china and silverware and nearly toppling several glasses. "That's enough. You can just forget this foolishness. I won't allow it."

"You won't have any say in the matter. I'm going to be eighteen in a few weeks. Then I can do whatever I want and you can't stop me!"

With that, she turned on her heel and tore down the terrace steps, leaving a stunned silence behind. Maggie and the others at the table watched her tear across the dewy backyard and disappear into the long, six-car garage. Seconds later her sporty red Mustang shot out through the wide doors and she barreled down the drive without so much as a glance toward the terrace.

"Well. That was interesting," Nan drawled after a moment.

Maggie sneaked a peek at Jacob. He looked pale and shaken. So did her mother. "I'll go get Charley," she murmured, and rose from the table.

"You're the cause of this, you know," her father said before she'd taken a half-dozen steps.

Maggie stopped in her tracks and turned. "What?"

"Jacob, really! This is too much," Nan scolded, but he paid her no mind.

"Jo Beth has always been a sweet, biddable girl. Then you show up and she starts getting these harebrained ideas. Just because you ran off to New York and became a model, she thinks all she has to do is

walk into a theater and someone will make her a
star.''

Maggie tossed her head back and laughed. ''I
wondered how you were going to make this my
fault.''

As a rule, out of old habit and deference to his
illness, Maggie let her father's criticism roll off her.
If she bothered to counter at all it was with flippant
humor, but this was more than she could swallow.

''First of all, Daddy, *I* went to college, remember?'' She cupped her hand to the side of her face
and widened her eyes in mock surprise. ''Oh, wait.
Of course you don't. How could you? You didn't
attend my college graduation, did you. Just Momma
and Aunt Nan came, as I recall.''

Jacob frowned. ''There was a cri—''

''Yes, I know. A crisis at the cannery. Which was
miraculously solved by the next day when we got
home. But the point is, Daddy, I went to college.
And if you'll recall, I didn't 'run off to New York.'
You threw me out on my ear.

''I'll take the heat for my own sins, but don't you
dare try to blame me for Jo Beth's. Now, if you'll
excuse me, I'll go find Charley. You look as though
you need him.''

She whirled around to leave and pulled up short,
startled to find Dan standing just a few feet behind
her. She could see by the look in his eyes that he'd
heard the whole thing.

Quivering with hurt and humiliation, she side-
stepped around him and hurried inside, for once unable to dredge up so much as a smile.

* * *

Maggie spent the remainder of the morning in her room, at first pacing and raging and calling herself a fool for returning home, but in her heart she knew she was whipping up her anger as a way to fight off tears.

When she'd calmed down some she passed the time with busywork. After hand-washing her delicates, she gave herself a facial and painted her fingernails and toenails a sassy fire-engine red.

Then she bit the bullet and spent an hour on the telephone with Val, scheduling a photo shoot in New York.

Val wanted to set it up for the following week, but Maggie managed to push the session back another two. It was studio work, thank heavens, which was quicker than going on location, but it still meant she would be gone for three days minimum, probably four.

When she went downstairs for lunch, to her delight, Laurel was seated at the dining room table. Her sister had stopped by every day to visit with Jacob, but if Maggie was there she never stayed long.

"Hi, sis, good to see you," she greeted, and bent to kiss Laurel's cheek before she could shy away. Ignoring her stiff 'Hello,' Maggie sat down next to her.

"Where's Daddy?" Laurel asked, glancing at the empty chair at the head of the table.

"He's not feeling well. He's having lunch in his room with Charley. Today it will be just us girls."

"Oh. Well, in that case, I, uh…I think I'll just run along," Laurel said. "I have a dozen things to do. I just stopped by to visit with Daddy for a few minutes before I got started.''

"Wait a minute, sis. I have an idea. I have an appointment in Tyler this afternoon with Dr. Sanderson to discuss Daddy's treatment. Why don't you come with me? We can leave now and have lunch at Mario's, just the two of us, the way we used to. Maybe do some shopping afterward.''

"Oh. No...no, I...I couldn't.''

"Nonsense,'' Nan chimed in. "Martin won't be back until late Saturday night. I'm sure whatever you have to do can wait a day. Anyway, you have to eat lunch somewhere. It'll be good for both of you to spend some time together.''

"Nan's right,'' Lily agreed. "You're always so busy, Laurel, you've barely spent five minutes alone with your sister since she's been home.''

"Oh, but—''

"C'mon, sis. It'll be fun, I promise. And look at it this way, it'll give you a chance to talk to Dr. Sanderson about that experimental drug study you want Daddy to join.''

Three hours later Maggie wondered why she had bothered to twist Laurel's arm. During the drive to Tyler her sister had stared out the side window of the Viper, speaking only when Maggie asked a question, and then replying with a curt yes or no, or a silent shrug whenever possible.

It wasn't like Laurel to hold a grudge. She was the most forgiving person Maggie knew. There had to be something more behind her behavior than just the rift between them. Laurel seemed edgy and distracted, almost frightened.

Throughout the drive to Tyler, Maggie had tried subtle probing but Laurel had remained mum. Finally she'd given up and used the direct approach.

"Sis, I know you're still upset over what you think happened, but there's more, isn't there? Something else is bothering you."

"No!" Laurel denied too quickly, shooting Maggie a horrified look. "No, of course not. You're imagining things."

"Oh, Laurel, we used to be so close, you and I. We could tell each other anything. Everything. Remember? I miss that. I miss you. Can't we talk this through and maybe get back what we once had?"

If anything, Laurel looked even more panicked than before. "I told you, there's nothing to talk about. Now, will you please just drop it."

Lunch hadn't been any better, and Laurel had been equally uncooperative during their brief shopping excursion afterward. Exasperated, Maggie had finally given up and driven to the offices of Drs. Lockhart and Sanderson, even though it meant arriving forty-five minutes early for her appointment.

For what seemed like the hundredth time, Maggie glanced at her watch, then went back to flipping through the six-month-old magazine. She did her best to ignore the excited glances she was receiving from the receptionists and the other patients waiting to see the doctors. She was in no mood to exchange pleasantries with strangers.

Maggie glanced at Laurel and ground her teeth. Her sister sat on the other side of the room, as far away from her as she could get, calmly reading a paperback novel she'd pulled from her purse. So much for renewing their sisterly bond.

The inner door opened and the nurse stuck her head out. "Miss Malone, Dr. Sanderson will see you now."

Neil Sanderson stood up and extended his hand across the top of his desk when Maggie walked into his office. "Miss Malone, how nice to see you again. Won't you—"

His eyes suddenly lit up. "Laurel! I didn't know you would be here, too. What a nice surprise." Dropping Maggie's hand in midshake, he hurried around the desk and took both of Laurel's in his. "It's so good to see you again. How are you?"

"I'm fine, Doctor."

Maggie raised one eyebrow at her sister's shy tone. To her surprise and amusement, a flush followed, flooding Laurel's cheeks.

"Good, good. And please, I told you to call me Neil. Why don't we sit down over here where it's more comfortable?"

Bemused, Maggie watched him solicitously lead her sister to the small furniture grouping in the corner of his office and take a seat beside her on the sofa. Maggie followed and sat in a chair across from them, but she had the feeling that Dr. Sanderson had forgotten she was there. He seemed to have eyes only for Laurel.

Picking up one of Laurel's hands again, he gave it a pat. "Now then, how is your father today?"

Maggie leaned back in her chair and let Laurel do most of the talking, interrupting only occasionally to add a comment of her own or ask a question. Her sister explained that Jacob wasn't feeling well today, but that generally he seemed to be holding his own. Then she launched into an excited explanation of the experimental drug study that was being conducted in Houston, and her talks with the doctors who were in charge.

Neil listened attentively without interrupting, but when Laurel was done he grimaced and sighed. "I'm so sorry, Laurel, but in my opinion, and I'm sure Dr. Lockhart would agree, your father isn't a candidate for any kind of study. His cancer is too advanced."

Laurel's eyes filled with tears. She gazed at him pleadingly, shaking her head. "No. No, there has to be something he can try. There *has* to be."

"Oh, Laurel, I'm so sorry. I would give anything if only I could save Jacob for you, but I can't." In an unconscious gesture, he cupped her pale face and wiped a tear from her cheek with the pad of his thumb and gazed at her with such abject tenderness that Maggie's jaw dropped.

Why...he's smitten with her!

Maggie stared at the pair, both of whom seemed oblivious to her presence, filled with both delight and despair.

Neil Sanderson was perfect for her sister, exactly the kind of man Maggie would have chosen for her—kind, gentle, intelligent. Best of all, everything about him—from the lovesick look in his eyes to his warm tone to his body language—revealed that he adored Laurel. And from her sister's girlish blushes, the attraction was mutual.

The trouble was, Laurel was married to that creep, Martin. And of her sister's many virtues, absolute loyalty headed the list.

Ten

That evening, after returning from the visit with Dr. Sanderson, Maggie went to the office as usual. However, no matter how hard she tried to concentrate on the business at hand, every few minutes she'd catch herself staring off into space, her thoughts on her sister and the handsome young doctor.

She wondered if Laurel knew how Dr. Sanderson felt about her. How could she not? All you had to do was look at him. The man wore his heart on his sleeve.

Maggie sighed and tapped the pencil eraser against her chin. But then again, knowing how naive Laurel was, she probably didn't have a clue.

The hopelessness of the situation made Maggie sick at heart. They were so perfect for each other. If only Martin weren't in the picture.

Maggie sighed. But Martin was very much in the picture, and as much as she detested him, she couldn't interfere in her sister's marriage. Anyway, even if she tried, it probably wouldn't matter. Laurel was committed to making her marriage work at all costs.

With a little huff of annoyance, Maggie tossed the pencil on the desk and stood up. It was pointless to try to work anymore, since she couldn't seem to concentrate on anything but her sister's star-crossed love life.

She quickly tidied up the desk and returned the files to their proper places, then left the building and locked up behind her.

Leaving behind the security lights around the cannery buildings, she pulled her small flashlight from the pocket of her skirt and turned it on as she entered the darkness of the orchard. A hundred yards into the trees, Maggie cursed herself for forgetting to change the batteries. The small pool of light was so weak she could barely see. A few yards farther along the flashlight began to flicker and after a moment went out altogether.

Maggie cursed and stopped to get her bearings and let her eyes adjust to the darkness, then struck out again in the direction of home.

Though she knew it like the back of her hand, there was something spooky about the orchard at that hour. Maggie knew if she walked between the same two rows of trees she would come out at the back garden gate, but it was difficult to stay in the middle when you couldn't see two feet ahead of you, and low hanging branches kept snagging her hair and slapping at her face.

She was deep into the trees when she thought she heard something behind her. She stopped and listened, but there was nothing but the chirp of crickets and the gentle soughing of the wind through the trees.

"Get a grip, Mag," she scolded. "This is Ruby Falls, not New York."

Barely ten yards farther the sound came again—a rustling that had nothing to do with the wind. Maggie stopped, and the sound stopped an instant later. Her heart began to pound. She peered through the darkness behind her.

"Is somebody there?"

Silence.

She started off again, and again the rustling followed her. This time she heard twigs cracking underfoot and the soft thud of footfalls. There was definitely someone behind her, and he was no longer bothering to conceal his presence. Somehow, that frightened her even more.

She stopped and whirled, and the sounds stopped, too.

"Dammit, I know you're out there. Who are you? What do you want?"

She waited, but there was nothing. Even the crickets had stopped their night song.

Uneasiness shivered through Maggie. She picked up her pace, but the footsteps speeded up, too. She walked faster still. So did her pursuer. Her heart pounded in her chest like a tom-tom.

Out of the darkness behind her came a soft, sinister laugh that made Maggie's skin crawl.

After hundreds of hours of self-defense classes, she'd thought of herself as strong, capable of facing anything, but there was something so innately evil in that sound that all her confidence fled. Nearly suffocating with fear, she broke into a run.

Behind her, the laugh came again.

Giving in to panic, Maggie ran headlong, thrashing her way through low-hanging tree limbs, stumbling over roots, bumping into trunks in the stygian darkness. With each ragged breath, small whimpers escaped her. So terrified she lost all sense of direction, she simply tore, pell-mell, through the grove of trees, heedless to everything but the horror on her heels.

Maggie's throat was so tight her breath made a harsh, rasping sound as it tore from her throat. Her lungs began to burn.

The sounds behind her were coming closer. Unable to resist, she glanced over her shoulder and saw the shadowy silhouette of a man running behind her. He laughed and reached for her, and her scream pierced the night.

Dan stood on the front porch of his cottage, one foot braced on the railing, his eyes on the tattered clouds scudding across the night sky. If you could believe the weather channel, a front was due to blow in the next afternoon, bringing rain. Tomorrow he would have to hustle the pickers along to finish the Anderson Road orchard before the storm.

A noise from the orchard drew his attention—low moaning and thrashing. He frowned and stared in the direction of the sounds. Someone, or something, was in there, and from the sound of it, they were tearing up the orchard.

The hell with that.

He removed his foot from the railing and loped down the steps and into the yard, heading for the orchard on the north side of his house with long, angry strides. Halfway there, he heard the scream.

Startled, Dan stopped in his tracks, and the hair on the back of his neck stood on end.

Another high-pitched, blood-curdling scream followed, then another and another.

"Jesus!"

Dan broke into a run, but he halted after only a few strides when Maggie burst into the clearing. Not even in the dark could he mistake that glorious red mane.

Looking back over her shoulder, she ran flat out, screaming every breath as though the hounds of hell were after her.

Dan stepped into her path. She slammed into his chest, and her screams cut off abruptly—but only for an instant. Then they resumed at a higher pitch, more frantic than ever, running together like a banshee's wail.

"What the hell—"

He wrapped his arms around her, trapping her arms between them and holding her tightly against his chest.

Maggie went wild. Shrieking, she instinctively bucked and twisted and fought to get free, but he held her close.

"Easy, easy. Dammit, Maggie, stop fighting. It's me. Dan. What the hell is the matter with you? Easy, now. C'mon, Maggie. You're safe now."

At first his words failed to penetrate, but he held on tight and repeated them over and over. Finally her screams stopped and she went utterly still against him, though her breathing remained ragged and harsh.

"Da—Dan?"

"Yeah, it's me. You're safe now. I've got you."

He didn't think it was possible, but she pressed closer to him, as though she were trying to burrow her way right inside his body. Her hands clutched the front of his shirt so tightly he felt two buttons pop.

"Oh, Da-Dan," she gasped, pressing her face against his chest. "Thank God you're he-here. Thank God."

She began to shake.

"Hey, take it easy," he crooned, rubbing his hands over her back. "Just calm down and tell me what's wrong."

"Th-there's someone ou-out there. He fol-followed me from the office, and ch-chased me through the orchard."

"What?" Dan tensed, and his head snapped toward the trees. "You stay here. I'll go have a look."

He grasped her shoulders to set her away from him, but she surged forward again and clutched him tighter.

"*No!* No, don't leave me. Please…do-don't leave me. He's still out there! I know he is!"

"Maggie—"

"No, please."

Dan cast a frustrated look at the shadowy rows of trees, hesitating. Finally, he sighed and wrapped his arms around her again.

She was shaking so hard now he was amazed that she could stand. Shock.

"Come along, let's get you inside." He tried to ease her back again, but Maggie was so shaky she could barely move. In any case, she refused to let go of his shirt. In the end he swooped her up in his arms.

Inside the parlor of the Victorian cottage he placed her on the sofa. When he saw the angry red scratches on her face and arms he swore under his breath, but what worried him even more was her obvious shock. He quickly pulled the afghan from the back of the sofa and wrapped it around her, but when he started to straighten, she grabbed his arm.

"Wh-where are you going?"

"Easy, easy. I'm just going to get you some brandy. It will settle your nerves and warm you."

"No! Don't leave me!" Her voice rose in pitch, taking on an edge of hysteria again. She clutched his arm so tight her fingernails dug into his skin.

Dan looked into those panicked emerald eyes, and something shifted and cracked inside his chest. For the first time since he'd known her, all her sparkle, all that maddening, delightful sass and spunk was missing.

And that, he was shocked to discover, infuriated him.

He wasn't convinced that a man had chased her, but something had sure as hell spooked her out in that orchard. And Maggie didn't strike him as the hysterical type who jumped at shadows. Whatever it was, it had reduced this strong woman to a mass of quivering fear.

Hunkering down on his haunches in front of her, Dan pulled the afghan more snugly around her, tucking it under her chin and lifting her hair free, plucking out a few leaves and twigs while he was at it.

Then he took both her hands in his and looked into her eyes.

"Maggie, listen to me. You're safe here. I locked the door behind us. I promise you, no one can get in. Now, I'm just going into the kitchen and get you that drink. I'll be back in less than a minute. Okay?"

Fear still swirled in her eyes and her breath puffed between her parted lips in ragged shudders, but he could see her struggling for control. There were tears just beneath the surface, but she squared her shoulders and refused to give in to them.

No, she wouldn't, Dan thought wryly. Not a saucy rebel like Maggie. Not if she could help it. He'd learned when he'd found her crying outside Jacob's room the day she'd arrived just how much she hated letting her emotions get the upper hand. Especially in front of others. No, her style was to crack a joke and pretend nothing bothered her.

She glanced at the window, and a hard shiver rippled through her. The lace curtains that Lily had hung throughout the cottage offered little protection from prying eyes but, living as he did in the middle of the orchard, Dan had never felt the need for anything more.

Finally, she nodded. "Go ahead. I'm...I'm fine."

She was far from fine, and he wondered if maybe she would be better off if she did cry and let it all out.

Dan left her just long enough to fetch the drink and a first-aid kit. She took the snifter between her shaking hands and eagerly sipped the brandy, so fast, he had to caution her to slow down. He sat beside her on the sofa and watched her closely, monitoring her symptoms, but gradually the liquor did its job. As her trembling eased he could almost see that fierce pride of hers begin to reassert itself.

She swirled the remains of the brandy in the snifter, her downcast gaze locked on the amber whirlpool.

Then she turned her head and gave him a wobbly smile. "You don't have to look so worried. I'm okay now. I'm not going to go berserk or faint on you."

"Good. I'm glad to hear it. Now I can tend to those scratches."

"Scratches?" She looked at the red welts crisscrossing her arms, then gingerly touched her face and groaned. "Oh, great. Val's going to kill me. I have a modeling job in two weeks."

Dan stopped in the act of opening the first-aid kit and sent her a sharp look. "You're leaving?"

"Just for three or four days. Then I'll be back."

He continued to stare at her and she rolled her eyes. "I'm not running out on my responsibilities here, but I do have commitments to fulfill, you know. Legally binding contracts. I can't just ignore them."

"I guess not," he conceded with a shrug, but deep down he was surprised and annoyed at how relieved he was that she would be returning.

He soaked a cotton ball with alcohol, then cupped her chin with his free hand and tipped her face up. "Anyway, I wouldn't worry if I were you. These scratches don't look too deep. They should be gone by the time you leave. So, you want to tell me exactly what happened out there?"

He felt her tense again and dabbed at the welts on her cheek and forehead. Maggie flinched and sucked in a hissing breath but otherwise endured the stinging without complaint.

"I was a hundred yards or so into the trees when I heard something behind me," she began.

While Dan cleaned her wounds and smeared antibiotic cream on them, Maggie explained what had occurred in the orchard.

"And you're sure it was a man?" he asked when she was done.

She didn't answer, and when he'd finished recapping the tube of medicine and returned it to the first-aid kit, Dan looked around and discovered that she was staring at him. Her expression wasn't so much hurt as resigned.

"You don't believe me, do you. You think I imagined it. That I'm just a silly woman who panicked in the dark."

"I didn't say that."

"You didn't have to, sugar," she said with the first hint of her usual boldness. "It's written all over that handsome face of yours."

"Maggie—"

"Oh, don't worry about it, sweetcakes. It doesn't matter."

Despite her denial, he could see that she was annoyed, but he didn't care. He was too pleased to have the old Maggie back.

She threw off the afghan and stood up, wobbled a bit, then started for the door, doing a shaky imitation of her usual saunter.

"Thanks for the booze and the first-aid. And, of

course, for scaring away the bogeyman." Looking back at him over her shoulder, she fluttered her eyelashes. "My hero."

Dan caught her before she'd taken three steps and pulled her to a stop. "Where do you think you're going?"

"Home. I've taken up enough of your time."

"Don't be ridiculous. You're still so weak in the knees you can barely stand."

"Nonsense. I told you, I'm okay."

"Fine, if that's the way you want to play it, but I'm driving you."

"Don't bother. I can walk."

"Dammit, Red, hasn't it occurred to you that if there was a man in the orchard he's probably still out there waiting for you?"

Dan could have kicked himself the instant the words left his mouth. Every last vestige of color drained from her face. She stared at him, frozen to the spot. Then her chin began to wobble and the tears she should have shed earlier came gushing up into her eyes and spilled over.

"Ah, hell. Come here, Red."

He pulled her into his arms and cradled her against his chest. She resisted, but Dan wouldn't let her pull away, and after a moment she quit trying and sagged against him.

The small surrender opened the floodgates. Huddled against his chest, she let it all out.

At first her cries were so harsh they almost choked her, great, gulping sobs that seemed to tear from some place deep inside her soul. They were awful to hear, and several times Dan winced.

Her shoulders convulsed with each wretched cry. Tears soaked the front of his shirt. All Dan could do was hold her close and rock her and wait for the storm to pass.

She cried so long and so hard he began to worry that she would make herself sick. His gut told him there was more behind the jag than just fright.

Nuzzling his jaw against the top of her head, he continued the gentle rocking, moving his palm over her back in a circular motion. Gradually her cries tapered off into sniffles, then long, hitching sighs.

Exhausted, she remained snuggled against him. Dan wasn't sure if she was too tired to move or too embarrassed. Either way, he didn't mind. As a rule, a woman's tears made him antsy, but, strangely, it felt good to hold this woman in his arms and give her comfort. He was in no hurry to let her go. Beneath her cheek, his shirt was soaked and plastered to his chest, but he didn't mind that, either.

After a while, he felt her stir, and he hooked a finger under her chin and tipped her face up until she had no choice but to look at him. He cocked one eyebrow. "Feel better now?"

Maggie blushed and wrinkled her nose. "Sorry about that. I don't know what came over me. I usually don't lose it like that."

"No problem. You had a fright. It's a perfectly normal reaction."

He still held her close, their bodies touching from knees to chest, but neither made a move to break the embrace. She fit in his arms as though she'd been made for him, her body warm and soft against his.

Slowly, Dan inspected her face. Her eyes were puffy, the tip of her nose red, but not even the ravages of a crying jag or red scratches slicked with ointment could diminish her beauty.

He sensed the change in Maggie, a fine tension that vibrated through her.

He looked into those emerald eyes. Neither moved. Then his gaze drifted down to her mouth. He stared, drinking in the lushness of those lips, full and sensuous and soft, beautifully curved. Exquisite.

He could not have resisted kissing her if the ground had suddenly opened up beneath them. Drawn like a moth to a flame, his gaze fixed on that trembling mouth all the while, he slowly lowered his head. The quick intake of Maggie's breath an instant before his lips settled over hers sent fire streaking through him.

It took every ounce of restraint Dan could muster, but he kept the kiss gentle so as not to frighten her, a sensuous rub of flesh upon flesh, a nibble, an exchange of breath, a quick touch of tongues. Yet, for all its softness, the caress packed a wallop. Dan felt as if he'd been run over by a semi.

It was like drowning in ecstasy—voluptuous and sweet and shimmering with pleasure. It beckoned to him, pulled at him like a siren's song. His heart caromed. His pulse pounded. Every cell in his body cried out for him to lower her to the floor and take her, sate himself with her.

Appalled by the strength of his need, Dan wrenched his mouth from Maggie's.

Disoriented, she hung motionless in his arms for a few seconds, her head still tipped back, eyes closed, lips slightly parted. She looked so tempting it was all he could do not to kiss her again.

As though weighted with lead, Maggie's eyelids slowly lifted. Breathing hard, they stared at each other in the throbbing silence.

Finally Dan grasped her shoulders and stepped back.

"C'mon, I'll take you home."

In the early dawn light all was still, the only sounds the drip of dew from the peach trees and the buzz of bees. Dan walked carefully between two rows of trees, studying the ground. About fifteen yards from the clearing he spied what he'd been searching for and knelt for a closer look.

The previous afternoon the orchard had been weeded, then smoothed with a drag, and the dirt between the rows of trees looked as though it had been swept—except for the two sets of footprints. Maggie's and a larger set belonging to a man.

Dan looked up and down the row. To his right, as far as he could see toward the cannery, both sets of footprints followed the same path, the man's often overlaying Maggie's smaller ones.

"Looks like you were right, Red," Dan muttered. "Some yahoo was definitely following you."

To his left he could see that Maggie's prints continued in an erratic path down the row all the way to the point where the orchard opened into the clearing surrounding his house. The man's, however, continued to follow her for only a couple of feet beyond the point where Dan knelt, then veered off.

He rose and followed the larger footprints. They

led him over two rows to a tree adjacent to the clearing. A small area at the base of the trunk was compacted by multiple overlaying footprints. Staring at the patch of tamped ground, Dan cursed. The bastard had hidden behind the tree and watched him and Maggie while they had stood in the clearing.

At least he hadn't crept up to the house and played Peeping Tom, Dan thought grimly, eyeing the trail of footprints leading away from the tree toward the west side of the orchard.

Dan followed the footprints, but, as he had expected, they ended at a set of car tracks on the shoulder of the gravel road that ran along the side of the orchard.

Standing with his fists planted on his lean hips, he stared in the direction the vehicle had taken, his eyes narrowed beneath the brim of his straw work hat.

"Who are you, you bastard? And just what the hell are you up to?"

Eleven

With a sigh, Maggie tossed her pencil on the desk, slumped back in the chair and rubbed her face with both hands. The deeper she dug, the more concerned she became. And the more puzzled.

There didn't seem to be any one thing that she could put her finger on that could account for their dismal profit picture. More like a whole laundry list of things.

And they had occurred in every phase of the operation, from the orchard to the cannery to the big rigs that delivered their products.

It was all documented in various reports from the different department heads, but as far as Maggie could tell, no one had put them all together.

After hours of poring over production reports, memo files, purchase orders, lab tests, shipping dispatches and various other documents, she had compiled a chronological record of mistakes, bad breaks and just plain odd or unexplainable occurrences.

In the last year they had suffered frequent machinery breakdowns, huge shipments of sugar and other supplies going astray, customers' orders lost, shipments arriving at the stores damaged or shorted, others being delivered to the wrong place, expensive repairs and tire failures on their fleet of over-the-road trucks, and orchard irrigation systems mysteriously malfunctioning, flooding some trees and parching others.

Worst of all, and potentially the most damaging, there had been an abnormally high number of food batches that had tested positive for contaminants, in some cases, even dangerous microorganisms, something that had never happened in their company before.

The Mother Malone's brand had maintained an exemplary record for hygiene and safety for more than eighty years. Luckily, thanks to their rigorous testing, the contaminated batches were discovered before the food left the cannery. Had they gotten onto the supermarket shelves, the results could have been disastrous.

Even if no one had become ill from eating the products, a recall would have been a public relations nightmare that would have done irreparable damage to their reputation and hurt sales.

As it was, the destroyed batches of food added up to big losses—hundreds of man hours, tons of produce and canning supplies and sundry other operating costs, all gone to waste.

Taken singly, no one occurrence could have done serious damage to their P & L statement, but when added up, the cumulative effect was staggering.

On the surface, the incidents appeared unrelated, just a random series of bad breaks. But were they?

Could they be clever and systematic attempts to cripple the company? Maggie wondered.

It was a stretch, but not a difficult one. Her mind

immediately latched on to the name of the person she thought most likely to do such a thing.

Martin wanted her father to sell Malone's, had been pressuring him to take the steps that would allow the sale to happen.

Maggie frowned. The question was, why? They wouldn't be dealing from a position of strength, which meant they'd have to settle for a depressed price. Martin had to know that over the long haul he stood to gain much more if the business remained healthy and in the family.

Maybe he was shortsighted and just wanted to make a quick buck. Maybe he had debts that no one knew about. Maybe he gambled or drank. Or maybe he was so lazy he wanted to stop working. Not that Martin killed himself working.

Maggie's mouth twisted. ''Or maybe you're just paranoid when it comes to the creep and looking for a way to blame him,'' she murmured.

Giving the matter a bit more thought, she realized that there were others who could be behind the scheme. If there was a scheme.

The Tolivers hated the Malones, and had for generations. Their family owned Toliver Feed and Grain, the Double TT Registered Hereford Farm and had interests in several other local businesses, including a small pulpwood company and the bank, but they still coveted Malone Enterprises, and were openly antagonistic toward Maggie's family.

Then there was the possibility that a dismissed employee might be seeking revenge. Over the years, Malone's workforce had been fairly stable. Small-town folk were generally honest and hardworking, and in a place the size of Ruby Falls, people were happy to have a decent job. Still, there were a few disgruntled ex-employees who had gotten the sack for one reason or another.

If a Malone employee suffered some sort of misfortune or financial setback, her father had been known to help out, even to the point of generously retiring the debt himself, but he would not tolerate theft or malingering or dishonesty in any form.

It was also possible, Maggie supposed, that someone from Bountiful Foods was trying to force them to sell. If so, they'd probably bribed an employee to do their dirty work. But who?

There was one other possibility. Maggie didn't want to believe it, but it occurred to her that even Jo Beth could be responsible for all the mishaps.

Like herself and Laurel, their younger sister had had the run of the place all her life. Also like them, Jo Beth had undoubtedly picked up a general knowledge of the operations simply through being exposed to it on a daily basis.

Which meant that the opportunity was there. And her little sister was desperate to escape the yoke of responsibility Jacob wanted to hang on her.

Would she go so far as to destroy the family business? Their legacy and source of income? Would it even occur to her to cause some of the setbacks they'd suffered?

No, of course not. She was just a kid.

But then…kids did crazy things. Impulsive, irrational things. And Jo Beth had always been clever and creative.

"No, dammit!"

Disgusted with herself for having such thoughts, Maggie shot out of the chair and started pacing. When she reached the glass wall a movement in a patch of bright light on the cannery floor caught her eye and her heart leapt right up in her throat.

Instinctively, she jumped back from the glass and unconsciously kept moving in reverse until she came up against the wall beside her great-grandmother's photograph.

She stood absolutely still, struggling to calm her jangled nerves and thudding heart. It annoyed her that she was behaving like such a ninny, but she couldn't seem to help it. Since the episode in the orchard three nights ago she'd been jumping at the least noise or unexpected movement.

Gathering her courage, Maggie eased forward again and peered down at the cannery floor. Her gaze zeroed in on the brightly lit area and the man who was bent over a piece of machinery. Suddenly he straightened, and she let out the breath she had been unconsciously holding. Dan.

Her relief soon turned to unease as she watched him. She hadn't spoken to him since he had driven her home three nights ago. Neither of them had uttered a word during that short drive, and the instant he had stopped his truck she had mumbled a terse ''good-night'' and bailed out.

Maggie sighed. She didn't know which bothered her most, that sizzling kiss, or that he'd seen her cry. Twice.

So she'd been avoiding him. Which was just plain dumb, not to mention cowardly. The last really chafed her pride. Maggie Malone did not run from anyone or anything.

Watching him, it suddenly occurred to her that Dan had access to every inch of the cannery and orchards. He could easily have tossed contaminants into the cooking vats or jammed machinery or misdirected shipments, or caused any of the other catastrophes.

Trouble was, he had no motive to ruin them. Just the opposite. If they sold to Bountiful Foods, he would most likely lose his job.

Maggie tapped her chin with her forefinger, her gaze fixed on Dan. Coming to a decision, she muttered, "All right, Mag, time to face the man and get past it."

She grabbed the legal pad that contained her scribbled notes and left the office through the side door out of her father's office, which led directly into an enclosed stairway. At the bottom, Maggie pushed open the heavy steel door and stepped out onto the cannery floor.

In the vast quiet, her footsteps echoed hollowly, alerting Dan to her presence. By the time she drew near the spot where he was working he had straightened and was wiping his hands on an orange work rag, those pale eyes tracking her approach.

Maggie was used to people staring at her. That came with the territory. But there was something about that steady, silvery gaze that rattled her. Especially after what happened the other night.

To compensate, she held her head high and returned the stare with a bold one of her own. For good measure, she added a sultry smile and put a tad more hip action into her walk than normal.

She was so intent on holding his stare and keeping her composure, not until she was only a few steps away did she notice that he had stripped to the waist.

Maggie's mouth went dry. Jeezlouise, she thought, staring helplessly. If the man was something to behold fully clothed, half naked he was awesome. She didn't dare even try to imagine what he's look like completely nude for fear her heart couldn't take it.

"Something I can do for you, Red?" he drawled after she'd stood in front of him for several seconds, speechless as a stump.

"I, uh…" Maggie forced her gaze up past the wedge of silky dark hair sprinkled over impressive pecs, only to encounter broad shoulders and bulging biceps covered by smooth bronze skin. She swallowed, hard. "I wanted to talk to you about the problems Malone's has been experiencing."

She had meant to sound brisk and businesslike, but her voice came out husky and deep, with a hint of a quiver.

Annoyed with herself, she cleared her throat and looked around. "What are you doing down here at this time of night, anyway?" she demanded in a sharper tone than she had intended.

"I could ask you the same question. Please tell me you didn't walk here."

Though cursed with a redhead's fair skin, Maggie rarely blushed, but even that oblique reference to the other night brought a rush of warmth to her cheeks.

The faint twitch of Dan's mouth told her he'd noticed, but all she could do was brazen it out.

"No, I drove. But what's it to you, anyway, handsome? You didn't believe anyone chased me."

"I was wrong. I found footprints."

While he told her what he'd found Maggie's uneasiness grew. She felt exposed and vulnerable. The thought of that creep standing in the shadows watching them made her skin crawl.

"Of course, it could have just been a teenager," Dan said when he'd finished. "I've run high school kids out of the grove a few times. It's a favorite make-out spot, and once a group of boys got liquored up and as a prank they stripped a boy who'd passed out and left him in the middle of the orchard buck naked."

"I see. Do *you* think it was a teenager?"

Dan hesitated, but only for an instant. "No. This guy was obviously waiting for you when you left the office. Which means someone's been watching you and knows that you've been working late every night. Most likely he was just trying to scare you off, but we don't know that for certain."

"Which means someone doesn't want me nosing around."

"That would be my guess. The question is, who?"

Maggie shook her head. "My first choice would be Martin, but he was in Little Rock Thursday night."

"Mmm. Well, maybe it was just a kid playing a prank."

"Maybe." She glanced at the open toolbox.

"You never did tell me what you're doing here so late."

"The pump on this machine blew out an hour before closing yesterday and shut down two lines. I'm trying to install a new one before the shift starts in the morning."

"Another mechanical problem?" She consulted the list she'd complied. "That's the ninth one this month."

"Not surprising. It's only to be expected with machinery this old. Most of it has been here since Jacob was a boy. There's not a piece of equipment in the place that I haven't repaired a dozen times or more."

"That doesn't sound very cost effective. When machinery begins to break down repeatedly, generally speaking it's time to replace it."

"You're right. The whole system needs to be updated. I've suggested that to Jacob, but he says the company can't afford that kind of expenditure." Dan shrugged and picked up a wrench. "So I try to keep it patched together as best I can."

"What about all these other problems?" She handed him the yellow legal pad on which she'd listed the various incidents that had occurred. "Since you're the general manager, I assume you know about these."

He scanned the list, then handed it back to her. "Yeah, I know about them," he said over his shoulder, bending over the disabled machine again.

The action drew Maggie's gaze to his tight butt, and her brains scrambled.

Dan stretched to break loose a stubborn bolt, and

a thin line of white skin appeared above the waist-band of his jeans, in stark contrast to the deep bronze of the skin above. It occurred to Maggie that he must often work in the orchard without his shirt. The mental picture that brought to mind did nothing for her equilibrium.

The bolt refused to budge, and Dan held his hand out behind him. "Get me that mallet out of the tool-box, will you?"

"What? Oh. Just a sec." Maggie shook herself out of the trance and pawed through the tools until she found the mallet and put it in his outstretched hand.

"Thanks," he muttered, and gave the end of the wrench several solid taps.

Struggling to put her brain back in gear, Maggie tore her gaze away from the rippling muscles in his back and tapped the yellow pad. "Uh, don't you think there's something odd about all these inci-dents?"

"Every company has accidents and foul-ups."

"But Malone's has never had so many over such a short period of time. I checked."

Dan bore down on the wrench and the bolt broke free. He removed it and turned to face her. She no-ticed there was now a smudge of grease across his shoulder and another on his right forearm. Exertion had beaded his upper lip and forehead with sweat and more sheened his shoulders and chest beneath the haze of dark hair.

"So what are you saying?"

"That maybe they weren't accidents or mistakes. Maybe someone caused all these things to happen."

She expected him to laugh or look skeptical, but he appeared to seriously consider the idea.

"It's possible, I suppose. Do you have any thoughts on who it could be?"

Encouraged, Maggie told him her theories about Martin, the Bountiful Foods people and a possible disgruntled ex-employee. She didn't mention Jo Beth.

He mulled the matter over, then nodded. "You could be right. But even if you are, which one is it? And how're you going to prove it?"

"I don't know. I was hoping you'd have some suggestions."

"Not offhand. We sure as hell can't hire the kind of security we'd need if the company is scraping bottom like Jacob says."

Unhooking the shop light he'd rigged over a pipe, he thrust it into her hand. "Here, hold this close to the machine for me."

Maggie obeyed without question, though she did wonder just when and how she'd lost control of the situation.

Of necessity, she had to stand close and lean over him to aim the light on the area where he was working—so close her left breast brushed against his shoulder with each breath she took.

Dan seemed not to notice. His concentration was focused on repairing the machine. He worked steadily for several minutes in silence, except for an occasional grunt of exertion and a mild curse when he barked his knuckles loosening another bolt.

Then, without warning, he turned his head and looked into her eyes.

Their faces were mere inches apart, so close she could feel his breath feather over her skin. The smell of clean sweat and grease drifted to her nose, mingled with a scent that was all male.

His gaze locked with hers for the space of three heartbeats, then drifted over her face, touching each feature like a caress before returning once again to her eyes.

"Do you have any idea how damned beautiful you are?"

The question came out on a raspy whisper that conveyed both anger and desire, and sent a shockwave of heat coursing through Maggie.

She was a master at batting down pickup lines with a sassy quip or a laugh, but at that moment her tongue seemed to be stuck to the roof of her mouth.

Not that it mattered. She was so befuddled she couldn't have remembered her name if someone had asked. All she could do was stare back into those mesmerizing silver eyes with their tiny radiating spokes of charcoal, while her heart beat like a kettledrum.

She felt her blood pulsing in shockingly intimate places on her body, and panic began to flutter in her stomach. What in heaven's name was wrong with her? The compliment was far from the most elegant she'd ever received. Come to that, she wasn't even sure it *was* a compliment. More like an accusation.

Yet all she could think about was what it would be like to have his mouth on hers again, to feel his arms pull her against that magnificent body.

She finally managed to unstick her tongue, but it was no use—her brain refused to engage.

"I...um..." She drew an unsteady breath and licked her dry lips.

Dan's gaze dropped to her mouth, his eyes growing hot beneath heavy lids as he tracked the provocative action.

Closing his eyes to mere slits, he leaned closer, and Maggie's heart leapt right up into her throat and hammered wildly.

Anticipation thrummed through her, tightening her chest so that she could barely breathe. Every cell in her body tingled with yearning as she felt the pull of him, drawing her closer. Her breath shuddered out on a ragged sigh and her eyes began to drift shut.

The steel door at the bottom of her father's private stairway burst open and banged against the adjoining wall like a gunshot.

Maggie jerked back with a strangled cry. Dan cursed.

"Maggie! Stay right where you are," came Martin's furious shout as heavy footsteps echoed through the building. "I want to talk to you. Now!"

Her appalled gaze shot to the glass wall of her father's office. He had to have spotted her and Dan from there. After a moment of panic she realized that from that angle he couldn't have seen much, just the two of them standing close together. Nevertheless, heat rushed to her cheeks. Her alarm had barely begun to subside when it returned, stronger than before. Jeezlouise, what had she left spread out on the desk?

Martin charged around the end of a line and stomped toward them. Willing the color in her cheeks to fade, Maggie squared her shoulders and waited, braced for a fight.

Dan calmly went back to work.

"Dammit, Maggie! Just what the hell are you up to?"

"Me?" Maggie batted her lashes and flashed an innocent smile. "Why, I'm just holding the light for Dan. See?" She held the shop light up to Martin's face, making him blink and take a step back. Suppressing a smile, she hooked the light over the edge of the machine, close to Dan's shoulder.

"Don't give me that. I saw the ledgers and files spread out on my desk upstairs. Elaine telephoned me in Albuquerque last week and told me you'd been snooping around the office, but when you didn't come back I figured you'd just done it to annoy me."

So Miss Udall had reported to Martin, had she? From the start she'd had a hunch the two were thick as thieves.

"But you've been poking your nose in where you have no business, haven't you," Martin charged. "Well, I won't have it. I expect Jacob will toss you out again any day now, but for as long as you're here, the cannery is off-limits to you. Got it?"

Outrage left her speechless. She couldn't believe the man's gall. Before she could find her voice he turned and jabbed his forefinger in Dan's direction. "And as for you, what the hell do you think you're doing, Garrett?"

"What does it look like? I'm repairing a downed filling unit."

"I didn't authorize you to make any repairs. If I

want something repaired, I'll hire a professional. Pack up your tools and get out of here. Now. And in the future, you're not to enter this building outside of normal working hours. In fact, hand over your keys. Right now.''

Maggie's mouth dropped open. Dan was the company's general manager, for Pete's sake.

Dan merely shot him a dismissive look and kept on working. ''Forget it. I don't take orders from you, asshole. I answer directly to Jacob.''

''Why, you—''

Martin's face turned purple. He was so furious the veins in his neck stood out. He looked as though he would explode at any second.

Maggie had seen that look before, and as his hands curled into fists at his sides she took a quick step back.

''That's it! You're fired, Garrett. Get the hell out. I'll give you one hour to pack up your possessions and vacate the superintendent's house. If you're not off this property by then, I'll call the sheriff and have you thrown off.''

Dan's face registered no reaction, but Maggie saw his shoulders tense and the icy glitter in the look he shot Martin. He calmly finished what he was doing, then pulled the shop rag from his back pocket, wiped the wrench and laid it in the open toolbox. Wiping his hands on the rag, he turned to face Martin.

A contemptuous smirk twisted her brother-in-law's mouth as he watched him, and Maggie marveled at his arrogance. The fool seemed oblivious to the danger behind Dan's precise, unhurried movements and steely control.

"You can't fire me. You don't have the authority."

"The hell I don't! Now that Jacob is so ill, I'm running Malone Enterprises."

"That's where you're wrong, Martin."

Maggie had not planned on showing her hand quite so soon, but Martin's presumptuous claim was more than she could take. She stepped forward, positioning herself between the two men, and looked her brother-in-law square in the eye.

"Regardless of what you think, you are not in charge here. In Daddy's absence, I will be running Malone's, not you."

"You?" Martin gave a contemptuous bark of laughter. "That'll be the day."

"Oh, I don't know about that. I have more right to the job than you. I'm a member of the family, after all. And a shareholder."

"I wouldn't count too heavily on your status as a family member if I were you. You're hanging on by a thread these days. And that measly six percent of stock your grandfather left you hardly entitles you to run the company."

"Oh? And just how much stock do you own, Martin?"

The flush of angry color that had just begun to recede came rushing back to his face. "That's beside the point. I'm an officer of this company. And if it comes to that, I own just as many shares as you do."

"Correction. Laurel owns those shares. Not you."

"Same difference. Laurel's my wife. What's hers is mine."

"I'm sure you'd like to think so, but I doubt a court of law would agree. My sisters and I all inherited the same amount of stock, but there's one big difference between us. Neither of them wants to get involved in the company. Nor are they trained to do so. I am. Whether you like it or not, I'm taking charge."

His face tightened. The look in his eyes turned murderous. His hands curled into fists again, and he took a half step toward her before restraining himself. Maggie knew that if Dan hadn't been there he would have struck her.

Or, at least, he would have tried. She wasn't quite the same defenseless girl she'd been seven years ago. Since then she'd regularly taken kick-boxing and self-defense classes. She might not win against him, but this time she'd sure as heck inflict some serious damage.

"We'll just see about that," he snarled when he'd regained enough control to speak, and turned on his heel and stomped away.

Watching him, Maggie just couldn't resist getting in one more dig. "Oh, and Martin," she called after him. "Please leave through one of the cannery exits. I'll be using Daddy's office, so in the future it's off-limits to you. Unless I send for you, of course."

She had the pleasure of seeing him jerk to a halt and stiffen. His whole body quivered with barely controlled rage. Even from behind she could see his jaw muscles work.

After a few tense seconds, without a word, he

changed direction and stomped away, out of sight. His angry footsteps echoed through the building for a few seconds, then the outer door by the loading bay slammed with a bang that reverberated through the cannery like a cannon shot.

The jarring sound brought Maggie back to reality, and the brief crest of victory she'd dared to ride collapsed like a breaking wave. She exhaled a long sigh.

"Nice going, Red. I'm impressed," Dan drawled. "I doubt anyone has ever put him in his place like that before. He'll be smarting for a month."

Maggie turned around in time to see Dan relax. Only then did she realize that he had been braced and ready to defend her.

The corners of her mouth twitched. "Yeah, well. Don't be too impressed, sugar. To tell you the truth, he just made me so damned angry I kinda got carried away. My tenure as head of the company probably won't last past tomorrow morning. Martin is sure to complain to Daddy, first chance he gets."

"I wouldn't worry about it. I've always found Jacob to be a fair man."

The only response Maggie could manage was a sad smile.

After a restless night and a punishing long run, Maggie was the first one to arrive on the terrace for breakfast.

She had barely settled down with her first cup of coffee when Dan came through the garden gate. She winked and raised her cup in a mock salute. "Hi, handsome. You're early this morning. You come to witness the beheading?''

''Why do you assume that? Maybe I came to prevent one.''

''Why, sugar,'' she purred, batting her lashes. ''I didn't know you cared.''

He sat down beside her, poured a cup of coffee and took a sip before answering. ''Nice try, Red, but you're not fooling me. I spotted you running through the orchard this morning before dawn. You looked like a demon was after you. I figure you'd had difficulty sleeping and were trying to outdistance your nerves.'' His silver gaze did a slow inspection of her face. ''Even now, gorgeous as you look, you seem edgy.''

Surprise flashed through Maggie, at both the compliment and his perception. Before she could think of a response the back door opened, and her nerves ratcheted up several more notches when Charley wheeled Jacob out on the terrace. Nan, Lily and Jo Beth followed right behind them.

As soon as the greetings were exchanged and Jacob was helped to a chair at the table, the nurse disappeared back into the house and they settled down to their meal. Nan and Maggie's parents got into a discussion about an article in the local paper concerning a disturbance at Rowdy's Bar and Grill the night before.

''You ask me, that place should've been shut down years ago. Nothing but a hangout for riffraff and troublemakers.''

''Oh, Jacob, don't be so stuffy,'' his sister chided.

"It's just a place where young people gather to relax and let off a little steam."

"That's right, dearest," Lily added. "You even took me there a few times when we were dating."

Jacob frowned and looked uncomfortable. "Yes, well...things were different back then."

As usual, beyond an occasional rude remark to Maggie, Jo Beth said little.

They had just finished eating when Dan leaned toward Maggie and murmured, "Brace yourself, Red, here he comes."

"Jacob, we have to talk," Martin snapped, striding toward the table.

"Certainly. But first sit down and have something to eat. There's plenty left."

"I don't want to eat, and this can't wait." He shot a venomous look at Maggie. "Well? Have you told him yet?"

That got Jacob's attention. His gaze narrowed on Maggie. "Told me what? What have you done now, Katherine?"

"She's trying to take over Malone Enterprises, that's what," Martin answered for her. "I found her at the cannery last night. She'd been going through the books and files in your office. When I ordered her to leave she refused and informed me that she was in charge now."

"*What?* The hell you are! Explain yourself, girl. This minute!"

Maggie glanced at her mother, but Lily shifted in her chair and kept her eyes on her plate.

With a sigh, she met her father's glare and shrugged.

"It seemed like the thing to do at the time."

"Don't you dare take that flippant attitude with me. I did not, at any time, authorize you to take over the business. I won't have—"

"What are you getting so upset about, Jacob? Maggie was merely doing what Lily asked her to," Nan said.

"What?" Jacob's head snapped toward his wife. "Lily? Is this true?"

"Well...I..."

"Oh, for heaven's sake, Lily, spit it out," Nan snapped.

"Ye-yes, I asked her to, uh...to take a look at the company and see if she could salvage it. I didn't know what else to do, Jacob. You're too ill to work, but if something isn't done soon we're going to lose the company. You told me so yourself."

Martin made a derisive sound. "And you thought *she* would work a miracle? Yeah, right."

Nan bristled like a cat whose fur had been stroked the wrong way. "I would be very careful if I were you, Martin. It so happens that I support Lily in this."

Watching Martin, Maggie almost laughed. The arrogant bastard knew he'd made a tactical error. Because Nan was a woman, he tended to forget that she had just as much clout as Jacob. Or at least she did as far as he and everyone else knew. Biting back a grin, Maggie watched Martin scramble to undo the damage.

"Now, now, Aunt Nan, we all know how fond you are of Maggie, but we can't let our emotions get in the way of sound business decisions, can we?

I mean, let's be realistic. Jacob has all but disowned Maggie because he doesn't trust her. You can't expect him to now suddenly allow her free access to the company records. Posing for pictures hardly qualifies her to act as a corporate troubleshooter.''

Nan's eyes narrowed. ''No, but graduating magna cum laude from Harvard Business School does. And as for you, Martin Howe, if you ever *dare* to address me in that condescending tone again I will smack you.''

Knowing he'd lost any hope of winning Nan over, Martin gave up all pretense of pleasantness. ''Nevertheless, I'm in charge now, and I will not tolerate any interference, especially from the likes of her.''

''If you ask me, my niece is Jacob's logical successor,'' Nan fired back. ''In fact, I think we should officially appoint her acting president of the company right now.''

''What! That's ridiculous. I'm an officer in the company. *I* should be the one running it.''

''No, that's where you're wrong. Malone Enterprises should be run by a Malone, the way it always has been.''

Nan's gaze switched from Martin to her brother. Though her voice softened, it was no less firm. ''The time has come to make a decision, Jacob. Is the family business going to be run by an outsider? Or by your daughter...the way our grandmother intended.''

Jacob stared at Nan with the desperate look of a man who has suddenly found himself with his back against the wall. ''Dammit, Nan—''

"It's fish or cut bait time, Martin," she said, returning his glare with a steady look.

Maggie watched the silent duel between brother and sister, and wondered what was behind it. She had the curious feeling there was more to the exchange than who to put in charge of the company.

"Please, dearest. Won't you give her a chance?" Lily urged in a trembling voice.

Jacob glanced from his wife to his youngest daughter, who had remained amazingly silent during the exchange, her gaze bouncing back and forth between the participants like a spectator's at a tennis match. "Well, Jo Beth. You're a shareholder, too. What do you think?"

Maggie's heart sank when the girl shot her an unreadable look. If the decision were left up to Jo Beth, she didn't stand a chance. However, to Maggie's surprise, her baby sister assumed a bored expression and hitched one shoulder. "Why not? She is a Malone."

"Jacob, you can't seriously be considering putting her in charge," Martin exclaimed. "So she has a degree. So what? She has no practical experience. Maggie has never run a company. She doesn't know anything about running a big operation or overseeing workers or making decisions."

"Oh, you mean like the decision you made to fire Anna?" Maggie asked innocently.

Jacob's face went slack with shock.

Out of the corner of her eye Maggie saw Dan start. "I thought she was on vacation this week. Christ, what the man lacks in common sense he sure as hell makes up for in gall,'' he muttered under his breath.

Martin shifted, looking as guilty as a thief caught with his hand in the till.

"You *fired* Anna? You idiot!"

"Now, Jacob, I thought—"

"You thought? *You* thought! If you'd had a half-way intelligent thought in that head of yours you would've known that was the last thing you should have done!" Jacob shook his head, as though unable to accept that anyone would make such a monu-mental blunder. "I'm surprised Anna didn't come to me and tell me what you'd done. She should have known I'd set it straight."

"She didn't because Martin threatened her," Maggie interjected quietly, drawing another startled look from her father.

"What?"

"Don't listen to her, Jacob. She's lying."

"When I found out what Martin had done, I vis-ited Anna at her home," Maggie continued as though he hadn't spoken. "She said he told her that you knew he planned to let her go, and that you approved. He also told her you were too ill to see anyone, and if she tried, he'd have her arrested for harassment."

For a moment Jacob was so furious he lost the power of speech, but the look he shot Martin made words unnecessary. "You presumptuous little pip-squeak," he growled when he found his voice. "How dare you. If you weren't Laurel's husband I'd fire you on the spot."

"Jacob—"

"Shut up, Martin. I'll deal with you later. Katherine, go talk to Anna and explain that Martin overstepped his authority. Beg her, give her a raise, do whatever you have to, but get her back. Understand?"

Relief and elation bubbled up inside Maggie. "Yes, sir. Right away." She started to rise, then paused. "Uh, just so we're clear, Daddy. Does this mean you're putting me in charge?"

Jacob stared at her, hesitating, and she saw a muscle twitch in his cheek. "For now, I don't seem to have a choice."

"Dammit, Jacob, you can't do this!"

"I've made my decision, Martin," he ordered without taking his gaze from Maggie. He jabbed his forefinger in her direction. "But remember, Katherine, this is only temporary, so don't go getting any ideas. You mess up or pull one of your stunts, and I'll jerk you outta there so fast you won't know what happened. You got that?"

"Yes, Daddy." She tried to appear calm and businesslike, but she'd waited too long for this day and simply couldn't hold in her elation a second longer. Flashing a grin, she bolted out of the chair. "I'll go talk to Anna right now."

Before he could change his mind she raced toward the garage.

She left behind a taut silence, and as the others on the terrace watched her go, Dan sipped his coffee and watched them, waiting for the explosion. He didn't have long to wait.

"I don't believe this," Martin raged. "How could

you do this to me, Jacob? I've worked for you for seven years.''

"Worked? You've had a free ride for seven years. The position you hold was created for you because I couldn't think of another job in the company you could handle. Believe me, if you hadn't been Laurel's husband you wouldn't have lasted six months. Now, get out of my sight before I do fire you.''

Martin's face reddened.

Every muscle in Dan's body tensed. If ever he'd seen a man ready to do violence, it was Martin. He stood up and stepped behind Jacob's chair. "You heard the man.''

Something flared in Martin's eyes. Something violent and hate-filled. Dan braced himself, but at that moment Maggie's Viper shot out of the garage and rumbled down the drive past the terrace.

Turning his head, Martin watched her with a look of pure venom on his face. When she disappeared from sight he spat out a curse.

"All right, I'm going. But this isn't the end of it, I promise you.''

"Well. That was unpleasant,'' Nan drawled when he'd disappeared from sight. "And exhausting.'' She stood up and beckoned to her sister-in-law. "Come along, Lily. Let's leave the men to their business talk and take a walk through the rose garden. That always soothes my nerves. And you'd better get along to school, Jo Beth, or you'll be late.''

The moment the three disappeared around the corner of the house, Jacob turned to Dan.

"I want you to keep an eye on Katherine and report back to me everything she does.''

"You want me to *spy* on your daughter?"

"Yes. That's exactly what I want. I'm not convinced that putting her in charge is the smart thing to do. I intend to keep close tabs on her."

"Look, Jacob. I don't know what the problem is between you two, but...hell, man, this is your *daughter.*"

Jacob clenched his jaw. "Katherine isn't— Never mind. You'll just have to trust me on this, Daniel. It's important. I wouldn't ask it of you if it weren't."

A feeling of repugnance crawled through Dan. "I don't know, Jacob. I'm not comfortable being a snoop."

"Dammit, Dan, I can't watch her myself, and you're the only one I can trust. You have to do this for me."

Dan stared at his boss. He owed Jacob. He owed him a lot. But, dammit, this really stuck in his craw. He turned his head and stared out into the orchard, gritting his teeth.

Ah, hell. How could he say no? Anyway, what difference did it make? After that creepy episode in the orchard, he'd already decided to keep an eye on her, just to be on the safe side.

Twelve

"Here, now, you can't just barge in there unannounced."

Maggie looked up from the lab report she was reading in time to see Martin storm into her office looking like a thundercloud, with an outraged Anna on his heels.

"What the hell is this?"

"I'm sorry, Maggie. I tried to stop him."

"It's okay, Anna." Leaning back in her chair, she aimed a calm look at her brother-in-law. "Is there something I can do for you, Martin?"

He waved a sheet of paper at her. "You can start by explaining these deductions from my expense account check."

Instead of returning to her desk in the outer office, Anna shot Martin a defiant look, stepped around him and busied herself tidying up around the office.

"I instructed the accounting department to deduct the difference between first-class airfare and business-class. Also the difference in car rental fees for a BMW and an ordinary full-size, and to do the same with any other luxury items you tried to slip in."

"Those were all legitimate expenses," he blustered. "I have the receipts to prove it."

"Oh, I don't doubt that you spent the money. The point is, the charges are in violation of company policy, as I'm sure you know. Malone's will pay for you to travel in reasonable comfort, but we won't fund your extravagant life-style."

"This is an outrage. Your father would never have—"

"Oh, yes, he would. Don't try to bamboozle me, Martin. I checked your expense account file. Daddy held you to a reasonable standard. These sort of excessive charges only started showing up in the last few months since his illness has kept him out of the office. You've been taking advantage, and it's going to stop."

"As company rep I have to project a certain image when I'm entertaining customers."

"Oh? And just who were you impressing the night you dined alone and ordered a one hundred dollar bottle of wine?"

Martin's face tightened. "If you think I'm going to start penny-pinching just so you can impress 'Daddy,' think again. Martin Howe travels first class."

Maggie shrugged. "Fine with me. As long as you pay for any upgrades out of your own pocket."

His mouth pinched so tight a white ring formed around the edge. He looked angry enough to bite a nail in two. Then again, Maggie hadn't seen him look any other way since her father had put her in charge three weeks ago.

"You're enjoying this, aren't you. Well, don't get

too comfortable in that chair. You're not going to have it long. Bitch,'' he added under his breath as he stalked out.

"Insufferable toad," Anna muttered. "You ask me, Rupert Howe has a lot to answer for. He's spoiled that boy so rotten all his life, he thinks he's entitled to whatever takes his fancy. Reminds me of a two-year-old throwing a tantrum. Imagine, storming into the boss's office raging like that."

Maggie chuckled at Anna's outrage. "Yes, well, I doubt that Martin will ever think of me as the boss. And actually, compared to some of our other run-ins, that one was nothing."

With Martin every day was a battle. He fought her on every issue, on every procedural change she put in place to help her keep closer tabs on things, questioned every order she gave, ridiculed every question she posed and in general did his best to thwart her at every turn.

Maggie would like nothing better than to fire him, but she couldn't do so without appearing vengeful in Jacob's eyes and hurting Laurel.

At first Elaine Udall had been just as big a pain in the posterior. Fortunately, Maggie had no such compunction about firing the woman, and it had done her heart good to tell her so. The warning had ended Miss Udall's outspoken criticism if not her snippity ways and venomous glares.

Maggie only wished she could handle the other workers and the people around town that easily.

There were many things about living in a small town that she loved, but there were disadvantages, too. For one, it was almost impossible to keep anything a secret for long. Word had gotten out that Malone Enterprises was in trouble, and there was an undercurrent of panic around town.

Since Malone's employed a large portion of the town's workforce, almost everyone had a husband or wife or relative of some sort on their payroll. Therefore everyone felt they had a stake in the company, and few had any inhibitions about making their feelings known when something didn't suit them.

The workers and almost everyone else in Ruby Falls were upset that Maggie had been put in charge. They had no confidence in her ability to pull the company out of its financial slump.

Maggie couldn't really blame them. The employees were worried about their jobs, and others were concerned because the economy of Ruby Falls depended heavily on the cannery.

There was a lot of grumbling among the workers and townspeople, and rumors were flying. Wherever she went, whether walking through the cannery or warehouses or shopping at the local grocery, she was treated with suspicion and coolness.

Maggie knew she was still battling her old reputation as a wild and rebellious teenager and that she had to prove herself to the locals, but still, their snubs were difficult to take.

"How's it going, ladies?"

Maggie looked up to see Dan standing in the doorway, and her heart gave a little skip. It was the first time she'd seen him, except at a distance, since she'd returned the day before from the photo shoot in New York. He stood with one shoulder propped against the frame, the opposite hand hooked over his outthrust hip. Dressed in his usual attire of boots, jeans and a chambray work shirt with the sleeves rolled up, he looked so utterly male he took her breath away.

Why, she wondered, for perhaps the hundredth time, did she feel such a strong attraction to this particular man? It was annoying and exasperating, and just plain foolish, but there was no denying it. Whenever he was around she was so acutely aware of his quiet strength, those "go to hell" good looks and all that raw masculinity that she could barely concentrate.

It didn't make any sense. She worked with drop-dead-gorgeous male models all the time, and she'd met dozens of other handsome, successful, sophisticated men. Some were celebrities in their own right—actors, athletes, titans of industry—men of wealth and power. Yet not one of them had appealed to her except in the abstract, the way one would admire beauty of any kind.

So what was it about this man that made her heart jump?

Dan tipped his head toward the outer door. "I passed Martin in the hall. He's practically foaming at the mouth. Has he been giving you a hard time again?"

"Always. But it's nothing I can't handle. Did you want to see me about something?" The question came out sharper than she'd intended, but merely being around Dan put her on edge.

"Yeah. I've got good news and bad news. The

good news is, I got the new thermostat installed on cooking vat three and it's back in service.''

"Great. And the bad news?''

"We've got a conveyor out. It shut down production on five lines. I called the manufacturer and they're expressing us replacement parts, but it'll be tomorrow before they arrive. Which means we fall further behind in production. That's going to play hell with our shipping schedule. With all the problems and delays we've experienced lately we're low on inventory. What we have won't cover our orders. We're going to be late delivering on several large accounts.''

Propping her elbows on the desk, Maggie cupped her forehead in her hands and groaned, "Not another mechanical breakdown. That's four since I officially took over." She raised her head and looked at him. "What caused this one?''

"A crowbar in the gears. Stripped most of the teeth off a half-dozen of 'em before we could shut it down. It could have been an accident, I suppose, but I don't think so, not the way the thing was jammed in there. It looks like we've got ourselves a saboteur.''

Maggie sighed. "Great. Just great.''

"Don't you think it's time we told Jacob what we suspect?'' he asked quietly, watching her.

"No, not just yet.''

"Maggie, I have to agree with Dan on this one,'' Anna said. "Your father has a right to know what's going on.''

"I know, but until we know for sure that someone

is deliberately vandalizing Malone's, I don't want to upset him, not as ill as he is.''

"Well, if you ask me, he'll be more upset to learn that you've been keeping something like this from him."

"Anna's right. I think you should tell him now."

"Maybe," Maggie agreed, torn between protecting Jacob and exposing herself to his wrath. "I'll think about it."

Dan looked at her for a long time, then shrugged. "You're the boss."

"You have a visitor, Mr. Malone," Ida Lou announced from the doorway of the family room.

Annoyance rippled through Jacob. Lily and Nan were upstairs looking at dress patterns, or some such thing, and Jo Beth was still at school. He had been enjoying a few moments of solitude, lying back in his recliner and gazing out at the orchard. He wasn't anxious for company, especially not when he saw who his visitor was.

"Jacob, how good to see you looking so fit," Rupert Howe exclaimed, brushing past Ida Lou without waiting for an invitation and striding into the room. "How're you feeling, my friend?"

"I'm hanging in there." Rupert stuck out his hand, and Jacob had no choice but to shake it. He wanted to tell the smarmy bastard that they had never been friends. As far back as when they attended grade school together, Rupert had rubbed him the wrong way. However, as always, for Laurel's sake, he held his tongue.

"Good, good. I'm happy to hear that. I hope

you'll forgive me for not coming to see you more often, but I've been swamped down at the bank. You understand how it is, being a businessman.''

Jacob nodded.

"Of course, that boy of mine keeps me informed of your condition, but today I happened to be in the neighborhood and I thought, 'By George, I'm going to drop by and see for myself how my old friend is doing.'''

Ida Lou came in carrying a coffee tray, relieving Jacob of any need to comment. When she'd poured their coffee and left, Rupert sipped his quietly for a moment, then placed the cup and saucer on the end table and leaned forward, his expression turning from fake friendly to earnest.

"You know, Jacob, there is a small matter we need to discuss."

Instantly on alert, Jacob narrowed his eyes infinitesimally. He couldn't imagine what they had to talk about. Over the years he'd made sure he never did business with Rupert's bank, and as far as Jacob knew, everything was fine with Laurel and Martin.

He took a sip of coffee, even though he didn't want it, and eyed his guest. "Oh? And what would that be?"

"This business of putting Maggie in charge. Now, I know you made that decision in the heat of the moment, and perhaps my son did overstep his authority a bit, but Jacob, really...*Maggie?* Running Malone Enterprises? Why, that's absurd."

Muscle by muscle, Jacob stiffened. "Oh? And just how do you figure that?" he questioned, carefully keeping his voice neutral.

"Well, for one thing, she's a woman."

"What does that have to do with anything? You forget, this company was started by a woman."

"Well, yes, but your poor grandmother had no choice. I'm sure if your grandfather had survived World War I he would never have allowed her to soil her hands in business.

"Besides, you must admit, there is a great deal of difference between the original Katherine Margaret and your Maggie. Pardon me for saying so, Jacob, but the people of this town have long memories, and your daughter's reputation is not the best. She's wild and irresponsible and, well to be frank, some say immoral. I'm telling you, Jacob, your workers won't tolerate having her for a boss."

"Is that so?"

Either Rupert failed to notice or refused to heed the dangerous note in Jacob's voice and plowed on. "Look, I realize that you just put the girl in charge to punish my boy, and I understand that. But, Jacob, this has gone on long enough. It's time to put an end to this farce. By rights, my son should be the one to take over as president of Malone Enterprises. After seven years with the company, he's entitled. Everyone knows that."

"First of all, Rupert, the workers have no say in the running of this company. Neither do you or your son. Malone Enterprises is a family-owned business. Malones run it—always have, always will. Period.

"I have made Maggie acting president, and whether or not you and the rest of the people in this town like it, that's how it's going to be. I will not tolerate interference of any kind." He smacked the arm of his leather recliner for emphasis. "By heaven, I'll shut the damn doors before I'll let outsiders dictate how the company is run."

For an instant, Rupert looked ready to rage at Jacob, but he wisely reined in his anger.

"I'm sorry to hear that, Jacob. I truly am. With you incapacitated the way you are, I would have thought you'd welcome help. Talk around town is, Malone's is in trouble. Seems to me this isn't the time to let family tradition overrule good business sense."

"I don't happen to think the two are mutually exclusive. This family is perfectly capable of tending to its business. I suggest that you and others do the same."

Rupert gave him a long, frustrated look, then sighed. "Very well, if that's the way you want it. I was just trying to help. As your daughter's father-in-law, I felt it my duty. If you should change your mind—"

"I won't. Now, if there's nothing else you'll have to excuse me. It's time for my medication."

Rupert's face turned a mottled red. As the local banker, he fancied himself an important man in these parts, and clearly, he was not accustomed to being dismissed. Rising with stiff dignity, he gave Jacob a curt nod.

"Certainly. I'll just see myself out."

"Oh, Rupert."

At the door, the other man paused and looked back. "Yes?"

"One thing I want to clear up before you go. Katherine may have a mischievous nature and I will

admit that from time to time she has behaved reck-
lessly, but neither you nor anyone else can honestly
say that she has ever done anything immoral. I will
not tolerate anyone spreading that sort of talk about
her. Do I make myself clear?''

Rupert looked taken aback. ''But I thought...that
is, everyone knows...''

''Knows what?''

''That you and Maggie don't get along. I mean,
be honest, Jacob, that girl has always been a thorn
in your side. It's common knowledge around town.''

''You and the rest of the people in this town know
nothing about my relationship with Katherine,'' he
ground out. ''Absolutely *nothing*. You got that?''

''Of course. Whatever you say.''

When Rupert had left, Jacob realized he was so
angry he was shaking. Grinding his teeth, he stared
out the window. The raw fury that had shot through
him when Rupert maligned Katherine had caught
him by surprise.

But dammit, it was one thing for him to criticize
her, and quite another for someone else to do so,
particularly an outsider.

Even more troublesome than his instinctive defense of her was Rupert's shock that he'd done so.
All these years, he had assumed that no one else—
at least, no one outside of Lily and Nan—had been
aware of his ambivalent feelings toward Katherine.
He should have known better. This was Ruby Falls,
after all.

Damn. How could he have been so blind, not to
have known that sort of tittle-tattle was going
around? Hell, it probably had been circulating all of

her life. Which meant that Katherine had known. She was too sharp and intuitive not to have.

Dear God, what must it have been like for her as a child growing up, knowing that everyone believed her father didn't love her?

Hell, maybe Nan was right. Maybe all that teenage rebellion and impudence was just her way of getting his attention.

Jacob's fist hit the arm of the recliner again with a solid thud. Dammit! Whatever his feelings for Katherine, he'd never meant for her to be hurt by malicious gossip.

"So, are you going to tell me about her or not?"

Dan fought back a grin. Taking his time, he signaled the waitress to refill his iced tea glass and cut another bite of chicken-fried steak. "Tell you about who?"

"You know perfectly well who," Lucy Garrett snapped, shooting her oldest son a pithy look. "Maggie Malone, that's who."

"What do you want to know?"

"For starters, is she as beautiful as her pictures?"

"Yes."

"What's she like?"

Dan chewed thoughtfully and swallowed the bite. "Let's see. I guess smart and sassy about covers it."

"Really?" Lucy grinned, delighted by the description. "Good. I'm glad to hear success hasn't changed her."

"That's right, you were working in the high school cafeteria when she was a student there."

"Yes, but I can't really say I knew her." Lucy

scooped up a forkful of salad, but hesitated with the bite halfway to her mouth. "Couldn't help but notice her, though. Back then she was a skinny beanpole. When you looked at her all you saw was a full mouth that was way too big for the rest of her face and a mop of red hair. I guess the rest of her face caught up with that mouth." She chuckled. "Life's funny. Just the other day I read in a woman's magazine that in a recent poll men voted her lips the most luscious in the world."

Instantly, Dan thought about the kiss he'd shared with Maggie. Oh yeah, they were that, all right.

"Back in her high school days others called her wild, but I always admired her gumption." Lucy paused to chew the bite of salad, then continued on another track. "Rumor has it that Malone's is losing money. Do you think Maggie's going to be able to turn things around?"

"It's too soon to tell. She works hard and she's smart, and she appears to know what she's doing. But so far that hasn't been enough to turn the tide."

"Mmm." With her forefinger, Lucy idly doodled in the condensation on her iced tea glass. "Did you know there are some in town who want to organize a delegation to go talk to Jacob and demand that he remove Maggie as president?"

Dan shot his mother a sharp look, his knife and fork suspended over his plate. "No, I didn't. Who's behind it?"

"The usual bunch. Pauline Babcock and her husband and all her cronies. Dorothy Purdue has convinced Leland that their pharmacy will go belly-up if their customers lose their jobs, and he's agitating all the other local merchants. Rumors are feeding on rumors.''

''Damn.'' Dan put down his knife and fork and stared out the window at the Saturday afternoon traffic around the square. It wouldn't surprise him to learn that Martin was behind the rumors. He'd used the local gossips to his advantage before.

Dan applied himself to his steak again and made no comment, but he turned the matter over in his mind. Lucy picked at her tuna salad and left him to his thoughts, but not for long.

''So, you haven't mentioned Debra,'' she said, deftly changing the subject. ''How is that going?''

Dan's mouth twisted. Before she'd dropped her little bombshell he'd been wondering how long it would be before his mother got around to this. She wanted him to get married, and took every opportunity to nudge him in that direction.

Since he'd reached the point in his life when he was ready to settle down, he didn't mind. Lately he'd been seeing a lot of Debra Karnes, hoping she might be the one.

''It's not. I broke it off with her a few weeks ago.''

''Well, thank the Lord for that.''

Dan blinked. ''I thought you liked Debra.''

''I do. She's a nice young woman, and I'm sure she'll make some man a good wife, but not you. She's bland as dishwater and too meek. She'd bore you silly in a month. What you need is someone with spunk and sass.'' She waited a beat, then sent him a sly look. ''Someone like, say...Maggie Malone.''

Dan stared. His mother's keen insight and intuitiveness never failed to astound him. Somehow she had hit on his exact reason for breaking off with Debra.

On the surface she'd seemed ideal. They came from similar blue-collar backgrounds. She was attractive and sweet-natured, and easy to be with, a perfectly nice woman.

Then, during the week after Maggie returned to Ruby Falls they'd gone out twice, and he'd realized that if he had to spend the rest of his life with her he would go quietly out of his mind.

So he had ended it. Debra had cried, but it was the honorable thing to do. It just wasn't fair to any woman to compare her with Maggie, and he'd finally realized he'd been doing that during most of their last two evenings together.

Maggie had the kind of looks that could stop a man's heart, but it was more than that. Debra had no sparkle, no sass, no wicked sense of humor or pugnacious courage. Hell, compared to Maggie, she *was* dull as dishwater.

Though he was beginning to suspect that Maggie's wild reputation was largely undeserved, he still wasn't thrilled about the attraction he felt for her. It was too powerful. Hell, he hadn't felt desire like this since he was a randy teenager, trying to seduce Mary Lou Hunsacker in the back seat of his '52 Chevy. Worse, he imagined more than half the men in the world felt the same pull of lust every time they looked at Maggie's picture.

"Look, Mom, don't go getting any ideas about

me and Maggie, okay? Trust me, it just isn't going to happen.''

"Why not?"

"Why not? For Pete's sake, Mom, we come from different worlds."

"What nonsense. She's a local girl."

"Trust me, Maggie may have started out in Ruby Falls, but she's moved light-years beyond anything this town has to offer, including me. Not only is she Harvard-educated, successful, wealthy and gorgeous, she's the boss's daughter, for Christ's sake."

"So are you telling me that Maggie is a snob?"

"No, I didn't say that. Look, I'm proud of what I've made of myself and I like my life. I like living in Ruby Falls, I like my job and being near my family. But I'm strictly a small-town, working stiff. Supermodels like Maggie Malone are so far out of my reach they might as well be on another planet. So forget any ideas about Maggie and me, okay?"

"Oh, all right. But I still think you're wrong."

Dan didn't agree, but the sad truth was, as long as Maggie was around, every other woman paled in comparison. Which was why he'd made the decision to put his social life on hold until she was gone.

That shouldn't take long. If Maggie managed to pull off a miracle and get Malone's back on its feet, after Jacob passed on, no doubt she'd put a competent person in charge and flit back to New York and the sophisticated life-style she was used to leading.

Then he could get on with his own life.

The bell over the café door tinkled. Lucy sat facing that way, and instantly her eyes lit up. "Well, now, look who's here."

From the abnormal silence that spread through the café, Dan knew before he craned his neck around the edge of the high-backed booth whom he would see.

Maggie stood just inside the door, next to the Please Wait to Be Seated sign. The booth right behind the one he and his mother occupied was empty and so were a couple of stools at the counter and a table, but Mabel Jean, the owner of the City Café, and Dinah, the day-shift waitress, both stayed behind the counter and ignored her.

"Go ask her to join us," Lucy insisted.

"Mom—"

"Go on."

With a resigned sigh, Dan tossed his napkin on the table and slid out of the booth.

"Hey, Red." Something like relief flickered in Maggie's eyes as he strolled toward her. "The place is kinda crowded today. Why don't you come join us?"

Maggie cast a quick look at the vacant places and sent him a droll look. "Yes, so I see. Thanks, sugar, I believe I wi— Wait a minute. We? You're here with someone?"

"Yeah, come meet her."

"Oh, uh…no, on second thought—"

"C'mon, Red, she won't bite. I promise."

Maggie tried to dig in her heels, but he grasped her arm and frog-marched her past the empty booth. "Mom, meet Maggie Malone. Maggie, this is Lucy Garrett, my mother."

For the first time since he'd known her Maggie seemed at a loss. For an instant she looked as though she didn't know whether to be relieved or horrified, but true to form, she recovered quickly.

Flashing a dazzling smile, she extended her hand. "Mrs. Garrett, how nice to meet you."

The women exchanged a few pleasantries, but when Lucy invited her to sit down Maggie shook her head.

"Thank you, but I've already eaten. Anyway, I don't want to intrude on your lunch with your son."

"Nonsense. You're not intruding at all. Sit."

"No, really, I just dropped in for a cup of coffee. I'm killing time while Leland refills one of Daddy's prescriptions," she said, with a vague wave toward Purdue's Pharmacy on the opposite side of the square.

"You might as well give in, Red. Mom doesn't take no for an answer. Anyway, I'm sure you can handle a piece or two of Mabel Jean's chocolate pie with that coffee. C'mon, scoot in," he ordered, and all but stuffed her into the booth, then slid in beside her.

Dan signaled to Mabel Jean. She didn't looked happy about waiting on Maggie, but she didn't dare refuse him.

To Dan's amazement, Maggie seemed ill at ease with his mother. She was polite and pleasant, but she squirmed on the padded vinyl seat, and he noticed a slight tremor in her hand. Most telling of all, she didn't behave in her usual breezy manner. And she didn't flirt with him once.

Lucy wasted no time launching a deft interrogation, which both exasperated and amused Dan. While Maggie polished off a huge piece of pie, his mother peppered her with chatter, now and then slipping in seemingly innocent questions. Within ten minutes she managed to pry more personal information out of Maggie than he'd learned in the five weeks that she'd been home.

Most interesting of all, she got Maggie to reveal that she wasn't in a relationship, and that she'd never been seriously involved. When Lucy mentioned the newspaper stories about her attending movie premieres or glittery parties on the arm of some actor or rock star or pro athlete, Maggie laughed.

"I hate to tell you this—I know that people around here find those stories and photos titillating—but the truth is, most are pure fabrication. Those that weren't were dates that were arranged either by one or both of our press agents for the publicity."

"Really?" Lucy imbued the one word with such abject disappointment that Dan nearly rolled his eyes. He had a hunch what his mother was up to, and despite her long face he knew the sly little devil wasn't in the least disappointed.

"Actually, I don't date much at all," Maggie continued. "I know it doesn't seem like it to most people, but modeling involves a lot of hard work and long hours. You can't party all night and appear at a photo shoot at dawn looking your best. Anyway, I prefer a quiet life, so most evenings I stay home. Between you and me, life in the fast lane is incredibly boring."

"Imagine that. A pretty girl like you, and no young man to keep you company," Lucy said guilelessly. "Maybe you just aren't suited for the big city."

Maggie gave another throaty laugh that sent a prickling sensation skittering over Dan's skin. "You may be right." She glanced out the window, and those famous green eyes swept over the stone courthouse and the quaint shops lining the square. "I know I've missed this place like crazy."

"Do you think you'll ever move back here?"

Maggie pulled her gaze away from the scene outside the window and shot Lucy a surprised look. "I already have. I'll keep my apartment in New York for when I go on modeling assignments, at least for as long as my career lasts, but from now on, Ruby Falls is home."

Dan jolted as though he'd been startled awake from a sound sleep. He couldn't believe she was serious.

The bell over the door tinkled again.

"Uh-oh, here comes trouble," his mother muttered when two women entered the café, chattering to each other ninety to nothing.

"Tully says she's making changes right and left and questioning everything. Says she marches through the place like she owns it."

"Well, it's a disgrace, if you ask me."

"Be right with you," Mabel Jean, called out, hustling toward the back of the café with a tray loaded with food.

"Don't worry about us, Mabel Jean. Dorothy and I will just take this booth right here," Pauline Babcock called back, and she and Dorothy Purdue settled into the booth behind Dan and Maggie.

"Anyway, as I was saying, it's just scandalous the way that girl is taking advantage of her daddy's weakened condition. Everyone in town knows that Jacob never would have let her come in and take over the way she has if he'd been in any condition to stop her. Why, he wouldn't have let her set foot on the property. He washed his hands of that wild hellion when he tossed her out. And I say, good riddance."

Lucy bit her lower lip and sent an uncomfortable look from Maggie to Dan. Maggie sat perfectly still, her gaze fixed on the empty plate in front of her.

"Some are saying that his mind has been affected by all that medication he's taking," Pauline confided.

"Could be. I know my Leland fills prescriptions for him all the time. Maggie came in just a little while ago to pick up another one."

"That fancy-schmancy car of hers is still parked in front of your store. I can see it from here."

Dorothy chuckled. "Leland has already filled the prescription, but he's making her wait. He told her he was out of the drug and waiting for a pharmaceutical order that was being delivered from Tyler."

"Good for Leland. That girl is gettin' too big for her britches. It's time somebody took her down a notch or two."

The two women shared a laugh, and beside him Dan could feel Maggie's anger growing. Out of the corner of his eye he saw that her hands were gripping the edge of the table and she'd clenched her jaw.

"Easy, Red," he whispered. "They're just a couple of harpies, flapping their gums."

She glanced at him and attempted a smile, but it was strained.

"You know, if Jacob refuses to oust Maggie, maybe Lily and Laurel could be persuaded to have him declared mentally incompetent. That way they could put Martin back in charge."

"Anyone would be better than that awful girl. Did you see *The Sports Gazette* magazine where she was parading around in those skimpy swimsuits? They were downright indecent. I don't know how she had the nerve."

"Mmm, I know. Shameful."

"That's it." Leaning across the table toward Lucy, Maggie murmured, "It was nice meeting you, Mrs. Garrett, but please excuse me. I have to go now."

"Certainly, my dear. I understand."

She elbowed Dan. "Move, so I can get out."

"C'mon, Red, don't leave," he whispered back. "Don't let those two gossips drive you out."

"Leave? I'm not leaving. I'm going to go tie two wagging tongues together. Now, get out of my way, handsome, before I have to hurt you."

Looking into those flashing emerald eyes, Dan grinned and stood up.

Dorothy glanced up, but she went right on talking—until Maggie slid out of the booth.

"Heard that— Oh! Oh, dear." Turning red to the tops of her ears, Dorothy Purdue could only stare at

Maggie, her mouth opening and closing like a banked fish, not a sound emerging.

"What? What's the mat— Maggie!" Pauline gasped.

The silence returned as every customer in the café stopped what they were doing to watch the confrontation. Across the aisle, Emory Perkins, Harold Duff and Alvin Dooley, three farmers who met at the café each day to complain about crop prices and cuss the government, gaped like young boys at a peep show.

"Hello, ladies." Smiling pleasantly, Maggie turned her attention on Pauline. "You know, Mrs. Babcock, I'm curious about something. Maybe you can clear it up for me. Neither you, your husband nor any of your sons work for Malone's. And since you're not a relative of ours, I know you don't own stock. So why are you so concerned about our company?"

"I...well...uh...my nephew, Steven, works there."

"Ah, I see. And your nephew...that would be Steven Muckleroy, your sister's boy, right?" At Pauline's nod, she went on in the same curious tone. "So tell me, has Steven ever missed a paycheck?"

"Well, no—"

"I thought not. Has he ever gotten paid late?"

"Not that I know of, but—"

"Then what is your gripe? Kindly explain to me why you think you have the right to stick your long nose in the Malone family business."

Beginning to regain her composure, Pauline puffed out her scrawny chest and jutted her chin. "Everyone knows that the economy of the whole town is tied to the cannery. You can't blame us for being concerned. We've heard that if things get any worse, Malone's will have to sell to Bountiful Foods. Why should we trust our futures and the future of Ruby Falls to a reckless hellion like you?''

"All right, listen up, people," Maggie said, raising her voice and turning to address everyone in the café. "Since the grapevine works so efficiently around here, I want you all to spread the word. For the record, Malone's will not be sold to Bountiful Foods or any other firm. Nor are we going belly-up."

"You say that, but I have it on good authority that your profits are dropping monthly, and if the trend continues you may not be able to meet payroll," Pauline interjected with belligerent smugness.

"Don't worry, Mrs. Babcock. We'll meet payroll, and any other expenses we incur. If I have to, I'll cover them out of my own pocket."

A murmur of surprise ran through the café, but Maggie wasn't finished with the two gossipy women.

"Now that we have that settled, let's talk about that swimsuit layout you ladies found so offensive. I don't think everyone agrees with you on that.

"Take Dooley, here," she drawled, moving across the aisle to stand by the table where the three farmers sat gaping. Smiling seductively, Maggie winnowed her crimson-tipped fingers through what little hair was left on top of Dooley's head and curled the wispy tuft around and around her forefinger. "I'll bet you weren't offended by those pictures, were you, Dooley?''

Alvin Dooley's Adam's apple bobbed like a cork on a fishing line, and he turned the color of a tomato all the way to the top of his nearly bald pate, but he gaze at Maggie with a stupefied expression and shook his head. "No, ma'am, I surely wasn't."

"Thank you, sugar." Maggie released Dooley's hair and planted a kiss on his weathered brow before turning back to the women. "There, you see? You ladies see evil where others see beauty."

"You were practically naked!"

"Well, you know what they say," Maggie drawled. "If you've got it, flaunt it."

Dorothy gasped and Pauline's mouth drew up in a tight pucker, as though she'd tasted a lemon, but Maggie ignored them both and headed for the door.

"Excuse me, all," she said over her shoulder. "I'd like to stay and chat some more, but I'm afraid I can't. Now I have to go kick Leland's sorry ass."

"There, you see? Now *that's* the kind of feisty woman you need."

Lucy's emphatic statement barely registered on Dan. He stared out the window, a grin slowly spreading over his face as he watched Maggie head for Purdue's Pharmacy on the opposite side of the square, strutting her stuff.

Thirteen

The grandfather clock in the hall struck midnight as Maggie climbed the stairs, bone weary and sick at heart.

The night before, someone had poured antifreeze into the soil around eleven of their best trees, killing them. Now she had no choice. Tomorrow morning she had to tell her father about all the incidents, and that she suspected someone was trying to drive them out of business.

After confronting Pauline and Dorothy in the café two weeks ago, she had been so sure that whoever was responsible for the vandalism would back off, once word got out of how committed she was to keeping Malone's going. Then three mornings ago she went to get her car and discovered that someone had entered the garage and slashed all four tires on her Viper.

She'd had the tires replaced without mentioning the slashing to anyone, not even Dan. Still, it gave her the willies to think that someone had sneaked into the garage while the family slept and done such a thing.

At the top of the stairs, Maggie tiptoed past her parents' room and slipped into her own at the end of the hall. She dropped her car keys and purse on the dresser and raised both arms over her head. In midstretch a curious lump in the middle of her bed caught her attention, and she paused.

Puzzled, she walked over to the bed and tossed back the bedspread and top sheet. A strangled cry tore from her throat before she could stifle the sound.

Clamping a hand over her mouth, she jumped back, staring in horror at the dead rat that lay in the middle of the floral sheet.

Maggie's gaze flew to the door. She waited, half expecting her mother or Charley to come running in to find out what was wrong. After a few seconds, when no one appeared, she forced herself to look back at the bed.

"Oh God, oh God, oh God."

Someone had invaded her room and put that filthy creature in her bed. Who would do such a thing? And why? It had to be someone they knew, someone who was welcome in their home.

The thought made Maggie sick, and she pressed her palm against her churning stomach.

She had to get rid of the carcass. She didn't want the whole household upset. If her father found out that someone hated her this much he might reconsider their agreement and tell her to leave.

Heart pounding, Maggie edged close to the bed. Doing her best not to look at the revolting creature, she tossed the bedspread back all the way, stripped off the top sheet, then quickly unfastened the corners of the bottom sheet, gathered them together and ran to the window. Working furiously and trying not to be sick, she raised the sash, unhooked the screen and tossed the rat out into the side yard.

Dropping the contaminated sheet on the floor, Maggie wrapped her arms around her middle and shuddered over and over again. Finally, when she'd gained a measure of control, she made herself gather up the sheets and stuff them into the hamper in her bathroom.

She had just shaken out the fresh bottom sheet when the telephone rang.

Maggie gasped and jumped, but she pounced on the phone before the ring could sound again and wake her father. Who in the world? She glanced at the bedside clock. It was twenty minutes after midnight.

"Hello."

"Is this Maggie Malone?" a gravelly voice asked.

She gripped the receiver tighter, her heart pounding. "Yes. Who is this?"

"Rowdy Williams, down at Rowdy's Bar and Grill. I'm real sorry to be calling so late, Miss Malone, but I think you'd better come down here and get your little sister."

"I..." Her gaze fell on the bed, and she turned away and raked her shaking hand through her hair. "Uh, what?"

"I said you need to come down to my place and get your baby sister."

"Jo Beth? She's *there?*"

"Yes'm. She came in here a while ago, drunk as Cooter Brown. I refused to serve her and took her car keys away so she couldn't drive, but she's pitching a fit to have 'em back. I sure as heck don't want to call the sheriff. I know your daddy wouldn't appreciate that a'tall, but if somebody don't come fetch her soon, I'm gonna have to.''

''I'll be right there.''

Clamping down on her frazzled nerves, Maggie grabbed her purse and keys and on trembling legs retraced her steps as quietly and quickly as she could. She prayed as she crept passed her parents' room that the telephone hadn't woken them. Downstairs, tiptoeing through the kitchen, she kept an eye on Ida Lou's door, half expecting to see a light come on at any second. Once she'd let herself out the back door she took off for the garage at an unsteady run.

Resisting the urge to floor the Viper, Maggie eased the car down the drive past the house, all the while railing silently against her sister.

What in heaven's name was wrong with that girl? Sure, at Jo Beth's age she had done some stupid things herself, but their father hadn't been dying then. Besides, Jo Beth had always been Jacob's little princess. Dammit, how could she pull a stunt like this? And on her birthday?

Maggie smacked her forehead with the heel of her hand. ''Duh! She turned eighteen today. *That's* why she went out and got plastered—just to show everyone that she could. You should've seen this coming, Mag,'' she muttered to herself as she approached the end of the drive.

Jo Beth had fidgeted throughout her birthday dinner, and as soon as Charley had carried their father upstairs, Jo Beth had dashed out to celebrate with her friends.

"If you hadn't been anxious to escape yourself, you might have caught on," Maggie scolded.

Because it had been a special occasion, they had all been there, even Laurel and Martin. Once their father had retired for the night and Jo Beth had left, rather than endure Martin's company, she had gone back to the office.

Maggie had almost reached the road when Dan's truck came around the curve and turned into the drive. Even as upset as she was, she wondered whom he'd been out with, and she experienced a little pang at the thought.

Maggie slowed and pulled over for him to pass, but when they drew even Dan signaled for her to stop and he did the same.

"What's wrong? Where are you going at this time of night?" he demanded, leaning out the window. "Is it Jacob?"

"No. He's fine. Sleeping, I hope." She hesitated to reveal her sister's stupidity, but then, what did it matter. Very little went on in their family that this man didn't know about, anyway. "It's Jo Beth. I just got a call from Rowdy's. She's there, drunk and belligerent. I'm on my way to get her. I just hope I can sneak her back into the house without Momma and Daddy knowing."

"I'll go with you. You might need some help persuading her."

Maggie wasn't about to argue. She was too grateful for his support and his company. After finding that nasty little surprise in her bed, she still felt shaky and was in no shape to play Superwoman.

In any case, he didn't give her a chance to refuse.

Dan reversed out of the drive and waited, and when Maggie shot out onto the road his pickup fell in behind the Viper and stayed on her bumper all the way to Rowdy's.

When they entered the bar Rowdy looked up from drying a beer glass. He nodded toward the opposite end of the bar, where Jo Beth sat swaying on a stool and making eyes at a biker type in black leather pants and vest and no shirt.

Located on the main highway, Rowdy's Bar attracted a lot of people who were just passing through. One look told Maggie this guy was definitely not a local.

The man looked to be about thirty, with long, dirty hair and a beard. Tattoos covered both arms from shoulder to wrist. An earring pierced one eyebrow, and beneath the leather vest another glinted in his right nipple when he moved.

Maggie slipped her hand inside her purse and gripped the stun gun she had started carrying after that frightening episode in the orchard and headed that way.

The usual Friday night crowd filled the bar. People stared as she wound her way through the patrons, and a few old acquaintances called greetings. Maggie waved and smiled, but she didn't stop to talk.

The man talking to Jo Beth glanced up at Maggie's approach, and his eyes widened. Immediately a wolfish look settled over his face.

"Well now, hell-*lo*, gorgeous."

Attempting to see who had caught his eye, Jo Beth twisted around on the stool and nearly fell off.

When she saw Maggie she scowled. "Whad're you doin' here?"

"Hey, don't I know you?"

"No." Trying to ignore the three studs piercing the man's tongue, Maggie picked up her sister's purse from the bar and hooked it on her shoulder with her own, then slipped her arm around the girl's waist. "Come along, honey. Time to go home."

"No, I don't wanna go home. An' you can't make me. I'm eighteen now, ya know."

"Yes, I know."

"Hey, I *do* know you from somewhere."

"Naw, you jush think you do. Thish is my big-shot supermodel sithter," Jo Beth declared with drunken scorn.

The biker snapped his fingers. "Yeah, right. You're that Maggie Malone chick! Yo, mama, how 'bout I buy you a beer an' you and me get acquainted."

Maggie felt Dan stiffen, but before he could intervene she shot the man a blistering look. "Not interested."

"You think you're something, don'tcha. Big schel-leb-ritty." Jo Beth hiccoughed and banged her fist on the bar. "Hey! I need a drink down here!"

"It's time to take you home."

"Maggie's right. Let's go, short stuff."

With an effort, Jo Beth fastened her blurry gaze on Dan and gave him a sloppy grin. "Well lookie who's here. Hey, Dan, you know what? I'm eighteen."

"Yeah, kiddo, I know."

"Nuh-uh. Not a kid anymore. I'm all grown-up now."

"Uh-huh. But it's still time to go home," he said, lending his support on her other side as Maggie tugged the girl off the stool.

"Hey! Whadda you think you're doing? Me'n her was talkin'."

The biker, for all his brawn, was several inches shorter than Dan. Thrusting his jaw out, Dan bent over and got in his face. "Yeah, well, you're done now. Get out of our way, asshole. We're taking this girl home."

The other man tensed, and for what seemed like an eternity to Maggie the two men stared each other down, eyeball to eyeball, each spoiling for a fight. She held her breath, but finally the other man stepped back and curled his lip.

"Hell, take her. She's just a snot-nosed kid, anyway. She ain't worth it."

"I am not either a kid, you jerk. Hit 'im, Dan. Go on, punch his lights out."

"Will you pipe down?" Maggie said, and hustled the girl away and out of the bar.

Though humid and still warm for November, the night breeze was refreshing after the smoke and stale-beer smells of the bar. Maggie drew a deep breath the instant they stepped outside and firmly steered the wobbly girl across the parking lot toward her car.

"You know, sugar, not that I don't appreciate your help," she drawled over Jo Beth's head. "But the whole point of this little excursion was to get her home without Daddy ever finding out. When you and Marlon Branflakes squared off back there I could see tomorrow's headline. Maggie Malone and Sister Arrested in Barroom Brawl.''

"It never entered my mind that he wouldn't back off. That type usually does. But if he hadn't you were supposed to duck and run and haul short stuff outta there before the sheriff arrived.''

"Oh, I see. *That* was the plan.''

"I wisch you woulda hit him,'' Jo Beth mumbled. "He called me a kid.''

"Yeah, well, maybe next time. Now, in you go, short stuff.''

When they had Jo Beth buckled into the passenger seat and Maggie got behind the wheel, Dan leaned down beside the driver's window. "I'll be right behind you.'' With a thump on the Viper's hood he strode away and climbed into his pickup.

Rowdy's was about three miles north of the city limits. As Maggie turned south and headed toward Ruby Falls, she glanced over at her sister.

The girl sat with her head resting against the back of the seat, her eyes closed. Maggie pressed a button and lowered the passenger window. "If you feel sick, holler and I'll pull over.''

Jo Beth grunted.

The night air rushing in blew her dark hair every which way, but it seemed to sober her a bit. Opening her eyes, she rolled her head on the seat back and looked at Maggie.

"You think I'm dumb, don'tcha?''

"Dumb? No. A little foolish, maybe, but that's not fatal. Or permanent. At least, it doesn't have to be.''

A few seconds of silence ticked by. When Maggie glanced at her sister again she had turned sideways and sat facing her, huddled in a ball. Tears of misery rolled down her cheeks.

"Hey, don't cry, sweetie. It's not that bad."

"Ye-yes it is. I-I don't want to upset Da-Daddy. I don't. Esch-pechially not now. But he jusch makes me so ma-mad."

"Yes, he can do that, all right," Maggie agreed, but she didn't pressure her for more. Instead, she pulled a couple of tissues from the console and handed them over.

After a period of sniffling, Jo Beth dabbed at her eyes and blew her nose, then grew quiet—but only for a moment.

"I'm not going to college. I don't care what he says," she declared defiantly, as though expecting Maggie to argue. When she didn't, the girl gave her a wary look. "He hasn't given up on that, you know. He sent in all those applications himself. I keep tellin' him I'm not a brain like you, but he jush wo-won't listen. He still thinks I'm gonna run the company shum day, even though you've already taken over."

Maggie's hands tightened around the steering wheel. *Well, what did you expect, Mag? He said it was just a temporary arrangement.*

"I won't do it. I *can't*. I'm like Momma, I don't have a head for business and math and all that kinda boring stuff. No matter what Daddy says, I'm gonna be an actress."

Maggie sighed. "Jo Beth, I hate to say this, but I have to agree with Daddy."

"*What!* Oh, thas so unfair! You followed your dream an' went to New York an' became a model, even though it broke Momma's heart. But I can't follow my dream? That sucks!"

Maggie winced. She had not planned to become a model at all. It had not been a dream, but a nightmare that had sent her scurrying to New York seven years ago. Her little sister seemed to have conveniently forgotten that fact, but she didn't bother to point it out to her. Instead, she said gently, "Ah, but if you'll recall, I had already finished college when I went to New York."

"I don' care. I'm not wasting four years of my life on somethin' I have no intenshun of doing."

"Look, I don't mean you shouldn't pursue an acting career, if that's really what you want. I'm just saying it would be smart to get an education first so that if it doesn't work out, you'll have something to fall back on.

"Go to college, but choose one with a strong drama department so that you can learn the craft. That way you'll satisfy Daddy by getting a degree—maybe not in business, but in something that will prepare you for life. At the same time, you'll be getting experience and honing your talent so that when you do give show business a try, you'll have a better chance of success."

A glance at her sister revealed that a contemplative frown had replaced the girl's belligerent expression, but how much of what she'd said had penetrated Jo Beth's alcohol-befuddled brain was questionable.

"So how does that sound to you?"

"I donno."

Turning into their driveway, Maggie felt an urgent need to convince Jo Beth, aware that she might not have another chance to talk to her this way. "You don't have to decide tonight. Just promise me that you'll think about it. Okay?"

Jo Beth again sent her a blurry-eyed look of suspicion. "Wha's it to you, anyway?"

Maggie brought the car to a stop at the front of the house and glanced in the rear mirror at Dan's headlights coming up behind them. She looked at her sister through the dimness and put her hand on the girl's arm. "Believe it or not, I do care about you. I love you, sis."

Jo Beth blinked owlishly at her.

Dan opened the passenger door, and the moment passed.

"Everything okay?"

"Yes," Maggie said, and climbed from the car.

He helped guide Jo Beth as far as the front door, but Maggie declined his offer to carry her to her room.

"The fewer people tromping around upstairs, the less chance of waking Momma and Daddy. I can take it from here, thanks," she whispered. "Oh, and Dan," she added when he started to leave.

He turned back and cocked one eyebrow. "Yes?"

Maggie gazed at him through the darkness. He was so rock steady and reliable, so strong, and she thought how wonderful it would be to put her head on that broad chest and unload, to tell him her worries and fears, to share with him that someone had slashed her tires and put a rat in her bed, and how violated that made her feel. To feel his arms around her.

"Thanks for going with me."

For several seconds he returned her gaze, his pale eyes intense and unfathomable, glittering in the darkness of the porch. Finally he nodded. "No problem."

Then he loped down the steps and strode away, and Maggie sighed.

Though the going was a bit wobbly, they managed fairly well until they reached the top of the stairs and Jo Beth let out a groan.

"I'm gonna be sick," she gasped.

"Shh. You'll wake everyone."

"Ooooh!"

"Hold on, hold on," Maggie whispered urgently. "We're almost to your room."

"Oh! Oh! Here it comes!"

Half carrying, half dragging her, Maggie shoved her sister into her bedroom and ran her to the adjoining bathroom. They barely made it in time.

Like a collapsing sack of feed, Jo Beth sank to her knees in front of the commode and hung over the rim.

"That's it. Get it all out. You'll feel better when you're done," Maggie crooned. She held the girl's dark hair back with one hand and cupped her forehead with the other while she lost the contents of her stomach in a series of violent and noisy convulsions.

Through it all, every few seconds Maggie glanced over her shoulder, worrying about whether she'd shut the bedroom door, worrying that Jo Beth's loud retching and moaning would reach their parents' room. Lily, particularly, had ears like a hawk whenever one of her chicks was ill.

"Ooooh, I'm gonna die," Jo Beth moaned. "I'm gonna die right here, on the bathroom floor with my head in a toilet."

"You're not going to die. You're just going to wish you would. Now, look up. That's a girl." Hooking her finger beneath Jo Beth's chin, Maggie tilted her head up and wiped her face with a cool cloth. Then she handed her a paper cup filled with water. "Swish and spit. There you go. Good girl. Now again."

When Jo Beth was done she helped her to her feet.

"I feel awful," the girl groaned.

"I know. You're probably going to be sick several more times before morning."

"Don't *say* that."

"Sorry, but that's the price you pay. I'll put a plastic trash can beside your bed. Now, let's get you out of these clothes and into a nightgown." With her arm around Jo Beth, she gently turned to guide her back into the bedroom but stopped short when they came face-to-face with their father.

"Daddy!"

Somehow he looked both fierce and pathetically fragile, standing there in the doorway, leaning heavily on Charley Minze for support, his face gray from the effort. Lily hovered behind the two men, pale and upset and wringing her hands.

"Daddy, I know this looks bad, but please don't be too hard on h—"

"How *could* you?"

Maggie blinked. "Pardon me?"

The male nurse gave her a sympathetic look, and belatedly she realized the raw fury in her father's voice and eyes was directed not at Jo Beth, but at her.

"You took that child out carousing and got her drunk."

"No! That's not—"

"I was beginning to believe you'd changed. You seemed to be working hard, taking your responsibilities seriously. I should have known better. You just couldn't resist falling back into your old ways, could you?"

Maggie's chin came up. "Before you start throwing accusations around, you might get the facts. I didn't—"

"No. I don't want to hear any of your lies and excuses."

"Daddy, you've got it all wro—" Jo Beth started to shake her head, then groaned and twisted back around to hang over the commode again.

"Oh, my poor baby." Lily squeezed past the two men and Maggie to tend to her youngest daughter.

"What in the world is going on in here?" Nan strode into the room, tightening the sash on her robe. "Doesn't anyone in this house know what time it is?"

"Stay out of this, Nan," Jacob ordered, never taking his eyes from Maggie. "I warned you what would happen if you caused trouble. I will give you until noon tomorrow to pack your things and leave this house. And this time, don't come back."

"Jacob!" Nan and Lily gasped in unison, but he ignored them both.

"Take me back to my room, Charley. I've seen enough."

"Jacob Malone, have you lost your mind?" Nan started after him, but Maggie put a hand on her arm and stopped her.

"No. Let him go, Aunt Nan."

"But, Maggie—"

"Don't worry." Maggie's gaze followed her father's slow progress down the hall. Her expression remained calm, but inside the old hurt churned.

Shaking off the pain, she managed a weak smile for her aunt. "We'll get it all sorted out in the morning. By then Jo Beth will be able to tell him what really happened. Now, why don't you and Momma go back to bed? I'll take care of Jo Beth."

Lily would have argued, but Nan took charge and guided her out, reminding her that Charley probably needed her assistance getting Jacob settled again.

When they had gone Maggie helped her sister get into her nightgown and tucked her into bed. She placed a cool wet cloth in a decorative dish on the nightstand, along with a glass of water, and put a plastic trash can beside the bed. When she was done she hung Jo Beth's discarded clothes in the closet.

"There, I think you're all set." She glanced at the empty twin bed next to the one in which Jo Beth lay moaning and thought of what had awaited her in her own. "You know, if you'd like, I could sleep in here tonight. Just in case you get sick again."

Jo Beth opened one bleary eye. For an instant Maggie thought she saw relief there, but her sister's expression turned sullen and she closed her eye again and shrugged. "Makes no difference to me. I can take care of myself."

"Fine, then I'll see you in the morning."

She turned to leave, but her steps faltered when a familiar photograph caught her eye. It lay next to an open album on her sister's desk. Curious, Maggie walked over for a closer look.

The picture had been cut from a magazine. It was a full-page ad for Eve Cosmetics showing a close-up of her own face, with her trademark provocative smile and laughing eyes. She'd done the shoot months ago.

Maggie stared at the open album. "What is this?" she asked, but Jo Beth didn't answer, and when she glanced over her shoulder she saw that her sister was asleep.

She looked back at the album and hesitated, but curiosity won out. Slowly, she paged backward, all the way to the beginning. Her amazement grew with every page she turned. Each contained clippings of the various ads that she'd done during the past year.

On the shelf above the desk, Maggie noticed other albums. On closer inspection, she found that they were all filled with her clippings, and each one bore a number, one through six. She flipped over the album on the desk and saw that it was labeled with the number seven. One for every year that she'd been modeling.

Maggie stared, dumbfounded. Her little sister had been keeping scrapbooks of her career. It appeared she had a copy of every photo ad she had ever done, plus clippings and pictures from gossip columns and society pages of various newspapers.

Maggie looked back at the sleeping girl. Why, Jo Beth Malone, you little fraud. All that antagonism is nothing more than a defensive shield.

But it was a defense that Maggie understood all too well. Loving and not being loved in return hurt. It was easier to pretend you didn't care.

Maggie ran her fingers over the scrapbooks and glanced at Jo Beth again, then quietly left the room. Five minutes later she returned, dressed in her nightgown, and climbed into the twin bed beside her sister's.

Fourteen

The next morning, Maggie returned from an early run and rousted the hungover girl out of bed at seven, ignoring her groans and whines and claims of imminent death.

"C'mon, get a move on, little sister."

"Ooooh, I can't. My head. My head."

"Yeah, well, that's what happens when you overindulge in that 'who hit John.'"

"I'm dying, I tell you. I gotta go back to bed."

"Oh, no you don't. I need to get to work, but you have some explaining to do before I can. I did my best to shield you, but I'm not taking the fall for you on this one, kiddo. There's too much at stake. So move it."

"Okay, okay. I'm going. Just stop shouting, will you?"

With the advancing season, breakfast had been moved back into the dining room a few weeks before. The whole family was already there when Maggie and Jo Beth arrived downstairs.

However, Jacob was no more in a mood to listen than he'd been the previous night.

He watched in grim-lipped disapproval as his youngest daughter eased herself into a chair with excruciating care, propped her elbows on the table and cradled her head between her palms. Slowly, in a voice that reflected her misery, she recited her sins of the night before.

"So don't blame Maggie. She had nothing to do with it," she ended in a reedy whisper.

"If I find out you're lying to protect your sister—"

"She isn't lying," Dan said from the doorway, and every head swiveled in that direction. "I went with Maggie to Rowdy's to bring Jo Beth home."

He ambled into the dining room and poured himself a cup of coffee from the pot on the sideboard, then sat down across from Maggie and looked at Jacob. "She was just trying to help."

Jacob stared at him. "I see. Well, that, uh…that does put a different light on things."

"Yeah," Jo Beth mumbled, still holding her head. "Instead of ragging on Maggie, you oughta be thanking her. We had a talk on the way home last night, and she convinced me that I should go to college."

Maggie shot the girl a startled look. Considering Jo Beth's condition at the time, she was surprised that she remembered their conversation, and she certainly hadn't had time to think it over. Jo Beth had to have made a snap decision just now.

"Oh, thank heaven," Lily exclaimed.

As Jacob and Nan added their approval, Maggie eyed her little sister. She couldn't help but be suspicious. Had the announcement been an attempt to help get Maggie back in Jacob's good graces? Or

had it been merely a clever ploy to take the heat off
herself?

"Aaah. Please, y'all, keep it down, will ya?" Jo
Beth begged, gripping her head tightly. "And before
you get too excited, you might as well know, I'm
not going to study business. I'm going to major in
theater arts."

"What? Now, see here—"

"Easy, brother," Nan cautioned. "The important
thing is, she's going to college. At this point I think
you'd be wise to just smile and count your bless-
ings."

Jacob didn't like it. He glared and huffed, but
after a moment he resigned himself and agreed. He
even congratulated Jo Beth and told her that he was
proud of her for making the right choice.

"And it appears that I owe you my thanks for
talking some sense into her, Katherine." He cleared
his throat. "I, uh...I also owe you an apology. I
shouldn't have blamed you for your sister's folly.
That was unfair of me, and I'm sorry."

Maggie stared at him. Never once had her father
ever apologized to her for anything.

Realizing suddenly that her mouth was hanging
open she snapped it shut and murmured, "That's,
uh...that's all right."

Maggie had no idea what she ate or how or if she
responded to the conversation around her. She knew
it was foolish to be so affected by a simple apology.
It was long overdue—a mere crumb, really. Nevertheless, she couldn't remember ever being so happy.

When she and Dan met with Jacob in the family
room after breakfast and told him about the vandal-

ism and their suspicions, not even his explosive reaction could dim the glow of happiness deep inside her.

More than she dreaded her father's anger, Maggie hated to burden him with bad news. In the two months that she'd been home he had steadily declined.

They had taken him back to the hospital twice more to have his lungs drained, and each time it took him longer to bounce back, and never as much as the time before.

He was so weak he required assistance merely to stand. Consequently he spent most of his time in bed or propped up on a mound of pillows in his recliner in the family room.

Her mother fussed over him and daily Ida Lou tried to tempt him with his favorite foods, but his appetite was almost nonexistent. He'd lost so much weight his skin seemed to hang on his bones and his complexion had such a deathly gray cast it wrung Maggie's heart every time she looked at him.

Bit by bit, he was slipping away from them, and there was nothing they could do about it. For Maggie the knowledge was especially painful, knowing that the hope she'd carried in her heart all of her life would die with him.

However, no matter how much the insidious disease ravaged Jacob's body, nothing could rob him of his mind or his spirit, and when his anger came, Maggie was braced for it.

"Dammit, why the hell didn't you come to me with this before?" he demanded after scanning the list of incidents that she'd compiled.

"What was the point? You wouldn't have believed me. Anyway, at first it was just a suspicion. I had no proof that the incidents were anything more than a string of incredible bad luck. Now there's no longer any doubt. It appears whoever is doing this has decided that he wants us to know we're under attack."

Jacob shook his head. "It's still difficult to believe. The people in this area depend on the cannery for a living. Why in God's name would anyone do this?"

"The Tolivers aren't exactly fond of us," Maggie offered.

"Maybe. But they've hated us for over seventy years. Why go on the offensive now?"

"Maybe they heard about the offer from Bountiful Foods. I'm sure they'd be tickled if we were forced to sell out."

"True. Still, I can't see them stooping to something like this unless they stood to gain, and gain big. The Tolivers never stir themselves to do anything unless there's a profit involved."

"There's always a ticked-off ex-employee," Dan said, speaking up for the first time. "Someone with an imagined grudge."

"Hmm. Maybe."

Maggie exchanged a quick look with Dan, then cleared her throat. "Martin seems anxious for us to sell."

"What are you saying? That Martin is out to ruin us? Don't be ridiculous, girl. He's a vice president, and his wife will be a major shareholder soon. That would be cutting off his nose to spite his face. Martin's not the brightest bulb in the box, but he's not stupid.''

"Yet he has repeatedly urged you to take Bountiful's offer.''

"Only because he wants us to salvage what we can before it's too late. And he certainly wouldn't do anything that would devalue the company before the sale.''

Jacob scowled and pointed a bony finger at Maggie. "Just because you resent Martin isn't any reason to make unfounded accusations. Do you have a shred of evidence linking him to even one of these acts?''

Maggie exhaled a long sigh. "No, none.'' The truth was, Martin had been out of town almost every time something had occurred.

"I thought not. Any more theories?''

She shook her head. She didn't dare mention Jo Beth. Anyway, she had all but ruled out her sister.

"All right, so we have no idea who's doing this,'' Dan said. "The question is, what do we do about it?''

"I don't think we have any choice,'' Maggie replied. "We have to hire twenty-four-hour security to patrol the orchards and the cannery.''

"What? Don't be absurd. This is Ruby Falls, not New York. You expect me to guard my business from friends and neighbors? Folks around here would take that as an insult. Next thing you'll be saying, we should all lock our doors.''

Maggie thought about her slashed tires and the rat she'd found in her bed the night before, and barely suppressed a shudder. She had yet to mention either incident to anyone and had no intention of doing so. They had both seemed so…so personal, so obviously intended to frighten and degrade her. It was humiliating. Besides, she was still leery of what her father's reaction would be.

"Actually, I was going to suggest that."

"Oh, for— What's next? A moat with alligators?"

"Daddy, I know it's difficult to accept, but someone around here is behind all this, and his acts of vandalism are escalating."

"Yeah, well, you can just forget hiring any security. We can't afford to do that."

"We can't afford not to," Maggie insisted in a quiet voice.

She pulled papers from a file folder and passed them out to her father and Dan. "The top few pages are a breakdown on what the incidents have cost us so far. While they don't totally account for our plunge in profits, they are hurting us. Badly. At the back you'll find bids from three security companies, two out of Dallas and one out of Houston. As you can see, their fees for the same span of time would have been much less than the damage cost us."

"Hmm." Jacob scanned the papers. "Well, you've certainly done your homework, I'll say that for you."

He looked up and drilled her with a penetrating stare. "If this malicious mischief doesn't account for all our losses, what does?"

"I don't know yet. But I'm going to find out. I think the answer lies in the books. I can't put my finger on what exactly, but there's something that's just not quite right there.''

"Are you suggesting that someone in the office is embezzling?''

"I'm not suggesting anything yet. At this point all I can do is go with my instincts.''

She didn't bother to mention that those same instincts were telling her that Elaine Udall was somehow involved in whatever was going on.

At the moment she had no proof and no real reason to dismiss the woman, beyond disliking her intensely. Elaine was frosty and officious, and she pushed Maggie's patience to the limit, but she never quite stepped over the line into outright insubordination.

"That's why I've been going through the books after hours. If someone is doing some creative bookkeeping I don't want them to know that I'm suspicious. But I intend to find out what's going on and put a stop to it.''

"See that you do.''

"So. Do I have your okay to hire security guards?''

Jacob looked at Dan. "What's your opinion?''

"I think Maggie's right. We've taken it on the chin long enough. We don't have any choice but to protect ourselves.''

Jacob scowled, clearly uncomfortable with the idea, but finally he nodded. "All right, see to it. But don't sign any long-term contracts. If we don't see results fast, they're out.''

"Okay." Maggie stood up. "I'll get on it as soon as I get to the office. Now, if you'll excuse me.''

Maggie left the house through the French doors leading out of the family room. Through the windows, both men watched her cross the terrace with that leggy stride and lope down the steps, heading for the garage. When she was out of sight, Jacob turned to Dan.

"Well, you were right. You said that she would tell me what she suspected, and she did."

Dan frowned and shifted in his chair. "She was just waiting until she had enough proof to convince you."

"I noticed she didn't say anything about someone chasing her through the orchard, though."

"I imagine she was afraid that would upset you."

Either that, or she's afraid that it won't, Dan added silently. He suspected the latter, and that bothered him. He didn't like having such thoughts about Jacob, but he'd have to be blind not to notice the man's coolness to his oldest daughter. He'd never known Jacob to treat anyone as harshly as he did Maggie. Dan didn't understand it.

"She never worried about upsetting me in the past. Used to go out of her way to rattle my cage. I'm telling you, that girl used to pull some of the most outlandish stunts imaginable."

"Hell, Jacob, that was more than ten years ago. She's not a kid anymore. Look, I'm through doing this. Reporting on everything Maggie does makes my skin crawl. I don't know what you're worried about, anyway. She's bright and hard-working, and if you ask me, she doing a helluva good job under trying conditions."

"Maybe. You don't think she's up to something?"

"Like what, for Christ's sake?"

"Like maybe trying to wreck the business. Or steal it from her sisters."

"If she wanted to ruin the company all she had to do was sit back and do nothing. We were already in trouble and heading down a slippery slope when she took over. Remember? And how could she steal the business?"

"I don't know," Jacob mumbled. "But Maggie is smart. If there's a way, she'll figure it out."

"Look, Jacob, you're worrying for nothing. As far as I can tell, all she's guilty of is working like a Trojan to save Malone Enterprises."

"Maybe you're right. But I'm not totally convinced yet. Look, just keep your eyes open a little while longer, okay?"

"Dammit, Jacob—"

"A few more weeks, that's all. Just until I'm sure she's competent. That's not too much to ask, is it?"

Maggie turned the key in the Viper's ignition. Silence.

"No, this can't be." Frowning, she turned the key again. Again the action produced not a sound.

"No-o-o-o," she wailed, and hit the dashboard with the sides of both fists. Slumping forward, she rested her forehead against the steering wheel. "What next?"

It had been a beastly day, starting with a whining call from Val and culminating with an unpleasant clash with Elaine Udall just before quitting time for the office staff. Now, after putting in a fifteen-hour day, here it was after eleven and her car wouldn't start. Great. Just great.

"Something wrong?"

Maggie let out a squeak and jerked upright, then slumped back against the seat with her hand on her heart. "Dan—for Pete's sake, don't sneak up on me like that! You scared me half to death."

"Sorry. But I saw you sitting here with your head down and I thought I'd better see if you were okay."

"It's my car. It won't start. Barely two months old, and already it's giving me trouble."

"You got a flashlight?"

Nodding, Maggie fished the light out of the console and handed it to him.

"Good. Now pop the hood and I'll take a look. Could be it's something minor like a loose wire."

She did as he asked, then climbed out of the car and peered over his shoulder while he bent over the engine. In only seconds he straightened and slammed the hood shut. "You won't be driving this thing tonight. The wire harness to the onboard computer has been cut."

"Cut? You mean someone deliberately disabled my car?"

"Yes."

Maggie's gaze darted around the dimly lit parking area, and she unconsciously took a step closer to Dan.

Without warning, the wind began to gust.

"Oh, my." Maggie first grabbed her hair, then abandoned it to the whipping wind and fought to keep her skirt from blowing over her head.

"Looks like a front is blowing in." Dan scanned the night sky and sniffed. "Rain's coming."

"Oh, great."

"You got a coat? It's going to get cold in a hurry. You do remember what a Texas blue norther is like, don't you?"

"Of course I remember. And no, I didn't bring a coat with me. It was seventy degrees at nine o'clock. Besides, you don't have one either, so what are you on my case for?"

He gave her a wry look. "When I came back to the office after dinner I didn't plan on being here long."

"C'mon." He grasped her arm and steered her toward the orchard. "If we hustle we might make it to my place before it starts to rain."

"Where's your truck?" Maggie raised her voice to be heard over the wind, hurrying along beside him.

"At the cottage," he yelled back. "It was such a nice night when I left I decided to walk."

Lighting the way with the flashlight, Dan kept his grip on Maggie's arm and hurried her through the orchard.

"Brrr. It's getting colder by the minute."

"Yeah, let's pick up the pace."

Their long, quick strides ate up the ground. Breathing hard from the exertion and the cold, neither spoke.

They were two hundred yards shy of the clearing when the first fat raindrops splattered down.

Maggie gave a shout when several icy drops smacked her face.

"C'mon, run!" Dan grabbed her hand and they took off.

The sky opened up and the sprinkles turned into a torrent of sleet and rain. Water and ice pounded down, falling in sheets so thick they could barely see two feet in front of them. Maggie and Dan were soaked to the skin before they'd gone ten yards.

The noise was deafening. The heavy drops pounded the ground, turning the bare earth to mud. Ice crystals rattled the leaves overhead and stung their skin, and tiny particles slid down their necks and slipped beneath their clothing.

Maggie shrieked and shivered, but she kept pace with Dan's long strides.

Finally they burst into the clearing. They tore across Dan's neat patch of lawn and up the steps. The porch, though dry, offered no shelter from the freezing temperature, and they burst through the front door at top speed and slammed it shut behind them.

"Damn!" Dan spat, coming to a halt in the middle of the foyer.

"Oh! Oh, I don't be-believe it!" Dripping water, gasping for breath and shivering violently, Maggie collapsed back against the door and gave in to a fit of choking laughter.

Dan looked at her as though she'd taken leave of her senses, but before long his mouth began to twitch. Finally he bent over, braced his hands on his knees and joined her.

For several minutes they laughed like fools, relieved, exhausted, overcome with hilarity.

After a while, though, their laughter faded, and

there was only the sounds of their breathing and the ponderous ticking of the grandfather clock.

As they straightened, their gazes met and held, and the silence grew thick. Awareness vibrated in the air, stretching the silence tighter still.

A wave of gooseflesh rippled over Maggie's skin. She shivered helplessly and felt her nipples pucker.

Dan's silvery gaze dropped to her breasts, and when she glanced down she saw that her white blouse clung to her like a second skin, revealing the twin hardened nubs pushing against her lacy bra.

Her gaze snapped back to Dan's, and the heat she saw in his eyes sent another shiver through her.

Resisting the urge to clamp her hands over her breasts, she attempted a blasé smile. "We're, uh…we're soaked," she said needlessly into the awkward silence.

Dan remained silent. He started toward her, his steps slow and deliberate, his sizzling gaze locked with hers.

Maggie swallowed hard. "A-and I'm afraid we're, uh…"

Her eyes widened as Dan kept advancing. She took a step back and bumped into the door. Immediately he braced his forearms against the door on either side of her head and leaned in, pinning her with his lower body.

Shock slammed through Maggie. Following hard on its heels came electrifying desire.

First she felt the cold clamminess of wet jeans, then his searing body heat seeping through. Struggling to hold on to her train of thought, Maggie stared into those heated eyes and licked her suddenly dry lips.

"We're, uh...we're dripping all over your floor."

"Shut up, Red," Dan whispered, and covered her mouth with his.

Maggie moaned and clutched his hair with both hands. She realized with sudden blinding clarity that she had been waiting for this almost from the moment they met.

The pleasure was almost unbearable. She could not get enough of him. With an urgent little sound, she wrapped her arms around his shoulders, answering passion with passion, greedily kissing him back with a hunger that matched his own.

Without taking his lips from hers, Dan straightened and pulled her away from the door. Maggie felt his arms tighten around her, molding her upper body to his chest. Then, remotely, she felt herself being lifted and carried with her feet dangling mere inches from the floor.

When he sat her on her feet again he tore his mouth from hers and nibbled her neck while his big workman's hands worked at the tiny pearl buttons on her blouse.

Instinctively, Maggie arched her neck to give him better access. Gazing through glazed, half-closed eyes, she vaguely realized that they were in his bedroom.

"D-Dan, this is crazy."

"Insane," he agreed, nipping her earlobe.

"We can't. We mustn't..."

"I know." He kissed and nipped his way down the side of her neck. She felt her blouse fall open and his hand slipped inside and closed around her breast. Maggie moaned. An instant later she sucked in a sharp breath and shivered when his thumb swept over her nipple.

They were breathing hard, gasping, their hearts pounding.

"This is senseless," he agreed in a raspy voice. He trailed a line of nibbling kisses along her collarbone. "Foolish." His mouth slid downward over the soft swells above her bra. "A huge mistake."

"Ye-yes."

"We have to stop."

"Yes, we—" Maggie cried out as he closed his mouth over her breast and suckled her through the fine lace.

She clutched his head and arched her back, her body instinctively seeking the intense pleasure.

"Please. Oh, please!" she cried, but what she was pleading for exactly she couldn't have said.

Dan raised his head and held her away from him at arm's length. His face was flushed and his chest heaved. "I know this is reckless and unwise, but I don't want to stop. But if that's what you really want, I will."

"I..."

"Do you want to stop, Maggie?"

Want? It was the smart thing to do, the safe thing. But want?

Breathing hard, her heart thundering, she stared at the passion in his eyes and felt it pull at her, felt the same burning heat pulsing through her body. Caution and common sense went flying. She surged forward and threw herself against his chest, her arms wrapping around his neck as her mouth claimed his.

It was all the answer Dan needed.

It was as though her impulsive response opened a floodgate. They strained together, kissing greedily while they frantically worked to divest each other of their soggy clothing. Hands clutched and tugged and snatched at buttons and zippers.

Maggie shoved Dan's shirt off his shoulders, then paused to string kisses over his chest. He tasted of rainwater and a lingering hint of soap. She slipped her hands beneath his sodden jeans and shoved them down, as well, and gave a low moan of pleasure as she felt his manhood pressed against her.

Dan was just as busy, and soon they were naked in each other's arms, warm flesh to warm flesh. Maggie closed her eyes and reveled in the feel of his callused hands sliding over her body, caressing, arousing.

"Oh, yes. Yes, sugar."

"No!" Maggie gasped as Dan fell with her onto the bed, twisting to take her weight. Quickly rolling her onto her back, he rose up partway and looked at her, his face hard. "Say my name, dammit."

Maggie blinked at the fierceness in his eyes, in his voice. "Wha-what?"

"Not sugar, or handsome or sweetcakes or any other of those meaningless pet names you throw around to adoring males. When we make love I want to hear you say *my* name. Say it!"

Understanding dawned. Maggie gave him a melting look and cupped his face in her hands. "Make love to me, Dan," she whispered.

Fifteen

Maggie felt glorious. Eyes closed and limp with delicious lassitude, she luxuriated in the sensation of floating.

Then Dan shifted and rolled off her and onto his back.

Her eyes popped open, and she experienced a sudden chill that was due only in part to the loss of his body heat. Dear Lord, Mag, what have you done? Instinctively, she started to turn away, to flee.

"Come here," Dan murmured.

Surprise shot through Maggie as she found herself being hauled against his side. She didn't know what she had expected, exactly, but certainly not that he would loop his arm around her and pull her close.

She lay still and tense in his embrace, nestled against his side, her cheek on his shoulder, and stared across the room at nothing as Dan rubbed his hand slowly up and down her arm. She'd never felt so awkward or unsure of herself in her life.

Rain pounded the roof and lashed against the windowpanes. Everything had happened so fast Dan hadn't turned up the heat, and, with the temperature plunging outside, the room had grown chilly. Everywhere her skin touched Dan she was warm, but gooseflesh covered the rest of her. She shivered and pressed closer.

"Cold?" Without waiting for a reply, he reached down and drew up the covers, tucking them around her with surprising tenderness before settling back in his former position.

Maggie told herself to get up and get dressed, make some flippant excuse and get out of there. But she couldn't seem to move from the delicious warmth.

She bit her lower lip. This was a big mistake, Mag. Big, *big* mistake. You have to work with this man every day, for Pete's sake. What were you thinking?

She almost laughed at that. That was the trouble. She hadn't been thinking at all. In the heat of the moment she had simply gone with her heart and her emotions.

Over the last two months she'd fallen in love with Dan, and she had been so caught up in that mad maelstrom of love and desire she had forgotten that for men lovemaking did not necessarily have anything to do with love. To them, sexual intimacy was often just about pleasure—an itch that needed scratching.

Dan had never so much as hinted that he had feelings for her, so it was pointless to fantasize about love and marriage or even romance.

Maggie peeked up at him through her lashes. From that perspective his face was all hard angles and planes, and his eyes were fixed on the ceiling.

He's probably trying right now to think of a way to put some distance between the two of you. So go ahead. Do both of you a favor and let him know you don't expect anything of him.

Drawing a bracing breath, Maggie gave his chest a pat and rose up on one elbow. She tossed back her damp, wildly curling mane and smiled. "Well, sugar, that was great, but I gotta run."

"Whoa. Where're you going, Red?" Dan's arm clamped tighter around her, holding her in place when she tried to roll away.

"Home. A girl needs her beauty sleep, you know, handsome."

"You're not going anywhere just yet. We need to talk, Maggie."

"Talk? About what?" She fluttered her lashes and looked at him with feigned puzzlement. But she knew what was coming. She could see it in his eyes.

"About us. About what just happened."

"Don't be silly, sugar. There's nothing to talk about. We simply got carried away by the exhilaration of the storm and shared a few moments of pleasure. No harm done. We're both adults here. Don't worry about it, sweetie." She made another attempt to get up, but Dan tightened his hold again.

"Now, sugar, let me go. Look, you don't even have to get up. Just tell me where to find the keys and I'll drive myself home in your truck. If it's still raining in the morning I'll pick you up," she said reasonably, but he wasn't about to be sidetracked.

"What is this, a brush-off?"

"No, of course not."

"Sure sounds like one to me. A quick roll in the hay, then so long, sailor."

"Oooh, I didn't know you were in the navy, handsome."

"Knock it off, Maggie. I'm not in the mood for any of your flippant remarks. I want to know what the hell is going on. One minute you're melting in my arms, and the next you can't wait to get away from me."

Maggie sighed. Why couldn't he just let her leave and spare both of them an awkward scene? "Look, I didn't want you to feel cornered, okay? I thought if I kept it light you would know that I don't expect anything to come of this. That there are no strings."

He stared at her so long that she began to squirm. "That's what this is about?" he said finally. "Did it ever occur to you that maybe I *want* something to come of this? That I *want* strings?"

"No!" she blurted out in amazement before she thought.

"Why not?"

"I, uh, I'm not..." She groped for an evasive answer that would satisfy him and drew a blank.

"Yes?"

"I'm not exactly the kind of woman that men..."

"Go on. That men what?"

Now Maggie felt cornered, and she didn't like it. "Do we have to talk about this?"

"Yes, I believe we do. That men what, Maggie?"

"I'm not lovable, okay?" she spat at him. "There, are you happy now?"

"Lord, no. You can't be serious. Have you looked in a mirror lately, Red?"

"Oh, men drool and pant over me and try to get

me into the sack, but that's just because of the way
I look.''

"That's just plain crazy.''

"Is it? Would we be here in this bed right now
if I looked like a troll? I don't think so.''

Dan chuckled. ''A troll with a smart mouth. Now,
there's an image.''

"That's no answer.''

"All right, so the way you look is a factor. But
physical attraction is the first step toward deeper
feelings. It has to be. It's impossible to fall in love
with someone if they revolt you or leave you cold.''

His use of the word *love* set up a fluttery sensation
in the pit of her stomach that was part yearning and
part stark terror. ''That may be. I wouldn't know.
I've never gotten beyond the first step. You may not
believe me, but before tonight, I've had only two
lovers. With both Brian and Hank I thought that
maybe—just maybe—I'd found the man of my
dreams, but neither of them stuck around long.

"To most men I'm just a trophy date. They love
to be seen and photographed with me at parties and
premieres, gallery openings, that sort of thing. It's a
way of saying to the world, 'Hey, look at me, I'm
dating Maggie Malone, supermodel.' But they don't
fall in love with me.''

Dan slowly shook his head, his eyes full of sor-
rowful amazement. ''Ah, Maggie, Maggie. What has
Jacob done to you?''

She stiffened. ''This has nothing to do with my
father.''

"The hell it doesn't. You've convinced yourself
that he doesn't love you, and if your own father

can't love you, then it stands to reason that no one can, particularly a man. Rather than risk more rejection, you hide behind flippant remarks and a facade of unconcern and don't let any man close enough for anything deeper to develop.''

''That's not true.''

But it was, and Maggie knew it. That was why she'd never been seriously involved with any man, why she seldom even bothered to date. She flirted outrageously precisely to keep men off balance.

That Dan had seen through her so clearly shook Maggie to her core and left her trembling inside.

''Sure it is. You do it all the time. Whenever you feel threatened or pressured or anyone gets too close, that glib tongue of yours goes into action. Well, I'm warning you, Maggie, now that I know what's behind it, that little trick isn't going to work on me anymore.''

''What does that mean?'' she demanded, eyeing him warily.

''What it means, Red, is I care for you. And I'm not going anywhere.''

She stared at him, speechless, her heart pounding.

Dan's mouth curved into that rare hard smile of his that did devastating things to her insides. His gaze drifted down her face and settled on her mouth. Beneath heavy lids, his silvery eyes smoldered. Slipping his free hand beneath her heavy mane of hair he cupped the back of her neck and tugged her closer.

Against her lips he whispered, ''And neither are you. Not tonight. Not ever, if I have anything to say about it.''

* * *

The next morning, Maggie came awake slowly, stretching like a satisfied cat. A feeling of bone-deep pleasure and well-being permeated her body. Smiling, she lifted her heavy eyelids, but blinked as her gaze focused on the unfamiliar room.

She became aware of a delicious warmth all along her backside from her neck to her heels, and she realized with a jolt that she was lying, spoon-fashion, against a man's naked body.

Before panic could seize her completely, memories from the previous night came flooding back. With a sigh, she relaxed.

It had been a magical night. She and Dan had made love twice more before falling asleep in each other's arms. Then sometime before dawn he had kissed her awake. Ignoring her protests that she had to go, with his lips and tongue and tormenting touch, he had seduced her until she was weak and quivering with need. Taking his time, he had made slow, sweet love to her, while the rain kept up a steady patter on the roof.

Maggie smiled. Dan was a wonderful lover, strong and forceful, yet wonderfully sensitive and giving. No one had ever taken such tender care with her before, or brought her to such heights of pleasure. She could almost believe that he really cared for her, as he'd said. Almost.

"Mmm, morning, Red," Dan mumbled against her neck an instant before she felt his lips nibbling there.

Laughing, she hunched her shoulder. "Uh-uh,

none of that. This time I really do have to go. The family will be getting up soon. Dan, cut that out!''

"Oh, all right." He released her and flopped onto his back with his arms spread wide. "Spoilsport."

Before he could change his mind she scooted off the bed, scooped up her clothes and dashed into the bathroom. Still clutching her clothes to her breasts, she caught sight of herself in the mirror and stopped short.

She looked wanton and well loved. Her hair was tousled every which way, she hadn't a speck of makeup left, her lips were slightly swollen from Dan's kisses, and that looked like... Frowning, Maggie leaned closer to the mirror and groaned. Dear Lord, it was. She had a *hickey* on her neck.

If that wasn't enough, to top it all off, she was positively glowing.

"If Val could see me now she'd have a photographer in here clicking pictures right and left," she muttered to her disheveled reflection.

"So much for discretion. You might as well have I Spent the Night Having Great Sex stamped on your forehead."

And the pitiful part was, if he tried, Dan could have her back in that bed with very little effort, and to hell with her reputation or work or anything else.

Making a low, desperate sound in her throat, Maggie turned her back to the mirror. Time to get out of here, my girl, while you still have an ounce of self-control left.

After scrambling into her clothes, she washed her face, squeezed some toothpaste on her forefinger and rubbed it over her teeth, then located Dan's hairbrush and attacked her tangled mane. When done she studied her reflection and sighed. She looked only fractionally less debauched, but it was the best she could do.

Dan was dressed and waiting when she emerged from the bathroom. His hair was damp and he smelled of shaving cream and toothpaste, and she realized that he'd made use of the guest bathroom while she had been fretting over her appearance.

On the short drive neither spoke until the pickup came to a stop in the driveway beside the terrace and Dan announced, "I'll come in with you."

Maggie paused with her hand on the door handle. "You don't have to do that."

"I know that, but I want to."

"Really, Dan, it isn't neces—"

"What's the matter, Maggie? Are you ashamed of me? Is that why you don't want your family to know you were with me last night?"

"*No!* It's not that at all!" It had not occurred to her that he would think such a thing. "Just the opposite, actually."

"Meaning?"

"Meaning I don't want to ruin your relationship with Daddy. He isn't going to be happy about this, you know. I was just trying to prevent him from finding out."

Dan's eyes narrowed. He gazed at her for a long time in that disconcerting direct way he had. Finally he nodded. "Let me worry about Jacob. If he has a problem with me seeing his daughter, he can take it up with me."

Maggie snorted and shot him a wry look as she

opened the passenger door. "I was thinking more along the lines of him having a problem with me seeing his right-hand man."

She bailed out of the truck without giving him a chance to comment, and Dan followed. They dashed up the short path and across the terrace through the sprinkling rain and rushed inside through the first set of French doors, which led directly into the den. Laughing and shaking off raindrops, they slammed the door quickly, but their laughter died when they turned and saw Jacob, scowling at them from his recliner.

"So. That's where you've been all night."

"Daddy. What're you doing up so early?"

"Your father had a bad night. Since he couldn't sleep, he wanted to sit down here and watch the dawn."

Maggie's gaze swung to the sofa in time to see Charley Minze rise to his feet. Her attention had been so focused on her father, she hadn't noticed him before.

She took a quick step toward Jacob, concern wiping out every other thought. "Are you all right? Should I call the doctor?"

"Charley already has. I don't need any help from you."

Looking uncomfortable, Charley edged toward the door. "I'll, uh…I'll go see if Ida Lou has made coffee yet."

"Dammit, just look at you, girl. You stay out all night and come dragging in at dawn still wearing the clothes you had on yesterday and looking like a shameless hussy. I suppose I should have expected as much from you. Disgraceful. Absolutely disgraceful.''

Well, what did you expect, Mag? Understanding? Parental tolerance? Approval? Yeah, right. In your dreams.

Reining in her concern, Maggie ruthlessly squelched her hurt and flashed an irreverent grin.

''I wouldn't want to disappoint you. But let me remind you that I'm a big girl now, Daddy. My private life is nobody's business but mine.

''Now, if you'll excuse me, I need to shower before I go to the office.'' She glanced at Dan and winked. ''Thanks for the ride home, sugar. And for everything else,'' she added in a sexy purr, and sauntered out of the room.

Dan watched her until she was out of sight, then turned to find that he had become the focus of Jacob's glower. ''Was that necessary?''

''Was it necessary for you to seduce my daughter?'' the old man shot back. ''When I asked you to get close to Katherine, that wasn't what I had in mind.''

Guilt and fury tangled in Dan's gut. Along with the feelings came a fierce need to protect Maggie. He glowered back at the older man, and when he spoke his voice was low and intense. ''Let's get this straight right now, Jacob. What happened between Maggie and me has nothing to do with you or Malone Enterprises. Nothing at all. I care for your daughter, and I'm going to keep right on seeing her, and if that doesn't set well with you, too bad. I guess you'll just have to fire me.''

* * *

No sooner had Maggie parted from Dan than she began to have doubts. He couldn't possibly be serious about her. Oh, sure, the night before he'd claimed to care for her, but what else could he say under those circumstances?

By the time she had showered and dressed she was convinced that she was right, and as she left her room she resolved to let him off the hook as soon as she saw him again. Halfway down the stairs, however, Maggie's steps faltered and all thoughts of Dan flew right out of her mind when she spotted her sister and Dr. Sanderson in the foyer below.

The good doctor held Laurel in his arms, tenderly stroking her back and murmuring in her ear while she wept on his shoulder.

Starting down the stairs again at a slower pace, Maggie cleared her throat and murmured, "Excuse me." The couple sprang apart like two guilty teenagers caught making out.

"Miss Malone. I, uh, I was just comforting your sister." Neil Sanderson straightened his tie and tried to look professional, but his face turned a painful red.

"So I see. Is there something I should know about?"

"I'm afraid I brought her some bad news."

"Oh, Maggie, Daddy's latest tests aren't good. Dr. Sanderson says he's failing faster than he and Dr. Lockhart expected. He's changed his medication, but if it doesn't slow down the cancer he says we'll be lucky if he lives to see the New Year in."

The statement hit Maggie like a fist to the heart. She caught her breath and would have staggered back had she not been gripping the newel post. Thanksgiving was only a little over two weeks away.

"So soon? Are you sure, doctor?"

"As sure as one can be in a case like this. But on the plus side, your father is a fighter. I was just telling Mrs. Howe not to give up hope. Jacob may surprise us all." He sent Laurel another sympathetic glance and picked up his bag. "I'll be running along now. If you need me, day or night, just call."

"Oh, wait, Doctor." Laurel sniffed and dabbed at her eyes with a man's white handkerchief before handing it back to him. "Thank you for all you've done. And for being so kind."

Neil gazed at Laurel like a starving man, then looked down at the tear-soaked handkerchief and closed his fingers tightly around it and slipped it into his pocket. Maggie had the feeling the scrap of cloth would never see the inside of a washing machine again. "Think nothing of it. It was my pleasure."

When he had gone Maggie moved to her sister's side, and through the etched glass panel beside the door they watched the young doctor drive away.

"He's a good man," Maggie murmured.

"Yes. Yes, he is."

"I can't believe it. Oh, Laurel, we're going to lose Daddy." Laurel did not reply, but when Maggie turned her head she saw a tear slip down her sister's cheek.

"Oh, sis."

Instinctively, she reached out to offer comfort, but Laurel flinched away and snapped, "Don't. Just don't touch me."

Hurt shot through Maggie. Tears sprang to her eyes before she could stop them.

"Maggie, I'm sorry—"

Laurel reached out to her when she turned to flee, and the sleeve of her sweater pulled back an inch or so. Maggie had already taken a step, but she stopped in her tracks when she spotted the dark smudge on her sister's wrist.

She grabbed Laurel's hand and pushed the sleeve back and stared at the mark, ignoring her sister's attempt to free herself. Her horrified gaze locked on Laurel. "How did this happen? Where did you get this bruise?"

"It's not a bruise." Laurel tugged at her hand again, but Maggie refused to let go.

"It most certainly is." Maggie's eyes narrowed, zeroing in on the patch of discolored skin on her sister's cheek that makeup couldn't quite hide. "And so is that." And she was willing to bet that her sister's turtleneck sweater hid more marks that she didn't want anyone to see.

"Don't worry about it. It's nothing. Really."

"Nothing? How can you say that? And don't you dare try to tell me this was an accident. Martin hit you, didn't he? *Didn't* he?"

"All right, so maybe he did slap me once or twice, but only because I made him angry. It's nothing to make a fuss over."

"The hell it isn't! It's called domestic violence, Laurel. You can file charges and have him put in jail, for Pete's sake. Which I think we should do right now. C'mon, I'll go with you."

"*No!* No, I can't do that!" Laurel pulled free and

stepped back, wringing her hands. "You don't understand. It's not like that. Martin isn't a wife beater."

"The hell he isn't. He hit you, didn't he?"

"Well…yes. But it was all my fault. Martin can't help it if he has a bad temper. If I didn't do or say things that upset him he wouldn't hit me. Anyway, he's always sorry afterward."

"Good Lord, Laurel, listen to yourself. You're the victim here. You are in no way to blame. How can you defend that creep?"

"He's my husband," she said simply. Her chin came up a notch, and she looked at Maggie with a fragile dignity that wrung her heart.

Frustration and fury trembled inside Maggie. She should have known that Laurel would defend the slimebag. Her sister had always had an idealistic view of love and marriage, and she was loyal to the core. For Laurel, marriage was forever, no matter what she had to endure. Her sweet, biddable nature made her the perfect whipping boy for an abuser like Martin. And how typical of her to think that if things weren't quite as rosy as she'd hoped, then she must be the one doing something wrong.

"A marriage licence doesn't give him the right to hit you."

"Maggie, just leave it alone. This isn't your concern."

"You're my sister. I can't just stand by and do nothing. Just wait until I see the bastard. I'll put the fear of God into him. When I'm done, he won't dare lay a hand on you again."

"No! Maggie, you mustn't!" Laurel's face turned

white and her eyes darted around as though she was afraid that Martin had somehow overheard. Maggie had never seen such terror in anyone's eyes before. She gripped Maggie's hands so tightly it felt as though her bones might snap. "Please. You have to promise me you won't say anything to Martin. Or to Momma or Daddy, either."

"Laurel—"

"Please, Maggie, I'm begging you. Promise me."

Maggie gritted her teeth. It went against every instinct, everything she knew was right, but in the end she could not deny the pathetic plea in her sister's eyes.

"All right, you win. But I don't like it."

"Promise me. Say it, so I'll know you mean it."

Maggie almost smiled. It was the same childish demand they had made of each other thousands of times when they were little girls.

"I promise, I won't say anything to Martin, or to Momma or Daddy."

Sixteen

No sooner had Maggie made the promise to Laurel than she regretted doing so. Five days later, sitting in the first-class section on a New York-to-Dallas flight, she was still brooding over the situation.

As the plane started its decent toward DFW Maggie stared out the window at the winter-brown ranch land around Dallas and Fort Worth, the vehicles darting along highways like busy ants, not really seeing either. All she could think about was her sweet sister, at the mercy of that pig, Martin.

After leaving Laurel that morning, Maggie had barely arrived at the cannery when Martin had stormed past Anna and into her office with another of his complaints. The mere sight of him had turned her stomach and filled her with rage. It had been all she could do not to leap across her desk and tear into him, claws bared. Instead, because of that stupid promise, she'd had to grind her teeth and listen to him rant.

"I just got off the telephone with Ken Burrows over at K&W Wholesale Grocers. He said you called him and worked out new shipment quantities. Is that true?"

"Yes. The problems we've been having have left

us short on inventory. I felt it would be better to scale back on all the orders now and catch up later, when we have things under control again. To that end, I'm personally contacting all our accounts to explain our situation and ask for their cooperation. In return, I'm offering a discount off their contracted cost. So far, they've all been agreeable.''

"I don't give a rat's ass if they're shouting for joy. You keep your nose out of my business. *I'm* the company PR man. *I* deal with the buyers, not you. I won't stand for you going behind my back and making deals with my accounts.''

"*You* won't stand for it?'' Shooting to her feet, she'd braced all ten fingertips on the desktop and leaned over the shiny surface toward him. "Why, you insignificant, worthless piece of pig flop. *You* don't have any say in the matter. I'm running this company, and if I want to talk to a customer, I will. Furthermore, they are not *your* accounts, they're Malone Cannery accounts. You just work here. And only because of my sister, at that. Now, get your sorry hide out of my office. And the next time you want to talk to me, make an appointment.''

Maggie smiled at the memory. Oh, that had felt good. Really good. Not as good as giving him the horsewhipping he so richly deserved, but good.

Martin's face had turned an apoplectic purple. He'd looked ready to hit her. Actually, she'd been hoping he would try. She had been in just the mood to practice some of her kick-boxing moves on him. But after a lot of sputtering, fist-clenching and nostril-flaring, he had swallowed his rage and stormed out.

At first she had felt victorious—until she started worrying that Martin would take his fury out on Laurel.

That thought had haunted her for the last five days while in New York shooting the Stephano Perfume ad and making an appearance on *Oprah*. Twice she had telephoned Laurel. Her sister had insisted that she was fine, but Maggie still felt uneasy.

At one point she had almost called Dan. She had desperately needed to confide her worries to someone.

Maggie's mouth twitched. C'mon, Mag, be honest. That's not the only reason. You also wanted to hear his voice.

She had gotten as far as dialing his number, but hung up after only one ring.

Since that rainy morning five days ago she hadn't talked to Dan. Except for glimpsing him a couple of times through the glass wall of her office later that morning, she hadn't seen him, either.

She'd left the office earlier than usual because she had to drive to Dallas before dawn the following morning to catch her New York flight. She'd half expected him to call her that evening at home, and like a lovesick teenager, she had jumped every time the telephone had rung. But he hadn't called or dropped by.

Which merely confirmed her doubts about the veracity of his feelings for her.

Lost in her troublesome thoughts, Maggie hadn't realized they were actually landing until the wheels touched down on the tarmac.

A few minutes later when the seat belt light

blinked off, she slung her carryall over her shoulder and wearily started up the jetway behind two other first-class passengers. It had been a grueling five days, and she was beat. She wasn't looking forward to the two-hour drive home.

As happened wherever she went, heads turned when she stepped into the terminal. Normally Maggie would have smiled, maybe signed a few autographs if anyone worked up the nerve to ask, but she was too tired to deal with fans. Fixing her eyes straight ahead, she kept moving and pretended not to notice the stir she was causing.

"Hey, Red, can I bum a ride?"

Maggie jerked to a halt. "Dan!"

He stood waiting just a few feet ahead to her right, a shoulder propped casually against a post, looking so wonderfully rugged and masculine he took her breath away.

Grinning at her flabbergasted reaction, he pushed away from the post and ambled toward her. "What's the matter? Cat got your tongue? That must be a first."

"Wh-what are you doing here?"

"What do you think? Come here, Red." Reaching out, he hooked his big, workman's hand around her nape and hauled her in.

His other arm wrapped around her and pulled her close, and Maggie's carryall slipped to the floor, forgotten. There in the middle of the concourse they kissed passionately, hungrily, oblivious to the deplaning passengers veering around them on either side like water seeking its course.

A flash went off, and Dan's head jerked up.

"What the— Hey, you! Come back here!" he yelled, but the photographer was sprinting away, dodging through the crowd.

When he would have given chase Maggie grasped his arm. "Don't bother." She made a wry face. "Gawking people and paparazzi are something you'll have to accept if you're going to be with me, I'm afraid. If that's going to be a problem for you, say so now."

He gave her one of those steady looks. "I can handle it. And, honey, when it comes to us, there is no 'if' about it." He stroked his callused fingers down her cheek as his eyes caressed her, and Maggie's heart thumped.

"C'mon." Scooping up her carryall, he looped his other arm around her waist and started down the concourse.

When they approached her Viper in the long-term parking garage, Dan said, "I know you're tired after that long flight. If you'll trust me with this thing, I'll drive."

"You're on," Maggie replied, and tossed him the keys.

The instant they were seated inside the car, Dan leaned over and planted another kiss on her mouth.

He took his time about it. Cupping her breast with one hand, he rubbed his thumb back and forth across her nipple in rhythm with his stroking tongue. Maggie speared her fingers through his hair and clutched his head, making a low sound in her throat as she gave herself up to the sensual pleasure.

After a time, Dan pulled back a few inches. His eyes smoldered and his breathing was raspy and not quite steady. "This car wasn't built for where this is heading. Anyway, if we don't stop now, we're liable to get arrested."

"Mmm, that would never do."

With controlled movements he straightened and cranked the engine. He reversed out of the slot and started down the spiral ramp. Maggie kicked off her shoes and curled sideways in the seat, unable to take her gaze from his strong profile.

"You still haven't told me how you got here."

"One of our rigs was making a haul to Dallas. I hitched a ride."

"But how did you know I'd be on that flight?"

"Easy. I got a copy of your itinerary from Anna."

She smiled, inordinately pleased.

"I'm sorry I didn't see you before you left. We had a break in the irrigation system at the orchard out on the Corsicana highway. By the time I got it repaired and drove home there weren't any lights on at the house. Then the next morning I found out you'd left for New York. I thought about calling your apartment, but with the time difference it was always late by the time I got home. I figured you'd be asleep."

"It wouldn't have mattered. I wish you had."

"Next time I will," he said quietly, sending her another smoldering glance.

Happiness effervesced inside Maggie like champagne bubbles. Smiling, she snuggled her cheek against the leather seat back. "You do realize that photo will most likely be in the papers. By tomorrow everyone in Ruby Falls will know about us."

Dan slanted her an amused look. "Honey, everyone already knows."

"You're kidding me. But how? Daddy wouldn't say anything."

"Charley told Ida Lou."

"Oh, I see." She loved Ida Lou with all her heart, but there was nothing the dear old soul loved better than talking about "her girls" to her best friend Clara. Clara Edwards could not have kept a juicy tidbit like that to herself for five minutes.

"You don't mind everyone knowing about us?"

"Why should I mind?"

"I'm not exactly the most beloved person in town."

He shot her another one of those intense looks that made her toes curl. "You suit me just fine. That's all that matters."

Yes. Yes, it was, she thought, hugging the reassuring words to her heart.

A comfortable silence fell between them as they left the outskirts of Dallas. Maggie didn't mind. She was happy and content merely to be with Dan, and to drink in the sight of him.

The last thing she expected was to fall asleep, but the next thing she knew she awoke with a start when the ride turned bumpy.

"Wha…?"

"Relax, we're almost there."

Looking around, she saw that they were on the gravel lane leading to her family home. Yawning, she arched in a sinuous stretch. "Sorry, I didn't mean to conk out on you."

"That's okay. You were tired. Anyway, the music drowned out your snoring."

Maggie shot him a horrified look, then slugged his arm when he grinned. "You beast. I don't snore."

Dan turned in at the gate and started up the long drive before aiming another teasing look her way. "No, but you do make cute little sighing noises."

"I do not do any such th—"

Maggie twisted around in her seat as the Viper shot past the house. "Where are you going?"

"My place." Without slowing, he drove past the point where the driveway forked to the left toward the garage and headed down the other branch toward the orchard where it narrowed into the dirt lane leading to his cottage.

"Oh, sugar, there's nothing I'd like better. Truly. But I really should go home. The family is expecting me, plus I need to check on Daddy."

"He's doing fine. The last couple of days he's actually improved. He's feeling better since he started taking the new medication. Dr. Sanderson is amazed."

"Really? Oh, that's wonderful news."

"As for the other, you don't have to worry. I told Ida Lou where you'd be. She'll calm any worries your momma might have."

Maggie smiled sadly. She noticed he wasn't concerned that her father would be worried. "You've thought of everything, haven't you, sugar. Still, I am terribly tired. I wouldn't be the most exciting companion tonight, I'm afraid."

Dan brought the Viper to a stop before his cottage

but left the engine running. He looked across the dim interior at her. "I didn't bring you here to ravish you, Maggie, although I'll admit, that would be great. I'll be content just knowing you're here, to have you sleeping next to me." He reached out and touched the corner of her mouth with his callused thumb, caressing her with his eyes. "I've missed you, Maggie, and I want you with me tonight."

Maggie's heart did a slow roll in her chest. Emotion clogged her throat, and her eyes grew misty as she gazed back at him through the dimness. With that simple statement he had made her feel loved and cherished and needed in a way she never had before.

Covering his hand with hers, she turned her head and placed a kiss against his palm, watching him all the while. "Let's go inside," she murmured, and reached for the door handle.

The days that followed were a time of paradox for Maggie. She hadn't known it was possible to experience such extremes of emotions all at once, but existing right alongside the walking-on-air happiness her relationship with Dan had brought her was despair over her doomed relationship with her father, concern about his health and constant nagging worry about the business.

Now and then she felt guilty about being so happy when everything else was so horrible, but she couldn't help it. She was in love, and though Dan hadn't said the words yet, his every action, look and touch said that he loved her, as well.

Dan was proving to be a wonderful lover and

companion. Maggie had been attracted to him almost from the moment they met, but she had not suspected that beneath that strong, almost stern exterior was a thoughtful and caring man. Daily, however, he continued to surprise her with his tenderness and sensitivity to her moods and needs.

At least once or twice a day he found an excuse to come to her office. If the draperies were drawn he would swoop down and give her a passionate kiss while she sat at her desk. If they were open and the cannery hands could see, he contented himself with merely making love to her with his eyes. Either way, when he walked out of her office he left her weak and quivering with desire and love.

Whenever Maggie worked late, Dan kept up his vigil, regardless of the guards patrolling the buildings. He would find work to do somewhere in the building where he could keep her in sight, and when she left the cannery, he stayed by her side.

Two or three nights a week Maggie stayed at Dan's cottage. Her father still scowled and made caustic remarks, but the rest of the family seemed to accept, even approve of the relationship. Her mother, in particular, took pains to let her know what a fine man she thought Dan was. Even Jo Beth gave her a left-handed compliment on her taste in men.

In Ruby Falls, tongues were wagging and there were bets being made on how long the affair would last, but that was no more than she and Dan had expected.

One bright spot was that after the security guards

began patrolling, the vandalism had stopped. Or at least so Maggie thought.

One evening a week before Thanksgiving when Dan walked her to her car, they were both so absorbed with each other that neither of them noticed the damage at first. Then a chance glance made Maggie gasp. "Oh, no!"

"What the *hell?*"

Written in bright yellow spray paint along the driver's side of the Viper and on the hood were the words "Get out, bitch!"

"Who the devil would do this? And why?" Dan gingerly touched the paint and discovered it was still wet. Immediately he pulled Maggie close and darted a hard look around the parking lot. "And where the hell is that security guard?"

As though he'd heard him, the guard stepped out of the building they had just left.

"Evening, Miss Malone, Mr. Garrett. You heading ho—" The man stopped and stared, bug-eyed, at Maggie's car. "Holy, jumpin' Jehoshaphat!"

"Where the hell were you when this happened?"

"I...I just stepped inside to take a leak...uh, sorry, Miss—to use the men's room. I wasn't gone more'n a couple of minutes, Mr. Garrett. I swear it."

"That's all whoever did this needed. He must've been watching, waiting for you to take a break. Which means he might still be around. You stay here and guard the car while Miss Malone and I go get something to clean this off. If we hurry we might be able to wipe it off before it ruins the paint job."

Maggie and Dan ran back inside the cannery and returned moments later with bundles of clean shop rags. The three of them worked like demons, but despite their best efforts, dried smears of yellow marred the Viper's emerald-green paint when they were done.

"Well, at least we obliterated the words," Dan said. "We'll take it to a paint shop tomorrow. They can put it back like new."

Maggie shook her head. "Who could hate me so much? Why do they keep doing these things to me?"

That earned her a sharp look from Dan. "What do you mean 'keep doing'? Has something like this happened before? Something personal aimed at you?" The truth must have shown on her face, because he spat out an obscenity that made her jump. "Dammit, why didn't you tell me? I want to know what happened, and I want to know right now. Start talking."

"Now, sugar—"

"Knock it off, Maggie. You're not going to flirt your way out of this. Tell me."

She flinched and glanced at the security guard, who was avidly taking in every word. Dan ordered him to go search the rest of the parking lot, then turned back to Maggie with a face like granite. "Now, spit it out."

Reluctantly, Maggie told him about the tire slashing and finding the rat in her bed. When she was done, he looked as though he could cheerfully throttle her.

"Dammit, Maggie, why the devil didn't you tell me?"

"I didn't know you that well then. And I was

worried that if Daddy found out he would want me to step down.''

"You know me now. You've had plenty of time to tell me in the last couple of weeks. So why haven't you?''

Maggie's lips curved. "The truth is, I've been so happy lately, I forgot all about it.''

Dan narrowed his eyes and studied her face, trying to decide if she was telling him the truth. Finally he gave in and snatched her close. "Don't you ever, *ever* keep something like that from me again. You hear?''

"I won't. I promise.'' She returned his hug, then eased back and looked up at him. "But, Dan, I still don't want Daddy to know. There's nothing he can do, and knowing would just upset him.''

Dan hesitated, frowning, but finally he nodded. "Okay. You're probably right.''

He cast another grim look at the Viper. "Well, this settles it. You're moving in with me.''

"What? Dan, I ca—''

"No arguments. Until this thing is over, I'm not letting you out of my sight.''

Though she spent every night with Dan, Maggie did not agree to move in with him. Somehow, though, over the following week more and more of her personal belongings found their way to his cottage. Maggie suspected collusion between Dan and Ida Lou, maybe even her mother.

She didn't really mind. The week following the spray-painting incident was the most blissful of her life. Then Thanksgiving morning, just as Maggie padded into the kitchen for her first cup of coffee, Dan dropped his bombshell.

Barefoot and wearing one of his T-shirts and a pair of bikini panties, her curly mane in a wild tangle, she was still half asleep, and it took a moment for his words to register. Even then she was sure she'd misunderstood.

She blinked at him. "What did you say?"

"I said, we have to hustle. Mom gets on a tear if all her chicks aren't there early on holidays."

"Whoa! Wait just a minute! You can't be serious. You want *me* to go with you to your mother's for Thanksgiving?"

"Sure I'm serious. I thought it was understood we were going. And don't look at me like that. Hell, you'd think I was asking you to commit hara-kiri in the middle of the town square."

Might as well, Maggie thought frantically. "Are you crazy? I can't spend a holiday with your family."

"Why not?"

"I have to spend Thanksgiving here with my own family," she said quickly, grasping at the first excuse that came to mind.

"First of all, I checked with Lily. In deference to Jacob, she's planning merely a quiet dinner at the usual time. Thanksgiving at my mom's is around three. Anyway, knowing your appetite, you can easily handle two feasts."

Maggie twisted her hands together. "I...I still can't go. Don't you realize what kind of conclusions your family will draw if you bring me to a family gathering?"

"That this is not just a fling? That I'm serious about you? Maybe even that I'm in love with you? Yeah, probably." Dan shrugged. "So what? They'd be right."

"I still can't—" Maggie gaped at him. "You love me?"

"Yeah, I do," he said quietly, watching her in that piercing way he had.

Joy exploded inside Maggie like a Roman candle, but she ruthlessly quashed the emotion and narrowed her eyes at him. "You're just saying that so I'll agree to go with you."

"I don't believe this," he muttered, looking heavenward. "In every other way you are without exception the strongest, brightest, bravest, sassiest, most self-assured woman I know, but when it comes to love I've never seen anyone so insecure and suspicious. Dammit, woman! I just told you that I love you, and I damn well want to hear you say it back."

His anger startled her at first. Then, as she stared at his furious face, a flood of warmth swept through her, turning her insides to mush. Her eyes grew misty, and a smile blossomed on her face as the joy she could no longer contain broke free. Her chest was so swollen with emotion she could barely speak, but she managed a quavery "I love you, too, Dan."

"Good." He pointed to the floor in front of his feet. "Get over here, woman, and kiss me. Now."

Laughing, Maggie covered the space between them in one leap, threw her arms around his neck and fastened her mouth to his.

The kiss was hot and hungry and exultant. They clung to each other, desperately straining to get closer still, as though they would each climb right inside the other's body if they could. Feverishly, hands stroked and clutched, lips and tongues rubbed, teeth nipped, as low, hungry sounds issued from them.

When at last the kiss ended Dan leaned his forehead against hers and they both struggled to catch their breaths. "Come here, Red," he said at last, and leaned his hips back against the kitchen counter and brought her to stand between his braced legs. "There, that's better. Now, say it again."

Looping her arms around his neck, Maggie leaned back in his embrace with a sultry smile. "I do love you, handsome. With all my heart. And if you ever use that dictatorial tone with me again I'll put a knot on your head you can wear a hat on," she said sweetly.

Dan threw back his head and laughed. "That's my Maggie." He hugged her close, and she snuggled her cheek against his chest, relaxing as he rubbed his hands over her back in slow, hypnotic circles.

"So, you are going with me to Mom's, right?"

Maggie groaned. "You just never give up, do you?"

"Hell, Red, it's just a meal with my family. What's the problem?"

She leaned back in his arms again with an exasperated expression. "If you must know, mothers don't like me. Okay?"

"That's nuts. You met my mother. She thinks you're fantastic."

"Yeah, well, that was before you and I were involved. Now that I'm practically living with her son, I'll bet she wishes I'd never come back here.''

"Honey, you *are* living with her son. You just won't admit it. And I'll take that bet.'' He turned her around and hustled her toward the bedroom. ''Now, shake a leg, Red. We don't have much time.''

Dan won the bet. Lucy Garrett welcomed Maggie as though she were a long-lost daughter, enveloping her in a hug the minute they arrived.

Matt Garrett, his wife, Caroline, and their two children had arrived from Dallas the night before. Mary Alice Garrett Trent, husband Joe and their brood of five lived in Ruby Falls and had come over early that morning.

The younger Garretts and their spouses, though gracious, were at first intimidated by Maggie's celebrity and more reserved than Lucy. Their stiffness dissolved quickly, however, when Maggie joined in a rough-and-tumble game of touch football with gusto and later pitched in to help in the kitchen.

At dinner, when Maggie ate second helpings of every dish on the table, Lucy beamed her approval. The others could only stare in dumbfounded amazement.

"Holy cow, does she eat like that all the time?'' Matt blurted out when Maggie helped herself to a second slice of pecan pie.

"Several times a day.''

Maggie grinned. ''My momma says I was born hungry.''

"It's not fair," Mary Alice wailed. "If I ate half of what you do I'd weigh three hundred pounds."

"And I always thought models ate like birds," Joe marveled.

"Now, you children leave Maggie alone." Lucy shot a reprimanding look around the table at her brood. "These days it's refreshing to see a young woman with a healthy appetite."

"Healthy, my arse. Hell, Maggie, sumo wrestlers don't put away what you do." Matt grinned at Dan. "Damn, bro, you're gonna need a second job just to feed her."

Ignoring Lucy's scolding, Maggie laughed right along with the rest of them.

By the time she and Dan left that evening the whole Garrett clan was treating her like family.

"Now, aren't you glad you came?"

"Mmm. I like your family, and your mother's a great cook," she replied, patting her tummy.

Maggie rested her head on the seat back and closed her eyes.

The day had, indeed, been relaxing and fun and had given her a needed break from the problems she wrestled with every day, but the respite was over. The time had come to face hard reality. Maggie rolled her head on the seat back and peeked at Dan through her lashes.

"I've been thinking that tonight would be a good time to broach the subject of refitting the cannery to Daddy."

Dan glanced at her. "You sure you want to do that?"

"No. But it has to be done, and soon. I wanted

to spare him this argument, but the company can't wait until he's gon—'' She bit her lower lip and looked out the side window. ''We can't wait any longer. Unless we increase our production and efficiency we're just going to fall further and further behind. Our accounts are being understanding right now, but if we don't start catching up on the back orders we're going to lose them.

''There probably won't be a better time than today to approach Daddy. He's feeling a lot better since Dr. Sanderson changed his medication, and he loves holidays and having the family around, so he's sure to be in a good mood.

''The proposal and cost analyses I put together have been ready to present to him for days now. I've just been too chicken to give them to him, but I can't put it off any longer.''

Dan reached over and squeezed her hand. ''He won't like it, but Jacob's a smart man. You've done a thorough job. Once he looks over all the facts and figures, he'll see reason. Just expect some fireworks at first.''

Fireworks didn't come close to describing Jacob's reaction. *Explosion* was more accurate.

The entire family, Martin and Laurel included, were gathered in the family room for cocktails when they arrived. Encouraged by Jacob's chipper mood, Maggie decided to seize the moment.

''Daddy, we need to talk.''

''About what?''

''About modernizing and refitting the cannery. Now, before you say no, I'd like for you to take a look at these,'' she said, handing him her proposal and cost analyses. "I've given this a lot of thought and researched it all thoroughly. As you can see, by refitting we can increase our production by forty percent and our efficiency by 62.2 percent."

Giving the analysis and the production figures merely a cursory scan, Jacob flipped through the papers straight to the bottom line. His eyes bugged out when he found it. "My, *God!* Have you lost your mind, girl? We can't afford to do this! For the first time in over eighty years Malone's is losing money, and you want me to spend millions? Absolutely not!"

"Daddy, we don't have any choice. The machinery is falling apart. Dan spends half his time making repairs. And even when everything is working, it's all so slow, compared to modern equipment, that we can't keep up with our orders. If we don't modernize, we're going to go under. It's as simple as that."

"Is this all that big-shot Harvard degree taught you? Throw money at a problem? Well, the answer is no. We don't have the money for refitting, and I won't borrow."

"I wasn't suggesting that we do," Maggie said quietly. "I plan to use my own money."

"Your own—" Jacob stared at her, flabbergasted. He glanced down at the figure on the page. "Are you telling me that you've made *this* kind of money posing for pictures? I don't believe it."

"I know it seems incredible, but it's true. Look, Daddy, I'm perfectly willing to finance—"

"No, that doesn't change anything. I'd sooner borrow from a bank than be indebted to you."

"Good for you, Jacob," Martin piped up, sending

Maggie a gloating look. "You stick to your guns. Things aren't as bad as she's making out. She's just trying to get her hooks into the company any way she can, that's all."

"That's not true. Daddy, if you'll just read my analysis—"

"It won't make any difference."

"But—"

"Dammit, girl! *I* am the head of the company and the major shareholder—along with Nan, of course, but she leaves these matters to my judgment. *I* make these decisions. And my answer is no."

Maggie's shoulders slumped. She had hoped things wouldn't come to this, but he'd left her with no choice. "No, Daddy, you're not the major shareholder any longer. I am."

"What? What are you talking about?"

"I purchased all of Aunt Nan's shares in the company a year and a half ago."

Jacob's face turned ashen. He slumped back in his recliner as though he'd been shot. Outraged, Martin jumped to his feet and spewed out a string of curses that turned the air blue, while Lily and Maggie's sisters sat as though turned to stone, too astonished to speak.

Jacob glared at Nan. "Is this true?"

"Yes, it's true."

"But the shares are in your trust fund. The stock reports still come to you."

"The Malone-Endicott Trust is Maggie's. As the executor, I get the reports, but the stock belongs to her."

"It was all a trick to keep me in the dark! How could you do this to me? My own sister!"

Tilting her chin, Nan faced her brother's wrath squarely. "I'm sorry you're upset, Jacob, but it was the right thing to do. Maggie is the only one of your children who is qualified to take over the company. At the time of the sale I also felt that she was entitled to her fair share. I still do."

"The hell she is!" Jacob erupted. "Dammit, that sale was illegal. The stock can only be sold to a family member!"

Taken aback, Maggie blinked. She glanced around at the others for an answer, but everyone, with the exception of Nan, looked just as perplexed as she felt. "Uh...Daddy, I *am* a member of this family. Even if you've legally disowned me without notifying me, that doesn't change my bloodline."

"That's just it. You aren't my daughter!"

"Wh-what?" Maggie paled and staggered back a step.

"What's this?" Martin rubbed his hands together with relish. "Well, well, isn't this an interesting development."

"Shut your mouth, asshole, or I'll shut it for you," Dan snarled. He stepped close to Maggie and put his arm around her waist. "Easy. Easy, sweetheart."

Maggie didn't hear him. Nor did she hear Lily's gasp or notice her sudden agitation.

"Jacob, I don't think now is the time for this," Nan cautioned.

"Maybe not, but it has to be said." He looked

directly at Maggie. "Your mother was raped nine months before you were born."

"Jacob! How *could* you? You promised you would never tell anyone. You *promised!*" Covering her face with her hands, Lily doubled over and began to weep. Laurel and Jo Beth rushed to her side, their faces full of shock and concern.

Maggie was too stunned to move.

"I'm sorry, my love," Jacob said, regarding Lily sorrowfully. "You know I wouldn't hurt you for the world if I could help it. I've kept quiet all these years, but I have to speak out now. I can't stand by and let another man's child take over my family's company. You see that, don't you?"

"Y-you never told me you doubted that Ma-Maggie was y-yours. All th-these years...and I...I ne-never knew."

"Then I'm not a Malone?" Dazed, Maggie tried to take it in. She felt oddly fragile, as though she might shatter into a million pieces at any moment, like old, brittle glass.

"Jacob doesn't know that for certain," Nan snapped. "He's just let his anger over what happened to Lily eat at him all these years. There was never any sort of test done to determine paternity, one way or the other."

"You *knew* about this? All along, you knew?" Maggie stared at her aunt, feeling the sting of betrayal almost as keenly as Jacob's denouncement.

"Oh, no! It wasn't like that. I only recently found out. Jacob confided in me shortly after I got here."

"And you didn't tell me?"

"Oh, dear, don't look at me that way. I wanted

to. Truly, I did. But it wasn't my secret to tell, and Jacob made me promise not to say anything to anyone.'' Nan reached out her hand. ''Please, Maggie.''

''It doesn't matter,'' Maggie said in toneless voice, and looked away, ignoring the pleading gesture.

I will not cry. I will not let him see me cry, she told herself fiercely. She felt weak and shaky and sick to her stomach, but she hugged her arms tightly around her middle and held her chin high, determined to get through the nightmare with what little dignity she could salvage.

She looked at Jacob and attempted a careless chuckle, but to her horror the sound that came from her throat was closer to a sob. ''Well, at least now I know why you've always disliked me. Funny, as a kid I thought of dozens of reasons for your coldness—I wasn't pretty enough, or dainty enough, or smart enough. I was too tall, too skinny, my hair was too red, my mouth too big. But it never occurred to me that I wasn't yours, that every time you looked at me you saw some monster's spawn.''

Lily's wails rose to a hysterical pitch, but Jacob frowned.

''Katherine, it wasn't like that. I never—''

''No, please don't. Just…don't.'' Maggie pressed her lips together and looked up at the ceiling, widening her eyes to hold back tears. I will not cry. I will not cry.

''Actually…I understand. Lord, how you must have hated the sight of me.''

''Katherine, don't. That's not—''

''Given the situation, I suppose you did the best

job of fathering that anyone could expect. I just wish I had known the truth. I wouldn't have wasted the last twenty-seven years trying to win your love." Another pain-filled bark of laughter escaped her, this one bordering on hysteria. "What a hopeless effort that was."

Dan's hand tightened on Maggie's waist. "Don't do this to yourself, sweetheart."

Martin fidgeted anxiously. "Why don't I go call the company attorney right away and instruct him to take whatever steps necessary to have that stock sale nullified?"

"You'll do no such thing," Nan snapped.

"She has no right to that stock. Or to run Malone Enterprises."

"You don't know that. No one does."

"Then let's find out. Tomorrow I'll see Dr. Lockhart about DNA testing." Maggie looked at Jacob. "I suggest that you and Momma do the same. You should have your answer in a few weeks.

"If I am not your daughter, I'll step down from Malone Enterprises and return the stock to Aunt...to your sister."

"Oh, Maggie, don't you know that I'll never stop being your aunt? And you don't have to resign. Jacob and Lily were married when you were conceived and he has acknowledged you as his own all these years. Legally you are a Malone, no matter who fathered you."

"No, for once I agree with Martin. If I'm not a descendant of Katherine Margaret, I'm not entitled to any share in the company. Or to hold any position in it."

Nan whirled on Jacob. "Do you see what a mess you've caused? You've hurt and humiliated Lily and Maggie, blurting out that horrible secret in front of everyone. If you had taken my advice and told Maggie the truth you could have handled this whole thing discreetly and in private."

"I would have if I'd known you sold her those shares behind my back. And as for you," Jacob charged, pointing a finger at Dan. "You're sleeping with Katherine. You should have pried that information out of her before now and reported back to me, like you were supposed to."

"Dammit, Jacob—"

"Oh, my God."

"Maggie, let me explain," Dan began, but she spun away from him and backed away several steps, shaking her head, her hand unconsciously pressed against her heart.

"You were spying on me. That's why your attitude toward me changed. Why you seduced me. Not because you cared for me, but so you could get close to me and report everything I said and did back to Da—to *him?*"

She was reeling like a fighter who'd received a one-two-three punch, but of all the blows she'd taken in the last few minutes, this one was by far the worst. This one threatened to take her to her knees.

"No, sweetheart, it wasn't like that. You've gotta believe me."

"What a fool I've been. What a love-starved fool."

"Maggie, listen to me. I'll admit that in the beginning, before I got to know you, I did agree to keep an eye on you for Jacob. I didn't want the assignment. But how could I refuse? After all he'd done for me I owed him that much. But I swear to you, all my reports to Jacob were made before we became lovers and they were all positive. After that first night we spent together I told him I was through keeping tabs on you. That's the truth, I swear.''

"You used me, betrayed me. Why should I believe anything you say?'' She back away another step, shaking her head. "We're finished. Through. I'll have Ida Lou collect my things from the cottage tomorrow.''

"Maggie, I'm begging you, don't do this. I love you, sweetheart.''

"Oh, please.'' She laughed, a harsh sound full of pain and bitterness. "You can drop the act, Mr. Garrett. You did your job, but it's over now. It's my own fault, really. The day after I arrived you did warn me that you'd do whatever it took to protect Jacob.''

Lily still sobbed quietly on Laurel's shoulder, but everyone else watched them with varying degrees of discomfort and concern, taking in every word. Maggie flashed a strained smile to the group. "Now, if the rest of you will excuse me, I think I'll skip dinner. I'm sure you'll understand that I'm not in the mood to give thanks just now.''

Struggling to hold on to her fragile dignity, she held her chin high and headed toward the door on shaky legs.

"Maggie, wait!'' Dan rushed forward to stop her, but when he tried to grasp her hand she reacted with explosive anger, whirling around and furiously slapping his hands away.

"Don't touch me! Don't you *ever* touch me again."

"Maggie, don't. I can't let you do this. Please, sweetheart, we have to talk."

"No! I don't want to talk to you, I don't want to see you, or even hear your name," she ground out through clenched teeth. "For as long as I remain here you will speak to me only when necessary, and then only pertaining to business. Is that clear? Otherwise, I will file harassment charges against you."

When she spun around Ida Lou stood in the arched doorway with tears streaming down her cheeks. "Oh, child," she said with infinite sadness, and opened her arms wide, as she had done countless times in the past whenever Maggie had fallen and skinned her knees or sustained any sort of hurt.

This time, though, Maggie shook her head and scooted around the elderly woman. She simply couldn't bear to be comforted. She would splinter into a millions pieces at the first touch.

Seventeen

Word of Lily's rape and Maggie's doubtful parentage spread through Ruby Falls like wildfire.

Maggie had known that the story could not be kept a secret within the family. She was quite certain that Martin had delighted in spreading the word, never mind that in doing so he caused great pain and humiliation to his mother-in-law.

Wherever Maggie went—in the cannery or the office, in town, people stared. Some gave her pitying looks. Others, less charitable, acted as though she were something that had crawled out from under a rock, and avoided direct eye contact. Still others, like Pauline Babcock and her cohorts, would sniff and assume that smug "I always knew you were a bad seed" expression.

The weeks while they awaited the results of the DNA testing were tense and uncomfortable for everyone involved. Maggie had thought the period seven years ago after her father had thrown her out was the most miserable life could get, but she was wrong. She felt like an earthquake victim whose world had crumbled around her, moving through her days by rote, functioning somehow, but still dazed and traumatized.

Heartbroken over Dan's betrayal and riddled with doubts about who she really was, about her place in the family, her right to run Malone Enterprises, she withdrew from everyone.

Though she returned to the big house, what little time she spent there she stayed holed up in her room. Her mother and Nan protested and pleaded, but she refused to join the family in the dining room at mealtime. If she ate at home at all it was in the kitchen with Ida Lou. More often than not she merely picked up something at the drive-through of one of the fast-food restaurants in town and ate at her desk while she worked.

Work became her escape. Maggie arrived at the office before dawn and stayed late, long past the time the household retired for the night.

Jacob and Dan she avoided whenever possible. For his part, Dan abided by the orders she'd issued and made direct contact with her only on matters concerning business. However, he often gave her long, intense looks, as though trying to communicate with her silently, but she ignored them.

Occasionally while working late in the office she would see him working in the cannery, but he seemed to have abandoned his role as bodyguard, for which she was grateful. It hurt her to be around him at all. Every time she glimpsed him walking through the cannery or orchard her heart felt as though it would crack in two.

Maggie considered ordering Dan to stay out of the cannery in the evenings altogether, but she needed him to keep things running. Plus, she didn't want him to know how much his nearness affected her.

Between Thanksgiving and Christmas Maggie went on two more modeling assignments, and each time she was sorely tempted to simply stay in New York and not return to Ruby Falls ever again. Make a clean break and walk away—from the family, from the business, from the town. From Dan.

But there was that tantalizing possibility that she was Jacob's daughter, after all.

Often Maggie thought about the times as a kid when she had felt isolated from the rest of the family, the times she'd wondered why she couldn't have been born dainty and pretty like her sisters, and she would tell herself it was foolish to hope. But until she knew for certain, she could not walk away.

On Christmas morning everyone had already gathered in the family room when Maggie came downstairs. When she walked by the doorway her mother rushed out into the hall and intercepted her.

"Maggie, sweetheart, where are you going? Surely you're not going to work today. It's Christmas."

"Yes, actually, I am."

"But the family always opens gifts together on Christmas morning. Aren't you going to join us?"

Maggie glanced into the room where the others were gathered around the tree. They all watched her and waited to see what she would do. Her eyes met Jacob's briefly and she could have sworn that even he looked hopeful. But she was through with impossible dreaming. She shook her head. "No, I'm not."

"Oh, but Maggie—"

"I'm sorry, Momma. You'll find presents from me for everyone under the tree. Now, if you'll excuse me, I have to go."

Maggie knew her actions were hurting her mother, and she was sorry for that. The last thing she wanted was to cause Lily more pain, but she didn't have her capacity to simply push hurtful and unpleasant things aside and pretend they had never happened. Nor did her mother understand that for Maggie, merely being around the people she had always thought of as her family was excruciating and degrading beyond measure. So Maggie avoided them all and drove herself to the point of exhaustion so that she wouldn't have to think about the day of reckoning that was bearing down on them.

One morning during the first week of January, Anna came into Maggie's office with an odd expression on her face.

"Sorry to interrupt, Maggie, but there's a Mr. Henry Kincaid on line one. He asked for your extension, but I get the impression he's expecting to speak to Martin."

"Henry Kincaid? Should I know him?"

"He's the CEO of Bountiful Foods."

"Oh, really." Maggie picked up the telephone. "Mr. Kincaid, this is Maggie Malone. What can I do for you?"

"Actually, Miss Malone, I called to speak to the acting president of the company. I think I was put through to the wrong office."

"You are speaking to the acting president, Mr. Kincaid."

"You? That is, I thought Mr. Howe was filling in for Jacob Malone."

"No, that job has fallen to me." Temporarily, she added silently. "Mr. Howe is out of the office at the moment. Perhaps I can help you."

"Well, it was Mr. Howe who approached us, but I suppose I really should be dealing with you. Martin told us that once Mr. Malone passed on he would head the company, and that he would immediately move to change Malone Enterprises's articles of incorporation to allow it to be sold to outsiders. Anticipating that, we made an offer some weeks ago. I'm calling to inquire if your shareholders are ready to consider it."

"I'm afraid you've been misled, Mr. Kincaid. The Malone Cannery is not for sale."

The man laughed. "Miss Malone, I can tell you're a savvy negotiator, but let's cut to the chase, shall we. We were just testing the waters with that figure. We are quite prepared to go higher. I must say, after examining your books and seeing your splendid profit picture, we here at Bountiful Foods are most impressed with your company."

Splendid profit picture? "I see. I didn't realize that Mr. Howe had given you access to our books."

"Yes, he provided us with a computer-generated copy of your company records for the past two years. He's been most helpful in facilitating this deal. Most helpful."

"Oh, I'm sure he has. However, I'm afraid Mr. Howe has wasted your time. Jacob Malone is still very much alive, and when he's gone the company will remain in the family."

Mr. Kincaid argued some more, but Maggie finally convinced him there would be no deal. When she hung up, she frowned and tapped her pencil against the desktop. If Mr. Kincaid and his board thought their profits looked splendid, he was looking at a different set of books than she was.

Maggie shot out of her chair. "I'm going to accounting," she said, marching past Anna's desk in the outer office.

The door to Elaine Udall's office was closed, but Maggie could hear a keyboard clacking. Grasping the knob, she started to barge in, but when she opened the door a crack something about Elaine's demeanor stopped her, and she paused to watch.

With quick, nervous moments the woman was entering figures onto a computer spreadsheet, every now and then casting furtive glances toward the door, as though fearful that someone would walk in and catch her. Maggie's eyes narrowed. Why so secretive? She was about to knock and announce her presence when Elaine finished her work, withdrew a diskette from the Zip drive and slipped it into her purse.

Giving the door a quick tap, Maggie pushed it open. Elaine started guiltily and shoved her purse into the bottom drawer of her desk.

"Miss Malone, is there something you want?"

"Yes. I want to see all the purchase orders, invoices and all expense receipts for the past two years."

"Very well," she said in her snooty schoolmarm voice, and turned back to the computer. "It will take me a few minutes to print them out, though."

"No, I don't want a printout of the books. I have that. I want to see the actual orders and invoices and all other pertinent documents."

Maggie wasn't sure, but she could swear she saw panic flash in Miss Udall's eyes. "I'm afraid that's impossible. We don't keep that sort of thing."

"Don't try to play me for a fool, Miss Udall. I know what the law requires, and I also know that we keep thorough substantiating records going back decades in our storeroom. I want the past two years' worth in my office within the hour."

Elaine puffed up like a toad. "Are you questioning my accounting?"

"Are you questioning my right to review company records?" Maggie fired back.

"Mr. Howe says you're not even a Malone. He said you won't be here much longer. I don't think I should turn over company records to you."

Maggie braced her hands on top of the woman's desk and leaned toward her. "I don't give a rat's ass what Mr. Howe says. I am still acting president of this company. Now…you can either have those records brought to my office immediately, or you can clean out your desk right now. The choice is yours."

It took Maggie less that two hours to uncover gross discrepancies. The printout of the company's financial records that she had did not tally with the actually receivables and payables during any month she'd checked.

Fuming, Maggie buzzed Anna and told her to have Martin and Miss Udall come to her office immediately. A short while later Anna walked into Maggie's office alone.

"Sorry, Maggie, but Martin left the office at noon. He told his secretary he had a golf date with a customer, but he didn't say which one."

"And Elaine Udall?"

"According to Susan in accounting, she shot out of here like a cat with its tail on fire about two hours ago, right after she had those archive records brought to you."

Maggie grabbed her purse and headed for the door. "If anyone wants me, I'll be at Martin's house."

She had not been to the Howe home since she returned to Ruby Falls, and when she brought her car to a halt in the circular driveway she looked with distaste at the white colonial. The place belonged to Martin's father and was the biggest, most ostentatious house in town. Rupert could not have borne anything less.

As president of the First National Bank, he liked to think of himself as the town's leading citizen, but to most folks around these parts that position belonged to Jacob.

A wicked little smile twitched Maggie's mouth. Though Martin's father had always treated Jacob with hearty friendliness, she knew that fact secretly galled Rupert.

Overriding Laurel's objections, Martin had insisted that they move in with Rupert on returning from their honeymoon. He had claimed that he couldn't possibly leave his father all alone in the big house.

Personally, Maggie didn't believe that was the reason. Not for a minute. Rupert had spoiled his son rotten, and never in his sorry life had Martin ever given a thought to anyone else's needs or wishes. The way Maggie figured it, he simply hadn't wanted to trade the grand home for one the size he and Laurel could afford, or give up the lavish life-style that his father had always provided.

The front door was ajar, but Maggie rang the doorbell, anyway, and stood impatiently while the elaborate chimes echoed inside the house. When no one answered she glanced toward Laurel's BMW parked in the side driveway. Maggie eased the door open and stepped inside.

"Hello. Laurel, are you here? It's me, Maggie." She eased farther into the foyer. "Anybody home?"

Maggie thought she heard a faint sound and stopped, cocking her head to one side. It was coming from upstairs. It sounded almost like a muffled moan, like an animal in pain.

Reaching inside her purse, Maggie closed her hand around her stun gun and started cautiously up the stairs. At the top the sounds grew louder as she followed them down the hallway to a large bedroom at the end. The first thing she noticed when she stepped inside were several red stains on the carpet that looked like blood. Maggie's heart rate speeded up.

Her gaze darted around the room, but there didn't appear to be anyone there. She was wondering if she should call the sheriff when she heard a moan from the bathroom. Maggie hurried across the bedroom toward the sound, but at the bathroom door she stopped in her tracks.

"Oh, my God! Laurel!"

Her sister lay curled in the fetal position on the floor, clutching her stomach and groaning, her face a battered and bloody mess. Maggie rushed inside and knelt beside her. "Oh, Laurel, you poor darling." She snatched a towel from the rack and ran it under the cold water tap, then knelt again and tried to gently blot away the blood, but Laurel moaned and put her hands up and tried to hide her face.

"No-o-o. Don't lo-look at me. Oh, go a-away, Maggie. I don't wa-want you to see m-me like this." Her lips were cut and swollen, and the words came out mumbly and slurred.

"It's too late for that. And I'm not leaving this house without you, so don't waste your breath. Anyway, the important thing right now is to get you some medical attention. Here, press this towel to your cheek while I go call for an ambulance."

"No, don't." Laurel clutched Maggie's arm. "Pl-please, don't do that. Ev-everyone will know. I couldn't bear that."

"Laurel, you need to see a doctor. Besides, once we call the sheriff, it's all going to come out." Maggie pushed a bloodied clump of hair away from her sister's face and gritted her teeth. "Damn Martin! He did this to you, didn't he?"

Laurel nodded, then moaned piteously when the action caused more pain.

"That bastard. That sorry, worthless— That settles it. You're getting out of here, and this time you're going to press charges. And don't you dare tell me you're not. No way am I leaving you with that beast."

"I—I won't...argue. I told him I was going to di-divorce him. That's why...why he b-beat me."

"You were finally leaving him? Well thank heaven for that. That's the best news I've heard all year. And don't you worry about Martin coming after you. He'll have to get through me first. I almost hope he tries."

"He will try. Hel-help me stand up. We have to get out of here be-before he comes back."

Maggie winced at the pain each movement caused her sister. "Laurel, you really should go to the hospital."

"No, please. Just take me home."

Every instinct Maggie possessed urged her to put her sister in the car and burn rubber all the way to Tyler, but she couldn't risk Laurel becoming hysterical on top of everything else. She huffed an exasperated sigh. "All right, you win. But I'm calling Dr. Sanderson. And the sheriff."

Laurel was in so much pain it seemed to take forever to get her down the stairs and out of the house. Maggie had just buckled her into the passenger seat of the Viper when Martin's Mercedes came roaring up the U-shaped drive.

"Oh, God. He'll kill me now for sure," Laurel whimpered.

"Like hell he will. Just sit tight. And don't worry. I'll take care of Martin."

The Mercedes slammed to a halt a few feet behind the Viper. Martin bailed out and came storming toward them. "What do you think you're doing? You get the hell away from my wife, bitch. You're not taking her anywhere.''

"Wanna bet?" Maggie stepped in his path and raised her hand to his arm.

Pzzzzt.

Martin dropped like a stone. Leaning over her brother-in-law's twitching body, Maggie smiled. "You lose."

"Wh-what did you do to him?" Laurel asked when Maggie climbed into the Viper.

"Zapped him with my stun gun. If I weren't so anxious to get medical attention for you I would've wiped up the ground with him."

Jacob, with Lily and Nan walking on either side, was being pushed through the central hall in his wheelchair by Charley when Maggie struggled through the front door, half carrying Laurel.

"Dear God in heaven," Nan murmured.

Lily gasped. "My baby, oh, my poor baby!"

"What the hell happened to you, Laurel?" Jacob barked.

"Martin happened to her, that's what," Maggie replied for her.

"Martin? *He* did this to her? I can't believe it."

"Well you'd *better* believe it. And it isn't the first time, either. He's been knocking her around ever since they married."

"Laurel, is this true? Why in God's name didn't you tell us?"

Maggie started to ask him why he hadn't seen what was right under his nose all these years, but at that moment Laurel groaned and would have sagged to the floor if Charley hadn't rushed forward and caught her before she could slip from Maggie's hold.

Sweeping her up in his arms, he headed for the stairs. "I'll put her to bed. Someone call a doctor."

"Yes. Oh, yes. Nan, would you see to it?" Lily dithered, following in his wake.

"Don't bother. Dr. Sanderson is on his way. I called him from the car on the way here."

"Good. I'll go help with Laurel."

When Nan had disappeared up the stairs, Maggie looked at Jacob. "You might as well know, I also called the sheriff and told him to arrest Martin, that Laurel would be filing assault charges. I expect Sheriff Dunwitty will be here soon to take a statement and photograph Laurel's injuries."

"Where is Martin?" Jacob demanded.

"Last time I saw him he was sprawled on Rupert's front lawn, flopping like a fish out of water."

"He was doing *what?*"

Maggie shrugged. "I zapped him with my stun gun when he tried to stop me from leaving with Laurel."

Jacob shook his head. "How could he have done that to her? How can any man do such a thing to a woman? Do you know what set him off?"

"On the drive over here Laurel told me that she found out he'd been having an affair with Elaine Udall. Apparently, the woman came to the house a while ago to warn Martin that I'd found out that she'd been keeping duplicate sets of books."

"What! Why would she do that?"

"To force us to sell to Bountiful would be my guess. She doctored the books we saw to make it

appear as though the company was teetering on
bankruptcy, and Martin gave Bountiful Foods a set
that made it look like we're raking in the money.
From what I've been able to piece together so far,
I'd say the truth of the matter is somewhere in between. We've been hurt, but not so badly that we
can't recover. Plus, there's still the question of what
happened to the profits that didn't show up on the
books.

"Anyway, from what Laurel said, when Elaine
arrived at their house she was babbling hysterically
and revealed everything, including their affair.
When Laurel got upset and told Martin she was going to file for divorce, he attacked her. I found her
a few minutes after he'd stormed out and left her
unconscious on the floor."

"That *bastard!* The man is an animal."

"Yes, I know. I tried to tell you that seven years
ago."

Jacob winced and hung his head. "I know," he
whispered. "I know."

Maggie turned to follow Nan.

"Katherine, wait."

Halfway up the stairs she stopped and gazed
down at him in silence. Jacob looked old and sick
and utterly forlorn. He also looked riddled with guilt
and regret.

"This is my fault. I should have at least suspected
something like this. I realize that now. Instead I dismissed Martin's controlling, overbearing treatment
of her as just part of his domineering personality and
ignored all the other signs. I guess I so wanted everything to be perfect for her that I turned a blind

eye." He rubbed a hand over his face and sighed. "That, and, to be honest, I didn't *want* to believe that you were telling the truth about Martin all those years ago."

"I know. Is that all?"

"Thank you, Katherine, for getting her out of that house and bringing her home to us."

Maggie lifted her chin. "You don't have to thank me. I may not be your daughter, but Laurel and Jo Beth will always be my sisters."

Eighteen

On the drive from Tyler to Ruby Falls, Dr. Sanderson must surely have set a world land-speed record. His sedate sedan screeched to a halt in front of the house a mere twenty minutes later.

He was livid when he saw Laurel, and would have gone after Martin himself if Maggie hadn't explained that he was already under arrest.

Sheriff Dunwitty came and took Laurel's statement and Polaroid shots of her injuries.

The news that Martin was in jail for beating Laurel spread through town like a firestorm. It was Ida Lou's day off, and she was in the City Café having dinner with her friend Clara when the story reached her. She left her meal half-eaten and hurried straight home. The dear old woman was so appalled and upset when she saw what Martin had done to Laurel that she broke down and wept.

A few minutes after Ida Lou returned Maggie answered a knock at the terrace door and found herself staring into Dan's stern face.

"How is she?" he asked without preamble.

Maggie's first impulse was to put her head on his shoulder and seek comfort in his arms. Immediately furious with herself, she subdued the foolish weakness and stepped back and motioned for him to come in. "Battered and in a lot of pain, but she's still refusing to go to the hospital. Dr. Sanderson isn't happy about it, but he says her injuries aren't life threatening, and she'll recover with no permanent physical damage. Emotionally...who knows."

A muscle rippled along Dan's jaw. "How is Jacob holding up?"

Maggie glanced toward the recliner where Jacob lay among a pile of pillows, staring into space. His complexion had taken on a gray cast that worried Maggie. He looked like a defeated shell of a man.

The emotions of a lifetime were not easily shed. Maggie held Jacob and Lily at least partly to blame for not seeing the signs that Laurel was being abused, and she was hurt and angry and struggling to come to grips with the past, but this was the man she had always thought of as her father, and no matter what, she still loved him.

"Not well, I'm afraid. This has depressed him terribly, which isn't good in his condition."

"I'll go see if I can distract him."

When Dan crossed the room to talk to Jacob, Maggie stayed by the French doors and stared out at the dimly lit terrace, keeping her back to the room.

Get a grip, will you. The man only pretended to love you so he could spy on you for Jacob. You can't still love him.

But she did. God help her, she did.

Maggie squeezed her eyes shut. Jeezlouise, you're pathetic, Mag. Really pathetic.

Throughout the evening friends called to express

their concern and inquire after Laurel. Most were also openly delighted that Martin had been arrested. His arrogance and overbearing manner had not earned him many friends in Ruby Falls.

From those who called they learned that Rupert had been furious when he heard that his son was in jail, particularly so when he discovered he could not bail him out until morning.

Typically, Rupert was insisting to anyone who would listen that the whole thing had been nothing more than a little domestic spat, that Laurel had simply overreacted. She was sure to drop the charges once she was thinking more rationally.

That he would dare to cavalierly brush off his son's brutal attack in such a manner and imply that her sister was at fault infuriated Maggie. She was so riled she could not settle and roamed the house like a restless soul.

Throughout the evening the entire family expected Rupert to descend on them in a rage. Maggie suspected that was why Dan appeared in no hurry to leave, and though his presence tore at her heart, for that, at least, she was grateful.

By nine that evening there had been no sign of Rupert, not even a telephone call. Laurel was resting comfortably, thanks to Neil Sanderson, the calls had stopped and the household had settled down somewhat. The young doctor remained at Laurel's side, and apparently he had every intention of staying right there all night. Feeling superfluous and antsy, Maggie left the others discussing the situation and went to the office where she could possibly be of some use.

When she entered her office she caught a whiff of a peculiar acetone smell and wondered what it could be. A cleaning solution they used down on the cannery floor, perhaps?

Her gaze fell on the boxes of accounting papers that still littered the room and the printout of the company books lying spread open on her desk exactly as she'd left it, and the mystery smell was forgotten. She settled in the chair and picked up her examination of the books where she'd left off that afternoon.

Twenty minutes later she was so immersed in the job she had no idea she was no longer alone.

"I thought I'd find you here."

Maggie jolted and her head jerked up. Her heart gave a hard thump when she saw who stood in the doorway. "Rupert! What're you doing here?" Her gaze shot past him. "How did you get past the security guard?"

A sly smile curved his mouth. He reminded Maggie of a fox. "It was a simple matter to walk up behind that idiot and conk him over the head. Currently, he's out cold in the parking lot."

Maggie's uneasiness went up several notches. She had known that Rupert would be angry, but it had not occurred to her that he would resort to violence. Although, in retrospect, she realized that it probably should have. Behavior like Martin's was usually learned. Like father, like son.

Okay, fine, Maggie thought, and rose slowly, bracing for a struggle. She didn't relish the idea of exchanging blows with a man Rupert's age, but if he made a move to hurt her she *would* defend herself. "I see. What do you want?"

"I came here to take care of a problem, once and for all."

"Oh? And what is that?"

"You. You've been a thorn in my boy's side for years. First you tried to stop Laurel from marrying him. Then you come back here and take over the cannery. Everybody knows that job should have been Martin's. He deserves to head this company. Come to that, the whole shootin' match should be his. Your sisters are incapable of taking over, and it turns out you're not even a Malone.

"Now, not only are you trying to ruin the deal Martin's got going, you're interfering in his marriage. Dammit! My boy is sitting in jail right now because of you! Like some common criminal."

"Martin is in jail because of what he did to my sister."

"If it hadn't been for you she would never have filed charges or threatened him with divorce. She would never have had the nerve to defy him.

"Well, you're through interfering in my boy's life."

He pulled a small, lethal-looking pistol from his pocket and pointed it at her, and Maggie felt the first acid taste of fear in her mouth. "Rupert, for God's sake, what are you doing?"

"Isn't it obvious? Once you're out of the picture, Laurel will do as she's told, and when Jacob dies the Bountiful deal will go through, as planned. It will require a bit of renegotiating and fancy footwork on Martin's part, thanks to you, but the deal can still be salvaged.''

Maggie stared at the obscene black hole in the end of the pistol barrel and panic nearly choked her. "Rupert, wait, this is insane.''

"I'm through waiting. I have to take action now before you ruin everything. You brought this on yourself, you know. I tried to force you to sell. I even tried to scare you away, but you wouldn't give up. You've left me with no choice.''

Maggie's mouth dropped open. "*You* were the man in the orchard? You put that rat in my bed, and slashed my tires and vandalized my car?''

"Yes.''

Hardly able to take it all in, she shook her head. "And the contaminated food batches, the 'accidents' and breakdowns, the poisoned trees? *That* was you.''

"Of course. I used Martin's keys to get into the cannery during the middle of the night when no one was here." He smiled his foxy smile. "You never even suspected it was me, did you. Neither will anyone else. After all, I'm a pillar of the community, a respected and influential man.''

"You'll never get by with murder. Guns can be traced through ballistics." Maggie glanced at the stairwell door and calculated her chances.

"Oh, I'm not going to shoot you, my dear. Not unless you do something foolish and leave me no choice. Your death is going to be a tragic accident. You'll perish in a terrible fire.

"And you can stop looking at that door. I've already blocked it, and the one at the bottom of the stairs, as well. I've also taken the precaution of disabling your sprinkler system. So you see, my dear, there's no escape. I suggest you say your prayers."

"Rupert, wait!" she cried, but it was too late. Even as Maggie sprang across the room he flipped the lock on the inside of the door, stepped back into the outer office and pulled it shut after him. Maggie grabbed the knob and the small lever and tried to unlock the door, but it wouldn't turn.

Her nose wrinkled as the pungent odor she'd noticed before suddenly became stronger. At first she couldn't figure out where the smell was coming from or what it was. Then her confusion turned to horror. Dear God! Rupert had squirted Super Glue into the lock.

Maggie beat on the door with her fists. "Rupert! Rupert, let me out of here this minute! This is crazy! You can't *do* this!" She grabbed the knob and rattled it, but it wouldn't turn. "Rupert, dammit—" A new smell entered the room, and like a deer scenting trouble on the wind, she stilled and sniffed the air.

A movement by her feet attracted her attention. She stared down at the wisps of smoke curling under the door, and fear grabbed her by the throat.

Maggie ran to the stairwell door and tugged on the handle, but the lock was glued, as well. This, she realized, was the smell she'd detected earlier.

Frantic, she darted back to the desk and snatched up the telephone receiver, but there was no dial tone. She jiggled the disconnect button but it was no use, and with a curse she slammed the receiver down. Panting, Maggie gripped the edge of the desk. Dear God, there was no way out!

Panic threatened to suffocate her, but she closed her eyes and took several deep breaths and gritted her teeth. "Think, Maggie. Think! You're not going to die here tonight. You will *not* let him win. Dammit, *think!*"

Forcing herself to breathe slowly, she looked around again and saw that smoke was now pouring in under the door. Already the room was hazy with it. "All right. First things first," she muttered, grabbing her sweater off the coatrack. She dropped to her knees and stuffed the soft garment under the door as tightly as she could. It didn't block the smoke completely, but it slowed it down to a seep and bought her time.

"All right now, Mag, think logically. You can't get out through the doors and you can't bust through the paneling."

Her gaze shot to the glass wall.

She dashed across the office, placed both palms on the plate glass and tested it with a push. It was strong, but she might be able to break it.

Her gaze dropped to the cannery floor, and her shoulders slumped. Even if she managed to break the window, a jump from this height would kill her.

A movement at the far side of the cannery floor caught her eye. Dan!

From that distance she couldn't see exactly who was down there working, but her gaze zeroed in on the shop light. It had to be him. It *had* to be.

She called his name and knocked on the glass with both fists, but he didn't come. Maggie coughed and choked. She glanced over her shoulder and saw smoke pushing in under the door, faster and thicker

than before. Now she could hear the crackle of the
fire in the outer office and feel the heat of it.

"Oh God, oh God." She banged on the glass wall
with the sides of her fists. "Da-a-a-an! Da-a-a-an!
Look up!"

Another spasm of coughing seized her, bending
her double. Kneeling low, she gulped in the cleaner
air next to the floor. Finally, drawing in a deep
breath, Maggie shot to her feet, snatched up the arm-
less chair beside the desk and swung it at the glass
with all her might. It hit with an impact that sent
shock waves up her arms, but the glass held. Making
desperate whimpering sounds Maggie swung the
chair again and again and again.

Dan heard the crash and looked up in time to see
a chair come flying through the wall of Maggie's
office amid a shower of broken glass. Turning end
over end, it arced downward and crashed into a conveyor with a tremendous racket.

"What the *hell?*"

Without conscious thought, he started in that direction. Maggie appeared in the opening in the broken glass wall, and the hair on the back of Dan's
neck stood on end. Clouds of gray smoke poured
out all around her.

Holy shit! The place was on fire!

"Da-a-an! Dan, help me! Help me!"

He broke into a run, his heart pounding. "I'm
coming, sweetheart!" he shouted. "I'm coming!
Hang on!"

He ran for the door at the bottom of the stairs,
intent on reaching her.

"No, the lock is jammed with glue!" Maggie shouted when she saw where he was heading.

Dan skidded to a halt beneath where she stood, the full implication of what she'd said sinking in. Bloody hell! This was no accident. Someone had locked her in and started a fire.

He cupped his hands around his mouth. "Can you get out through Anna's office?"

"No! That door is jammed, too, and the office is in flames! The only way out is to jump, but it's too far!"

Damn. Somehow, he had to reach her. They had extension ladders, but they were in the equipment barn on the other side of the complex. There wasn't time to go after one. Desperate, he looked around for something to use to reach her. Then it came to him and he broke into a run.

"Da-a-a-an!"

"I'll be right back," he shouted over his shoulder. "Stay low and hang on."

Arms and legs pumping, Dan streaked toward the loading docks on the other side of the cannery. As he ran he fished his cell phone out of his shirt pocket and punched in 911.

Emergency calls in Ruby Falls were routed through the dispatch desk at the sheriff's office. Nancy Eggelston, who worked the desk on the night shift, answered on the second ring.

"Nine-one-one. What's your emergency?"

"Nancy, this is Dan Garrett," he shouted into the phone. "Malone Cannery is on fire! Get the trucks out here, fast! And send the sheriff, too. Maggie is trapped inside her office!"

"They're on their way."

Dan flipped the phone closed and stuffed it back in his pocket just as he reached the loading dock where all the outgoing conveyor belts converged. Without breaking stride, he jumped up into one of the forklifts that were used to move cases of canned goods to the warehouses a few hundred yards away. The one he chose was a reach truck that could lift heavy pallets of goods onto shelves thirty feet high.

Dan cranked the engine and scooped up a double-decked pallet with the forks. He swung the machine around, opened it up to full throttle and headed back toward the offices on the other side of the building. "Go. Go, damn you!" he snarled at the machine, but even top speed seemed agonizingly slow.

Thick smoke was billowing out into the cannery now. Dan ground his teeth and alternated between praying and cursing the poky forklift.

When at last he backed the lift truck to a halt beneath Maggie's office he didn't see her at first, and fear squeezed his chest like a vise. "Maggie! Maggie, where are you?"

"Here."

She waved, and he realized that she was crouched on the floor with the heavy window drapery wrapped around her head.

Dan sent the lift carriage climbing. "I'm going to raise this pallet as high as it will go," he shouted. "It won't quite reach you, but when it stops I want you to jump down onto it. Okay?"

Jump? Maggie stared down at the wooden pallet, slowly rising toward her. He wanted her to jump onto *that?*

She waited, her gaze fixed on the tiny platform, her heart clubbing against her ribs. Keep coming, keep coming, she silently urged, but when the lift arm stopped the pallet was a good five or six feet shy of the office floor. Maggie stared, and her parched throat tightened painfully. She knew the pallet was four feet by four feet, but from where she crouched it looked like a postage stamp.

"Jump, Maggie. Jump!"

Holding the heavy drapery over her lower face, she climbed to her feet and stood at the edge, staring down through the smoke at the minuscule square of wood.

"Jump, Maggie!"

She shook her head. "I can't!"

"Yes, you can! You can do it, sweetheart!"

"What if I miss? What if I can't hold on?"

"You won't miss. You'll make it. C'mon, Maggie. You have to jump! There's no other way!"

"But the impact might topple the lift."

"It won't! I promise you, this rig is strong enough to take the strain. C'mon, baby. *Jump!*"

He was right. She knew that. But the thought of jumping terrified her so much she wasn't sure she could move.

She heard a crackling sound and glanced over her shoulder. Instantly, her terror multiplied tenfold. The fire had consumed her sweater and flames were licking up the inside of the door.

Screwing up her courage, Maggie drew a shaky breath and leapt into space.

With a strangled cry, she hit the pallet a little to the left of center. Her knees buckled on impact, and she went sprawling onto her belly, clutching for purchase, all the while making desperate little sounds.

The instant she hit, the rig began to sway ominously. In what seemed like slow motion the whole rig began to teeter to one side, and Maggie screamed as she felt herself sliding. She flailed about for a handhold but here was nothing to grab on to but the flat boards. Her scream reached a crescendo when she slipped over the edge.

In a last desperate effort she somehow managed to snag one of the pallet's side stringer boards.

"Hang on! Hang on!"

Dangling from the side of the pallet thirty feet above the concrete floor, her body swinging like a church bell on Sunday morning, Maggie clutched the stringer with both hands in a death grip. Whimpering and gasping, she looked down and saw Dan leaning hard to the other side and realized that he had managed to arrest the topple and bring the rig upright again.

"Hold tight. I'm going to lower you now," he yelled.

The whole rig gave a little jerk when the carriage began to descend, and despite Dan's warning Maggie shrieked.

It seemed to take forever to reach the floor. Maggie's hands were raw and stinging from scrabbling around on the rough pallet and her arms felt as though they were going to pull right out of their sockets.

Her toes finally touched the floor, but before her heels could follow Dan jumped out of the cab and snatched her into his arms.

"Thank God! Thank God!" He held her close and rocked her, his hands clutching her as though he'd never let go. Beneath her ear, Maggie heard his heart thundering wildly. "Are you all right? Are you hurt?" Holding her slightly away from him he ran his hands up and down her arms, over her head and shoulders and back, all the while looking her over. Maggie knew that her face and hair, like her hands, were covered with soot.

"I'm okay." She looked up and cried out. Flames were visible in her office now, greedily climbing the walls and spreading over the ceiling. "We have to do something! C'mon. We have fire extinguishers every twenty-five feet along the walls. We'll grab some and go around the outside to the main entrance. We can get up to the offices from there. Let's *go!*"

Before Dan could stop her she darted past him and snatched an extinguisher off the wall beneath the burning offices.

Dan ran after her as she raced toward the next extinguisher. "Maggie, wait! I called the fire department. They're on their way. Listen. You can hear the sirens now."

He could have saved his breath. With an extinguisher hanging from each hand, Maggie ran for the side door.

"Dammit, Maggie, stop!"

The air outside felt wonderfully cool and fresh sliding into her parched lungs. Maggie sucked in great gulps as she ran the short distance to the main entrance. As she had hoped, Rupert had been in too much of a hurry to lock the doors behind him when

he left. Barely breaking stride, she shouldered open
the doors into the small lobby, but before she could
climb the stairs, a strong arm hooked around her
waist, jerking her to a halt.

"Let go of me. Let *go!*"

"Not on your life!" Dan shouted, hauling her,
kicking and bucking, back out the door. "You're not
going back into that fire, you little idiot!"

"But my office! I can't just let it burn!"

"You don't have the gear or the know-how to put
out that inferno. Leave it to the pros."

Right on cue, two fire trucks roared into the parking lot, sirens clanging, followed by an ambulance,
the sheriff's cruiser and Dr. Sanderson's car. The
men of the Ruby Falls Volunteer Fire Department,
dressed in yellow slickers and gas masks, hit the
ground running. One, Cris Patterson, their leader,
paused long enough to be sure they were okay.
When satisfied, he ordered them to get clear of the
building and dashed in after the others, who were
already dragging a fire hose through the lobby doors
and up the stairs.

Neil, Charley, Jo Beth, Nan and Lily had already
climbed from the doctor's car when Maggie and Dan
staggered over to them. She halted abruptly when
she spotted Jacob sitting propped up with pillows
and covered up to his chin with blankets in the back
seat.

"Have you all lost your minds?" she demanded.
"Why in heaven's name did you bring him here?
He shouldn't be out in the cold night air. And he
certainly doesn't need to see this."

"Maggie? Is that you?" Lily asked. "Oh, my word! It *is* you. Oh, dearest, are you all right?"

Neither Maggie nor Dr. Sanderson paid her any heed.

"I'm afraid I'm to blame for bringing him, Maggie," Neil answered. "When he heard the sirens approaching he got so agitated nothing would do but he come see what was going on. I figured he'd be better off here with us than working himself into a frenzy at home."

A back window on the sedan lowered and Jacob stuck his head out. "What're you doing with those fire extinguishers, Katherine?"

"What?" Maggie looked down, surprised to see that she still gripped an extinguisher in each hand. She had forgotten she had them. "I, uh..."

"She was about to rush back inside and fight the fire single-handed," Dan supplied, prying the cylinders out of her hands and tossing them aside. "She fought me like the devil, but I wouldn't let her go back into that blaze. She barely escaped being burned to death once already tonight."

"Good God, girl! What were you thinking? You could've been killed!"

Neil stepped close to her, instantly switching from family friend to medical professional. "How're you feeling, Maggie? Any pain anywhere? Trouble breathing?"

"I..." Without warning, as though her bones had suddenly turned to mush, Maggie's knees gave way beneath her and she sank to the pavement, landing hard on her rear end.

"Dammit, Red," Dan barked, and hunkered down beside her.

Lily cried out, and Nan took a concerned step forward, but Neil waved them both back and knelt by Maggie's other side. Dazed, she looked around in confusion and began to shake.

"Delayed reaction," Neil said. "I'll go get some blankets from the ambulance. And some oxygen—just in case."

"Hang on, honey." Dan moved in close and wrapped his arms around her, chafing his hands up and down her arms.

Neil returned and wrapped a blanket around her, then draped a fireman's slicker over it. Kneeling beside her again, he poured coffee from a thermos. "Here, I got this from the paramedics. They carry it for shock victims. It's sickeningly sweet, but it's good for what ails you."

Maggie held the cup with both hands, but she was shaking so hard she couldn't bring it to her mouth without assistance from Dan. She nearly gagged at the sweet taste, but the hot brew felt wonderful sliding down her throat, and within a few minutes the bone-rattling shakes tapered off.

Sheriff Dunwitty came over and hunkered down in front of her. "You okay, Maggie?"

She huddled deeper into the blanket and slicker and nodded.

"Well, now...y'all will be glad to know that the boys have the fire under control. It should be out soon. They managed to contain it to two offices and a small section of hallway."

They all expressed their relief, but Sheriff Dunwitty's expression remained grave. "The thing is…Cris says the fire looks like arson. You know anything about that, Maggie?"

"Dammit, Woodrow!" Jacob thundered from the back seat of the car. "Are you accusing Katherine of deliberately setting that fire. You fool. She was nearly killed tonight."

"Now, Jacob, I have to ask—"

"No, it's okay," Maggie said. "Actually, Sheriff, I do know who set the fire." In detail, Maggie recounted the events of the evening. Several times her story drew shocked gasps from the others. By the time she was done they were outraged.

"Why would Rupert do such a thing?" Nan asked.

"All I know for certain is he and Martin were trying to force us to sell to Bountiful Foods. When I figured out what Martin was up to and put a stop to the negotiating, it infuriated Rupert. He figured if I was out of the way, Martin could salvage the deal and push it through. Why they wanted the sale so badly, I have no idea. In the long run, Martin stood to gain more if Malone's remained in the family." Maggie shook her head. "It doesn't make any sense to me."

"Well, all I know is it's sure gonna do my heart good to slap the cuffs on ole Rupert," the sheriff drawled. "Never could abide the arrogant little pissant."

"Speak of the devil," Jo Beth muttered. "Look who just drove up."

All eyes swung toward the maroon Mercedes that cruised to a stop behind the ambulance and fire trucks. Rupert climbed out and stopped to speak to the paramedics and a passing fireman before heading their way.

"I don't believe it!" Nan snapped.

"He's got one helluva nerve, showing up here," Jacob growled.

Dan surged to his feet. "Son of a bitch! I'll kill the bas—"

"Whoa. Take it easy. Let me handle this," the sheriff cautioned, putting a restraining hand on Dan's shoulder. "Everybody keep quiet and let's see what he has to say. Give an arrogant fool enough rope and he'll usually hang himself."

Rupert headed straight for the car when he spotted Jacob. "Jacob, I came as soon as I heard the sirens."

Sitting huddled on the ground, Maggie watched the two men from beneath the cover of the blanket. Jacob's face looked as though it were carved from granite.

"You've got some nerve showing your face around here, Rupert."

"Now, now, Jacob. I know you're angry with that boy of mine right now, but you and I have been friends too long to let our children's spats come between us." He sighed and assumed a tragic expression. "I heard about Maggie and I had to come offer my condolences. Even if she isn't your flesh and blood, you raised her. You and Lily must be devastated. To perish in a fire that way...well, it's tragic. Just tragic. You have my sympathy."

Maggie could keep quiet no longer. She tossed the blanket off her head and stood up. "They don't need sympathy. Especially from the man who tried to murder me.''

Rupert could not have looked more shocked if she had risen out of a grave. ''Maggie! How did you—''

''Sheriff, I want you to arrest Mr. Howe for attempted murder. He filled the locks on my office doors with glue to trap me inside, then set the fire.''

''What nonsense! I did nothing of the kind.'' He sent Sheriff Dunwitty an indignant glare when he started toward him, unclipping the handcuffs hanging from his belt. ''See, here, Sheriff, you can't arrest me. It's her word against mine.''

''Not quite, Rupert,'' Maggie said with hard satisfaction. ''The security cameras I recently had installed caught the whole thing on tape. They're in fireproof casings, so I'm sure they'll provide all the evidence I need to back up my story.''

''You bitch! I should have shot you while I had the chance!''

''Okay, that's all I need. Come along. I got a nice cell waiting for you right alongside your son's.'' The sheriff shoved Rupert up against the car and snapped the handcuffs on his wrists before he realized what was happening. ''Rupert Howe, you're under arrest for attempted murder and arson. You have the right to remain silent. Anything you say can and will...''

''I'll get you for this! You see if I don't! You're dead, bitch! You hear me! Dead!''

Grabbing Rupert by the back of his shirt collar, the sheriff led him away, continuing to recite his Miranda rights over the invectives Rupert shouted at Maggie.

"Lord have mercy, what a day this turned out to be," Nan said as they watched the sheriff's car roll out of the parking lot.

"Yes," Maggie agreed. She turned to look at the smoke-blackened building. "It's just lucky for me that Dan happened to be working tonight."

"Lucky, hell." Dan grabbed her shoulders and turned her to face him. "Luck had nothing to do with it. I've been here every night that you worked late."

Maggie blinked, shocked by his anger and the fierce emotion in his eyes. "You were here? But...why?"

"*Why?* Because I love you, dammit. No matter what you believe. Did you think I'd just walk away when there was a lunatic threatening you? He put a dead rat in your bed, for Christ's sake. Slashed your tires, sprayed obscenities on your car. It was just a matter of time until he came after you personally."

"What's this? What's this about a rat?" Jacob demanded. "And attacks on your car? Why wasn't I informed?"

Maggie's gaze darted from Dan to Jacob and back. "You didn't tell him?"

"No. I tried to explain before, my reports to Jacob ended when I fell in love with you."

Maggie's heart thumped painfully. She gazed into Dan's harsh face, wanting to believe him. Because she so desperately wanted to believe, she held back, not trusting her love-starved heart to guide her. "And when, exactly, did you start loving me?"

Dan's mouth quirked with a hint of a grin. "I began to suspect that night you announced to Martin that you were taking over. I knew for certain the day you kicked butt in the café, then sashayed across the square to do the same to Leland.'' His face grew serious again. ''You're one helluva woman, Maggie Malone, and I will love you until the day I die.''

Maggie's heart did a slow roll in her chest. Emotions filled her, and as she stared into those silvery eyes, glittering like diamonds, she wondered how she could ever have doubted him.

''Oh, Dan,'' she said in a quavery murmur, and stepped into his arms.

It was like coming home. He held her tight, the way a drowning man clutched a lifeline. Maggie slipped her arms around his middle and rested her cheek against his chest, smiling as she heard the thunderous beat of his heart beneath her ear.

Dr. Sanderson cleared his throat. ''Well, now, I hate to break this up, but I think Maggie should go with the paramedics to the hospital in Tyler and get checked out. You may need to be treated for smoke inhalation.''

She looked at the young doctor over her shoulder and shook her head. ''No, I'm okay. Really. I just want to go home.'' She looked up at Dan with her heart in her eyes. ''Back to the cottage. Where I belong.''

Dan needed no second urging. With an abrupt ''We'll see you tomorrow'' for the others, he swooped her up in his arms and headed for his pickup.

Neither said a word on the short ride. A frightful fatigue settled over Maggie, and she was content to simply rest her head on Dan's shoulder. She sensed the coiled tension inside him, and knew he was holding his emotions in check because of all she'd been through.

Inside the cottage he led her straight to the bathroom. "First a shower, then it's bed for you," he announced, stripping away her ruined clothing as though she were a small child. After hurriedly removing his own he stepped with her into the shower.

Dan proceeded to wash away the soot and grime that covered her, muttering to himself when his scrubbing reddened her skin and cursing when he saw the splinters in her palms. "Damn, even your hair is black," he grumbled.

All the time, docile as a lamb, Maggie watched him through half-closed lids, both amused and touched by his fierce concern. She balked, however, when they stepped from the shower and he grabbed a towel off the rack to dry her.

"Darling, I can do that. I'm not an invalid, you know."

"You've had a bad shock and you're still shaky."

"Yes, but I'm fine now."

He hesitated, frowning, but finally handed over the towel. "Okay, I'll go get the first-aid kit while you finish. But sit down if you feel weak."

When he returned she sat on the edge of the bed wrapped in a towel and gritted her teeth while he plucked more than two dozen splinters from her palms, then blew on them after applying disinfectant.

"You don't have a nightgown here anymore. You can sleep in one of my shirts."

"Why bother?" She took the first-aid kit from

him and placed it on the nightstand. Giving him a sultry look, she ran her hand over his bare chest, twining her fingers through the mat of silky hair. "You'll just have to take it off." She flicked a tiny nipple with her fingernail and smiled when he jerked.

He scowled and grabbed her hand. "Maggie, cut that out. You need to rest."

Leaning forward, she nuzzled her face against his chest. "I need you more," she murmured against his skin. She blew on the silky thatch, and a hard shudder rippled through Dan.

"Maggie...stop," he ordered weakly, even as the hand holding hers tightened and he cupped the back of her head with the other.

"Oh, my love. I've missed you so much." With the tip of her tongue, she traced a wet pattern over his skin. "Make love to me. Now. Tonight. I need to feel alive. And loved."

"Maggie—" Arching his back, Dan squeezed his eyes shut as she continued the delightful torment. Running her hand down his flat belly, she deftly unfastened the loosely knotted towel wrapped around his hips. Her fingers closed around him in a delicate grip, and Dan moaned.

"Ah, Maggie. Maggie."

Nineteen

The ringing telephone jarred Maggie from a sound sleep. "Wha...?"

Like a startled deer, she raised her head off Dan's shoulder, but before she could sit up his arm tightened around her. "Take it easy, I'll get it."

Holding her snuggled against his side, he reached out with his other hand and snagged the telephone off the nightstand. "Hello."

Maggie felt Dan's body tauten, and she knew instantly that something was wrong. "What is it? What's happened?" she demanded, scrambling to her knees beside him.

"Right. We're on our way." He slammed the receiver down and looked at Maggie, and an icy sensation feathered down her spine. "It's Jacob," he said simply.

"No." Tears welled in Maggie's eyes. "No."

"He's asking for you, Maggie. We have to hurry. Dr. Sanderson says he won't last much longer."

When they entered Jacob's room only moments later everyone was there. Lily, with Nan beside her, stood beside the bed holding his hand, weeping softly. On the other side Laurel sat in a chair in her bathrobe, her bruised and swollen face streaming with tears. At the foot of the bed, Jo Beth sobbed against Ida Lou's amble bosom while the old woman murmured to her quietly, her own eyes misty, her face scrunched in grief. Dr. Sanderson and Charley hovered discreetly by the door.

As Maggie and Dan approached the bed, Jacob's eyes fluttered open. "Kath-Katherine? Is that... you?"

Laurel scooted her chair back to make room for them to step close to the bed. "Yes, it's me," Maggie murmured.

Jacob reached out a trembling hand to her, and she closed her own around it. The tightness of his grasp surprised her.

In his other hand he clutched a white envelope in the same crushing grip. Maggie idly glanced at the return address, then did a double take, her eyes widening.

It was from the clinic doing the DNA testing.

Her gaze flew to her mother, then to Nan. Her aunt nodded. "It came a short while ago."

Jacob tugged on Maggie's hand, and she leaned closer. The look in his eyes was one she'd never seen directed at her before, and her heart began to pound.

"Katherine. My beautiful...beautiful...Katherine."

He closed his eyes, and she could see unbearable pain in his face. "I've been a...fool. So many wasted years. My fault. My fault. I'm sor...sorry, Kath— Ma-Maggie. So sorry. Forgive me. I...beg you. Forgive me. Please..."

Maggie chin began to wobble. Her throat felt as

though she'd swallowed an apple whole and it had lodged partway down. Unable to speak past the painful tightness, she stared at his blurry image through the wall of tears banking against her lower eyelids.

Oh, God. A lifetime. A lifetime of yearning and hurting and hopeless striving and always being denied her father's love. When it should have been hers all along. It wasn't fair!

She looked at her father, felt his frail hand clinging to hers, and so many conflicting emotions swirled in her chest she could barely breathe—anger and acceptance, resentment and relief, unbearable sadness and the sweetest joy imaginable, all tangled together.

A part of her wanted to shriek and rage at the injustice of it all, the cruelty. But this was her father, the man she had adored from a distance all of her life, and no matter what he'd done or why, she loved him still.

And he was dying. How could she not forgive him?

Maggie's tears overflowed and splashed like warm rain onto their clasped hands. Her lips wobbled uncontrollably and her voice quavered, but she forced out the words he needed to hear. "I forgive you, Daddy. It doesn't matter now."

Jacob opened his eyes and looked at her. Tears streamed from their outer corners and streaked downward, soaking the silver hair at his temples, shocking Maggie to her core. Releasing the envelope, he raised his other hand and stroked her cheek, and the feeble gesture nearly cleaved her heart in two.

"You're a...good...girl, Maggie. A good daughter."

"Oh, Daddy..."

"Come here, child."

A weak tug on her neck was all it took. Maggie collapsed against his chest, and when his arms enfolded her the sobs she'd been holding in check poured out like water through a bursting dam.

"My daughter. My own...precious daughter," Jacob murmured, weakly stroking her hair. "I love you, Maggie. I...love you."

"Da-Daddy. Daddy," she sobbed, clutching him. "I love you, too. Pl-please don't leave us! Oh, please! Not now."

"Love...you. Love..."

His hand stilled and slid off her head. Beneath her ear, his heartbeat slowed, then stopped.

Maggie rose up and looked at her father's still face. "No! *No!* Oh, please, no...no...no..."

"Come here, sweetheart."

Dan pulled her into his arms and Maggie collapsed against his broad chest and wailed out the unspeakable grief that threatened to strangle her. All around her the other women were weeping, too, but Maggie was lost to all but her own staggering pain.

The wrenching sobs tore from some place deep in her soul. They were harsh and painful to hear and they hurt her throat, but she couldn't stop them. She didn't even try.

She cried bitterly for the loveless child she had been, for the lost teenager, for the woman who had

at last won her father's love, only to lose him. She
cried for what could have been, what should have
been, for what never would be.

Finally the first shocking wave of grief spent itself
and she gradually calmed. Standing within Dan's
strong arms, her cheek resting against his chest, she
became aware that they were alone, and no longer
in her parents' bedroom. At some point Dan had
maneuvered her into the small adjacent sitting room,
and she hadn't even known.

She also realized that she was clutching the envelope from the medical lab.

A cheery fire crackled in the fireplace, and the
room smelled of her mother's favorite potpourri. On
the mantel her great-grandmother's clocked ticked
softly.

"You okay now?" Dan asked, nuzzling the top
of her head.

Maggie released a shuddering sigh, but she was
too exhausted to move. "No, but I will be. Oh, Dan,
it hurts so much," she whispered, blinking back a
freshet of tears. Beneath her cheek, his shirt was
already soaked and plastered to his chest.

"I know, sweetheart. But at least now you know
that he was your father. And you got to hear him
say he loved you."

"Yes, there is that," she said in the same listless
voice. She had finally gotten her heart's desire, but
oh, how bittersweet it was.

She sighed again. "I just wish it hadn't taken in-
disputable proof that I was his flesh and blood for
him to love me. Why couldn't just being me be
enough?"

Grasping her shoulders, Dan eased her back a bit and looked into her eyes. "I don't know, sweetheart. I'll never understa——" He stared at the envelope clutched in her hand. "Wait a minute. Look at that."

Following the direction of his gaze, she looked down at the crumpled envelope. A prickly sensation crawled over her skin, leaving gooseflesh in its wake. "It's still sealed." She looked up at Dan, her eyes wide with disbelief. "He never looked at the results."

He smiled at the joy dawning in her eyes. "Looks like just being you was enough for him, after all."

"I can't believe it. This was the proof he wanted."

A quick frown replaced her smile. "What if...what if I'm not his daughter? What if I don't have a right to the name Malone? Or to run the company?" She stared at the envelope. "I really should look."

She slipped her thumbnail under the flap, but before she could tear it open Dan put his hand over hers.

"Maggie, does it really matter? You needed him to accept you for you. Maybe he needed you to accept him the same way. It's true that he wasn't the father he should have been to you, but like I always told you, Jacob was a good man. In the end he didn't need proof because he'd come to value you, and love you, for the woman you are. Isn't that all that really matters?"

The question hung between them, and as Maggie met Dan's steady gaze she felt all the tension drain out of her. She looked down at the envelope in her hand. After a moment, she smiled. "You're right."

She walked over to the fireplace and tossed the envelope into the flames. She watched it wither into a charred curl of ash and felt immense relief.

Dan pulled her back into his arms. "That's my Maggie."

For an interminable time they held each other close and let the profound silence envelop them.

"I've got a suggestion," Dan said finally.

"Oh? What's that?"

"If it's okay with you, I'd like to name our first-born son Jacob?"

Maggie leaned back in his arms, and despite her red-rimmed eyes, she managed a weak attempt at a saucy look. "Why, sugar. Is that a proposal?"

"Yeah, it is. So what's your answer, Red?"

"Well, I don't know," she drawled, and pretended to think it over.

"Maggie," Dan said in a warning voice.

"Although...I do like the name Jacob."

"Dammit, woman—"

Grinning, she flung her arms around his neck. "Yes. Yes. Yes!"

"Don't worry. It will go fine."

"Easy for you to say. They could vote against me. They could vote to hire an outsider to run the company. They could even vote to sell. Remember, between them they have more shares than I do."

"For Pete's sake, Red, they're your sisters."

"Dan's right," Anna said.

"Yeah, well, in this case, I'm not sure how much

that means.'' Maggie paced to the end of the long conference room and back. ''Laurel still acts stand-offish around me, and with Jo Beth...well, you never know how she's going to react.''

It had been ten days since Jacob's funeral. Maggie had delayed this meeting as long as she could, partly to give them all time to grieve, and partly because she was apprehensive of the outcome. Today marked the first convening of the new owners in a shareholders' meeting.

The faint smell of charred wood still lingered in the air, and the sound of power saws and hammering could be heard through the closed door. Down the hall the construction crew was busy rebuilding the burned offices. Most of the smoke had been sucked out of the broken glass wall in Maggie's office, and for the past two weeks a crew had been cleaning up the smoke damage in the cannery itself. If all went right today, Maggie hoped that within a week or so, the refitting would begin.

Maggie twisted her hands together and paced the room again.

''Sweetheart, will you quit worrying. Remember what they say. 'Never let 'em see you sweat.' Just sit down and relax. They'll be along in a minute.''

Giving Dan and her secretary a wan smile, Maggie went to the head of the conference table. She had just taken her seat when the door opened and her sisters, followed by Art Buchanan, the company attorney, walked in.

When they were seated, Maggie cleared her throat. ''Well, now that we're all here—''

The door opened again, and Laurel made a distressed sound. Dan shot to his feet.

"Martin! What are you doing here?" Maggie demanded. "Your employment with this company has been terminated, as you well know. I must ask you to leave at once." She had known he was out on bail, pending trial, but it had not occurred to her that he would dare to would show up at the cannery.

"You heard her," Dan growled. "Get out."

"I have every right to be here. When I married Laurel she signed her shareholder voting rights over to me. I've had a seat on this board ever since."

"That can be remedied." Maggie turned to the attorney. "Mr. Buchanan, please do whatever is necessary to rescind Mr. Howe's voting rights and return them to Laurel."

"I have the form with me." He snapped open his briefcase, removed a sheet of paper and a pen, marked the signature line with an *X* and slid both down the table to Laurel.

An angry flush reddened Martin's face. "Laurel, don't you dare sign that."

"Jesus, Martin. You have the hide of a rhinoceros." Dan shook his head. "Hell, man, you were served with divorce papers a week ago. You can't come in here ordering her around."

"We're not divorced yet, and if Laurel will listen to reason, we never will be." He focused on his wife, and Maggie grimaced as she watched him turn on the phony charm. "Laurel, sweetheart, you know I love you. You can't just walk out on me like this."

"I didn't 'just walk out,' Martin. You cheated on

me, remember? And when I found out, you beat me.''

''All right, maybe I got a little rough—''

''A little rough? My nose is broken and I have three cracked ribs and a bruised kidney. Not to mention the other cuts and bruises.''

Martin's mouth flattened, and for an instant fury flared in his eyes. Maggie knew that if he and Laurel had been alone he would have struck her again.

With an effort, he managed to conceal his anger and force a placating tone. ''Sweetheart, the affair with Elaine meant nothing. I had to string her along. I needed her to doctor the books.''

Art Buchanan cleared his throat. ''Mr. Howe, you really shouldn't be making such statements in front of an attorney. As an officer of the court, I must warn you, doctoring company books is a crime.''

''Only if you use them to steal. The records I gave the Bountiful people were legit. The doctored ones were just to convince Jacob to sell out.''

''Even so, if the Malone family wants to pursue the matter, I'm sure a case can be made against you.''

Maggie looked at her sister. ''Laurel, it's your call. What do you want to do?''

''I just want him out of my life.''

''You heard her. Personally, I don't know how you have the gall to even show your face around here, after what you did to her,'' Maggie said. ''Not to mention everything else you and your father tried to do.''

''I'm not responsible for my father's actions. The

crazy old fool took it on himself to get rid of you. I had nothing to do with starting that fire."

Martin's callous dismissal of his father so stunned Maggie and the others they could only stare at him, speechless.

No matter how wrong and misguided, Rupert had always been fanatically devoted to his son. All of Martin's life, his father had run interference for him. Whenever he'd landed in trouble Rupert had used his influence to smooth things over. If Martin wanted something, his father employed whatever means were necessary, whether it was a little arm-twisting or coercion or subtle threats, to see that he got it. Some even claimed that Rupert wasn't above paying bribes.

That he could so coldly turn his back on his father now was a shocking betrayal, even for Martin.

"Laurel, don't be a fool. Before you make a hasty decision, hear me out. I can make you all filthy rich. We change the company charter and sell the cannery to Bountiful Foods. They don't grow their own produce, so they're not interested in the orchards, just the cannery complex, which means we keep the land.

"Now, here's where the good part comes in. My dad has inside information that a major software company is moving into the area. They're going to build a huge complex and move in a whole army of high-salaried employees who are going to want up-scale homes. We can subdivide the orchards into one-acre residential lots and sell them for eighty or ninety thousand apiece. Malone Enterprises has over fifteen hundred acres under cultivation. We'll all be filthy rich in no time."

"So it was the land you wanted all along," Maggie said. "The sabotage, the altered books, the scare tactics—that was all just to panic us into changing the charter."

"Yeah. The profit from the cannery sale will be peanuts in comparison. And since Jacob wouldn't listen to reason, I had to do something."

"It was a wasted effort, Martin. Malone Enterprises was started by our great-grandmother. Four generations of Malones have poured their hearts and souls into the business and it supports a good portion of the people in this area. It is not now, nor will it ever be, for sale."

If looks could kill, the one Martin gave Maggie would have annihilated her on the spot.

"Don't pay any attention to her," he urged, turning to her sisters. "You don't have to let her run the show. Between the two of you, you have the controlling shares. You can do whatever you want."

He turned a coaxing smile on his wife. "Laurel, honey, you can't be serious about leaving me. Not after all we've meant to each other. I love you, baby. We've got problems, sure, but we can work them out. I promise.

"And Jo Beth, with your share of the money you can forget about college. You can go anywhere you want, do anything you want. You don't owe Maggie anything. Hell, you don't even like her."

Maggie held her breath and watched her sisters. She had no idea if family loyalty and tradition would be enough for them to say no to a fortune.

In the past the cajoling tactic had always worked for Martin when dealing with Laurel. She was silent so long, Maggie began to fear it would again.

Finally, without a word, Laurel rose and walked around the table. Standing behind Maggie's chair, she looked straight at her husband and put her hand on her sister's shoulder.

A moment later, Jo Beth did the same.

Martin looked ready to explode. "You're idiots!" he shouted. "All of you. You're sitting on a gold mine and you're letting stupid family tradition keep you from cashing in on it!"

He stormed out, and the instant the door slammed behind him Maggie shot out of her chair and embraced her sisters. "Thank you! Oh, thank you so much."

"Maggie, surely you didn't think we'd side with Martin against you?"

"Yeah, especially after what he did to Laurel."

"Well...he was talking about a lot of money."

"We're not exactly poor as it is. And Jo Beth and I are Malones, too, you know."

"Yeah. Besides, sisters stick together," Jo Beth said. "And I say good riddance. Martin's an asshole."

Maggie laughed. "I have to agree, but I wouldn't let Momma hear you use that expression if I were you."

Jo Beth rolled her eyes. "She'd have a hissy fit."

Laurel squeezed Maggie's hand. "Sis, I never have thanked you for helping me—"

"Shh. You don't have to thank me. As Jo Beth said, sisters stick together."

They hugged again, but when tears threatened Anna stepped in. "Now, now, none of that. We've still got business to attend to. Mr. Buchanan is a busy man. I'm sure he doesn't have time to sit around and watch the three of you get sloppy."

Their equilibrium restored, Maggie and her sisters grinned at one another and took their seats.

The meeting went smoothly. Unanimously, they decided to refit the cannery with modern equipment and make Maggie president and CEO, although her sisters did voice some concern about the last.

"Are you sure this is what you want to do, Maggie? What about your modeling career?"

Maggie laughed. "Trust me, running Malone's is what I've always dreamed of doing. As for the modeling, if I scale back a bit I can handle both. I've already been doing that for the past four months and I can continue for as long as it lasts. Believe it or not, at the ripe old age of twenty-seven, my modeling days are numbered."

"Why, that's terrible!" Laurel protested.

"It's plain stupid, if you ask me," their younger sister declared.

"True, but that's the reality of the fashion world. Anyway, it's not important. Everything that really matters to me is here. My family. This business." Her eyes sought Dan's across the table, and she smiled. "And the man I love. What more could I ask for?"

Once again, Anna took charge and defused the emotional moment.

"Well, then, it's all settled," she announced,

snapping her steno pad shut. "Why don't you bang
that gavel so we can all get out of here."

Maggie laughed and gave the table a rap. "Meeting adjourned."

When the others had left, Dan came around the
table and pulled Maggie into his embrace. With his
arms looped loosely around her waist, he looked
deep into her eyes. "It's taken a long time, but
you've finally made it. Welcome home, my love."

*From seduction in the royal sheikhdom to
high adventure in the hot Arabian desert comes a
breathtaking love story by international bestselling author*

DIANA PALMER

LORD OF THE DESERT

Gretchen Brannon was completely out of her element when she aligned herself with Sheikh Philippe Sabon, the formidable ruler of Qawi. They came from different worlds, but he made her aware of her own courage. She, in turn, aroused his sleeping senses like no other woman could.

But now that Gretchen's heart belongs to the Lord of the Desert, she's become the target for vengeance by the sheikh's most diabolical enemy. In a final showdown that will pit good against evil, can love and destiny triumph...?

**"The dialogue is charming, the characters likable
and the sex sizzling..."**
—*Publishers Weekly* on *Once in Paris*

On sale October 2000 wherever paperbacks are sold!

Visit us at www.mirabooks.com   MDP617

One small spark ignites the entire city of
Chicago, but amid the chaos, a case of mistaken
identity leads to an unexpected new love....

SUSAN WIGGS

On this historic night, Kathleen O'Leary
finds herself enjoying a lovely masquerade. She
has caught the eye of Dylan Francis Kennedy. The
night feels alive with magic...and ripe with promise.

Then fire sweeps through Chicago, cornering the young
lovers with no hope of rescue. Impulsively, they marry.
Incredibly, they survive. And now Kathleen must tell
Chicago's most eligible bachelor that he has married
a fraud.

But the joke's on her. For this gentleman is no
gentleman. While Kathleen had hoped to win Dylan's
love, he had planned only to break her heart and steal
her fortune. Now the real sparks are about to fly.

THE MISTRESS

"In poetic prose, Wiggs evocatively captures the
Old South and creates an intense, believable
relationship between the lovers."
—*Publishers Weekly* on *The Horsemaster's Daughter*

*On sale October 2000
wherever paperbacks are sold!*

MIRA®

FIONA HOOD-STEWART

Sometimes the closest distances
are the hardest to cross....

THE JOURNEY HOME

They met in the wilds of Scotland, as a winter storm
approached. India Moncrieff, a woman desperate to hod
on to Dunbar House, her family's majestic estate. And
Jack Buchanan, the American tycoon enchanted by the
land, who sees the house as a business opportunity.
Business and passion soon unite them. But shocking
revelations will alienate the lovers in their desperate
battle over a legacy neither will surrender.

*Available the first week of October 2000
wherever paperbacks are sold!*

MIRA

Visit us at www.mirabooks.com

MFHS606